An Empire of Stones
Book 1

By Stephanie van Rijn

An Empire of Stones

Copyright © 2023 Stephanie van Rijn

English translation copyright © 2024 Stephanie van Rijn

Edited by Kimberly Caissy-Lépine

Corrections Kimberly-Ann Pednault and Marie-Ève Rodrigue

Translation Stephanie van Rijn and Kimberly-Ann Pednault

Cover design Lesly-Ann Lagacée

ISBN 978-2-9821640-4-8 (trade paperback)

ISBN 978-2-9821640-5-5 (ebook)

First Edition: April 2023

Printed in the United States of America.

For Wes and Dean,

My little creatures, my motivations

Hierarchy of Balt'boec

Walderlake

Monarch - Hargon

Master - Toran Sius

Guardian - Brennet Reinhart

Cendril

Monarch - Tanyll Zylfaren

Master - Elyndel Arren

Guardian - Tanyll Zylfaren

Brilea

Monarch - Azura Kane

Mistress - Micelys de Bronet

Guardian - Azura Kane

Wynnorth

Monarch - Fabyan Netherborne

Master - Icarius Ancel

Guardian - Valera Netherborne

Guverl'yt

Monarch - Valera Netherborne

Master - Serval Andwin

Guardian - Valera Netherborne

Osthallvale

Monarch - none

Mistress - Eraza

Guardian – Eraza

TABLE OF CONTENTS

CHAPTER

1

THE ORACLE

Queen Valera's footsteps reverberated through the winding halls of Guverl'yt Castle, breaking the eerie silence that preceded an impending storm. Such spectacles were regrettably common for the guards stationed around the palace, but Her Majesty paid them no mind as she resolutely lifted the folds of her vermilion satin dress, adorned with gold threads and black pearls. Her sense of elegance never wavered, regardless of the circumstances.

She hurried down the stone staircase leading to the dungeons, leaving behind a trail of uneasy glances and hushed murmurs. It was uncommon for her to venture into the dusty and foul confines of the oubliettes, where the smell of mold and sweat pervaded the air. The woman, whose grace contrasted sharply with the state of the place, came to a sudden stop, disgusted. She covered her nose in disdain, suppressing a retch.

No. She refused to succumb to the temptation of turning back. Determined, she pressed on. The guards watched in awe as she ventured deeper into an isolated dungeon, reserved for hardened criminals. Her enraged expression did little to diminish her undeniable beauty. Finally, Her Majesty arrived at the remotest chamber, a thick door of wood and iron, secured with four locks at its extremities. The sentry standing before her bowed awkwardly, struggling to open the entrance to the tiny cell.

"My apologies, Your Highness. The latches are tricky!" the man stammered.

Valera's commanding presence took over, and she replied with a naturally suave, yet authoritative tone, "Show some decorum! You represent the crown, act accordingly."

The guard straightened his back, proudly displaying his metal armor adorned with a scarlet tabard, bearing the emblem of the kingdom of Guverl'yt—a golden snake coiled around an ivory willow. But the queen paid him little attention, her focus still on the closed room.

With a loud creak, the door finally opened. Her contentment was evident as her faint smile met the darkness before her. At that moment, her sense of grandeur was worth more to her than all the gold in the world. Her eyes fell upon a cowering figure, barely visible in the shadows.

"Is she conscious?"

"She is. However, Master Andwin administered a sedative. The poor soul tried to escape... again," explained the guard, lowering his head, attempting to conceal his compassion for the prisoner.

Valera's fascination granted him a reprieve from any reprimands. She entered the cell with an almost languid grace, reminiscent of a feline. There, lying on the ground in filthy, torn rags that once hinted at fine, satiny fabric, was a woman. Her face was hidden behind thick, dirty hair. Only rare silver-blonde streaks revealed the true shade. The frail prisoner shivered, whether from exhaustion or fever, it was hard to tell.

"By Itos, God of all gods! This humidity is overwhelming," Her Majesty exclaimed, brushing the jet-black curls from her neck, unveiling subtle moles that betrayed her fair complexion. Her amusement was evident as delicate lines formed on her mature face.

"Poor creature!" she continued in a honeyed tone. "It's time we found you a more suitable place. A place that feels more… welcoming."

The prisoner slowly turned her head, revealing pointy ears and what seemed to be a lovely visage, despite being covered with dirt, dried blood, and bruises. Valera's crystalline laugh rang through the dungeon, like a bell in the depths of a dark cave.

"There! I knew you would like it!" she simpered, approaching her.

The elf struggled to straighten with what little strength her battered body allowed. A gleam of hope shone in her piercing eyes.

"I could grant you a simpler existence. No more suffering! No more chains or dungeons! I could offer you a comfortable, easy life," the queen whispered.

The prisoner stared at her in disbelief.

"But first, I need you to reveal something to me. A simple fact which, I am sure, will bring immense relief to our respective peoples," Valera cooed. "Tell me who the person in this vision of yours is… that prophecy Master Andwin managed to extricate from your poor little mind… the one about the dragons."

The queen knelt beside the woman, feigning compassion. Removing a silk handkerchief from her bodice, she wiped away the beading sweat from the elf's soiled forehead. The prisoner gently grabbed Valera's wrist and closed her eyes, remaining silent for a few seconds.

"A comfortable, easy life?" she muttered in a quavering voice.

Her Majesty nodded, a good-natured smile playing on her plump red lips.

"Your salvation is now within your reach, Oracle," she whispered, her tone tempting.

"But… how can I live a comfortable existence if there's any chance you could end up on the throne our Emperor Galvrick once occupied?" the elf retorted, violently pushing Valera's hand away.

With this gesture, the Queen rose abruptly, swinging her ebony mane behind her shoulders with rage. Her delicate features twisted into a furious grimace, and her limbs trembled as her face flushed.

"I deplore your need to defy me at all costs. My intentions are in favor of the survival of my people… and yours, for that matter. I dare to hope that you will eventually understand that," she fumed between her gritted teeth.

"On the contrary, my conscience is begging me to ensure the salvation of Balt'boec by keeping you away from the woman that I saw… the one you would subject to the same treatment as me. I know that you would lock her up, torture her, and ultimately use her as a weapon."

The Oracle flashed a smirk that ignited Valera's anger. She glared menacingly while hovering over her with contempt. The elf braced herself for a slap or a kick, but nothing came.

Instead, Her Majesty turned on her heels and headed gruffly for the exit.

"GOOD. I shall have the pleasure of summoning Master Andwin. Maybe one more session with him will enlighten you," she growled cruelly. "I hope our journey to Wynnorth will give you some time to reconsider."

"Wynnorth?" the Oracle inquired, but Valera did not answer. Instead, she ordered the guard to close the door behind her. The Oracle fought the urge to scream, to let her rage explode. Swallowing a sob, she sank to the floor, wrapping her emaciated arms around her bruised knees. Aware of the impending torture she would face once again, she tried to console herself, knowing her suffering might ensure the survival of her people and perhaps prevent the disaster she had witnessed in her mind. The door slammed shut, plunging her back into complete darkness. She heard Her Majesty Queen Valera's thunderous footsteps receding, and after a few minutes, silence enveloped her.

CHAPTER

2

THE GUARDIAN OF WALDERLAKE

Brennet awoke abruptly, momentarily blinded by the light streaming into his room through the flowing curtains. Painful, hoarse breaths escaped between his pale lips, and sweat beaded on his wrinkled forehead. Restlessness had plagued his night, marked by terrible and repetitive nightmares. He inhaled deeply, quickly soothed by the delicious smell of bread that Minerva, his faithful cook, was preparing at the end of the hall. Despite the tempting scent, the old mage knew that overpowering fatigue would quash his appetite. He had resigned himself to endure these agonizing nights since this mysterious illness had taken him as a companion. In just a few months, his health had declined, and he, who had formerly been a model of vigor among the people of Walderlake, was now but a shadow of his former self. He likened himself to a wretched ghost, forever confined to his bed. His usually bright steel-grey eyes nowadays seemed veiled. His chestnut hair had thinned, making Brennet, who once made the women of Brevic swoon, appear elderly. The mage tried to wipe the sweat from his face with the back of his veiny hand but was frustrated by this disability he could not shake. His servants, whom he considered his own family, worried about his poor state. They had advised their master to rely on the good care of Brevic's sanatorium. However, the man's pride had commanded him to firmly decline. How could he, Brennet Reinhart, the Emerald Guardian of Walderlake, entrust his well-being to healing mages? He refused to be mothered day and night like a helpless infant. His household was not the only one fearing the worst. Hargon, ruler of the realm and Brennet's elder brother, had voiced his concern to the Council of the Emerald Order. The man's inability to assume his title stirred up Walderlake's court. The king had tried to shut down the gossip, hoping this would soothe the anguish that weighed on his usually serene subjects.

However, their apprehension was justified, as this gem was the beating heart of this flourishing realm, a colossal source of defense on which Walderlake could rely. Galvrick, the very first emperor of Balt'boec, had crafted the emerald over a hundred years ago. Anxious to preserve his masterful gifts, he had locked up a part of his soul there, thus creating a magical catalyst of phenomenal power. When Galvrick felt his end was near, he divided what remained of himself into five more stones. He entrusted them to the sovereigns of the most deserving kingdoms of the empire: Walderlake, Cendril, Osthallvale, Brilea, Guverl'yt, and Wynnorth. With this final gesture, he hoped to bring lasting greatness to the people he had ruled over for more than four hundred tumultuous years. However, the prosperity that Galvrick envisioned soon turned into a lust for domination. Wars erupted between the monarchies, and the smell of blood and smoke plagued Balt'boec. Many were corrupted by a desire for expansionism, attempting at all costs to seize neighboring gems. The union that once prevailed among the six powers gave way to a world of chaos, marking the beginning of the Eighth Age of the Empire, the most destructive of all.

It had now been over thirty years since Brennet had been appointed Emerald Guardian, a title in which he took immense pride. Hargon himself had inherited the gem following the sudden death of their father, King Edrick. Nevertheless, being deprived of magical gifts, the new sovereign was compelled to entrust the jewel to the most deserving magistrates of the Emerald Order, his own brother, Brennet. The latter was dedicated to this organization, eager to perfect the art of magic. However, this succession was not without consequences. The young mage's aptitudes frightened the ruler, but not as much as the loyalty the court felt toward him. He refused to constantly watch over his shoulder, fearing a potential usurper who was both Guardian and heir to the throne. The king offered him an ultimatum: the stone or the title of Prince of Walderlake. Without hesitation, Brennet renounced his royal privileges and devoted himself to the advancement of magic and, thereby, to the well-being of the people. Thanks to his incredible charisma and ingenuity, his popularity extended beyond his homeland. Soon, his influence rivaled with Hargon's. Few were fortunate enough to experience that level of respect in their lives. For that reason, he did not fear his own passing, and only a grateful smile lingered on his sickly face.

The mage chuckled when his gaze met the woman curled up at the end of the room in a large ruddy velvet armchair. A grimoire rested on her knees, her eyes closed, and her lips parted. Elissa, his adoptive daughter, had once again dozed off at his bedside. The old man's expression softened. Even though he had repeatedly told her not to worry about him, his protégée turned out to be much more stubborn than he was. She was still wearing her clothes from last night, her fiery dark hair cascading over her pale shoulders. He smirked at the sight of the silver pendant around her neck. He had given it to her the day he had brought her home, more than twenty years ago. He was flattered she kept it to this day. The Guardian coughed, and Elissa awoke immediately, her eyes scanning the room with a bewildered look on her face. Her gaze met her father's, and she sighed in relief. She hastily put her book down on a bedside table and rushed to the old man's side.

"You seem cheerful this morning. There's a hint of color on your cheeks," she said with a smile.

Brennet chuckled softly. "So much hope in this mind of yours, Daughter."

"Since you no longer have yours, I'll need to use mine instead."

"My mind?" teased the mage.

"Your hope!" exclaimed the woman, rolling her eyes.

"Would you be disappointed in me?" he asked in return.

She did not answer immediately, questioning herself about the intention of her own remarks.

"It's painful for me to see the man who inspired me so much through all these years just… give up," she admitted.

Brennet smiled once more, obviously touched by his pupil's words. Truthfully, it was not a lack of hope. He was simply resigned to this imminent end. Silence settled between the master and his apprentice. Elissa looked down and nervously twirled her pendant between her fingers. Brennet knew better than anyone that this meant she was upset… or anxious about asking for a favor.

"Yes?" preceded the mage with some apprehension.

"Well, I… I'm grateful for all the kindness you have shown to me for all these years," she began. "They were, of course, most precious to me. I… I understand that you have always preferred a more secluded life for me. This is a decision that I have respected until now, without questions or judgments."

"But…" he wondered.

He sat up with difficulty while waiting for her to continue. Elissa remained silent for a moment, as if afraid to offend the man responsible for her survival.

"I understand that every choice you've made was for my best interest. However…"

She stopped again, swallowing hard.

"Yes?" Brennet insisted.

"I'm confident my abilities would be put to better use within the Order."

The mage stared at her in disbelief. There was a hint of nervousness that betrayed her composure.

"You're so young, Elissa. Don't you think it would be wiser to wait a few more years?"

The apprentice frowned but kept her head high and her gaze assured.

"My youth is fading a little more each day. May I remind you that you were roughly the same age as me when you joined the ranks of the Emerald Council?"

"That's true. However, a little freedom never hurt anyone. Being part of the Order does not only give you a title. It's a lifestyle, a sacred responsibility," he insisted, his expression darkening.

"What do you expect of me, then? You have trained me rigorously in every conceivable sphere of magic. And more! You educated me in the different dialects of the world, you forged my knowledge … and why? Why would you if you refuse to let me enter the ranks of the Order?"

"Enjoy the life you have for a while," Brennet said stubbornly. "Normalcy will be impossible for you once you are bound to the Council."

"You talk about freedom, yet you've kept me isolated within this household since childhood. I've rarely ventured beyond the boundaries of this village, and when I have, it's always been with you by my side. I've been living in secrecy and restrictions for so long!" stormed the woman who could no longer contain herself.

Brennet did not answer. He only considered her words for a moment and simply nodded, pensive.

"So?" she insisted.

"Let me think about it. This is a request not to be taken lightly," he said in a low, strained voice.

Elissa pursed her lips and bowed with obvious frustration.

"I understand that's not the answer you were hoping for. For that, I am sorry," added the Guardian, slumping on his bed.

The young mage sighed, knowing that Brennet would not entertain further discussion. She got up with a gruff attitude and rushed for the exit.

"Elissa?"

The woman stopped short.

"Does the name Owen Strongbow mean anything to you?"

She immediately whirled around, her face lighting up with excitement.

"Of course! Who doesn't know Walderlake's most famous knight? His prowess is legendary!"

"Well, Owen and I happened to serve together many years ago… At the Battle of Ram'burc. We have remained great friends ever since."

The mage understood he had just enticed his protégée, who always loved his epic tales.

"Did you fight on the Ram'burc front? The first confrontation between the peoples of the West and the dragons!" Elissa exclaimed, retracing her steps.

"Among others!" he replied wistfully, giggling at his daughter's volatile moods.

"Please, tell me everything! I've read about this battle countless times, but I've never had the chance to discuss it with someone who was actually there. And you were right under my nose all these years! Shame on you," she growled with a mischievous grin.

"Let's keep this for some other moment, Elissa," Brennet said wearily.

"Oh… Of course…"

"To be fair, Owen tells this story with a lot more gusto. This man has a gift for bringing all his anecdotes to life. Why not ask him directly when he joins us in a few days?"

Elissa's expression lit up again, her eyes wide with bliss. She jumped on her feet, now bubbling with enthusiasm.

"Seriously?" she inquired in a quavering voice.

Before Brennet could respond, a violent fit of coughing gripped him. Elissa rushed toward him, intuition guiding her actions. The man struggled to catch his breath, his face turning livid under the concerned gaze of his apprentice. She reached for the mage's chest, but he immediately pushed her away.

"Elissa, no," he blurted out with difficulty.

Unperturbed, the woman placed her palm on her father's sternum, focusing her energy. She concentrated so hard that her whole body shook, her head boiling with indescribable power. A timid silver-grey glow emanated from her fingertips. The man's cough subsided almost instantly, and his face relaxed as the flicker intensified. His breathing became regular again, and serenity washed over him.

"Feeling better?" asked the apprentice.

She withdrew her numb hand, the radiance slowly fading.

"Elissa... I've told you hundreds of times never to use your gifts without your scepter!" Brennet protested. "You know very well that you don't fully control them!"

"That's why you refuse to let me join the Council? Because I don't entirely master my powers?"

"Making mistakes through magic can have devastating consequences. It's not like ruining a pie or a painting. Our gifts can have serious ramifications, especially without an adequate weapon to channel them."

"I can't just sit here and ignore your distress. Besides, I've never understood this obsession with those vulgar magical sticks. I don't use mine, and I have yet to experience any ill effects."

He studied her for a moment with a mixture of resolve and uncertainty.

"No more spells without your staff," he said hoarsely.

The woman lowered her head, a feeling of guilt taking hold of her. Who was she to question the Guardian of Walderlake, after all?

"Now leave me. I must think about all this," the man commanded.

Elissa nodded, annoyed. How did he always manage to have the last word? She pursed her lips, trying to conceal her irritation, and rose slowly with a defiant look.

She hurried out of the house. The fresh air, which usually soothed her, now made her feel dizzy. She did not stop to greet the servants as she normally did. Healing spells drained the energy of any mage who used them, and in her case, it was much more than that. Her throat constricted, her breath becoming short and erratic. Panic gripped her, and she felt trapped. Traversing the porch, her steps led her to the pond several minutes away from the mansion. But she didn't stop there. She wanted to go further, beyond the wheat fields that she skirted at full speed, past the stables and the old mill. She ran without pausing and finally reached the edge of Brennet's domain. That was the boundary the Guardian had asked her not to cross. But why? She had obeyed, never daring to question him. However, the desire to be somewhere else gnawed at her now more than ever. During all those years spent working hard, remaining cloistered from the rest of the world, Elissa had learned to be silent, without anyone explaining the reasoning behind it. She was eternally grateful to her adoptive father for giving her a quiet life. Without his kindness, she might have grown up in one of the county's orphanages, begging on the streets or worse. The future of a *traitor*'s offspring did not seem enviable. However, this bitter feeling had persisted in her for so many years. She had learned to bury her torment deep within herself, accepting this loneliness as a part of who she was. Her existence had become an enigma to which she no longer had any answers. Brennet had discouraged all her attempts to seek information on her past. Each time, he managed to find a cleverer excuse than the previous one, preventing her from discovering anything meaningful about her origins.

The mage recalled her childhood with her parents, but many details were now fading from her memory. Regret filled her heart as she realized she hadn't paid enough attention to that long-gone era, failing to truly understand those she was torn away from. They were a reclusive group of druids who resided in the forests of Valler, northeast of Walderlake. Although her time with them was brief, she unconsciously retained some of their customs, deeply ingrained in her. When Brennet risked his own life to rescue her, a child he had never met before, she became bound to that oath. A druid's norm. As she filled her lungs with the fresh country air, she leaned against the wooden fence. Her mind was a whirlwind of questions, each one weighing heavier than the last. Reluctantly, she closed her eyes. Lost in her thoughts, minutes turned into hours. Completely unaware of the passage of time, she eventually fell asleep.

———— ··●·· ————

Elissa's sudden awakening left her drenched in sweat, her breaths heavy and labored. Glancing at the position of the sun, she realized she had dozed off for most of the day, the toll of sleepless nights finally catching up with her. Feeling disoriented, she staggered to her feet and hurried back to the family estate, her hunger gnawing at her like a raging beast. The guilt of leaving her father's bedside weighed heavily on her heart. She desperately hoped his condition had not worsened during her absence, knowing she could never forgive herself if that were the case.

As she entered the bustling house, she noticed an unusual commotion among the servants, their hurried steps and agitated whispers standing out from the usual calm atmosphere. Elissa assumed it was because of Owen Strongbow's impending arrival, and she tried not to let worry overtake her. Attempting to satisfy her hunger, she headed for the kitchens, only to be stopped in her tracks by the high-pitched voice of her governess, Bruna. The maid's nervous clapping and flushed cheeks betrayed her excitement, and Elissa's heart skipped a beat.

"Where were you, Elissa?" Bruna scolded in her melodious southern Walderlake accent, crossing her arms with reprimand. Fear gripped Elissa, and she felt herself being led by Bruna toward the Guardian's quarters, expecting the worst.

The bedroom door swung open, revealing Brennet standing before her, donned in an elegant ruddy velvet jacket. Elissa could not help but gasp in surprise, questioning if her eyes were playing tricks on her.

"We have to hurry," Brennet said with impatience, wrapping a cape around his shoulders. Still stunned, Elissa asked hesitantly, "Are you feeling better?"

"A kinder day would be a more accurate way of describing it," he replied, adding to her confusion.

"Where are we going? Is it wise to leave the manor in your condition?" Elissa inquired, concerned.

"I don't need to be mothered, Elissa. We're heading to Richeroc for the Council meeting. Now, hurry up! The magistrates won't wait," Brennet insisted, alarming her. Elissa had never set foot in the Capitol, assuming it was off-limits to those outside the Emerald Order. This news was a welcome change for her, a moment she could not have imagined.

Stammering with awe and disbelief, she looked at Brennet. "It will be my greatest honor to accompany you. But does your condition allow such a grueling journey? The Capitol is days away."

"Do not trouble yourself. I can fulfill my obligations," Brennet reassured her. "Now, go gather your things. We leave within the hour."

Nodding silently, overwhelmed with emotions, Elissa mechanically rushed to her room. After changing into her traveling clothes and packing her satchel, she noticed the cart already hitched up, ready to leave. Brennet and Bruna were seated inside, their worry evident. The late hour and the uncharacteristically hasty departure raised her anxiety. There was something they were keeping from her, and she was determined to find out.

CHAPTER

3

THE PRINCE

In the kingdom of Wynnorth, a scorching summer had descended, particularly upon the capital of Eluin, where the relentless drought burdened the populace. Once prosperous and fertile, the land now lay barren. The nation was on high alert as the death toll rose due to unbearable heat and scarce resources. Some speculated that the extinction of dragons had disrupted the world's magical balance, while the country's leader stubbornly blamed the gods for their misfortune. The citizens grew impatient, no longer willing to remain unheard. Meanwhile, the eastern sovereigns urged them not to fall behind in repairing the extensive damage caused by the dragons over two decades ago. Amidst this turmoil, Prince Farklyn Netherborne seemed unconcerned about the impending rebellion threatening Wynnorth. He casually wiped a bead of sweat from the chest of the woman lying beside him, whose name he did not care to know. She exuded a wild beauty, which he preferred over the ostentatious aesthetics of the nobility. With a chuckle, he mused on his mother, Queen Valera of Guverl'yt, and her disapproval of his relationships with *country rats*, as she called commoners.

"Why bother?" he thought, relishing his unapologetic pursuit of pleasure over courtly customs. He enjoyed testing his mother's boundaries subtly, considering each tiny provocation a personal victory. Yet, he never openly challenged her, well aware of her volatile temperament. After all, he owed her his title and existence, even if her moods were known to be explosive.

"Are you satisfied, Your Highness?" asked the woman with a charming round accent typical of commoners.

Her words danced pleasantly, and with a seductive pout, she pressed her lips against Farklyn's chest.

"Absolutely lovely!" he thought as he lay back. "Not quite like the stable boy from last night, but magnificent, nonetheless."

Farklyn had difficulty keeping track of his conquests, as his title and pleasing physique were undeniable assets. His slender yet athletic figure exuded vitality, and his face charmed with a piercing gaze framed by cascading chocolate-colored locks. Many had told him that he had inherited his mother's beauty and spirited nature, but he often wondered about the traits passed down from his late father, King Baalhan of Wynnorth. Perhaps it was the appetite for lust? Regardless, he felt little attachment to a man who had remained a stranger to him. Baalhan's reign had been tragically short-lived, as he was assassinated just months after his official coronation. Farklyn's twin brother, Fabyan, now occupied the throne, while Valera acted as regent. Fortunately, jealousy never consumed Farklyn; he considered his brother's title a curse he wanted no part of. He gladly left politics and responsibilities to his family while indulging in pleasures and delights. The joys of good wine and lovely companions were more than enough for him, offering a perfect balance he embraced without reservation.

His lover admired the opulent room. The huge bed, covered in fine, shimmering fabrics, faced a mezzanine with a dazzling view of turquoise waters and ivory pebbles. The bedroom exuded an elegant white ambiance, adorned with subtle bronze accents. Farklyn found daily solace in the aroma of the sea and the soothing sound of the waves. Often, he forgot about the famine caused by the drought ravaging the kingdom.

"What incredible refinement!" the woman exclaimed, gently stroking the silken sheets.

"You get used to it," the man sneered, amused.

"Really? I can hardly imagine that such a life could be tiring!"

"And yet..." he sighed, a hint of bitterness coloring his tone.

But his lover climbed on top of him, her caramel complexion glistening in the morning light.

"So, it will be my duty to entertain you, Your Highness!" she whispered, her warm breath caressing his ear. With a seductive grin, she leaned over his chest, her wavy blonde hair tickling his neck.

The man chuckled hoarsely, his torment momentarily forgotten.

Suddenly, the bedroom door swung open, startling the woman, who hastily clutched the ivory silk sheets to shield herself. Meanwhile, Farklyn lay unperturbed, hands laced behind his head, more exposed than ever. He immediately recognized the almost childlike countenance of Guverl'yt's messenger—round and puffy, with nervousness evident in his watery eyes. Braylon, the king's adviser and a magistrate of the Sapphire Order, followed the young man. Beads of sweat rolled down Braylon's bald forehead, collecting at the tip of his snub nose.

"Highness," began Braylon breathlessly.

"What's going on, again?" asked the prince wearily.

The magistrate and the messenger exchanged a brief, uncertain glance.

"I'm listening," Farklyn insisted, annoyed.

He turned to them, revealing all his splendor. The two intruders looked down awkwardly, but their interlocutor did not cover himself. Braylon stroked his gleaming skull with a trembling hand before continuing.

"Your brother... the king. He... he..."

"A garrison of Brilean mercenaries has imprisoned His Highness," the young messenger finally blurted out forcefully, as if the words had exploded from his mouth.

Farklyn gaped before bursting out into hearty laughter.

"The Citrine Order? Who would have thought that a country as primitive as Brilea would overcome the despotism of my dear brother?"

"My prince!" the adviser protested, bringing his hands to his plump, rosy cheeks.

"You can't deny that Fabyan and my lovely mother took pleasure in tyrannizing our neighbors. A retribution was inevitable," Farklyn continued with detachment bordering on arrogance.

The two men stood uncomfortably in front of the bed, dancing from foot to foot.

"My lord... those words can be considered treason," Braylon whispered.

Farklyn shrugged. What could they really do to him, after all?

He then noticed the panicked expression of his lover, who had remained silent, sitting in the corner of the mattress.

"Thank you, my dear. You can grab the purse on the table when you leave," he said.

The woman complied, hastily gathering her scattered clothes from the foot of the bed. Mortified, she fled without hesitation, not bothering to fully dress herself.

The counselor cleared his throat before speaking.

"Prince Farklyn... Your brother's abduction plunges our kingdom into dire straits. We worry it may ignite a rebellion. The severe drought, the famine... They have reached a breaking point. In the absence of His Highness's iron fist, I fear Wynnorth will be pushed to the brink," the man stammered.

"Tragic," the prince retorted sarcastically.

Truth be told, the people's suffering did not leave him indifferent. However, he could not help but rejoice at the thought of the two sovereigns grappling with such a disastrous situation. Finally, their inflated pride was humbled by a real threat.

"Your Highness must act as steward of Wynnorth until the king's return," implored the magistrate.

He paused, hesitant to continue. He knew the prince would not welcome the rest of his news.

"Braylon?"

"My lord... Your mother... Her gracious majesty is coming here, to Ryre's Keep," the counselor mumbled, immediately lowering his gaze to the ground.

Farklyn felt as if lightning had just struck him. He jumped to his feet, his eyes wide and his complexion livid. If he could have avoided her presence forever, he would have willingly done so.

"Here? N-NOW?" he stuttered, panic evident in his hoarse voice.

"Within two days, at most," specified the messenger, still averting his gaze.

The prince let himself fall limply on his bed, dejected and perplexed. Whenever Valera appeared, it spelled trouble for him, and Farklyn loved his routine as it was. He remained silent for a moment, gathering his thoughts, alienated by the unfortunate news.

"Bring me my clothes and ready the chariot," he ordered, his tone both dry and absent.

Surprised to find an escort outside his chambers, Farklyn hastily dressed and made his way to Ryre's Keep, where he knew his mother was heading. Anxiety gripped him as he hurried, hoping she could not get ahead of him. She hated waiting...

——— ··●·· ———

Ryre's Keep, the empire's most imposing fortress, stood proudly in Wynnorth, commanding a view over the capital of Eluin from atop Mont Auberlon, a once-destructive dormant volcano. Through the years, this mountain had transformed into one of the only cultivable areas in the region, vital amidst the drought that plagued the kingdom. The four massive towers of the bastion rose behind an ancient facade of stone and obsidian, testaments to its enduring history. Arrowslits lined the walls, reminders of countless battles that had taken place on its grounds. Despite the dragons that had once roamed freely before their extinction, Fabyan diligently cared for the fort, seeing it as a reflection of himself— imposing and impenetrable. However, Farklyn viewed Ryre's Keep differently, considering it gloomy and uninteresting. His taste leaned toward beauty and refinement, qualities he believed the fortress lacked.

As anticipated, Valera's arrival was announced two days later. Farklyn awaited her in the main hall, a vast room dominated by a surprisingly simple granite throne. Paintings of distant landscapes adorned the walls, while tall iron chandeliers served as the only decorative elements. Practicality prevailed in Ryre's Keep, a sharp contrast to the opulent court villas Farklyn was accustomed to. Despite simmering nervousness, he masked it behind his detached and smug expression. His attire exuded luxury: a grey silk shirt with a plunging neckline, a sapphire velvet jacket embellished with silver buttons cascading down to his knees, ashen trousers, and tall black sphinx-skin boots. Royal jewels added a touch of nobility and refinement. His long hair, left untamed but meticulously styled, was a deliberate effort to avoid his mother's reproach about his appearance.

Staying true to form, the Queen of Guverl'yt made a grand entrance. Citizens cheered as she paraded through the streets in a vibrant procession, reveling in her presence as she soaked in the adoration. Despite Wynnorth's dire circumstances, Valera's popularity soared, sustained by her military triumphs, particularly the liberation of the East from dragons that had plagued the land for decades. The closing of the portal connecting their dimension to Razakstrom, the homeland of the flying reptiles, was a remarkable feat that earned her widespread acclaim. As the procession finally reached the hall, twenty armored sentries and ten lace-clad ladies-in-waiting led the way. Valera arrived last, emanating grace and charm. Her ebony hair was intricately styled into a braided bun, enhanced with a lavish rose-gold tiara encrusted with jewels. She wore a violet taffeta gown, the color of royalty, with veiled fabric sleeves fluttering on each side, casting a mystical aura around her. Completing her regal ensemble was her twisted bronze scepter, topped with the Stone of Guverl'yt—a fist-sized ruby with a shimmering flame at its center—further enhancing her majestic presence.

The courtiers bowed before her, their murmurs filling the great hall. Valera savored the adoration, then approached her son with an almost arrogant smile, her lips as full as they were in her youth at the beginning of her reign. She kissed him gently on the cheek and whispered in his ear.

"I see you're stubbornly hiding your lovely face behind that long mane. What a pity."

Farklyn sighed, knowing he would likely never gain her approval. She dismissed his efforts with calculated detachment, sometimes with subtle cruelty. He had once hoped that with each passing year, her attitude might soften, but that optimism had been in vain.

"Hello, Mother," he retorted politely, forcing a smile, and gestured gracefully toward the throne for her to take her seat.

"No, no! That's yours now," she said, opting for an adjacent chair.

"Temporarily," insisted the prince, hesitating to sit on the throne.

Valera chuckled softly, her laughter sending shivers down his spine. "We'll see," she replied.

"What do you mean?" Farklyn asked.

"In this kind of situation, one must always assume the worst," she explained in an almost absent tone, her lightness belying the fact that she was talking about her own son's imprisonment.

"Deplorable," he muttered through gritted teeth.

"Deplorable that your brother did not ensure his lineage in case of adversity, yes! If fate decided so, the title of king would be yours. I don't think anyone would appreciate such a turn of events," she continued, brushing off her own double-edged remark.

"Unfortunately, Fabyan and I share the same values when it comes to freedom and celibacy. We have different wells to drink from," Farklyn sneered, glancing at the ladies-in-waiting, who giggled coquettishly in unison.

"One does not prevent the other. We must remedy this situation at once," retorted Valera decisively.

He knew where his mother was heading, and his breath caught for a moment. He suspected she had a pre-established plan ready to be set into motion.

"Always so opportunistic, Mother," Farklyn answered.

His voice cracked, but he concealed his distress behind a mocking attitude. Meanwhile, Valera chuckled and shrugged. Gently, she placed her fingertips on her son's silk-gloved hand, and Farklyn felt a shiver run through him. Gestures of maternal affection were rare for him, a fact he particularly appreciated.

"So… what should I deduce from this announcement?" he asked, still feigning innocence.

"I know we understand each other. This charade you're so crudely orchestrating to gain my approval doesn't please me. We are more alike than you might think, my dear son," Valera replied.

She showed no sign of weakness, instead fixing her gaze on him defiantly. Farklyn pondered all the insults he wished to hurl at her. In an ideal world, he would not have held back.

"We must exercise extreme caution and discretion in selecting your future bride," continued the queen, her tone almost solemn. "The precarious situation of Wynnorth and Guverl'yt due to the severe drought does not permit us to invite animosity from our neighbors. Another ally could undoubtedly restore the supremacy of our two kingdoms."

"Another ally? The entire empire of Balt'boec wishes us dead! I thought you and Baalhan took care of that during his short reign," Farklyn replied slyly, knowing this topic was a jab at his mother.

The queen's expression darkened, and for the first time since her arrival, Farklyn perceived a hint of vulnerability in her. She could not hold his gaze and forced a smile that betrayed her inner turmoil.

"Your father... Baalhan... he would have sacrificed anything for the supremacy of his people," she explained in a weak, troubled voice. "I... I cannot deny that his actions burdened the empire, but..."

Her grief suddenly gave way to frustration. "You know it's impossible for me to clearly recall that period of my life, Farklyn! I've desperately tried to piece together those missing memories, but to no avail."

Her son stifled a groan as he observed once again her obstinate attempts to justify herself. The queen had consistently maintained her innocence regarding her late husband's actions, attributing her lapses in memory to inexplicable reasons. Always such convenient timing! Farklyn hated how she could so easily credit her behavior to these supposed moments of confusion. Despite numerous visits to mage healers, they assured her of her perfect health and believed that her troubles stemmed from a traumatic event. In the absence of further clarification, Valera accepted their diagnosis without question.

Apart from her bouts of memory loss, Valera rarely discussed the man who had spent his final years married to her. It was rumored that his assailants were rebels who remained loyal to Auda Verina, Valera's late aunt and the previous ruler of Wynnorth. Farklyn never quite understood the fascination with his unfortunate great-aunt, who had earned the moniker *the Demented Queen*. True, her reign had endured for more than twenty tumultuous years, during which she wielded absolute authority over her subjects. At the time, Valera, her young niece, had just ascended to the throne of Guverl'yt. Soon, she found herself under her aunt's sway, as Auda claimed it was her duty to restore order and justice in the East. However, Auda Verina's once vibrant and ambitious spirit swiftly deteriorated into madness. Paranoia consumed her, plunging Wynnorth into a nightmarish chaos that persisted for months. The queen became mistrustful of everyone around her, except for Baalhan, who remained her loyal adviser. Auda secluded herself in Ryre's Keep, isolating completely from her court and even her own servants, convinced that a coup was imminent. Lost in her delusions, she launched a merciless purge against her perceived adversaries. Thousands of citizens met gruesome fates in the public square, tortured for information that existed solely within the sovereign's tormented mind. Peasants, nobles, and magistrates alike fell victim to her indiscriminate wrath.

It was on a summer night, following one of the deadliest days, that Baalhan finally found her. In her left hand, she clutched a glass vial containing only a few drops of poison. Despite the adviser's evident grief, rumors swiftly spread throughout the empire. Those loyal to Auda Verina loudly proclaimed Baalhan as the true culprit behind the tragedy. They suspected him of manipulating the queen, leading to her gradual descent into madness. Now branded as a usurper and an assassin, Baalhan faced widespread condemnation. While Valera vehemently denied these accusations, Farklyn had long learned to be skeptical of his mother's protests. For a moment, the prince hesitated to reach for her hand, sensing her overwhelming distress. However, he refrained from the gesture, wary that even a small action might provoke one of the queen's unpredictable mood swings, further exacerbating the already volatile situation.

Valera looked up, her expression brightening. "I hope you won't mind, but I've taken the liberty of selecting a bride who will secure our dominance within Balt'boec."

She spoke casually, signaling to a servant to bring her a drink.

"Of course," Farklyn replied, once again masking his true feelings with a forced smile. There she was—the ruthless queen.

"I have Princess Satya of Cendril in mind, daughter of King Tanyll Zylfaren. This union would deal a significant blow to any who dare oppose us," she declared with unwavering conviction.

"An elf?" Farklyn pondered, struggling to conceal his disdain.

"I know! Their stern demeanor and eccentricity leave much to be desired. However, I cannot overstate the importance of such an alliance for our nations. With theirs combined, our army would reign supreme over the empire!" Valera's eyes gleamed with ambition. Rarely was she more animated than when envisioning grand schemes. Her son firmly believed this to be where she would one day meet her downfall.

"Why not form a coalition with Walderlake? I'm sure a half-elven lineage wasn't part of your plans," he remarked with subtle contempt.

Farklyn found it challenging to mask his lack of empathy toward the people of Cendril, known as Balt'boec's most formidable mercenaries. Moreover, it was one of them who had been accused of his father's murder.

"King Hargon has no female heir, and the Emerald Guardian has no children—except for an adopted daughter," Valera countered, her tone tinged with exasperation. "Surely you agree that a union with an orphan, tethered to a powerful magistrate by the whims of fate, is less than ideal."

"A Guardian's daughter? I believe it could be a prestigious alliance. They wield true power within Balt'boec," Farklyn replied, subtly challenging his mother's perspective.

"Really? Tell me, my son, can you name those who safeguard the empire's gems?"

"Of course! You, as Guardian of Guverl'yt and Wynnorth. Brennet Reinhart, the Guardian of Walderlake. Tanyll Zylfaren, of Cendril..."

Farklyn hesitated momentarily.

"Eraza possesses Osthallvale's Moonstone, and Azura Kane holds the Citrine of Brilea," the queen interjected.

Farklyn nodded uneasily. His mother always found a way to make him feel foolish to prove her point.

"Nevertheless, I believe the daughter of a Guardian is a worthy match for an Elven princess."

"An ADOPTIVE daughter. No. Satya Zylfaren seems like an excellent choice to me," Valera declared firmly and insistently.

She continued to stare at her son with unsettling intensity. Farklyn wanted to object but held his tongue. A sense of unease nested in his stomach, a feeling all too familiar in his mother's presence. He swallowed hard before conceding, "Satya Zylfaren it is," reluctantly averting his eyes from Valera.

CHAPTER

4

THE COUNCIL OF THE EMERALD ORDER

Elissa had only visited Richeroc once before. During that brief encounter, Brennet had kept her concealed, preventing her from freely exploring the city or interacting with its inhabitants. Though her recollection of the trip was somewhat blurred, she remembered feeling overwhelmed by a sense of suffocation. The metropolis loomed large with its bustling crowds, cacophony of noise, and ceaseless activity. Richeroc served as the abode of high society, bourgeois elites, and affluent merchants, epitomizing perpetual commotion. Its towering buildings, crafted from volcanic stone, stood in stark contrast to the architecture of Brevic. Renowned for its temples, Richeroc boasted magnificent facades adorned with gold and bronze— a hallmark of the town. The central library, housing the rarest books of Balt'boec, was hailed as a marvel known far and wide. Elissa found solace in witnessing the progress of the city's reconstruction efforts, a hopeful sign of recovery from the devastation wrought by the dragons.

The journey proved long and draining for Brennet, who spent most of the trip asleep. Elissa and Bruna exchanged only occasional whispers, if any at all. Truth be told, the mage had little inclination for conversation, as anxiety consumed her thoughts.

"I notice you're not wearing the dress I left in your room," the governess murmured in her high-pitched voice.

Elissa responded with an indifferent shrug. Indeed, she had witnessed the gaudy raspberry-colored taffeta dress on her bed. As usual, she had disregarded it, opting for more practical and inconspicuous travel attire. Bruna let out a sigh of exasperation, rolling her eyes with her typical dramatic flair. Despite her constant irritation, Elissa could not deny the fondness she felt for her. When the mage had arrived at Brevic Manor, Bruna had taken on a maternal and protective role for her. At that time, Bruna was in her prime, her beauty blossoming with each passing day. Her jet-black mane, rosy cheeks, and shapely figure caught the attention of many men in town. Yet she turned down all suitors to watch over the little orphan.

"I can't keep up with you!" Bruna exclaimed in frustration. "If only you'd let me style your hair in the fashion of the ladies in the capital! You know, with delicate adornments at the front!"

Elissa groaned, annoyed, and turned her gaze back to the window, ignoring the pleas. Of course, she wanted to comply! What would be the point? Matters of vanity and allure remained foreign to her. Despite Bruna's persistent efforts to introduce her to high society, Brennet had never permitted it. It seemed that arranging suitable marriages for their daughters was the primary concern for fathers in the region. But not for him... not Brennet. Elissa found it easier to feign indifference at each of the maid's attempts. She preferred to bury her thoughts deep within herself and discourage any inquiries about potential romantic entanglements.

As Bruna prepared to voice her protest, the chariot jolted to a sudden stop. The anxious mage peered outside and immediately recognized the distinctive turrets of the Itos temple. Brennet stirred, awakening with a start, and struggled to catch his breath amidst a fit of coughing. In a matter of seconds, the carriage door swung open, revealing Reynold, the coachman.

"Why have we stopped?" inquired the Guardian.

Reynold's already sun-reddened face deepened in color. He anxiously ran a hand through his greying goatee and glanced over his shoulder.

"Apologies, my lord... but there's a crowd gathering in the streets," he stammered.

"A crowd?" Brennet asked, still recovering from his sudden awakening.

"A protest," Reynold confirmed.

"I see... Take us to the south entrance," Brennet ordered.

With no need for further explanation, Reynold nodded briskly and closed the door. After a brief pause, the carriage resumed its motion. Voices reverberated through the avenue, filled with palpable anxiety.

"We refuse to remain powerless any longer! The stone must be protected at all costs!" urgently proclaimed one of the townspeople.

"What if the dragons reappeared?" another citizen asked.

Elissa cautiously cracked open the shutters and observed the concerned crowd gathering in the public square.

"What is happening?" she wondered aloud.

The Guardian remained silent, offering no immediate answers.

The carriage came to a second stop, this time with a smoother transition. Though less imposing than the main entrance, the south one exuded its own sense of majesty. The massive structure, a fusion of stone and gold, soared into the sky with its towering spires. Elissa marveled at the thought that humans had constructed such a splendor. She hurried to assist her father out of the carriage, her eyes wide with awe as they stepped into the corridors of the Capitol. Emerald-adorned carvings decked the walls, and crystal chandeliers hung from cathedral ceilings ornamented with gemstones. At the heart of the hall stood a statue of unparalleled magnificence—that of Galvrick, embellished with gold and precious gems. Between his outstretched hands, a sphere of sparkling light slowly revolved. Its radiance cast soft, multicolored glimmers that danced through the crystals of the chandeliers, creating the illusion of a starry sky suspended above them. Elissa had never witnessed such a captivating spectacle.

As they paused in the corridor, she noticed Bruna signaling for her to proceed without her.

"Why are we leaving Bruna behind?" Elissa inquired, her gaze lingering on the breathtaking room.

"She lacks clearance to access the conference chamber," the Guardian replied, his tone firm.

"Shouldn't I wait for your return as well?"

Brennet remained silent, his assured strides echoing through the halls. His stern countenance and icy demeanor persisted. With each resounding step, Elissa's confidence waned in the imposing grandeur of the Capitol's corridors. Her heart pounded in her chest, her hands trembling with nervous energy. It was then that she sensed her father's silent acknowledgment of her eagerness, his compliance to her impatience. This long-awaited day, so fervently anticipated, now seemed surreal and unsettling. They came to a stop before the imposing doors of the main hall. Two guards stood sentinel at the entrance, their imposing figures resembling stoic guardians. Clad in emerald-hued tabards gilded with the royal sigil—a griffin intricately embroidered in gold thread—they held formidable halberds at their sides, their points reaching toward the resplendent geode-lined ceiling. With an air of dignity and solemnity, Brennet released Elissa's arm and advanced forward. The doors creaked open slowly, revealing the expansive Council chamber beyond. Voices swelled like a tidal wave, echoing through the corridors. An aromatic haze enveloped the mage's senses; she had always found ceremonial incense unsettling. Brennet strode forth with unwavering poise, commanding the attention of the assembly with every movement. Elissa fought the urge to look away, her thoughts consumed by the prospect of escaping the monotony of Brevic. Reluctantly, she followed her father, only to be abruptly halted by the guards, who instinctively moved to block her path. A sense of helplessness washed over her; never before had she felt so small.

"You cannot enter this meeting room without permission," the sentry to her right declared in a resolute voice.

Brennet turned, engaging in a whispered exchange with the gatekeeper. The latter cast a puzzled glance at Elissa, studying her for a moment. To her surprise, he gestured for his comrade to allow her passage. With a respectful bow, the guards stepped aside, offering no further resistance.

The vast hall stretched across multiple tiers of ebony marble balconies, each filled with mages dressed in traditional Council robes. At the heart of the chamber, an ancient oak throne stood as a symbol of modesty amidst the surrounding opulence. This was the original chair of Galvrick I, preserved by the magistrates to remind the Guardian who would occupy it of the importance of humility—a principle that echoed the emperor's own life. A shiver ran down Elissa's spine as she grasped that her mentor was not leading her to the balconies, but directly into the spotlight. Trembling, she followed, struggling to maintain her composure. As Brennet took his seat, Elissa stood beside him, her unease evident. Magistrates stared, fingers pointing, whispers circulating—a mixture of astonishment and curiosity painted on their faces. In that moment, she realized that her presence had not been expected.

A slender yet imposing figure rose from the center of the dais, commanding immediate attention from the room. Elissa recognized him instantly: a man with a white beard that shimmered with golden undertones of his youth, eyes of piercing blue, and an aquiline nose that carried a haughty expression. Toran Sius, the Master of Magistrates. Second only to Brennet in influence within the Council of the Emerald Order. His icy gaze briefly settled on Elissa, causing her to hold her breath. Despite the passage of time, he appeared just as she remembered—the man she had seen on that fateful day when she lost her parents, when the Circle of Am fell. Toran Sius had commanded the troops dispatched by the king to expose the dragons allegedly harbored by the druids of her community. Since then, his praise had resounded far and wide, his popularity soaring. He was a war hero, a guardian of the people.

Turning his attention to the assembly, Toran began to speak. "Esteemed magistrates! I am grateful for your swift gathering today. Although the announcement of this assembly was sudden, I am proud to see such a considerable turnout. Let us stand together and recite the opening sermon in honor of Galvrick, the protector of our existence, whose spirit resides within the stones."

All rose solemnly, including Brennet, and in unison, they cited the sacred words:

"By Emerald's boundless might,

Light and jewel of our days,

In your care, our soul and form unite,

With your strength and shield, we'll find our ways.

Watch over us, brethren of this Sacred Council,

For Galvrick's will guides us without delay."

As the sermon concluded, everyone retook their seats in complete silence. Elissa dared not move, her anxiety gnawing at her. Toran Sius remained quiet for a moment, his gaze once again fixed upon the still woman. He smiled—a peculiar smile that sent shivers down her spine. She could not quite fathom his intentions, but she sensed deep within that it was not a mark of courtesy or benevolence. His eyes held something intoxicating, something that invoked dread and submission.

"I believe we are all eager to learn why our Guardian has convened us," Toran stated, a smirk tugging at his lips. "And naturally, our curiosity is piqued regarding the identity of the woman at his side."

A heavy pause filled the room. The Master's gaze remained fixed on her, almost as if he expected an answer from her.

"I… I am..." Elissa began, her words faltering.

However, Brennet's commanding voice cut her off immediately.

"Could someone please explain the cause of the commotion outside the Capitol?"

Once again, silence prevailed. An uncomfortable hush gripped the chamber, amplified by an echoing quality that made even the faintest movements startlingly audible. Brennet scanned the gathering, his presence commanding such formidable authority that Elissa momentarily forgot his ailment.

"The citizens of Walderlake are… concerned," Toran offered in a measured tone. "The ongoing tensions in Guverl'yt and Wynnorth, as you're aware, have stirred restlessness among the populace. Rumors circulate that Queen Valera Netherborne has seized an Oracle who shared an apocalyptic prophecy, one predicting the imminent return of dragons to our land."

"I see," Brennet responded, his skepticism evident.

"These are mere gossips, naturally, but if they were proven true, the consequences would be dire indeed," the Master continued somberly.

Once again, those on the balconies reacted strongly. Even though Elissa had only witnessed the tail end of the conflict between the Empire of Balt'boec and the dragons of Razakstrom, the news troubled her. Glimpses of destruction and terror still haunted her thoughts. After all these years, the mere mention of those winged giants was enough to stir her fear and distress.

"How are you, dear Brennet?" Toran Sius inquired, his voice soft. "As many of our esteemed colleagues here are aware, I've heard of your condition, which seems… how should I put it… precarious."

To the young mage, his tone feigned concern. His gaze lingered on the

Guardian with a faint smile, a look of subtle dominance. Evidently, he relished the opportunity to publicly showcase the elderly magistrate's vulnerability. Brennet's response was a sneer, accompanied by a defiant stare. Elissa felt a surge of pride at observing her mentor stand firm against his colleague's attitude. She would not have expected anything less from him.

"True, I've seen better days," Brennet acknowledged, his demeanor astonishingly composed. "This is precisely why I've summoned you all here. I understand that my ailment places our kingdom in jeopardy, especially in the light of the delicate political climate that surrounds us."

A delicate political situation? Brennet had assured her that Walderlake had no cause for concern among the other realms. Elissa had rarely felt as out of the loop as she did now. She was clueless about the true reason for her presence in the Capitol. Clearly, her father's intentions diverged from hers. Anticipation built in her, as it did for the rest of the Council, as they waited for him to reveal his explanations. Finally, he rose to his feet to speak once more.

"That is why…"

Then he fell silent, a strange pause following. He swallowed visibly, and for the first time since they had entered the room, Elissa sensed an unusual vulnerability in him.

"That is why it is now my duty to name a successor."

As soon as his sentence came to an end, the crowd erupted. Elissa's gaze, filled with distress, shifted to Brennet. It felt as if a knot had tied around her stomach, leaving her breathless. She knew there were only two ways a Guardian could sever their bond with the emerald and relinquish their title. The first was through death, and the second was the formal passing of their title to a successor in a ceremony involving the emerald itself. In the latter case, the Guardian's mortality was a certainty within weeks of the ritual. The body, stripped of its prolonged connection to the gem, deteriorated beyond repair. Unable to contain her horror any longer, bile crept up her throat. She felt like her abdomen was being crushed. Blinded by tears, she rushed to her mentor's side in desperation.

"Father... no," she pleaded in a barely audible voice.

Brennet gently covered her trembling hand with his own and offered a reassuring smile.

"It's going to be alright. Trust me."

But she could not. Not this time.

Toran Sius, with a hand gesture he had to repeat to silence the uproar, requested order.

"I understand that this news has caught us all off guard... left us all stunned! However, Brennet has nobly and effectively served as the guardian of the stone for over three decades. What an undoubtedly heroic decision from this exceptional man, who prioritized the prosperity of our realm above all else... a man who placed the lives of thousands before his own! This, dear brothers and sisters, exemplifies the conduct of a true magistrate. Therefore, with humility, I accept the responsibility of succeeding Brennet Reinhart as the Guardian of the Emerald."

The Master turned to Brennet and performed a respectful bow. Council members followed suit, breaking into a harmonious applause that transformed into a standing ovation for the old mage, a tribute that seemed to stretch on endlessly. Elissa could glimpse a faint smile on her mentor's lips, a smile that did not reveal much. Something was brewing, of that she was certain. As the cheers subsided, Brennet gradually straightened up to address the assembly.

"My valiant brethren! I wish to extend my gratitude to Toran Sius for his touching words, and to all of you for your incredible support. However..."

Brennet paused, letting suspense hang in the air, captivating the crowd, and his apprentice.

"I regret to inform you that Toran Sius may have been a bit hasty in his announcements," he declared with unwavering resolve.

The Master's countenance immediately darkened, his smug smile giving way to irritation.

"Regarding my selection for a successor…"

"Choose your words wisely, Brennet!" Toran Sius intervened, rising abruptly, his expression fraught. "Let's not forget the complexities that…"

"No, Toran. Permit me to refresh your memory of the Guardians' Code. A code established by Galvrick himself! It states that in the event of resignation, the stone's keeper has the authority to freely designate a worthy successor," Brennet interjected with an impassive tone.

"This is preposterous! You and I both know that this law is archaic. Numerous other kingdoms have discarded such primeval rules eons ago."

The Master's crystalline gaze locked onto him. Nervously, he ran his trembling fingertips over his pursed lips.

"Brennet is correct. The Guardian indeed has the prerogative to pass on their title to a chosen successor, as long as said aspirant is also adept in magic," chimed a woman wearing a purple turban, seated to the right of Toran Sius.

Elissa recognized her instantly: Lady Janile Mercyn, a cousin of Hargon and Brennet. She had gained fame due to her telepathic abilities that had played a pivotal role in many high-profile trials. Toran Sius was held back from protesting by the weight of her renown. A disapproving expression gripped the leader of the magistrates, one he could not conceal.

"Thank you, Janile!" he hissed through gritted teeth.

Brennet did not delay. He refused to grant the Master another chance to manipulate the crowd.

"Without further ado, let me unveil the name of my successor. This is a choice that I've pondered deeply. The dedication, integrity, and courage of this individual make me feel at peace in passing on the mantle. I trust that the stone will be in the hands of someone both competent and, above all, compassionate. Allow me to introduce your forthcoming Guardian, my daughter, Elissa Reinhart."

She was struck, as if by a bolt of lightning. There she stood, rendered speechless, frozen at Brennet's side, while his hand rested proudly on her shoulder. For a suspended moment, her ears hummed, and the world around her moved in an agonizingly slow rhythm. The magistrates surged from their seats. Their expressions of shock and awe seemed distant echoes in her bewildered mind. Despite her fervent desire to be among the Council, Elissa found herself unable to fathom the reasoning behind this evidently irrational decision.

"Brennet... your condition is clouding your judgment!" Toran Sius asserted, his voice edged with certainty. "I believe a period of rest would offer clarity. I suggest we adjourn this assembly to the next moon. This would provide time for reflection and reconsideration of this impulsive choice."

Toran Sius strode toward the man with an air of severity, a barely concealed fury in his gaze.

"My lucidity has never been sharper," the Guardian retorted with unshaken calm. "Furthermore, I made my decision for a successor several years ago... the very moment I began her training."

"She is utterly untested!" a magistrate exclaimed, his voice a mix of astonishment and dismay.

"Elissa possesses a gift greater than most of you can comprehend," Brennet replied with assurance.

Once more, the assembly sprang to their feet, the room palpably charged with tension, and Elissa found herself fearing for their safety.

"I do not doubt her talent," the Master retorted. "Yet, assigning such a grave responsibility to an outsider, someone without any history within this Council... Brennet, your decision is irrational! I will never consent to entrusting the stone to a worthless orphan!"

Elissa's insides churned, but she gritted her teeth and struggled to maintain composure. Her nails dug into the flesh of her palms, the physical pain offering a modicum of relief to her inner turmoil.

"I told you so, didn't I, Brennet?" Toran Sius snapped, descending from the dais toward the Guardian. "I warned you that adopting this impoverished girl would lead to disaster. And why? To soothe your conscience? I never imagined she would drive you to madness!"

In that moment, Elissa would have given anything to be leagues away from the Capitol. They were chastising her without even knowing her, without soliciting her opinion on the matter at hand. She wanted to align herself with those who shouted in disagreement and demonstrate that she did not presume to stand as their equal. Yet, her father exuded confidence in his decision, steadfastly refusing to dignify the Master's accusations.

Toran Sius assumed a more composed stance, attempting to placate the Guardian with soothing words.

"Brennet, I understand that your affection for this girl may be clouding your judgment," he asserted. "Your attachment to her is commendable, but it would be unwise to push this matter any further."

"Elissa is more deserving of this stone than anyone here," the Guardian persisted, his resolve unyielding.

He turned to his apprentice, his gaze conveying a fleeting smile imbued with pride.

"More deserving?" The Master's tone dripped with arrogance. "Were her parents not traitors, members in a rebel faction within the Circle of Am?"

"My parents were not traitors," Elissa growled, her voice a barely audible rumble.

A palpable tension swept across the breathless chamber. Fury coursed through Elissa like molten lava. Toran Sius shifted his focus to her, a contemptuous expression twisting his features.

"I must have misheard. For a moment, I thought this insolent girl dared to address me," he retorted in a belligerent tone before breaking into a malicious chuckle.

Consumed by rage, she could no longer contain her words.

"You heard correctly. My parents, Nora and Jeon Lothain, were not traitors!" she reiterated forcefully, her body quivering with anger.

"How dare you speak to me like that! I am the Master of the Emerald Order!" Toran Sius thundered.

"And I am the future Guardian of Walderlake!"

Elissa's utterance was met with immediate regret, a declaration she could not swallow. No one had ever spoken to the Council's leader with such unflinching audacity, not even Janile or Brennet. Toran's face shifted from livid to a deep scarlet. His features twisted into a grimace of fury, and he advanced a few steps toward Elissa and her mentor.

"I see that the welfare of our realm is not your concern, Brennet! I have no option but to take possession of this stone by force!" he roared, gripping the scepter held resolutely at his side.

Instinctively, the young mage's hand lifted toward the Master. Brennet's shout to halt came too late. A silvery beam of light surged from her fingertips, propelling Toran a few paces backward. His fall disrupted several candlesticks, their clattering creating a cacophonous eruption within the grand chamber. He lingered on the floor momentarily, a mixture of vexation and embarrassment evident in his grumbling.

"I see... so this is what you've concealed from us," the Master murmured, readjusting his attire with evident displeasure. Brennet remained quiet, withholding any reply.

"How can this be?" Lady Janile faltered, her hand covering her mouth in disbelief.

The gazes directed at Elissa spoke volumes of collective astonishment. She felt transformed into an oddity, simultaneously captivating and fearsome. Her anger faded, replaced by a creeping anxiety that knotted her stomach. She anticipated the guards stationed at the entrance to be summoned, ready to apprehend her.

But nothing happened…

"I propose we adjourn this assembly," the Master concluded, his composure still unsettled. "Brennet appears to have made his choice, and I will respectfully honor it. At the coming moon, we shall arrange a date for the final transfer ceremony. Until then… I await our next encounter, Miss Reinhart."

His grin was a sly promise, akin to a wolf preparing to pounce. She wished to retreat, sensing an ominous retribution, yet remained rooted to her spot. Her pride compelled her to stand her ground. Why had she not managed to control herself?

Brennet seized his daughter's arm, signaling her to lead the way. She offered an awkward bow and guided him out of the room, beneath the stares of the bewildered assembly. She dared not look back until they had exited the Capitol.

CHAPTER

5

WILHEM

Elissa could not shake the apprehension that their troubles had merely begun. Her impulsive attack on the chief magistrate had unfolded in front of a multitude of witnesses. Punishments for lesser transgressions were common in the kingdom. Yet, her foremost concern was her family's safety. Any misfortune she brought upon them would be an unforgivable burden to bear. Bruna, more agitated than ever, paced the inn's living room where they had taken refuge. Meanwhile, Reynold, informed of the incident, had sought solace at the nearest tavern. Merely hours had passed since their arrival in Richeroc, and an alarming predicament had already occurred.

"Do you think the Council will pursue us all the way here?" Bruna's voice quivered, a blend of anxiety and uncertainty.

"Calm yourself, my dear. No one shall face arrest, as no actual crime was committed," the Guardian responded, settled comfortably in a wicker chair, a cup of steaming tea in hand. His self-satisfied smile elicited a growl from Elissa.

"No crime, you say? I attacked the most influential magistrate in Walderlake!" Elissa's voice resonated, propelling her to her feet.

"Your actions align with those expected of a Guardian. Once you bear that title, protecting the stone becomes your duty against all who would seek to take it away," Brennet remarked.

"Even against Toran Sius?"

"Especially against Toran Sius," Brennet affirmed.

Elissa, her fingers knotting in her hair, resumed her pacing, reminiscent of a caged lion. Sighing in exasperation, she battled mounting restlessness and anxiety. How could Brennet be so dismissive, so bold? Then again, she reminded herself of who he was—the renowned Guardian of Walderlake. Perhaps he possessed knowledge beyond what he divulged.

Gradually, Elissa regained composure, sinking into a chair beside her mentor.

"Do you genuinely believe the Council will overlook my actions? Given the Master's reaction, I'm doubtful," she asserted.

"Toran's temper has always been heated. When his supremacy is challenged, his wrath ignites easily. However, remember he is not the sole member of the Council. Most magistrates uphold our code of ethics with unwavering dedication. Should Toran pursue any course of action, he will likely stand alone," Brennet offered, his voice imbued with reassurance.

Yet, Elissa's unease lingered.

"And that prophecy... It doesn't bode well," she added.

"I wouldn't invest much worry in that matter if I were you. Rumors and speculations have swept across the empire throughout history. The populace remains apprehensive after the Great Dragon War.

Nevertheless, I intend to discuss with Janile directly once tensions have subsided."

Elissa approached the window of the parlor, peering onto the streets with a nervousness previously foreign to her. She yearned to share her father's faith in the Council's justice, but doubt persisted.

"I believe it would be prudent to depart Richeroc as quickly as possible," she asserted resolutely.

"You're right. We shall set out at dawn," the Guardian concurred, taking another serene sip of his tea. "Furthermore, the assembly is scheduled for the next moon. Lingering here would serve little purpose."

Elissa nodded mechanically, her gaze still affixed to the inn's window. Nothing out of the ordinary on the horizon—the city's clamor softened as twilight enveloped the surroundings. Yet, the sense of oppression continued to weigh heavily upon her, and even the silence appeared deafening.

— • • ● • • —

Refusing to surrender to her apprehension, Elissa helped Bruna settle her father into bed. As always, he resisted each step, his dignity seemingly more important to him than his physical comfort. A sigh of relief escaped her lips when, finally, she extinguished the candles near his bedside. If only he understood that his unwavering pride burdened her more heavily than his ailment.

Despite her weariness, sleep eluded Elissa as she returned to the room she shared with her governess. The night seemed shrouded in an ominous aura, suffocating in its weight. The bustling atmosphere of the sprawling city felt foreign to her, and the evening breeze carried an unfamiliar scent tainted with the essence of Richeroc. There was a stale undertone that went unnoticed by the town's inhabitants. The noise of carts rattling over cobblestone streets, the sporadic squabbles of creatures on rooftops, and the drunken singing from below—the ceaseless cacophony grated on Elissa's nerves. Her fervent desire to leave her peaceful village of Brevic County had been overshadowed by an unrelenting yearning to return.

The image of Toran Sius's haughty expression materialized in her mind the moment she closed her eyes. "A worthless orphan..." his words echoed. How could she defend herself when her own identity felt foreign? Estranged for so long, she had suddenly thrust herself into their world like an unexpected cannonball. The rapid succession of events was overwhelming, each aspect careening uncontrollably.

Welcomed by the embrace of morning light, the mage breathed a sigh of relief. Swiftly, she gathered her belongings, as Reynold prepared the chariot for their departure. However, his demeanor remained noticeably evasive, avoiding her gaze, which she assumed was filled with judgment. How could it be otherwise? Fortunately, Bruna's attitude toward her had not changed. The same mixture of exasperation and ceaseless monologues reassured Elissa in an oddly comforting way.

"Will we be safe in Brevic, Mr. Brennet?" the governess inquired, her voice tinged with fear.

"As I've said before, I trust in the Council," the elderly man responded matter-of-factly.

Elissa found herself sympathizing with the maid's perspective, unable to shake off the feeling that Brennet's newfound attitude was amiss. Was it arrogance or mere negligence? She struggled to pinpoint the source of this sudden change.

Fortunately, their return to the family estate unfolded without incident. Upon arrival, Elissa helped the Guardian to his room, hoping he would find some much-needed sleep. To her dismay, his condition had worsened once more. She had fervently waited for a miracle, yet the sight before her felt like a cruel denial of her prayers. As he sank his head onto the feather pillow, the magistrate slipped into slumber. His hands, as pale as milk, rested on his emaciated abdomen, his features gaunter than ever.

Suppressing her tears, Elissa gazed at this heart-rending sight. The thought of facing the consequences of her actions without Brennet's steadfast presence gnawed at her. However, she knew she had to ignore these intrusive thoughts, for they would only cause her to lose what little composure she had left. Her own hunger pangs interrupted her contemplation, reminding her that she had not eaten in quite a while. In the whirlwind of anxiety, she had unconsciously prioritized others' needs over her own. With a final glance at the slumbering Brennet, she drew aside the heavy velvet curtains and slipped out of the room.

Already in the kitchen was Minerva, the cook, whose exuberant hug nearly took Elissa's breath away.

"So, how was Richeroc?" Minerva inquired with palpable enthusiasm.

The details of their journey had not reached the household, a fact that baffled Elissa, considering Bruna's insatiable appetite for gossip.

"Eventful," was all Elissa managed.

"Just that? What about the magistrates? Did you visit the city's shops or witness the grandeur of the Itos monument?"

"I barely ventured outside; our stay was fleeting," Elissa replied, her tone vague.

"That's a pity… but don't despair! Opportunities to explore will come again, sooner or later," Minerva added with genuine empathy, misinterpreting Elissa's apparent lack of enthusiasm for disappointment.

Elissa deftly redirected the conversation as she reached for a morsel. She knew better than to interfere with Minerva in "her kitchen"; that territory was sacred. "I've overseen the menu in this household for over forty years. Today won't be an exception, miss!" the cook declared tenaciously, flour-dusted rolling pin in hand.

Left to her culinary domain, Elissa's amusement stirred, a soft smile tracing her lips. With a generous slice of bread and a chunk of cheese in hand, she retreated to the parlor to seek some well-deserved peace and quiet.

Abruptly, four distinct knocks reverberated through the mansion, jolting Elissa. Her blood seemed to thicken in her veins. Had someone trailed them back to Brevic? Were they Richeroc soldiers, or worse, magistrates of the Order dispatched by Toran Sius to capture them? Rooted in the corridor, she felt her heart jump in her chest. The pounding persisted, a rhythm of urgency that left her no choice but to answer the door. With her mind racing, Elissa approached the grand entrance, thoughts swirling like a tempest. She gripped the handle, summoning every ounce of courage, praying that this would not mark her last action.

As she swung open the door, blinding light streamed in, momentarily obscuring her vision. Slowly, she discerned a figure standing before her, the details gradually resolving. Once her sight adjusted, the man on the porch came into focus—a man of impressive stature, robust and solid, with hair evoking fields of summer wheat. Clad in unpretentious traveler's attire, a leather belt adorned with a substantial sword studded with black tourmalines cinched his waist. Not a soldier's uniform or an Emerald Council tabard in view! Unlike the prematurely weathered countenances of the local young men, enduring the marks of rural life's toils, his face bore an intriguing constellation of scars, with one particularly pronounced on his upper lip, reflecting a distinct maturity.

Observing him, Elissa was taken aback by his vivacious, hearty expression. His turquoise eyes emanated kindness, his gentle smile assuring her that he harbored no intention of apprehension. Yet, her caution prevailed, and she left the door slightly ajar. Perceiving her wariness, the stranger hastened to speak.

"Apologies, Miss... Is this Brennet Reinhart's residence?" the visitor inquired.

"And may I ask who is looking for him?" Elissa responded, her voice cautious, her mouth still full of bread.

"Hmm... Wilhem?" he offered.

The name failed to strike a chord.

"Wilhem... Owen Strongbow's son," he clarified, accompanied by a friendly grin.

"Ah!" Elissa managed, feeling rather foolish. Owen Strongbow. Brennet had indeed forewarned her about the impending visit from the knight, but the recent tumultuous events had purged the conversation from her memory. Overcome by enthusiasm, she hurried out of the mansion, her feet navigating the stone path, snack still in hand.

"Are you searching for something?" he asked, amused.

"Where is Lord Strongbow? Could he have chosen a different route?"

Wilhem regarded her inquiry with perplexity, slipping a hand into his travel attire. Her apprehension resurfaced, and the man let out a low chuckle as he withdrew a parchment, its seal stamped with the Reinhart family crest. She examined the letter, recognizing Brennet's handwriting and confirming his summons for Wilhem's presence in Brevic—with clear emphasis on Wilhem's.

"I don't understand... Brennet said that Lord Strongbow would be visiting."

"My father's health doesn't permit long journeys... especially after the accident," he explained with a hint of unease.

"Accident?"

"A year ago, the chariot that carried him back from Richeroc met an unfortunate fate, tipping over into a ravine. He survived, but his legs weren't as fortunate," Wilhem elaborated.

"I'm truly sorry..."

A smile touched his lips, though it was evident that this jovial facade veiled a deeper sorrow. Why had Brennet omitted such a tragic detail and made a promise about the illustrious knight's visit?

"You seem disappointed," Wilhem ventured.

"No… it's just that I … my apologies. The past days have been exceptionally tumultuous for us."

Elissa swiftly extended an invitation, albeit with the awkward gesture of offering her cheese-laden chunk of bread.

Wilhem studied the opulent estate with a mixture of awe and respect, his gaze flitting from corner to corner.

"Excuse my manners; I'm a knight's son, and grand residences such as this still amaze me," he explained with a faint grin.

"Owen Strongbow is a legend! And isn't he also part of King Hargon's court?"

"Not quite, no. At least, not since he relinquished his titles…"

"Relinquished? Why?"

Wilhem's smile held a shade of discomfort, disconcerted by Elissa's forthright manner.

"Personal reasons," he supplied succinctly.

"Nonetheless, it's an honor to have been raised by an exceptional father, regardless of his status!" Elissa exclaimed, realization dawning about her earlier lack of tact.

"Yours isn't too shabby either!" Wilhem retorted with a wink. "I've heard amazing stories about you. The Guardian never seems to tire of praising your prowess."

Elissa's head dipped as her cheeks suffused with a warm flush. Prowess? Not quite.

An abrupt cough interrupted their conversation, drawing Elissa's attention to Bruna, who observed the scene from the staircase. The governess' sun-kissed face bore a familiar disapproving expression, one that the mage had grown accustomed to. In a heartbeat, Bruna descended the stairs, hastening to relieve Wilhem of his baggage. With a scrutinizing glance, she cast a condescending smile at him.

"You must be Mr. Strongbow, a guest of our master, Guardian Brennet Reinhart," Bruna remarked with an overly formal attitude.

Wilhem responded with a modest nod.

"Why not prepare a room for him, Bruna?" Elissa proposed, her tone carrying a hint of stiffness.

The maid glowered at her, then executed a curt bow before pivoting on her heels. Abruptly, she halted and spun back toward them.

"My room will be right next to yours, and I'm a light sleeper," she added, directing an accusatory gaze between the two young individuals.

"Thank you, Bruna. That will be all!" Elissa retorted in an authoritative, cutting tone. Rarely had her governess' demeanor caused her such embarrassment. Swiftly, Bruna returned to her duties, muttering a series of inaudible words that Elissa could well imagine.

"I apologize for Bruna's behavior, Mr. Strongbow. She can be... protective."

"Wil—"

"What?"

"Call me Wil."

Elissa's nervous nod was accompanied by a downward glance at her feet. Clearly, the two were already on familiar terms. Alright, then...

"Would it be possible for me to meet the Guardian?"

"He's resting at the moment. We've just returned from a long journey, and—"

"No need to trouble yourself, Elissa. I can receive Mr. Strongbow," interrupted Brennet.

The Guardian appeared in the doorway of his room, a figure both fragile and yet so commanding, as if he could marshal armies with his mere presence. Wilhem bowed respectfully, seeming somewhat overwhelmed by the magistrate's stature. It was a common reaction upon encountering him, one Elissa had grown accustomed to. Motioning for Wilhem to rise, Brennet approached him, his steps measured and deliberate. Placing a hand on the young man's shoulder, the mage scrutinized him with a wistful smile.

"Yes… Owen's likeness, almost deceptive!" he mused with a faint chuckle. "That same proud gaze, robust build, and the mischievous grin he was notorious for. Especially when he managed to embroil us all in some sort of trouble!"

"I assure you, I'm far more reasonable than he was," Wilhem responded, laughing.

A deep exhale, akin to relief, escaped Brennet's lips. He nodded as if lost in contemplation. Then, gesturing for Wilhem to follow, he led the way into his study, softly closing the door behind them. Elissa, on the verge of joining them, halted mid-step. She stood alone in the corridor, feeling inexplicably foolish. What had just transpired? Why had her father so casually excluded her from the conversation? Laughter and spirited exclamations emanated from the room, confirming that her presence had already been forgotten. Puzzled and, above all, upset, she turned on her heels, retracing her path to the parlor. In the wake of the Capitol's commotion, she struggled to understand how Brennet could remove her from this discussion. This secrecy, the persistent enigma surrounding her past and future—Brennet possessed knowledge she lacked. She begrudgingly admitted that jealousy was creeping in as well. The lively rapport that Brennet shared with a stranger, her father's jovial demeanor—Elissa ached for a similar connection, longing for that elusive warmth.

●

She lingered in the living room, her impatience mounting as the meeting dragged on. The need to distract her mind from the relentless grasp of the Council's concerns weighed heavily on her. Elissa sought respite in the gardens, where the sun blazed against a cloudless sky of azure. In contradiction, her demeanor seemed to darken. Amidst nature's grandeur, a solace that usually embraced her, her heart remained cold and unmoved. Restlessness surged within her, compelling her to pace along the paths that bordered statues of long-forgotten Guardians. Eventually, she leaned against one of them, the likeness of Auda Verina, Wynnorth's late queen. Carved from granite, the sculpture's gaze fixed on the horizon, its brow furrowed in an eternal aura of melancholy.

"I understand," Elissa murmured to the effigy with a bitter chuckle.

The warmth of the stone against her skin offered some semblance of relief. She sighed, her fingers caressing the pendant that hung around her neck, twirling it thoughtfully. The weight of numerous decisions loomed over her, decisions she had to accept without fully comprehending. Toran Sius' insinuation about her parents lingered, a venomous echo in her mind. Traitors? No. They were victims in the wake of a dragon hunt. At least, that was Brennet's explanation.

———— ··•·· ————

After an endless wait, Wilhem finally joined her in the gardens. His customary warm smile carried a hint of unease, casting a shadow on his demeanor.

"So? Did Brennet tell you all his secrets and unveil my dark past?" Elissa inquired brusquely.

Wilhem halted abruptly, his expression tinged with confusion. His furrowed brow betrayed his uncertainty in how to respond.

"Just kidding," the woman growled, rising from the ground nonchalantly. A wave of her hand brushed her coppery hair behind her shoulders as she sighed, visibly annoyed.

"Have I offended you?" the warrior asked, doubling in his discomfort.

Elissa did not answer immediately, uncertain of what to say to him. No, he had not offended her. She realized her anger was not directed at him, but rather at her mentor. Despite being unable to shake off the wave of jealousy gnawing at her, she attempted a more cordial tone.

"You didn't," she lied, offering him a smile.

However, her expression failed to convince him. He nodded resignedly, beginning to take his leave.

"Did Brennet mention anything about our current worries?" she ventured, her voice softer.

"He did tell me about the incident in the Capitol. You certainly made things quite hectic," Wilhem retorted, turning back to her.

"I do seem to have a knack for getting myself into trouble."

"Brennet also informed me of how you heroically rescued him."

"Heroically or foolishly?"

"Perhaps both?" the man replied with a smirk. His green-blue eyes sparkled, and Elissa found herself giggling, her cheeks tinged with a blush.

"May I … may I know what you two discussed?" she stammered.

"I must admit I'm not entirely sure myself. Does he always sound so cryptic?"

"You have no idea!"

"I see… However, he did make it clear that he wishes for me to accompany you to Richeroc next month," Wilhem explained, a hint of apprehension in his voice.

"As?"

"Your protector."

"Really? So Brennet does worry about our safety, after all."

"Was it truly a secret? A father always worries about his child."

"I wonder how much impact a lone man could have in the face of an attack. A man without magical powers, at that."

Wilhem burst into laughter, and Elissa immediately realized her comment had bordered on tactlessness.

"I apologize. I didn't mean to doubt your abilities..."

"If it's any reassurance, I was a member of King Hargon's personal guard after undergoing the same preparation as my father did in his youth."

"You're a Knight of Aegis?" exclaimed the mage with open admiration.

He nodded with a fleeting smile before looking away. That revelation indeed helped to quell her concerns. The King's guards were renowned for their rigorous training. Meticulously selected from childhood, they were molded into combat legends. Only a select few could claim to have been part of their ranks.

"I must admit, I'm surprised!" Elissa responded, her smile now stretching from ear to ear.

"Really? I don't quite fit the image you had of a knight?" Wilhem countered, a raised eyebrow hinting at his amusement.

"Not entirely, no! I always thought knights were more... intimidating?"

"Truly?"

"Yes! Like... like..."

"Like the way I may have envisioned the next Guardian of Walderlake?" the man asked with a teasing grin.

"I see your point..."

"If it offers any comfort, I wasn't too far off in my judgment," Wilhem declared with a wink.

Elissa looked down, her smile softening. Perhaps he did indeed intimidate her more than she had initially thought.

———— ··●·· ————

The remainder of the day passed swiftly. Wilhem proved to be excellent company, his presence rekindling the Guardian's spirit as he reveled in youthful memories. Bruna, unlike her master, seemed hesitant to welcome him into their home. Her stern looks and sparse words during dinner did not escape Elissa's attention. It was not until Brennet was preparing to retire for the night that Elissa decided to inquire about it. The governess immediately knitted her brows.

"You know, I have a vivid recollection of Owen... very vivid. And if this man's personality resembles his father's..."

She paused, her face growing even darker. With a deep frown and pursed lips, Bruna appeared to relive a distant memory.

"What I'm trying to say is that he's likely to dangle empty promises before you. He'll leave you waiting, stranded... like a... like a scoundrel," the housekeeper seethed with unusual intensity.

"I didn't know you and Owen had a relationship."

"A very, very brief relationship!" Bruna concluded bluntly. "Believe me, for your own sake, it would be wise to keep your distance from this Wilhem."

"Aren't you the one desperately trying to match me with the unsuitable bachelors of Brevic? Just a few days ago, you couldn't stop talking about the baker's son!"

"He'd be a much better match than Owen Strongbow's son, I'm certain," Bruna stubbornly asserted, raising her voice.

"Really? A baker's son who's nearly half my age and has a penchant for the county brothel appears more desirable to you than a knight of Aegis?" Elissa countered, a trace of arrogance lacing her tone.

Bruna groaned, clearly unwilling to continue this conversation. Abruptly, she stormed off toward Brennet's room. Elissa did not try to stop her. She understood that Bruna's aversion to Wilhem was rooted in her own personal history. She could not fault him for his father's actions, despite her governess's disapproval. So far, the knight had been courteous, empathetic, engaging… but nothing more. For a moment, Elissa hesitated whether to follow Bruna to her mentor's quarters. Brennet's enigmatic behavior still irked her, and she had no intention of conversing with him while that irritation lingered. However, she realized that her days with him were numbered if this arrangement went ahead. She could not afford to waste time in trying to change his mind. As she entered Brennet's room, she found the governess by his bedside, coaxing him to drink his customary herbal infusion.

"Thank you, Bruna, but I don't feel like it," he protested.

"Please, Mr. Brennet! The ingredients I've added will help your recovery."

"I fear I need more than just herbal tea."

"If not for yourself, do it for your devoted servant's peace of mind!" the woman insisted, pushing the concoction closer to the old man.

With an exasperated roll of his eyes, Brennet begrudgingly swallowed the contents of the cup.

"To your peace of mind, my dear Bruna!" he exclaimed, returning the empty goblet to her.

The governess nodded, a satisfied expression gracing her face, before she hastened out, avoiding the young mage's gaze. Elissa briefly contemplated stopping her, but held back.

"SO? What's your impression of our guest?" Brennet asked.

"I'm not certain. It's too early to tell," Elissa replied with a bitter tone.

Brennet observed her for a moment, his brow furrowing.

"Is something troubling you, my child?"

Elissa burst into laughter—a dry, bitter laugh, filled with irritation and bewilderment.

"A bodyguard? Really?"

"Sometimes, a bit of caution is wise," Brennet calmly explained.

"Granted. But caution against whom? The Council? Toran Sius?"

Brennet remained silent, his gaze fixated on her.

"You see? Silence! Perpetual silence! And for what reason? What's so astonishingly shocking that I can't know about it?" Elissa snapped.

"I've told you everything," the Guardian murmured.

She paced back and forth across the room, her steps heavy. She could no longer ignore the pressing need for answers.

"I noticed how the Council members were staring at me! The terror etched on their faces... I saw it... I felt it. You can't deny it!"

Brennet sighed. He studied her intently, his hesitation evident.

"It's your gift," he finally admitted, his voice barely a whisper. "Your magic—the one you can channel without your staff."

"I've been trying not to. I promise to control it from now on."

"It's not about that," Brennet continued in a serious tone. "Their fear stems from the fact that you're the only one who can do this. No one can wield magic without a staff, not anymore, at least."

"But... The Circle of Am, my parents... many mages didn't need a staff."

"You're different, Elissa. More so than I led you to believe."

"Why did you keep this from me?" she whispered.

Her mentor's face turned pale, beads of sweat forming on his drawn features. His breathing grew shallow, and a thin line of blood dribbled from his trembling lips. His body convulsed. Elissa instinctively rushed to his bedside. This time, Brennet did not intervene. A burst of light erupted from the mage's hands, settling on the man's chest. The coughing subsided, and she managed to calm him once more.

"Thank you, Elissa," Brennet whispered with a sigh of relief. "Soon, you won't need to worry about any of this."

"Don't say that, I..." Elissa began, her words trailing off as Brennet interrupted.

"I must rest, now. Please close the door on your way out."

Elissa's breath caught in her throat. She could not help but feel guilty about his deteriorating condition. Maybe her mood swings and questions had pushed him too far.

"Alright... good night, Father."

As she turned to leave, Brennet's quavering voice called out to her.

"Elissa... tomorrow, I'll tell you everything. I promise."

She nodded and left slowly. Promises. Always empty promises.

CHAPTER

6

PROPHECY

News spread swiftly across Balt'boec. As soon as Elyndel Arren, the Master of the Cendril Council, caught wind of the incident at Walderlake's assembly, he wasted no time summoning an urgent gathering. A selective group of the Order's magistrates were invited. Elyndel was certain that there had been a breach of confidentiality among their ranks. Months had passed since the sacred Oracle of Cendril was captured. In an attempt to safeguard the source of their precious visions, the elves had concealed her in a location known only to them. It was evident that a member within their Council was acting as an infiltrator, leaking information to their adversaries. Caution was imperative during this critical juncture to prevent the situation from spiraling into chaos.

Elyndel promptly made his way to the palace of the Cendril Guardian, King Tanyll Zylfaren. The Master had secured a concealed chamber for this very purpose—a room soundproofed and hidden from prying eyes. An underground passage led to it from beyond the castle walls. Its entrance was cunningly buried, tucked away near Loraven Forest within an abandoned crypt that had remained untouched for centuries. The place was bathed in muted light, its center dominated by a solid table hewn from ashen marble. Encircling it were a dozen intricately carved white birch chairs, similar to those found in the city. Elyndel could not help but smile at the irony. Never had a meeting been held in such an enigmatic and austere ambiance. It almost made him feel like a spy. An unquenchable thirst for adventure had persisted within him for decades, but as the head of the magistrates, he now understood the necessity of promoting rigorous discipline. Meandering for excitement was no longer a luxury he could afford. Despite being one of the oldest members in the Amethyst Order, Elyndel had managed to retain, as had his brethren, a nearly ageless physique. His countenance bore the grace of maturity, a blend of delicate and masculine traits. His features, slightly elongated compared to the norm, seamlessly melded into the rest of his face. His eyes, reminiscent of moonlit blue, emitted a comforting warmth. In spite of the gentleness he exuded, his profound wisdom and magnetic charm commanded respect among his people.

True to his punctuality, Elyndel was the first to arrive. He had chosen a simple attire for the occasion—a charcoal silk tunic and unembellished black leather trousers. He hardly ever donned the traditional vivid amethyst robes of the Order anymore. Taking his seat with an air of casualness, he poured himself water from a waiting pitcher. Intrusion during their meeting was to be avoided, and the identities of the participants kept undisclosed. The room was hence arranged with a tray of beverages and fresh fruits, each attendee responsible for accommodating themselves. Elyndel, naturally, had no qualms about this setup. He believed that an excessive number of servants weakened one's resolve and diluted nobility's inherent sense of reason. Sighing again, anxiety growing within, he took a prolonged sip from his cup. The gravity of the information he was about to share with those he regarded as his comrades gnawed at his thoughts.

Before long, the sounds of movement echoed from the staircase leading to the room. The ivory strands of a woman's hair were the first to surface atop the stone steps—Analera Naefiel. Though devoid of a smile, Elyndel knew there was no animosity between them. Her stern demeanor appeared to be her sole expression, except on rare occasions that she reserved exclusively for him. Despite this, she acknowledged the Master with a polite nod before settling beside him. Much like Elyndel, she had forsaken formal attire, opting instead for civilian clothing—a silvery taffeta dress concealed under a dark velvet cloak. It seemed as if she had not set foot in daylight in years, her skin almost translucent. She was a figure that drew attention, not due to her great beauty, but the distinctiveness of it. Her visage mirrored her nickname, the White Lady, derived from her snow-like complexion and hair. Her pronounced cheekbones bestowed her with an air of nobility, and her amethyst eyes echoed the hue of her kingdom's renowned gem. Though her bearing was haughty, Elyndel knew he could always confide in her. She had supported him for centuries, without ever demanding reciprocation, continually ready to offer invaluable counsel.

Then, Gareath and Nilyan Montallis made their entrance—the famed blood and arms brothers who once defended Ilsira Gorge against swarms of black dragons, long before their extinction. Elyndel had fought alongside them, forming an unbreakable bond of trust. Contrary to Analera's austere disposition, the Montallis brothers radiated warmth and camaraderie. Their resemblance was uncanny—towering stature, cascading dark locks, and a smile marked by an endearing asymmetrical dimple. Nonetheless, they differed significantly in character. Gareath exuded profound shyness, often choosing silence unless necessity demanded speech. Nilyan, in contrast, possessed an unparalleled charisma that could sway even the most stubborn of skeptics. Despite the fame that surrounded them, the essence of humility still thrived within the Montallis brothers.

"How is the family?" Elyndel inquired of Nilyan, the elder of the two.

"Wynn's starting to suspect that I've been having an affair with all these late-night meetings. Thankfully, Gareath's presence by my side tends to soothe her," his friend responded with a wry grin.

Laughter filled the air as Nilyan placed a hand on his brother's shoulder.

"I am, indeed, the voice of reason in the family," the younger sibling added serenely, offering a gentle smile.

The two men exchanged a chuckle imbued with mutual understanding. Gareath had perpetually chosen the path of celibacy, an option embraced by the majority of elves. Only a few possessed the fortitude to sustain love and passion with the same heart over centuries.

Syviis Arren, Elyndel's younger sister, breezed into the room. Her petite build, rosy cheeks, and ceaseless enthusiasm were a testament to her youthful spirit. The fervor that infused her every gesture was infectious for some, overwhelming for others. Her short, dark hair framed a mischievous face resembling that of a playful pixie, while her wide mouth was quick to illuminate the space with a sparkling smile. In stark contrast to Elyndel's poised maturity, Syviis exuded a childlike vibrancy that could occasionally make heads spin. This quality often garnered her disapproval from her elders, although her trustworthiness was beyond question. Her ingenuity and astuteness had earned her a place within the Amethyst Order mere months after graduating from the College of Mages. Seating herself opposite her brother, she bestowed upon him one of her most radiant smiles.

"Good morrow to all!" she chirped.

"Shhhhhh!" Analera interjected, pressing her finger to her lips. "Allow me to remind you that discretion is vital."

"Rest assured, Ana. I've personally cast a soundproofing spell on this room. No need to question its infallibility," Syviis retorted, her tone unyielding and confidently loud.

"I don't readily trust the supposed infallibility of other people's enchantments, especially one woven by a recruit," Analera countered in a judgmental expression.

Crossing her arms vehemently, Syviis huffed in frustration.

"You're certainly more pleasant when you wake up in my brother's bed," the young mage teased with a mischievous pout. "But judging by your demeanor, it seems that's no longer the case."

A flush of embarrassment swept across Analera's ivory complexion, a sharp contrast to her usual paleness. Nilyan barely stifled a chuckle, and Gareath averted his gaze, clearly uncomfortable with the tension.

"Syviis, please," Elyndel intervened with calm authority. This rivalry between the two women was nothing new to him, and he was accustomed to handling it. Syviis struggled to withhold a retort but managed to remain silent.

Finally, Tanyll, the king, entered the room. His Majesty's presence always exuded poise, elegance. He radiated natural splendor, a self-assuredness that demanded no validation. Braided hair adorned with a crown of silver chains and delicate leaves graced his brow. Like Elyndel, his visage carried a distinct maturity. His olive eyes, framed by subtle creases, sparkled with a playful demeanor against his ebony complexion. The members rose as a mark of respect, but Tanyll gestured for them to remain seated, a smirk tugging at his lips.

"Your Highness," Elyndel greeted with a salute, pulling a chair closer to him.

Tanyll took his seat, intertwining his fingers ceremoniously on the marble table. His gaze swept over each companion, carrying a touch of paternal consideration.

"I am pleased to see my most trusted allies gathered here. However, I am apprehensive that the reasons for which our Master summoned us may be less than pleasant."

"Indeed, my king," Elyndel concurred somberly.

"I dare hope that you've prepared a plan to retrieve Aelrie," Syviis interjected, casting aside social norms.

"I will address that," her brother replied, his tone both measured and authoritative. "I've received word from the Emerald Council. Brennet

Reinhart has declared that his adopted daughter will obtain his gem after an imminent succession ritual."

"Is this the ceremony where the Guardian parts from his stone and... dies?" Syviis questioned, her incredulity evident.

Elyndel nodded, and her eyes widened in shock.

The notion of anyone choosing to end their own life was incongruous to her. Strangely, those with near-immortality harbored the greatest fear of death.

"Forgive my astonishment! I thought this ceremony to be a mere myth, that nobody had actually done it," she continued.

"Indeed, the succession ritual is quite unconventional, which is why it's concerning," Elyndel clarified with a grave expression.

"Are you doubting his choice? Is the woman not qualified?" Nilyan asked, raising a quizzical eyebrow.

"No one knows. The future Guardian is a mystery to the public. According to our sources, she maintains no affiliations with high society, the political circles of her kingdom, or anybody beyond her immediate household. This has troubled many within the Council."

"So, she's unaffiliated with any group of mages? Richeroc College? No wonder the Emerald Council expressed disapproval of Brennet's decision," Analera exclaimed with a hint of outrage.

"Knowing Toran Sius, he would have been furious had Brennet chosen anyone other than him," Elyndel responded, his disdain for the neighboring Master evident.

"Indeed," Nilyan agreed with a derisive tone. "In my 627 years of life, I've rarely encountered someone as petulant."

"What truly troubles me is that the Guardian appears convinced that this ritual is the sole means to protect their stone," Elyndel continued.

"So, he doesn't trust the Emerald Order's magistrates?" the king queried, his concern evident.

"That's the root of my worries," the Master admitted. "Furthermore, I know Brennet well. He's never struck me as impulsive. He possesses a careful, methodical nature. I'm certain he has valid reasons for his choice."

"Don't you think…" Gareath began hesitantly, before stopping.

Nervously, he raked his fingers through his bluish-black hair, his gaze avoiding the others. Yet, Elyndel encouraged him to proceed, understanding that Gareath only spoke when necessary.

"Go on, Gareath."

With a fidgety shuffle in his seat, the reserved elf cleared his throat before continuing in a voice nearly a whisper.

"Do you suppose this might be what the prophecy alluded to?"

A heavy silence followed, gazes exchanged in mutual consideration. None had mentioned this vision since the Oracle's abduction.

"If that were indeed the case, the implications would be dire," the king spoke, his earlier enthusiasm dimmed.

"With all due respect, Your Majesty, whether the prediction unfolds imminently or at a later time, the ramifications will be catastrophic," Analera asserted. "Many anticipated it would ignite global uprisings, open warfare. The resurgence of the most destructive creatures ever known in Balt'boec could engulf our empire in flames."

"I agree, but we have the opportunity to prepare and mitigate the damage, to forewarn our people," Nilyan offered. "If this prophecy's fruition is imminent, it would thrust us into the heart of an unrelenting storm, affording no reprieve. However, prevention is possible. A solution can surely be found."

"Would the return of dragons truly be such a calamity?" Syviis queried nonchalantly.

All eyes turned to her, a mixture of astonishment and pain etched on their faces.

"What?" she wondered with childlike naivety. "I'm hardly the first to contemplate this."

"Many of our kin fell in battle against those winged giants… including our parents," Elyndel reminded with a reprimanding gaze.

"I don't dispute that. But you can't ignore that Balt'boec's magical equilibrium has been disrupted without their presence. The world is slowly unraveling, and you know it."

"The empire was in peril even when they were among us, if not more so," Nilyan retorted, his usual amiable demeanor replaced with a rare disapproving scowl.

"It doesn't matter! Our ancestors sealed the portal between our realms years ago. We successfully eradicated the dragons from our lands. There's no reason for concern here. Or perhaps you doubt the competence of those who closed the breach? That's where the real insult to their memory lies, in my opinion."

"While it's unlikely that the sealed rift would open again, one must consider a second occurrence," Analera interjected.

As Syviis prepared to respond, Analera raised a finger to halt her, signaling her to listen.

"I do believe the breach our people closed is secure. However, the Montallis brothers and I were present when your parents sacrificed themselves for our kingdom's safety. Elena… your mother… she never dismissed the possibility of other rifts."

Syviis's expression darkened, her excitement giving way to sorrow. Her mother's name had rarely been mentioned since her passing…

During the ensuing silence, Gareath hesitantly placed a hand on the young elven woman's shoulder, prompting a smile to return to her lips.

"We are still in disagreement regarding the prediction's true meaning and the significance of *Original Blood*," Nilyan interjected.

"Indeed, the prophecy remains open to various interpretations," the king remarked.

"Why don't we rescue Aelrie from Valera's dungeon and directly ask her about HER own vision?" Syviis interrupted assertively.

Analera groaned with indignation, finding it hard to fathom that a mere recruit could address their sovereign with such candor.

"It's alright, Analera. Syviis does have a point," Tanyll conceded, a faint smile playing on his lips. "Could someone kindly recite the exact wording of the prophecy?"

The task of refreshing the king's memory fell to the Master.

"Upon the return of the ancient winged creatures,

an empress shall ascend the throne.

Bound by the Original Blood,

mastery over the stones she shall have.

Under her rule, an era will unfold,

dismantling the very essence of the empire.

From the ashes, Balt'boec shall be reborn."

Though spoken softly, the words reverberated through the chamber, their weight hanging heavy in the air.

"Could the concept of *Original Blood* refer to us, the elves?" Nilyan questioned, a clear note of pride in his heritage present.

"It's a conceivable interpretation, but not indisputable. The Cendril people tend to lay claim to being the first in all matters," Elyndel countered.

"According to legend, the Abshanishs are the oldest of all races. Could it be about them?" Syviis suggested.

"But that's just it... a legend," Analera clarified. "There is no factual basis for the existence of such a people."

"Many have associated Galvrick with the Abshanishs, if I recall correctly," Gareath chimed in, seeking confirmation from Elyndel and the king.

"Those are mere rumors," Analera insisted.

"Regardless, this Original Blood entity would possess unprecedented power to manipulate the stones simultaneously, precipitating unprecedented change within the empire," Elyndel elaborated, aiming to quell the rise of a fresh argument.

"So, you suspect that this woman, the Guardian's adopted daughter, is the one described in the prophecy?" Analera inquired.

"It's a possibility that we should not dismiss," Elyndel replied.

"Is this truly such a dire prospect?" Syviis interjected with unabashed curiosity.

Silence ensued, the group exchanging puzzled glances.

"The prediction doesn't forecast the world's annihilation, but rather imminent transformation and rebirth," she continued. "I believe we can all agree that Balt'boec desperately needs such a transformation, however radical."

"I approve! Yet, the ordination of a new sovereign, or more accurately, an empress, is bound to raise concerns ... or objections," Elyndel contributed.

"I don't share your opinion," the White Lady interposed. "I recall the era of Galvrick's rule over Balt'boec. While it ushered in a golden age, it came at a cost. Our race's supremacy suffered greatly. We should not crave a tyrant on the throne, should we?"

"Some may not readily embrace a despotic rule," Gareath added cautiously, choosing his words carefully. "However, the glorification of this presumed supremacy has contributed to Balt'boec's current struggles."

"Tyrants, regardless of their intentions, have always plunged our empire into turmoil," Analera proclaimed, her voice no longer hushed.

"Our world did not deserve Galvrick and his blessings!" Syviis flared.

"That's enough," Elyndel intervened, his tone both commanding and slightly annoyed.

A hush fell, everyone yielding to the Master's authority and waiting for his words.

"Your Majesty, esteemed friends, isn't it time we reclaim control and defeat the corruption devouring Balt'boec? The woman in whom the Guardian of Walderlake places boundless faith deserves our attention. Within this prophecy, I see an opportunity to restore balance, to uncover a formidable ally in her," Elyndel proposed.

"Elyndel is right," the king acquiesced. "We must try to contact her quickly. Without doubt, she will draw the wrath of those fearing the resurgence of an empress. If a connection to this prediction, or even mere belief in it, exists, her safety will be compromised."

"Given Toran Sius's disposition, appointing a stranger as Guardian could expose her to grave dangers," Nilyan affirmed.

"We shall attempt to establish contact with her first," Elyndel stated solemnly. "At dawn, I'll dispatch a messenger to Walderlake."

"Have you considered the potential implications of getting close to her? The perils we might face? She's an outsider linked to an apocalyptic prophecy!" the White Lady exclaimed in disbelief.

"I understand your apprehension, Ana. Nevertheless, allowing someone else to approach the future Guardian first presents even greater risks.

Trust me, I have faith in this decision," Elyndel assured, his gaze softening as he looked into her eyes.

Her resistance eventually gave way. Despite her stubborn disposition, Analera inevitably yielded to Elyndel's influence. She nodded, acquiescing.

"We can only hope that Aelrie's vision hasn't already reached other ears, as we feared," Syviis grumbled.

"Which is why we must also locate the Oracle without delay," the king responded. "We must prevent such prophecies from sowing panic among Balt'boec's populace."

"Finally!" the recruit exclaimed, her astonishment at her own outburst evident. "Pardon me, Majesty… but Aelrie's capture constitutes a direct challenge from Valera."

"For once, I agree with Syviis. The Queen of Guverl'yt has crossed a line and must face consequences," the White Lady added, her voice laden with disdain when mentioning her eastern rival.

"Caution is advised. A confrontational approach will not yield results. Acting aggressively could place Aelrie in even greater jeopardy," Elyndel reminded.

"Excessive leniency could project weakness on our part," Analera countered.

"Appearances do not matter, particularly when a life hangs in the balance."

"Are you certain that your opposition to an assault on the East is solely motivated by concern for a friend? Especially considering our newfound advantage?" the White Lady taunted in a hushed voice.

The leader of the magistrates raised a skeptical eyebrow, genuinely perplexed by her comment's foundation. Deciding to disregard it, he refused to waste time on futile squabbles.

"We must formulate a strategy to recover the Oracle and, in the process, decipher the prophecy's meaning with clarity," he concluded in a resolute tone.

The motion was accepted despite the absence of unanimity. All that remained was to hope that the Master's judgment was sound and that the woman who was to inherit her kingdom's stone would indeed prove an asset. Unspoken but deeply felt, anxiety began to creep over Elyndel, a sensation he had not experienced in ages.

CHAPTER

7

"DON'T LOOK BACK."

The village of Brevic was engulfed in darkness, shrouded in a cloak of somber hues. Just as she thought she could finally enjoy an undisturbed night's rest, a sudden jolt woke her. Strong hands shook her shoulders, and in the dim light, she recognized the tousled blond locks of Wil.

"We must hurry," he whispered urgently as he hastily pulled her from her bed.

She could hear it too—intruders were present below.

"City guards?" she muttered anxiously.

"I don't think so."

"Then who?"

Wil's shrug mirrored her own confusion. Unlike the mage, he was fully dressed, and in the moonlight filtering through, Elissa caught the glint of his sword as if a phantom loomed beside him. They moved stealthily, their footsteps almost silent on the hallway floor.

"Bruna..." the apprentice murmured, groping her way toward her housekeeper's room.

To her astonishment, it was empty, the bed untouched.

At that moment, a shriek pierced the air, cutting through the stillness like an icy dagger. Elissa's hand instinctively covered her mouth to suppress her own scream. As she was about to rush below, Wilhem's strong grip stopped her.

"We can't be reckless. We don't know their numbers," he growled, grabbing her back firmly.

"I can't just stand here while they're in danger!" she protested, struggling against the warrior's hold.

"Your father entrusted me with your safety, no matter what."

"But they're my family!" the mage implored.

The cacophony of chaos grew louder—shattering glass, moans of pain, heavy footsteps echoing through the mansion. At Elissa's desperate plea, Wilhem relented, releasing his grip. He signaled for her to follow him quietly. She complied, her thoughts racing, her heart aching for her father, vulnerable, at the mercy of whoever sought the stone.

The stone...

A gaping pit of dread opened in her stomach.

Gradually, the tumult subsided. Wilhem raised a hand, motioning for her to halt. Peering cautiously around the corner, he counted—there were three intruders. Sheathing his sword, he opted instead for the twin bronze daggers at his sides—more discreet, more precise. With the grace and agility reminiscent of an Aegis knight, he slipped between them, his blades slicing through the air with deadly precision. The assailant let out faint, surprised groans, clutching at their throats before collapsing to the ground, blood pooling around them.

Elissa had not witnessed death in a long time—not since her parents...

Her stomach stirred, and her head spun. The sight was one she knew she could never become accustomed to. The attackers wore no recognizable Council robes or kingdom insignia. Their garments were entirely black, devoid of any identifying marks. Standing frozen at the foot of the staircase, Elissa realized her bare feet were stained with the blood of their victims. The warmth of the scarlet fluid against her skin induced a disorienting sensation. Her tear-clouded gaze shifted to Wilhem. He signaled for her to move, his usually cheerful countenance now etched with a blend of anxiety and resolve. She had to collect herself—her father was relying on her.

The two hurried toward the Guardian's quarters, the echoes of chaos still resonating throughout the residence. Amidst the disarray left by their assailants, they navigated the servants' corridor. That's when she saw her—Minerva's lifeless body sprawled just beyond her room. Her eyes, clouded and vacant, stared into the abyss; her features contorted in terror. She seemed untouched, devoid of visible injury. Elissa knew magic had been used. Suppressing a sob, she bit her lip. Who could have murdered this defenseless woman? Minerva was kind, empathetic, and utterly innocent. Blinking back tears, she forced herself to move forward, her determination to reach Brennet's quarters unwavering.

Though she anticipated the horrors awaiting behind half-open doors, she could not resist stealing glances. They were all there, lifeless, a terrible grimace marking their faces. Godfrik, the aging gardener who often spewed patriotic speeches... Reynold, the coachman who perpetually reveled in good humor... Una, the housewife whose off-key morning songs resonated with unmatched enthusiasm... they had all been her family. In that moment, a sensation of being drained, of emotions evaporating, consumed her.

Suddenly, she felt a forceful pull, a grip yanking her back. Instinctively, she recoiled, facing her assailant. An expression of fury mixed with an odd fear distorted his exquisitely delicate features.

"An elf," she whispered, shaken.

Before the aggressor could react, she placed her hand on his chest. A surge of lightning from her fingertips flung him several steps away. He writhed in agony but remained alive. Wilhem intervened, sword raised, and struck the elf down in a fatal blow. Yet, more adversaries were approaching—a dozen, prepared for battle. Wilhem seized Elissa's arm, propelling her into the corridor without relinquishing his grip. Crimson magical projectiles whizzed around them from all directions. Elissa retaliated, guided blindly by the man who, until yesterday, had been a stranger. Her blows landed, perhaps two or three, amidst the chaos. Her mind swirled, her body numbed. If she was struck, she scarcely registered it.

Finally, within the Guardian's room, they found respite. Immense relief washed over Elissa as her gaze met her father's. Brennet sat on his bed, scepter in hand. To her astonishment, several lifeless corpses lay on the floor. Her mentor's prowess had surpassed her expectations yet again. As Elissa and Wilhem barricaded the entrance, radiant beams of light bombarded the doorway.

"Are you hurt?" she asked her father, panic quivering in her voice.

"I'm unharmed," he whispered.

"What do they want from us?"

"I'm uncertain. These faces are unknown to me."

"One was an elf."

"More than one," the Guardian corrected.

He gestured toward two inert bodies he had personally felled—elves as well. The mansion trembled—their barricade could only withstand for so long.

"Is there another escape route?" Wilhem asked, straining against the door's pressure.

"Under my work desk, there's an underground passage leading to the forest," the elderly man replied.

He moved to his writing table with as much haste as his weary body could muster. From it, he retrieved a velvet pouch in a shade of dark green, extending it to his apprentice with solemnity. Elissa knew its contents without a word.

"Why are you giving me the stone? We must flee at once!" she insisted, gripping the satchel.

"Take it, Elissa. The time has come. I'll strive to delay them as long as possible to grant you a head start," the Guardian reiterated, his tone resolute.

"What are you saying?" she whispered, aghast.

"It's our only recourse, and you know that."

"But…"

"Listen, Elissa! I don't know who is behind this, but I suspect Toran Sius's involvement. You can't remain in Walderlake. You must head to Osthallvale."

"Osthallvale? Why?"

"The druids will provide sanctuary. I made arrangements long ago, foreseeing circumstances such as these."

With difficulty, Elissa nodded, words catching in her throat, unutterable. Without further delay, Brennet pressed the stone into her hands.

"Elissa… your lineage is invaluable. You're among the *Original blood*."

"*Original blood…*"

She had heard that term before.

"We must act swiftly!" cried Wilhem, straining to hold the barrier.

"Find Mistress Eraza. She resides in the village of Ashwick, near the sea. She'll protect you, guiding you to those who can hone your powers. I did my best, but my abilities differ from yours," Brennet continued, urging Elissa toward the desk.

With a deft movement, he turned the head of a Minotaur statuette, exposing a trap door beneath, revealing a stone staircase leading to the mansion's basement. Despite all these years, Elissa had been oblivious to its existence. Brennet grasped her face in his hands, pressing a gentle kiss onto her forehead.

"I owe you my life," she stammered, choked by emotion.

"No, Elissa. I owe you everything. You gave me years of pride by allowing me to call myself your father. Thank you."

Tears escaped her as the man bestowed an affectionate smile, a newfound vigor lighting his teal eyes. A sweep of his staff conjured an ivory radiance, forming a protective aura around the barricade. The relentless pounding on the other side momentarily ceased, granting Wil a much-needed pause to catch his breath.

"A protective barrier?" Wilhem inquired, his voice breathless.

Brennet nodded.

"How long?"

"A few minutes... please, watch over her, Mr. Strongbow," Brennet commanded solemnly.

He urged them both toward the secret passage, though Elissa's hand reached out for him.

"You'll be fine," he reassured her, his tone gentle.

Reluctantly, she let go.

The act of placing one foot ahead of the other had never felt so hard. Tears blurred her vision, her path obscured by grief. Amidst her own anguish, she knew she had to survive. This burden was now hers, one she would bear for Walderlake's sake.

"Elissa... don't look back," the Guardian commanded firmly, a reassuring grin on his lips.

Brennet stood tall, resolute, determination etched onto his features. As he turned the lever, the hatch began to close, obscuring her father's face behind the wooden door. Her heart ached—another instance of being torn away from her rock, for the second time in her life.

Don't look back. Don't look back. Don't look back.

The words became a mantra, her sole guide amidst the suffocating darkness expanding within her mind.

———— ··●·· ————

The mage and the knight of Aegis descended the subterranean tunnel with urgency, hindered only by the enveloping shadows. This passageway had long remained untouched, its damp and musty scent clinging to their senses. An odd, viscous substance underfoot impeded their speed, likely a layer of vegetative moss concealing the stone pathway. The clamor from the estate above slowly faded, replaced by the rhythm of their own breaths and footsteps resonating through the corridor.

Their flight felt unending. After what seemed like an eternity of walking, a glimmer of moonlight finally beckoned them toward the awaited exit. The hatch, sealed for countless years, yielded only to Wil's considerable force. He skillfully ascended to the surface and extended a hand to assist Elissa. She had hardly encountered such a demanding run in her life, her breath ragged and chest heaving. Nonetheless, she pressed on, knowing that their pursuers would soon scour the vicinity. Hesitation was a luxury they could not afford. Within the dense forest, mist resembling pea soup swirled amidst the towering maple trees. An owl's distant hoot jolted the already edgy mage. Fortunately, the full moon cast its radiant glow upon the sky, offering some visibility.

Then, a surge of intense sensation coursed through Elissa, an electric current that sent tremors down her spine. The feeling was overwhelming, compelling her to halt in her tracks against her own will. A cascade of tinkling, akin to a multitude of bells, chimed solely in her ears. The mage sank to her knees, her body soaring with such power that it felt on the verge of rupture. Wilhem also stopped, his brow furrowed in concern. Beads of sweat and blood dotted his wearied face as he urgently spoke to her. But his words remained unheard, drowned out by an almost unbearable resonance. Her gaze shifted to the velvet pouch she clutched in her hand. The stone within emitted an enchanting luminescence. Never had she beheld something so captivating, so intoxicating. An instinctual yearning enveloped her, an irrepressible desire to make contact. As her fingers brushed the gem's surface, the cacophony ceased, replaced by an ineffable equilibrium. Slowly, Elissa regained her composure, her breath heavy. Tears welled in her eyes as the realization dawned upon her. Following the path of her predecessors, the emerald had chosen her. Her father was gone.

"What happened?" the knight inquired, though he already knew the answer.

"I am now the Guardian of Walderlake," Elissa murmured, stifling a sob.

"I'm so sorry, Elissa," he whispered, his hand finding its place on her trembling shoulder.

She nodded, unable to articulate further. Wilhem extended his support, mindful of the immense loss she had just endured and the involuntary burden she was now destined to bear.

"We have to go," Elissa declared with a somber tone, her movements mechanical.

———— ··•·· ————

As the sun ascended, they neared the forest's edge. The mist gradually dissipated, yielding to the vibrant hues of summer and the invigorating fragrance of morning dew. A tranquil valley stretched out before them, bathed in a serene glow. Yet, despite this picturesque scene, the metallic scent of blood still lingered in the woman's nostrils. Pain numbed her, dulling her senses. Even the crimson blotches on their attire left her indifferent. Elissa became aware that she wore nothing but her nightgown, and her bare feet bore the evidence of her journey—scuffed and caked with mud. She did not care. The grip of suffering overshadowed everything else.

"We need to find a haven," Wil remarked, his words reflecting his consideration for Elissa's state.

"We must press on," she replied absentmindedly.

"You're worn out, covered in blood. We can't go on like this, attracting attention. Do you intend to reach Osthallvale barefoot and in a bloodstained nightgown?" he urged, compelling Elissa to halt.

She sighed, giving in to the man's pleas.

"Do you know a secure location where we can rest?" he inquired with a gentler tone.

"Given that we're oblivious to our assailants, we might still find ourselves with a dagger in our backs, regardless of where we stop," she grumbled, her gaze fixed on the ground.

A contemplative pause ensued.

"What is it?" her companion asked.

"There's a man who resides a few leagues from here... A hermit secluded near Pendard Forest. Only Brennet used to visit him."

"Do you believe he would help us?"

"I'm not even sure he's still alive, but I doubt he's associated with our attackers."

"Very well... Are you fit to continue?" he questioned with genuine concern.

Elissa remained silent. Her stubbornness had always been a defining trait, but this time, it was something more. She was overwhelmed by the dreadful conviction that admitting her vulnerability would shatter her irreparably, leaving no room for recovery. She recognized that her tenacity was her sole protection. Wil cast a final glance at her bloodied feet. Without a word, he gently hoisted her onto his back. Despite her resistance and attempts to break free, he did not relent. Thus, the new Guardian of Walderlake had no choice but to surrender to being carried by the very person she had unfairly envied just the day before. She would not admit it, yet she was grateful for this gesture.

CHAPTER

8

THE HERMIT

The morning's clear sky had given way to an impending storm. Thunder grumbled in the distance, while gusts of wind grew increasingly treacherous. Wil had shouldered the burden of carrying the new Guardian throughout their journey. Not once did he complain. Meanwhile, Elissa's demeanor remained stoic, almost detached. This was the same woman who used to struggle to restrain her emotions, yet now, feeling them was an arduous task. Elissa and Wil stopped as they reached the secluded cabin at the edge of Pendard Forest.

"I hope I'm not mistaken," she murmured, uncertainty shading her tone. The aroma of stew wafted from the vicinity as they neared the cottage, indicating that someone was indeed present. The exterior was surprisingly well maintained, adorned with a flowerbed and meticulously washed tiles. Hesitation gripped Elissa as she contemplated knocking on the door. Perhaps she had made a mistake; after all, she did not know the enigmatic man whom Brennet had mentioned only a couple of times. She stepped back, and the wooden porch creaked beneath her feet.

"Maybe we should reconsider," she whispered.

In that very moment, the door swung open. Startled, both Elissa and Wil involuntarily retreated a step. The person standing in the doorway clutched a rusty shovel, his weathered face etched with caution. His skin bore an almost orange hue, while thin, grizzled grey hair crowned his head, giving him an oddly pumpkin-like appearance.

"Who are you? What do you want?" he growled in a gravelly voice.

"I... I am the Guardian's daughter, Brennet Reinhart's apprentice," Elissa began, her uncertainty evident.

"Um... Ella... Elena?" he muttered hesitantly.

"Elissa."

The hermit scrutinized them, his bushy brows furrowing.

"Did you encounter trouble?" he asked, gesturing to their bloodstained attire.

"We were attacked... We need your assistance and a secure place to rest," the knight answered, purposefully vague.

"Where is Brennet?"

"The Guardian didn't survive, but we managed to escape," the mage disclosed with unsettling frankness.

The hermit's hand flew to his mouth, the rusty shovel slipping from his grasp, shock carved on his face.

"By Itos... I'm truly sorry to hear that... An attack?"

Elissa nodded, her emotions seemingly exiled from her body.

"Who are the assailants? Guverl'yt soldiers? Wynnorth's?"

"We have no clue. That's why we're here... Nothing is safe anymore," Wil interjected, casting an anxious glance behind him.

"The stone ... who has the stone? So the kingdom is vulnerable to invaders… I knew it! I knew it! That's why I've withdrawn from the world! Once Walderlake falls, I'll be far from the battlefields!"

"Calm down! The realm is secure," Wil reassured.

"But the stone!"

"It's safe. Don't worry!" the warrior insisted.

The hermit's eyes widened as he studied Elissa, the moment stretching into eternity.

"You… you're the new Guardian, aren't you? Brennet told me of his plan. I never thought this day would come in my lifetime!" he marveled.

Elissa, taken aback by the revelation, remained silent.

"So young," her interlocutor murmured, almost pityingly.

Wil cast another quick glance behind him, a movement the observant hermit did not miss.

"Well, I certainly can't have the Guardian exposed for all to see outside. Come in! Come in!" he urged, ushering them inside with eagerness.

As they stepped into the house, rain began to pummel the roof. Wil breathed a sigh of relief, recognizing their fortunate escape from the storm. Despite its rustic appearance, the cottage exuded a warm and inviting ambiance. Every detail seemed meticulously tended to, bordering on compulsive cleanliness. Intricately carved oak embellishments decorated the antique furniture, while a prominent fireplace commanded attention in the center of the immaculate dining room.

"You haven't told us your name," the knight remarked, surveying the surroundings.

"Call me Fergus," their host responded cheerfully.

He guided Elissa to a plush armchair decked in eggplant-colored fabric.

"Please, make yourselves comfortable. Are you hungry? Of course you are! After such a long journey!" he exclaimed, rushing out of the room.

His exuberance caught Elissa off guard, making her feel as if each moment unfolded in slow motion. Before she could respond, the elderly man reappeared, holding a cedar bowl filled with thick, steaming mutton stew. However, her inner turmoil had obliterated her appetite. Out of courtesy, she managed to take a spoonful into her mouth and offered a word of thanks.

"May I inquire about your destination? Cendril, perhaps? I must admit, those peculiar pointy-eared individuals don't impress me. Quite haughty creatures, if you ask me. I could never understand Brennet's affinity for their kind. At least their Master seems to have learned how to smile," Fergus continued, deeply immersed in his own speech.

"Actually, we're headed to Osthallvale," Elissa retorted, chewing on a second bite with reluctant compliance.

"That's quite the journey! I don't believe I've encountered anyone who's ventured there, aside from Brennet, of course!"

"My father visited Osthallvale?" Elissa's tone carried a hint of surprise.

"Yes! He entertained me with tales of a land inhabited by goblins and Minotaurs... Druid Minotaurs, to be precise! Can you imagine?"

"I had no idea," she confessed, a touch of concern coloring her words.

Why had her father never shared these adventures with her? He knew how much she loved stories of exploration. Wil, who had been occupied with devouring his stew until now, noticed Elissa's unease. Her gaze was vacant, lost in a sea of thoughts. She no longer seemed to hear their host's enthusiastic chatter. Recognizing the need to shift the conversation, he interjected.

"Do you happen to know of a swift route that would allow us to bypass major cities discreetly?"

"For a more inconspicuous path, I suggest taking the southeast passage toward Earnox village. I can also provide you with a map, should you desire one," Fergus offered.

Wil's gesture of gratitude was nearly drowned out by the resounding thunderstorm outside. Rain hammered against windows and rooftops, oscillating between a torrential downpour and a hailstorm.

"Well, that was a close call," Wil sighed, casting a glance toward the tempest outdoors.

"I still believe we should leave immediately," Elissa maintained.

"Are you serious?" Fergus interjected, his tone laced with dismay. "You should wait for this storm to pass. Traveling in such weather could prove fatal!"

"Staying here will be equally perilous if our assailants find us," Elissa responded impatiently.

"Not a chance!" Fergus sneered. "I've cast an impervious protective dome around the house since your arrival. It will remain invisible to anyone who approaches," he explained, pride swelling in his chest as he crossed his arms.

"So, you're a mage?" Wil inquired skeptically.

"That surprises you, doesn't it?" the old man replied with a chuckling wheeze, exposing the few teeth left in his mouth.

Wil offered a polite smile tinged with a touch of embarrassment, recognizing his lapse of tact. However, Fergus appeared blissfully unconcerned by his faux pas, continuing his bustling activities at full throttle.

"I still think we should leave as soon as possible," Elissa retorted with bitterness.

"While I understand that lingering here puts us at risk of an ambush, it might be wiser to wait out the storm," her companion suggested.

"I'm not bothered by the weather."

"Have you taken a look at yourself? You're worn out and in shock."

"So? I've already told you, I don't care."

"We will rest here for the night and leave in the morning. No sooner," the knight concluded with an air of authority.

Elissa glared at him but did not push the matter further. He had not persuaded her; she simply lacked the strength for further argument. Wil had seen countless colleagues in the same condition as her before. The sight of villages ravaged by war, the bone-deep weariness that accompanies the fight for survival, and the void left by the loss of loved ones—these were all too familiar to him.

———— ··●·· ————

Fergus did his best to uplift the Guardian's spirits over the ensuing hours. Yet, the weight of grief and fear stemming from such profound loss still clung to her thoughts. Despite his stories and antics, her stoic demeanor persisted. Meanwhile, Wil remained discreet, slightly more withdrawn. But he was never far from her side. Elissa felt the knight's concerned gaze upon her on numerous occasions. She had to admit, Wil's attention did manage to soothe her mind in some inexplicable way.

Fergus kindly offered the Guardian a chance to shed her soiled nightgown. In exchange, he provided her with buckskin trousers, a crimson tunic of sturdy fabric, and slightly worn yet well-fitting leather boots.

"They belonged to my wife... my late wife," he shared wistfully. "I've kept them in the best condition possible... much like everything else in this house, truth be told. I never could bring myself to change anything since her passing."

Elissa accepted the offered clothes delicately, a newfound appreciation for the meticulousness of the cottage. How she wished she could have held on to some of Brennet's belongings... Apart from her pendant and the stone... that vile stone for which she now bore sole responsibility, she had nothing of his. She would have to find contentment in that.

"Fergus... how did you come to know Brennet?"

"Your father... he was an extraordinary man. Truly remarkable!" the old mage responded, his tone tinged with reflection.

Elissa's probing gaze prompted the hermit to elaborate further.

"I first met Brennet nearly forty years ago. A span of forty long years! How young we were then! We had just joined the ranks of the Order. He, I, and Bella... my wife."

"Wait, you were part of the Council?" Elissa inquired.

"Once upon a time," the man replied with a soft chuckle.

"I had no idea Brennet knew your wife."

"Bella was a radiant presence, let me tell you!" Fergus recalled with a touch of regret. "I fell in love with her at first sight... her sweet honey-colored eyes... She kept her strawberry-blond locks cropped short, which beautifully accentuated her graceful neck... and her smile, no one could resist that smile... not even the Guardian. Back then, Bella was Brennet's lover. Your father... what can I say? He was a young lad in high demand with the fairer sex. And he wasn't one to shy away from such attention. His charisma was undeniable... a tall, handsome man, with fair hair and proud grey eyes. And then there was me... not particularly handsome nor ugly, with a wild mane and an unassuming build. A blend of ordinary traits, really! Today... I would gladly embrace what I once had! Life hasn't exactly been kind to me, as you can see. In any case... Of course, I couldn't compete with the king's brother, who was the more fitting candidate for the Order. I contented myself with their friendship, never daring to hope for more."

Elissa was taken aback, her surprise evident. Her mentor had never displayed any inclination toward women. It was a bitter revelation that she realized she knew her father even less than she had thought.

"I had no idea that Brennet had a lover," she whispered in disbelief.

"More than one, to be honest!" Fergus retorted with hearty laughter.

"Did that lead Brennet to leave Bella? For another woman?"

"Quite the opposite. Brennet did care for Bella, but his aspirations to climb the ranks within the Order took precedence. When King Hargon offered him the emerald, your father readily relinquished his noble title and disavowed any claim to the throne. That was the condition stipulated by Hargon."

"That does sound like him," Elissa murmured.

"Brennet had little time for anything beyond that… or anyone else. Left more isolated than ever, Bella eventually noticed my presence. Even now, I don't fully comprehend the blessing I received. But Brennet… I had never seen him so furious. Following that, the bond between us shattered."

Elissa struggled to keep up with Fergus's revelations, which seemed to paint a different picture from the one she had conjured in her mind.

"I'm sorry," she whispered, sensing the weight of remorse embedded in his expression.

The man nodded, his emotions palpable, his regret still lingering.

"Then came the Great War against the winged giants… a dreadful era," Fergus continued, each word heavy with significance. "Despite the horrors we endured, it was truly within the Circle that our destinies took a decisive turn."

"The Circle of Am?" Elissa asked, stirred by the mention of her long-lost home.

"So much suffering! An utterly senseless massacre!"

"I believe many dragon hunts concluded in bloodshed."

Fergus watched her with a mixture of confusion and sympathy.

"A dragon hunt, you say?"

"The one Brennet saved me from… the one that resulted in my parents becoming collateral damage."

"What... what did he tell you, exactly?"

His tone carried a note of caution, his concern evident. Elissa had a feeling that this conversation would not unfold in her favor.

"He mentioned that he needed to inspect the Circle because the Order had received information suggesting that the druids were harboring these creatures. The dragons turned against them, resulting in the decimation of my community. Isn't that right?"

The man did not respond immediately. Instead, he studied her with a mix of compassion and incomprehension.

"I'm not sure what Brennet told you, but it wasn't a dragon hunt that caused the devastation in Am."

"What else could it have been?"

"It was us... Brennet, Toran Sius, Bella, and myself... we alone bear responsibility for that tragedy," Fergus disclosed in a hushed tone.

The surge of emotions within Elissa was beyond description. Fergus's revelations seemed illogical. Brennet could never have concealed something so essential to the foundation of their relationship. Yes, he was a private individual, but this was an entirely different matter. He could not have been so heartless...

"Impossible," she snapped.

Bitter laughter escaped her lips as she grappled with the ridiculousness of such a reality. However, the mage's expression remained resolute, confirming the authenticity of his claims.

"Tell me everything," her words were more a command than a request.

"I'm not certain if I should... You've already endured more than your share of misfortune in the past hours," Fergus hesitated.

Elissa held his gaze with unwavering firmness, forcing Fergus to continue.

"Hargon had summoned us to apprehend the druids who were harboring these creatures. According to Toran Sius, they were offering them sanctuary, a refuge for sustenance. It was seen as a complete betrayal. When we arrived, the massacre had already begun, on the pretext that the Circle had resisted… but there wasn't a dragon in sight. Only the wounded, being tended to by the community, were present."

Indescribable fury engulfed Elissa. She had placed her trust in her mentor. She had given him her freedom as a token of her gratitude.

"Allow me to guess: Toran Sius, realizing their mistake, masked it by fabricating a tale of treachery on the druids' part?" Wil interjected, breaking the silence.

"Not exactly. After we arrived at the scene, it swiftly became apparent that Toran Sius and King Hargon were targeting those unfortunate druids. Something related to Original Blood, I think…" Fergus continued.

The Guardian's breath caught in her throat.

"So… Brennet is in part responsible for my parents' death," she gritted her teeth and uttered through the seething anger.

"He tried to halt the bloodshed. The moment we realized the true situation, he sought out survivors to protect… but it was already too late. Believe me, if we had known the truth behind our actions… we all would've deserted our posts."

"That's why Brennet took me under his wing? Out of guilt?" she questioned with a mix of bitterness and incredulity.

"I can't definitively claim to comprehend his motivations. But I can affirm that it seemed to be much more than mere remorse."

"And then?" her tone was sharp and piercing.

"With the tension remaining among us, he refrained from sharing his thoughts or decisions with me."

"Why did he visit you, then?" Elissa shot back with cutting precision.

Fergus's countenance became solemn, his demeanor downcast.

"What Bella witnessed when the Circle of Am fell... it haunted her. She was consumed by an insurmountable guilt. She wasted away. That's why we relocated. We hoped that a drastic change to the isolated countryside would bring solace to her spirit. Regrettably, Bella's condition never improved despite my unceasing efforts. A few years back, she died, exhausted. Brennet came to me to pay his respects."

Elissa exchanged a meaningful glance with Wil, seeing the compassion in his turquoise eyes. A storm of rage churned within her, but she understood that Fergus was not the real culprit. Toran Sius... He was the one who should face the consequences. Elissa swallowed her resentment, deciding to save it for the appropriate moment.

"I'm sorry," she managed to utter in a broken voice.

"Not nearly as much as I am. Your father... he was always like this: private, reserved. If I may say so, I believe you were the only person he held above his station. He never ceased to sing your praises. Whenever he spoke of you, his eyes sparkled with pride!"

Elissa nodded, deeply moved, but wrestled with the fear that her memory of the Guardian would be forever tainted.

"Why didn't you leave after Bella's passing?" Wil inquired.

"Brennet carried his burden, I had mine," Fergus responded, his remark veiled in vagueness.

"What do you mean?" the warrior insisted.

Fergus hesitated for a moment, contemplating how to put his thoughts into words.

"Pendard Forest, you see... it was once a gathering place for corrupt druids. It harbors potent energies, a catalyst for followers of blood magic."

"Blood magic?" Wil asked, seeking clarification.

"Sangre Majika, Malawet, the rites of the dead… it goes by many names. Its power is tied to the veil where spirits reside. Some spells demand different… quantities of blood," the Guardian explained.

"Pendard, relatively, isn't much of a threat anymore," their host interjected defensively.

"Relatively? Isn't that the only accessible way to reach Earnox?" the still skeptical knight pressed on.

"After Bella's passing, Brennet entrusted me with the duty of safeguarding the forest. I must not permit entry to anyone who could potentially be a practitioner of blood magic."

"Staying on constant guard is a challenging task, though…"

"Pendard has never been this secure. Of course, there are the occasional kobolds… but these rascals are more afraid of their own shadows… and some rare sylvan creatures that sometimes manage to elude me…"

"That doesn't sound very reassuring," Wil persisted, his suspicion unabated.

Fergus nodded, his annoyance evident, and let out a sigh.

"I know what you're implying, but I'm not inept."

With visible offense, the man abruptly rose, paying no heed to his guests, and left the room.

"Perhaps we should consider an alternative route," Wil suggested, his voice a murmur.

"Earnox is just a few hours away through Pendard. Taking another path would cost us days. The forest stretches for leagues, and we can't bypass it without losing precious time!" the Guardian responded firmly.

"You said it yourself; it stretches for leagues. I seriously doubt a single man can ensure its protection. Brennet seemed to have offered him this task out of sheer sympathy. To give him a purpose after his wife's death."

"We need to reach Osthallvale as soon as possible. Yes, the forest is risky. However, I believe that last night's assailants pose a greater threat."

Wilhelm wanted to counter, yet he held back. He looked at her for a moment, his expression softening. Frustration gave way to empathy as he realized the mage was not arguing out of caprice, but out of concern and prudence. After enduring all these hardships, he could afford her this victory.

"Alright," he concluded calmly, a faint smile forming on his lips.

———— ··●·· ————

Exhausted, Elissa sank into a plush, feather-stuffed lounge chair. Fergus, too, had succumbed to slumber in front of the crackling fireplace. His mouth hung open, snoring with surprising intensity. Even the howling storm outside could not drown out the old mage's rumblings. Meanwhile, Wil could not rest. He observed the woman, curled up on the sofa, tossing and turning in restless sleep. He felt as if he had failed in his task, despite his best efforts. The tragic loss of the Guardian's family haunted him. Wil struggled to understand the source of his turmoil, but the weight of responsibility pressed heavily on him. The knights of Aegis had instilled in him the importance of letting go of such emotions, emphasizing the protection of their charge as the sole duty that mattered. Why did this particular mission affect him so deeply? He hardly knew this woman, who, at first glance, had appeared unconventional, perhaps even a bit childish. Yet, there was something about her that stirred him—a unique combination of vulnerability and unwavering strength of character. She had faced her fair share of hardships and now deserved assistance, a chance to embrace her new responsibilities, to seek the retribution he believed she earned. He would watch over this woman who currently held the fate of their world in her hands. Elissa Reinhart... she was the last image he saw before finally surrendering to sleep for the remainder of the night.

CHAPTER

9

ELVES AND MEN

Despite his mother's presence, Farklyn carried on with his daily activities. These mostly consisted of indulging in drink and lust. He had barely seen the queen since her arrival, as she was busy portraying a charitable image by assisting the poor. Farklyn lounged on a marble bench within the fortress's inner grounds. The searing sun embraced his bare chest, lending a warm, amber hue to his skin. The relentless heat had persisted for far too long, with an azure sky stretching endlessly, free of any clouds. The once-vibrant gardens had withered due to the drought, leaving only a few cacti and desert flowers to adorn the terrace. The fragrance of white lilies no longer mingled with the scent of the sea as it had previously done. The statues of the gods of Balt'boec appeared solitary, remnants of the former grandeur of Ryre's Keep's inner courtyard.

A sense of weariness weighed on Farklyn's spirit. The queen's plans loomed, signaling the end of his years of freedom. While everyone spoke of Satya Zylfaren's extraordinary beauty, it held no interest for him. To him, she was just an elf, and nothing more. He felt an urgency to occupy his mind. Ordinarily, a hunting expedition would suffice, but the devastating brush fires caused by the drought had decimated the forests, leaving the poor animals to perish by the hundreds.

"The creatures have assumed their share of burdens," Farklyn responded when Braylon joined him.

"A ball, perhaps? It might lift everyone's spirits," suggested Braylon.

Farklyn sighed, feeling that nothing would ease his current state of mind. Irritation seemed to emanate from everything, and even Braylon fidgeting uncomfortably on his bench did little to improve his mood.

"You must come across a lot of gossip, Braylon," he finally said, breaking the silence.

"Well, I... I..."

"Don't feign innocence. I know the extent of your duties," the prince insisted. "You're always lurking, gathering information like a vulture. You must have heard your share of scandals!"

He sat up, fixing an intense stare on his flustered servant. Braylon, nervous, hesitated, his half-open mouth betraying his discomfort. Farklyn held his gaze, making it clear there was no escape.

"Well, I've heard that the Countesse d'Argenlet is soon to give birth," the adviser offered.

"And what about the Count d'Argenlet? Hasn't he been leading the military campaign against Brilea for over a year?" inquired the prince.

"He has..."

Farklyn chuckled, then abruptly stopped.

"Don't worry, Your Highness, the child is a bastard, allegedly fathered by the Duke of Clarence."

Braylon's reply was accompanied by a faint smile, as he understood his lord's brief moment of anxiety.

"Tell me something more... something with impact, not just about poor Count d'Argenlet's lineage," the young man urged after a sigh of relief.

"What would you like to hear, Your Majesty?"

Farklyn grew tired of beating around the bush and decided to pry on the real controversial topic that interested him.

"The kingdom of Walderlake is in turmoil. Something's happening with our dear rivals to the West."

"Brennet Reinhart was murdered... along with his entire household. Toran Sius's guards found them all dead. Well, almost all of them. There's no trace of his adopted daughter," Braylon explained.

"I've heard quite a bit about that woman in the past few days."

"Last I overheard, Toran Sius named her the main suspect in the massacre. Her escape, in possession of their emerald, has triggered a massive manhunt. He's mobilized their militia," the adviser continued, growing animated.

"Of course, Toran Sius blames her for the Guardian's death. She's the easiest target in this whole affair," Farklyn exclaimed, rolling his eyes.

"So you believe his suspicions are unfounded?"

"I've met Toran Sius once or twice... a petty individual. Perhaps even more so than my mother!"

"Majesty!" Braylon protested, disheartened.

"I'd wager my title that this man is the main instigator of this crime."

"The Master of the Emerald Order is immensely popular," the incredulous servant insisted.

"And? Valera is equally esteemed by the public, but that hasn't prevented her from committing her share of atrocities."

The counselor wanted to respond but held back. He knew he was futilely trying to justify his sovereign's actions. He changed the subject with what he hoped was subtle finesse.

"Your Majesty, if I may ask… you haven't yet shared your opinion on an upcoming ball. You do enjoy dancing, after all!"

"For what occasion?" Farklyn inquired.

"Do we really need a reason to hold a ball?" Braylon wondered with a chuckle.

Beads of sweat dotted his sun-reddened forehead, and his smile appeared more forced than ever.

"Me? Never. But you… and my mother?" Farklyn replied, scrutinizing him sternly. "Tell me, Braylon… whom do you propose we invite to this ball?"

The servant's breath quickened, realizing the prince had seen through him.

"The magistrates, of course! The nobles from Guverl'yt and Wynnorth… and perhaps even some from Cendril."

There it was! The truth revealed. Those awful elves would be part of the festivities. Farklyn felt his throat tighten, and his stomach churned. He no longer wished to continue this conversation. He sprang up and dashed down the avenue without so much as a backward glance.

"Your Majesty! Where are you going?" Braylon called out, rising to his feet.

The prince did not answer, his only goal being to escape and drown his distress in a bottle of wine.

Farklyn felt more disheartened than ever as the grand festivities began. In a matter of days, Ryre's Keep underwent a transformation into a lavish and unfamiliar ballroom. Flowers adorned every corner, courtesy of the Council's enchantments. Tables overflowed with a buffet: bison, quail, deer, pastries, cheeses… A stark contrast to the famine knocking on Wynnorth's door. The floors glistened, carefully waxed to embrace the couples poised to waltz the night away. The kingdom's most celebrated musicians and acrobats had been summoned for the occasion. The nobles of Guverl'yt were already making their grand entrance, wearing their most splendid attire. The fortress's numerous apartments awaited their arrival, each one meticulously redecorated for this special event. The once austere atmosphere of Ryre's Keep was now filled with vibrant activity.

Farklyn found himself drenched in sweat, attributing it to the sweltering heat. He could perceive the worry in the eyes of their guests, all eager to uncover the reason behind these sudden celebrations. He understood that after this evening, the life he had relished so much would soon come to an end. The lovely ladies who fawned around him left him indifferent, a fact that did not escape Braylon's notice.

"Cheer up, Majesty! No one expects you to forsake all pleasure. It's merely an engagement, a political arrangement," Braylon offered with empathy.

However, Farklyn had a different perspective. Satya Zylfaren would attempt to control him, to dominate him. How could it be otherwise? Elves, fueled by a sense of superiority, aimed to assert their power across the empire. Farklyn could not fathom sharing a throne, name, or bed with her.

Cendril's dignitaries finally arrived, showing up on the morning of the ball. The prince had hoped for their refusal, but it was clear his fate was sealed. Farklyn and Valera welcomed them, both dressed in Wynnorth's emblematic sapphire color. The queen radiated with elegance. Her raven-black hair cascaded in a twist over a plunging beaded bodice, revealing her graceful curves. A crimson hue adorned her lips, tracing a heart on her porcelain face, and her smoky eyes sparkled with passion. The prince, on the other hand, struggled to conjure a genuine smile. He had put considerable effort into his attire, donning a velvet frock coat paired with a billowy white silk shirt and form-fitting leather trousers. Yet, despite Valera's attempts to encourage his spirit, Farklyn could not shake the shadow from his angular features. He had genuinely tried to exhibit a jovial demeanor. However, the moment his gaze landed on Tanyll Zylfaren, anger seized him.

There were only a few guests from Cendril. The king was accompanied by the Master... Eryndal? Eryndel? Never mind. Their names felt hollow in the prince's ears. An elven woman with a visage as pale as snow clung to the Master's arm, emanating a disconcerting, almost wild aura. Typically, Farklyn was drawn to unconventional beauties, but this one left him cold. Behind them stood a dozen elven dignitaries, all interchangeable to him. Two individuals, the tallest among them, with dark manes and eyes, seemed to stand out from the rest. Farklyn's attention drifted through the procession, observing a gathering of arrogant faces. Their elongated, pointy ears jutted out a bit too proudly on either side of their heads. These diplomats bowed in respect, but against tradition, they did not lower their gaze.

Unperturbed, Valera approached her guests, gracing them with a warm and relaxed smile, looking more at ease than ever before.

"Your Highness, esteemed dignitaries of Cendril, I extend my humblest greetings!" she proclaimed with arms open wide.

A hush fell over the crowd, and for good reason. It marked the first time in at least twenty years that the peoples of the East and West stood near each other, outside the context of a battlefield. The court of Wynnorth collectively held its breath, fully aware of the historical significance of this moment.

Tanyll's delicate face remained impassive. Nevertheless, the Master showed a keen interest in Valera. Farklyn could not determine if it was infatuation or curiosity, but the intensity of his gaze indicated something was amiss. He bowed, almost entranced, yet he regained his composure as his king advanced toward the eastern monarchs. He loomed over the queen of Guverl'yt, his beauty rivaling hers. Farklyn begrudgingly acknowledged the magnetic presence of Tanyll, reminiscent of Soris, the sun god.

"Thank you for the invitation," was his succinct reply. Not unpleasant, but it lacked genuine gratitude. Valera, sensing the unspoken thoughts, awaited his continuation, which never came. She pursed her lips, a subtle expression, one that Farklyn alone in the room would notice.

"You must be exhausted after such a perilous journey!" she went on with feigned compassion, her smile maintaining its pleasant demeanor.

"Her Majesty need not trouble herself. We are accustomed to covering long distances without tiring," he responded.

"Well, I'm glad to hear it! Our valets will take care of you and lead you to your apartments. You can refresh yourselves before the ball," Valera concluded, her voice rising to ensure the rest of the crowd could hear.

"You shouldn't have," the king replied with bewildering impassivity, leaving a lingering sense of uncertainty in the room.

Valera emitted a high-pitched, disconcerted laugh. Tanyll and his entourage nodded politely before turning on their heels. Elyndel was the last to leave, bowing while keeping his eyes on her. A moment passed, a moment that Farklyn felt was a tad too prolonged. The Master and the Queen appeared disturbed, as if they had just seen a ghost. The elf eventually tore his gaze away from her and hastily joined his companions.

Valera maintained her facade, the practiced smile she often presented to her subjects. Farklyn's blood boiled as he watched the elven delegation disappear down the corridor. Despite differing opinions from his mother's, he could not deny Valera's attempts at civility. Once the group was out of sight, murmurs filled the room. The musicians struck up a cheerful tune, and attention shifted away from the royal pair. Farklyn took a seat on his temporary throne, a sensation of discomfort enveloping him. Valera approached her son, her smile vanishing to reveal a face flushed with anger.

"What abhorrent creatures!" she hissed through clenched teeth.

Farklyn was careful not to remind her that she was the one who insisted on inviting them.

"I wonder where Princess Satya is," she continued, "She was supposed to accompany her father. Considering she's your future wife, it's the least they could have done as a display of unity."

"I thought that disconcertingly pale woman was Satya," he replied.

"Of course not!" Valera snapped, her disgust evident. "That filthy thing is none other than Analera Naefiel, a trollop of the worst kind! An absolute tramp!"

A chuckle escaped the prince. He rarely heard the sovereign express such vulgarity, and, to be frank, he rather enjoyed it.

"Has she offended you in the past?" inquired the steward, struggling to suppress a laugh.

Valera rolled her eyes and groaned, displaying her annoyance. Farklyn knew better than to expect a response from her.

"Where could this princess be?" she repeated in a hushed tone.

"Ill? Running late? Poisoned during the journey? The possibilities are vast," Farklyn retorted with an almost optimistic attitude.

To Farklyn, the absence of his bride-to-be felt like a welcome respite. He could not ignore Valera's evident anxiety; her grand plan now hung in the balance, and uncertainty was taking its toll. Perhaps there was indeed a silver lining on the horizon, a glimmer of relief in the midst of turmoil.

"That king seemed so snobbish!" the young man continued, "I must say, I admire your composure."

She nodded absentmindedly but remained silent.

"And their Master!" Farklyn persisted, "I thought he was about to faint."

"Elyndel is probably the only one of them I can tolerate," the queen admitted, surprising him.

"Really?"

"I fought by his side during the Great War. He always seemed different from his peers. Less austere, less … how should I put it? Elvish."

Mother and son exchanged a rare smile, though the moment was short-lived, interrupted by Braylon's intrusion.

"What do you want?" Farklyn barked, clearly annoyed.

"Your Majesties… someone has attempted to enter your rooms," the counselor began in his quavering voice.

"What a surprise!" Farklyn sarcastically called out.

Valera swiftly rose from her seat, inquiring eagerly, "Have we caught the culprits?"

"Only the locks were forced, but without success. The militia is currently searching for any trace of the potential burglar and has increased vigilance."

"Good… good," the queen breathed, her relief not entirely masking her continued unease.

"Your Majesty should sleep soundly. The guards are taking this attempt seriously," Braylon reassured.

Valera cleared her throat agitatedly, whispering a barely audible, "pardon me…". She gracefully lifted the tails of her dress and hurried off without even glancing at her son. Farklyn observed his mother's rushed exit with a hint of amusement. For all the torment she had put him through, he felt he could let her handle her own troubles for once.

CHAPTER

10

THE PENDARD FOREST

The rain ceased as dawn began its ascent. Pendard Forest, looming ominously behind the cottage, was shrouded in a somber haze. Trees, darker than usual for the season, intertwined in a melancholic tableau, home only to the mocking crows. Fergus had assembled a travel bag for their journey, packed with rations for the road ahead. The pain of their abrupt departure was palpable in his demeanor. Though he'd chosen this solitude willingly, Elissa sensed his yearning for human interaction. He tried to elongate the moment by plying them with anecdotes and advice, each more eccentric than the last. If fate allowed, she vowed to return, to offer him some much-needed companionship.

Mischief-laden crows darted overhead, emitting sinister, shrill calls, throwing an unsettling shadow over the forest. Wil's concern was evident as he pressed on the chosen path, casting wary glances at the impish birds.

"Foul creatures," he muttered under his breath, his jaw clenched in annoyance.

As Elissa and Wil departed the cottage, the wind stirred once more, creating a hiss that seemed fit for a macabre requiem.

"Come back swiftly! We can't survive for long without the emerald!" Fergus hollered from a distance, his hands waving with urgency.

Elissa felt a lump in her throat. The absence of the emerald would leave Walderlake vulnerable, as the country relied on its protective stone to ward off potential invaders. Guardians rarely ventured beyond their realm's borders, reserving such actions for exceptional circumstances. During these brief periods, the city was fortified to withstand potential threats. Elissa was aware that her departure placed everyone's safety at risk. Her thoughts were interrupted by her companion, who, growing frustrated, muttered a few profanities. Annoyed, he threw a rock at the crows still observing them from the treetops, provoking a cacophony of piercing screeches.

"Damned demons!" he cursed, exhibiting an oddly aggressive demeanor.

"They're just birds, Wil," the Guardian calmly replied.

She examined him with concern. His features were tense, and she could not ignore the twitch in his jaw. An almost tangible anger seemed to emanate from him, a stark contrast to the warm conduct he had displayed during their initial encounter.

"Is everything alright?" she inquired, her voice tinged with anxiety.

The man nodded, offering her a forced smile as he tried to regain his composure.

"I'm just tired," he explained in a more composed tone.

Elissa did not press further, but she sensed that something else was troubling him... Wil was proving to be quite the poor liar.

Slowly but surely, they ventured into the maze of the forest, their steps uncertain amidst the dim surroundings. The once-vibrant presence of animals seemed to have abandoned this area; no tracks, no signs of beasts. An abominable scent of decay hung in the air, almost as if Pendard sought to punish those who entered without invitation. As they moved forward, the dense vegetation above their heads formed a canopy that barely allowed any sunlight through; it felt more like nighttime than day. Wil instinctively adjusted the belt around his waist, his hand resting on the hilt of his sword.

"This forest... you've been here before, haven't you?" Elissa finally asked, breaking the silence.

He nervously ran his fingers through his wheat-blond hair, avoiding her gaze.

"During my training, a few years ago," he admitted.

"I imagine it wasn't a leisure outing," she remarked.

"Hargon deployed us recruits through Pendard. It was a test of our composure..."

"Why Pendard, precisely?" she inquired, apprehension in her voice.

"There was... it's a bit complicated..."

He swallowed hard, and Elissa sensed his embarrassment.

"What were you supposed to do?" she insisted, her concern evident.

"A... a druid hunt."

The Guardian came to a halt, her face displaying shock.

"Yes, I'm aware of your heritage," he continued, his guilt evident. "Those we were tracking posed a threat to the realm; at least that's what we were told."

"I'm surprised you accepted my father's offer," she responded sharply. "After these revelations and those from Fergus, I'm surprised you'd stoop to protecting an outcast."

"I was so young during that mission… I had blind faith in my commanding officer. Challenging orders from my superiors was unthinkable. Regret… that's a feeling I've rarely known in my life, but that assignment was one of those times."

Elissa nodded, a peculiar emptiness settling in her stomach. She could not chastise him for something she herself was guilty of.

"I've spent an eternity working in complete darkness, afraid to question my mentor," she sighed.

"I assure you, Elissa, I'm devoted body and soul to this mission," he said, placing a hand on her shoulder.

She huffed once more.

"I can't believe my decisions are truly mine now," she uttered.

"And what better way to begin this journey than by embracing this newfound freedom to navigate this ominous forest!" Wil retorted with a wry smile. "You don't do things halfway!"

"Apparently," Elissa replied with a grin.

———— ··●·· ————

The path finally cleared after what felt like an endless walk. They arrived at a pond, a mirage amidst the forest. Judging by the area's state, it had likely been an ancient meeting site for the druids Fergus had mentioned. The grass was flattened, as if people had danced in circles for hours. White pebbles were placed strategically, reminding Elissa of the rituals she had witnessed in her childhood within the Circle of Am. In the center of these stones stood a menhir, adorned with runic engravings, which appeared to have served as an altar. Elissa approached slowly, her breath catching at a familiar scent. She could see them more clearly now: dried bloodstains splattered across the rock. Behind were bones of various creatures—kobolds, deer, smaller prey—but what struck her with dread were the remains that looked all too human. She knew of the twisted practices and sacrifices of those who indulged in the Sangre Majika. A shiver ran down her spine, and she quickly retreated toward Wil.

"Let's go. I can't bear to witness this sadism any longer," she whispered, as if the forest might overhear her words.

Suddenly, they sensed curious creaks behind them. The Guardian halted, glancing over her shoulder, but saw nothing. Wil had drawn his sword, scanning the surroundings for any signs of an enemy. The rapid transition from the jovial, gentle man he usually was to this formidable force of nature strangely fascinated her.

"I think we're being followed," he said in a deep, cold voice. "Stay close to me, and let's remain on our guard —"

Before he could finish his sentence, a small creature leapt out from behind a bush. Its skin covered with brownish scales, and its high forehead adorned with two short ivory horns made it resemble a furious devil. It rushed toward them, screaming shrilly. Just before it could pounce on Wil, the knight swiftly struck it with his weapon. The beast's tiny body was thrown back, crashing violently onto the ground, creating a pool of onyx blood around it.

"Damn kobolds," Wil growled.

He mechanically wiped away the thick, ink-colored fluid that glistened on his sword, then surveyed their surroundings.

"These creatures excel at setting traps and ambushes… we should be on the lookout," he explained.

Elissa nodded, adjusting her clothes, now decked with tiny droplets of blood.

No sooner had they resumed their journey, they heard more cracks, this time from all around them.

"We should quicken our pace," Elissa whispered.

The man stopped abruptly, shouting a "Don't move!" which froze her in place. He bent down, picked up a large stone, and hurled it directly into a pile of twigs in front of the Guardian. The load collapsed, revealing a vast crater with long, sharp wooden stakes, poised to impale anyone unfortunate enough to fall into it.

"Thank you," Elissa managed to utter, her relief palpable.

"Don't thank me too quickly. We're surrounded."

She heard it too—the rustle of leaves, getting closer. The woman held her breath, the glacial breeze caught under her cloak, causing her to shiver.

A horde of kobolds leaped from behind the bushes and rocks. There must have been about thirty of them, besieging them with incredible speed while emitting deafening cries. Despite their size, Elissa knew that these monsters became ferocious when in packs.

With a swift motion, she summoned emerald flames that sprang from her fingertips, hurling them at the kobolds. Some managed to scramble away in the nick of time, while others, engulfed in fire, dashed in all directions. Wil was quick to join the fight, his blade slicing through the air with finesse, knocking down the beasts that lunged at him. Echoes of agony reverberated across the forest as the creatures writhed in pain, their skinny brownish arms flapping frantically. The Guardian was taken aback by how adeptly they handled the situation. When the last kobold touched the ground, groaning, the two companions exchanged a proud grin, thinking they had overcome the challenge. But just as they were catching their breath, a new wave of the horned foes emerged... then another... and another. The fight raged on, and their strength began to wane as they panted, gasping for air. Soon, they found themselves back-to-back, the beasts encircling them.

"How can there be so many of them?" exclaimed the mage. "We can't keep this up forever!"

Elissa could not see his expression but felt the warmth of Wil's back against hers. She knew the knight was calculating his next move. After a moment, he separated from her.

"Run. Don't let them catch you," he whispered in a low, determined voice.

Breathing heavily, he charged toward the pack, roaring like a wild animal.

An infernal cry erupted, sending tremors through the forest and shaking the trees. Unlike the little creatures' screams, this one held an air of mastery, of immense power. The source of this sound must have been a monster at least a hundred times the size of a kobold. Another chilling growl followed, this time much closer. The beasts scattered, grunting in panic. Hundreds of crows swooped down from the sky, perching high in the treetops like sadistic spectators awaiting a gladiatorial showdown. Their cacophonous chorus reverberated through the air, causing an internal vibration within Elissa.

"Let's find cover!" urged the knight, gripping her arm.

Before they could seek refuge, the bluish-black birds abruptly fell silent. The ground quaked, and the companions watched in horror as the roar drew nearer. A colossal silhouette blocked the remaining sunlight filtering through the foliage. A mighty shriek shook the entire forest, a sound as formidable as the combined cries of all the crows. And then they saw it—the mythical sylvan creature hovering above. A colossal raven-like form, constructed from leaves, bark, and vines, but dark and diseased. Its eyes locked onto Elissa and Wil, and with a brief, mocking croak, it signaled its sinister intent. This beast embodied the forest's elements, but its verdant covering had transformed into a repugnant blackish hue, its body oozing a foul, putrid liquid. Its stone-like claws and beak crumbled with decay.

The creature fixated its dead gaze on the warrior. With a hoarse, macabre promise in its cry, the sylvan raven lunged down, aiming to seize its prey. Wil's blade struck the rotting animal's throat, and it recoiled with a mixture of fury and agony. It retaliated, viciously swinging its colossal talons, but Wil deftly escaped most of the attack. Elissa was not about to stand by. Flames erupted from her hands, scorching the creature in an attempt to engulf it. The beast struggled to evade the Guardian's fiery onslaught, and Wil seized the opportunity to counterattack. He plunged his blade into the sylvan raven's rotting skull. A resounding, almost endless cry burst from the bird as its massive head crashed to the ground, shattering into decayed fragments.

"Are you alright?" Elissa rushed to his side.

Wil exhaled heavily, wiping sweat from his forehead with the back of his hand.

"I officially hate birds," he growled, his breath ragged.

A gut-wrenching noise tore through the air, freezing Elissa in place. She turned, terror gripping her as she saw the monster they had just felled rise again. With a harsh croak, it hurtled toward the mage. Sword drawn, Wil leapt between her and the charging predator, shoving Elissa out of harm's way. This time, he could not dodge the attack. One of the talons slashed his arm, blood spurting from the wound. A groan escaped him as his weapon fell to the ground, leaving him vulnerable before the rampaging beast. He attempted to evade the creature's assault, but its hooked beak tore deeply into his flank. Elissa stifled a scream, rooted in place by sheer dread. Blood flowed from Wil's fresh wound, staining his pale linen shirt. The bird propelled itself back into the air, as if its prior injuries were minor. Elissa realized it would not cease until it was utterly annihilated. Wil's groans of pain echoed, his hand clutching his abdomen as the raven hurtled toward him with a frightening screech. A numbing terror gripped Elissa, watching helplessly as the massive creature descended upon him. A scream erupted from her lips, drowned amidst the birds' chaotic clamor. Her heart plummeted, witnessing the torment etched onto the man's face. She could almost envision the ebony horde fighting over his lifeless body, his eyes frozen in a plea for help, sealed by death.

Elissa saw the bird descending like a nightmare, a surge of fury replacing the icy dread that had ensnared her. A halo of emerald light blossomed around her, an uncontrollable torrent of power consuming her. In a blinding flash, an incalculable force erupted from Elissa, violently repelling everything in her vicinity. Trees splintered, revealing the decaying hearts within their trunks. She felt as though she were falling, plummeting into the abyss for eternity. Then all faded to black, and the once-deafening chaos reduced to a mere whisper.

———— ··●·· ————

When Elissa's eyes fluttered open, she found herself sprawled on the ground, battling intense dizziness. A grisly scene surrounded her—the earth hollowed, trees uprooted, and lifeless crows strewn across the scorched land. The sickening stench emanating from the sylvan bird's mangled corpse nearly forced her to retch. Gathering her scattered thoughts, she struggled to her feet, averting her gaze from the grotesque innards of the corrupted creature, preventing herself from succumbing to nausea. She looked upward, and at last, she saw it: a rift, undulating in a luminous, golden trail. What she beheld was anything but natural. Her index finger instinctively stroked the stone within its velvet pouch, hanging from her belt. The emerald, now warm to her touch, quivered in response to this energy fluctuation. She knew, without a shadow of doubt, that something that should have remained untouched had been disrupted by her loss of control.

And Wil? Fear clenched at her stomach, and she frantically scanned the vicinity for the man. A few paces away, he lay on the ground, seemingly lifeless. Still shaken, she rushed to his side, nearly stumbling in her haste.

"Elissa?" he managed to utter in a fragile voice as he saw her.

A sigh of relief escaped her, realizing he was alive. But panic surged back as she considered the extent of his injuries.

"Don't... don't worry," she mumbled, placing her hands on his chest. "I'm here... I'll heal you."

Now, with the true motives behind her father's warnings about healing spells clear to her, she hurried to act. However, her attempts granted no results. She tried again, but the wound stubbornly remained open. The energy used during the explosion had drained her, leaving her unable to wield her abilities to aid her companion. Swiftly, Elissa removed the leather belt from her tunic, fashioning a makeshift tourniquet for Wil's injured arm. His face was pallid and drenched. This would not be enough.

"We need to make it to Earnox," she whispered urgently, lifting him to his feet.

After a few faltering steps, he collapsed to his knees, releasing a poignant scream. He tried to rise, leaning on Elissa, but his strength betrayed him once more. He crumpled, pulling Elissa down with him.

"Go… get help," he mouthed.

"I will not abandon you in this perilous forest!" Elissa protested, her distress evident.

She scanned their surroundings, as if expecting a savior to come to their rescue. But there was nothing… only the sound of the cold wind weaving through the ailing trees.

"Elissa… hurry," Wil pleaded, his lips trembling.

She saw how rapidly he was deteriorating. She knew she had no time to lose. Grasping him under his arms, she managed to drag him to a shattered tree trunk, where she propped him up. He winced in pain, shivering uncontrollably. Elissa took off her cloak and covered him, but it seemed to bring little comfort.

"I'll be back," she whispered, gently touching his cheek.

She did not waste a moment, and she sprinted toward Earnox, fully aware that this was a race against death itself. The village still lay a few leagues away, and only a miracle could save Wil. She pushed herself without relenting, disregarding the branches that lashed her face and the cuts carved into her freckled skin. The frigid air seared her lungs, making each breath a struggle. She lost all sense of time, racing through the forest, driven by the desperate need to find their salvation.

CHAPTER

11

THE HUNTER

Elissa's eyes finally landed on it—a camp nestled in the heart of the forest. A simple satchel lay abandoned on the ground, and the remnants of a recently extinguished fire still emitted thin wisps of smoke. She could not discern who had been there or whether she should feel threatened by the presence of the campsite. At this point, with Wil's life hanging in the balance, caution was a luxury Elissa could not afford. However, she had the strange gut sense that she was being watched. She cast an apprehensive gaze around, but saw no one.

"Is someone there?" she called out.

Silence.

"Please... does anyone hear me?" she implored, this time with greater determination.

Still no response.

"I beg you... I... I need help!" Elissa's voice trembled, holding back a sob.

She waited, seconds stretching like eternity, then exhaled, tears brimming in her eyes. It was becoming evident she would not reach Earnox in time. With a heavy heart, she pictured leaving Wil's lifeless body in Pendard Forest, a gruesome offering for the malevolent birds.

Just as she was preparing to turn away, a man leaped from a tree to land right before her. Disheveled red hair framed his heavily freckled face. His lanky stature towered over her by at least a head, a sly smile playing on his lips. He appeared harmless, but Elissa knew all too well that looks could deceive.

She cautiously inquired, taking a step back, "Who are you?"

The man scrutinized her, his almost imperceptible eyebrow raised skeptically as he responded, "I could ask you the same thing! I'm not the one who stumbled into a camp, hollering for help," his arms crossed over his bony chest.

"I'm…" Elissa hesitated.

Revealing her true identity to a stranger felt unsafe with threats still lurking.

"Nora Lothain," she blurted out, surprising even herself by using her mother's name, trying to exude confidence. The man scrutinized her from head to toe, not entirely convinced by her less-than-stellar attempt at deception. He nodded with a playful smirk forming on his chapped lips.

"Finneus Anlys… but call me Finn," he introduced himself, extending his hand.

Elissa awkwardly shook it.

"My companion is gravely injured," the mage hurriedly explained, urgency evident in her voice. "We were attacked by a corrupted creature, there was blood… so much blood…"

Without another thought, she tugged the man in the direction she had left Wil.

"Let's not waste any more time," she implored, a hint of desperation in her words.

"Not so fast! We haven't discussed my payment yet," Finn interjected.

Elissa froze, her expression incredulous. "A payment?" she repeated slowly.

"Did you think I'd venture into the heart of the forest without compensation, risking my own life?"

"What sort of compensation are you asking for?"

"Three hundred crowns will do," Finn declared with a sly grin, holding out his hand expectantly.

"Three hundred crowns! That's absurd!"

"Alright, two hundred then."

"I… I don't have money. We fled in haste, leaving everything behind," the anxious Guardian explained.

"That's unfortunate," the redhead replied, his tone dripping with sarcasm. "Alright then! How about…"

He paused, scratching his head with grime-stained fingernails. Raising his index finger into the air, a wide smile spread across his emaciated face.

"That thick pouch attached to your belt… I'd like to see what's inside," he inquired with an impish expression.

"I… no … no, I'd rather not," the Guardian mumbled, her hand instinctively touching the stone.

"Then I sincerely hope you find a way to help your friend," Finn concluded, nodding curtly as he began to shuffle away.

"Alright!" she yelled out, feeling overwhelmed by the situation.

The young man halted abruptly and slowly turned around, a wicked smirk playing on his lips. He sauntered toward the Guardian, affecting a rather exaggeratedly lascivious stride, as he ran his fingers through his unkempt hair. Elissa gently pulled the purse's silk string, unveiling the dark-green stone that radiated a mystical glow. The hunter squinted, lowering his head to get a closer look at the gem, a sense of confusion creasing his brow.

"An emerald that size must be worth a fortune," he breathed, his voice tinged with longing.

"I can't trade it."

"Even to save your friend's life?"

"Even to save my own."

Finn's expression shifted, a hint of wariness evident.

"What's so special about it?"

"It… it contains a curse."

He instinctively took a step back, as if the gem itself was about to lunge at him.

"Then keep it away from me! I don't want to be struck by lightning or end up with boils covering my face."

"Are you going to help me anyway?"

"You're asking me to cross the boundaries that we, the BRAVE Hunters of Earnox, drew decades ago."

"But… he needs assistance!"

"And how is that my problem?" the man retorted with a shrug.

"You just claimed to be such a BRAVE hunter!"

"I didn't say suicidal!"

"We have to try to save him or at least bring him to Earnox and find someone who can!" the woman implored, a hint of anger marking her voice.

Finn hesitated. He seemed to be contemplating the idea of fleeing. Could she really blame him? Guilt surged within Elissa as she realized her actions had led Wil into this treacherous forest. He had attempted to warn her, and she had been stubborn. Tears traced paths down her wounded cheeks as she felt hope slipping away once again. Almost immediately, she saw a change in Finn's expression as he began to fidget, dancing from foot to foot in discomfort.

"I... don't cry... I ... alright! But I'm not a healer!" he groaned.

Elissa's face lit up, a glimmer of optimism rekindling.

"Thank you... With all my heart, thank you!" she whispered, her fingers gripping his hand in gratitude.

Finn responded with a grunt, bending down to retrieve his satchel. If Elissa had realized that shedding a few tears could have swayed him in her favor, she would have done it sooner...

———— ··●·· ————

When they finally located Wil, he lay on the ground, unconscious. His lips, tinged with a bluish hue, and his pallid complexion gave him the appearance of a cadaver. Convulsions intermittently shook his sweat-soaked body. Nevertheless, the fact that he was still breathing provided some relief. Finn approached cautiously, examining Wil's cuts with care, even going as far as to smell them. The acrid odor caused him to pull back, and he rubbed his nose vigorously, as if trying to erase the scent.

"Horrible! Fortunately, the wounds seem relatively shallow... nothing that I won't be able to mend with a few stitches," he said, but a hint of hesitation lingered in his voice.

"But?" the mage pressed.

"His injuries reek of sulfur and decay. I fear the creature passed on its corruption when it inflicted these cuts," the man explained.

"Can you help him?" the Guardian asked, anxiety apparent in her tone.

"Hard to say… Before I close his wounds, I need to apply a mixture of astragalus and mandrake. Sadly, I don't have any with me."

Finn retrieved a small leather case from his hunter's bag, carefully opening it to reveal a jar of beeswax, which he would presumably use as a base for an ointment.

"I'll get what's needed for you!"

"Good! Don't worry about the freshness of the plants. Surprisingly, the dried flora of Pendard will be an advantage for us this time."

Elissa nodded and hurried off in search of the required plants. In that moment, her thoughts turned to her father. He had encouraged her to study the basics of botany despite her apparent disinterest in the subject. If only she had known that this skill would one day prove invaluable!

In a matter of minutes, Elissa located the astragalus, which flourished abundantly in this region of Walderlake. However, finding the mandrake was far more challenging. This type of climate rarely hosted such plants. She ventured further, aware of the hostile path she was taking, unprotected. Still nothing. Her heart felt like it might burst from her chest, and despite the chilly temperature, sweat streamed down her neck. She had been away for way too long. The thought of Wil's life hanging in the balance, with her as the cause of his impending demise, loomed over her.

No, she could not allow such invasive thoughts to consume her. Time was of the essence, and self-pity would not save Wil. The Guardian steadied her breath and shook her hands, numb with emotion.

"Think, Elissa, think!" she whispered to herself as she searched her mind.

She recalled the stone altar surrounded by tiny purple flowers, fighting their way through the cracked granite. Mandrake… Elissa rushed to it without hesitation. She had been right. With a swift motion, she collected the plant from the damp ground, carefully gathering a few roots as well. Maybe the gods had not abandoned her after all.

When she finally returned to the two men, Wil remained unconscious, his breathing labored. Finn knelt beside him, blending the contents of his balm with dirt. Elissa handed him her miraculous finds, and the redheaded man quickly concocted an ointment that he applied to the knight's wounds.

"That should buy us some time," the hunter remarked. "I suggest we take him to the forest's edge, to my grandmother. She might be able to save your husband."

"He's not my… my … he's just a companion," the Guardian awkwardly muttered.

"I see, a *companion*. Very modern, I like it!" sneered Finn. He gave her a mischievous grin, causing Elissa's face to flush. She did not have time for explanations; she simply helped Finn lift the warrior onto his back. He immediately staggered under the weight of the unconscious knight. Refusing to accept defeat, the hunter raised a finger, indicating that an idea had just crossed his mind. He fashioned a stretcher out of branches, expertly securing them with thick vines. Together, they managed to drag the large, inert body without excessive difficulty.

"Is she a healer, your grandmother?" Elissa inquired.

"Kind of," Finn replied with a raised eyebrow.

Apprehensive, the Guardian followed him. She knew there was no time to waste, and Wil's fate rested in her hands. The risk of being guided by a stranger through the heart of Pendard Forest was outweighed by the potential for his survival. After all, what other choice did she have?

CHAPTER

12

THE WYNNORTH BALL

Elyndel could not help but acknowledge the grand efforts put forth by the Wynnorth court to impress their guests. The opulence of their quarters served as undeniable evidence of this. Beds covered with sapphire-blue silk sheets, and rooms decorated with trinkets of gold and precious gems created an aura of extravagance. Carefully assembled bundles showcased exotic gifts, like incense from the Ryn Desert and pearls from the Estriden Sea, hailing from the shores of Osthallvale. Despite the lavish display, Cendril's Master saw through the facade. He recognized it as an attempt to conceal the precarious state of the Eastern Kingdoms. The suffering of Wynnorth was evident, felt even beyond the fortress walls. The citizens clamored for food, and their grievances often led to harsh punishments, with many ending up imprisoned. The Sapphire Council struggled to quell the rebellion that loomed, a movement Elyndel secretly supported.

Syviis had sought solace in her brother's room since their arrival. While he diligently organized his paperwork, the young elf could not help but express her reproach about the state of the country. However, the Master's mind was preoccupied elsewhere. Amidst his sister's exclamations of "Ridiculous!" and "Terrible!" he found himself fixating on Queen Valera. Seeing her again after all these years had not stirred the emotions he anticipated. For the past two decades, a void had taken residence in his spirit, as if a part of him had been wiped clean. Despite his relentless efforts, certain memories eluded him, and unfamiliar sentiments lingered without clear origin. Above all, the face of Guverl'yt's queen had rekindled this disconcerting sensation, the nagging feeling of a missing piece within his mind. But what was it? His heart whispered that his presence in Wynnorth held the key to unraveling this torment. His senses, long dormant, hummed with anticipation. Why did a woman who had only evoked his disdain manage to awaken this emptiness he so fervently wished to dispel?

Like most of his compatriots, Elyndel bore a certain dislike for the denizens of the East. He openly criticized their susceptibility to corruption, their arrogance, and their volatile temper. Yet, he struggled to share the same level of animosity as his colleagues held for them. At times, he empathized with Valera, given the trials she had endured. Such resilience was a rarity across the empire. He regretted that such a dedicated and innovative woman found herself on the opposing side of the political spectrum. A certain admiration welled within him for her, and for the unwavering commitment she had shown to her people during the Great Dragon War. Apart from Valera and Auda Verina, few monarchs had actively participated. The sovereign of Guverl'yt had consistently fought on the front lines, shoulder-to-shoulder with her militia.

"Did you hear me?" Syviis barked, demanding his attention.

"Forgive me, my mind was wandering," Elyndel responded simply, his thoughts distant and distracted.

In truth, he felt no inclination to converse, nor to really listen. Not now, not when he stood on the brink of capturing the missing fragments that had eluded him for so long…

"The sooner we complete our task in this repulsive place, the sooner we'll return home," Syviis remarked, attempting to offer reassurance. A smile graced her rosy face as she gently placed her hand on her brother's shoulder.

"I don't particularly enjoy deceit," he fibbed, forcing a slight chuckle to mask his true sentiments.

"Valera gathered us here for this useless ball, and we shall honor it! If it isn't the primary reason for our presence here, then so be it!" she exclaimed in annoyance. "Sometimes, getting your hands dirty is a necessity for the greater good."

The irony that his sister's thought process often aligned closely with that of the woman she so passionately loathed was not lost on him.

"I'm aware. Yet, should anything go wrong, I'd never forgive myself," Elyndel confessed, revealing the doubt plaguing him.

"Don't you trust my abilities?"

"I do... I hope you're right."

Elyndel grappled with an impending sense of failure that Syviis had attempted, time and time again, to banish from his mind.

"Tanyll swears by the reliability of his sources. We'll find Aelrie in the dungeons of this fortress. Do you not have faith in our king?"

Elyndel hesitated, doubting his trust in anyone. He also recognized that their rescue mission could easily spiral into bloodshed with the slightest misstep. Moreover, this was the very reason Princess Satya remained in Cendril. They needed an heir ready to ascend the throne should misfortune befall Tanyll.

"After tonight, the balance may finally tip in our favor," Syviis asserted.

She was so confident, so naive...

———— ··●·· ————

As the sun dipped below the horizon, the "festivities" began. The Cendril delegation arrived resplendently attired for the occasion, maintaining the unique style distinctive to their kingdom. Analera had abstained from the restrictive corsets that humans seemed to prefer, confident that the grace of the female form needed no such contrivance. She wore an olive silk dress, adorned with delicate ruffles, which bestowed upon her an air of elegance. In contrast, Syviis chose burgundy leather trousers and a matching frock coat, the rich hue mirroring her bold and unrestrained personality. A golden tiara embellished her short, dark hair, serving as a subtle counterpoint to her raw charisma. The men, equally attired in their finest garments, donned the traditional Elven tunics in shimmering shades, their sleeves flaring gracefully. If not for their ever-stoic expressions, one might have almost believed they were genuinely invested in the proceedings. Nilyan and Gareath, however, seemed more comfortable in their training garb, constantly adjusting their formal outfits.

The ballroom was alive with vibrant music, its notes echoing through every corner. The delectable fragrance of the buffet infused the air with warmth, adding to the festive ambiance. Revelers indulged in drinks abundantly, and laughter reverberated all around. Elyndel entered alongside Tanyll, followed closely by Syviis. Valera, upon spotting them, gracefully rose from her throne. A satisfied "Ahhh!" seemed to carry a sense of release through the spirited conversations. She approached the Elven sovereign with a swaying stride, taking hold of his arm to escort him.

"Isn't she familiar with social conventions?" Syviis whispered indignantly in her brother's ear.

Elyndel remained unperturbed by her comment. She was right; one did not touch the king without his consent. However, the Master understood that the norms of decorum would need to be momentarily set aside if they were to proceed with their plan.

Tanyll yielded as Valera led him, and she eagerly introduced him to the influential members of the court. Elyndel observed this as a self-indulgent display to satisfy her ego. Gradually, she guided him toward Prince Farklyn, who was primarily keeping to himself. His long hair was neatly tied back with a silky, dark ribbon, revealing the chiseled contours of his statuesque face. If possible, his expression seemed even more austere than it had been in the morning. Nervously waddling beside him was a plump, bald man. Elyndel immediately recognized Braylon Micelt who had once advised the late King Baalhan. He had met Micelt in the past and harbored a bitter memory of his gossipy and cowardly nature. Farklyn executed a polite bow as Tanyll scrutinized him from head to toe. The Master dreaded this encounter between his sovereign and the intendant, acknowledging it as a pivotal moment of the evening. His throat constricted, and his heart pounded in his chest. They could not afford any missteps.

"Didn't your charming daughter accompany you?" Farklyn inquired, his tone dripping with false sympathy. "What a pity!"

The words sounded two-faced to Elyndel, who understood that their presence did not truly please their hosts.

"The princess remained in Cendril," Tanyll replied, mustering a forced smile.

"I trust she's doing well?" Valera asked sweetly, concealing her annoyance more adeptly than her son.

Tanyll chose to ignore the question and instead gestured toward a painting that covered half of the room's southern wall.

"An interesting piece," he remarked, raising an eyebrow in disbelief.

The fresco depicted a heroic battlefield scene, where the late Queen Auda Verina was at the heart of the action. She was portrayed with a scepter in hand, dramatically slaying a dragon. Several other smaller figures joined her in the war against the winged giants, all of them humans.

"Auda Verina! A sovereign firmly etched in our memory," retorted Valera, exhibiting a hint of discomfort.

"I had the honor of fighting alongside her on many occasions. I was also close to her during the battle in the gorge of Beron... a brutal struggle," Tanyll continued.

Valera remained silent, sensing the direction the king was taking.

"I notice very few elves depicted in this painting. Quite peculiar, wouldn't you agree? Especially considering the pivotal role we played in that battle," Tanyll insisted.

"It is an old portrait... the artists must have received their instructions from Auda Verina herself. I apologize for the lack of delicacy. I fully understand your dismay, and I will promptly ensure that this portrait be removed," Valera assured, feigning solidarity with her interlocutor.

"I vividly remember Auda. Her memory is as clear as the waters of Estriden," Tanyll continued, with a hint of defiance. "She was a noble ruler and a loyal ally. It would surprise me if she had overlooked her comrades in arms in such a victory."

"Those we believe we know can sometimes astonish us. Her unstable mind is a stark reminder of this," Valera countered, carefully choosing her words to soothe the king.

Tanyll nodded slowly, his lips forming a thin line. It was evident he remained unconvinced.

Elyndel's gaze searched for his sister. With a cup of wine in hand, she subtly made her way through the crowd and stealthily entered the main hallway. The moment had arrived. The Master worked to maintain his composure, so as not to arouse suspicion from their hosts, while Syviis embarked on her mission to reach the dungeons. After some time, Gareath too broke away from the courtiers, closely followed by his brother. Elyndel knew Tanyll would soon deliver a speech, effectively diverting everyone's attention away from their rescue operation to free the Oracle. His calculations proved accurate, and the king ascended the monarchs' dais. He assisted Valera in climbing the steps, gallantly holding her hand, a gesture that surely stung his ego. The proud queen, however, appeared unfazed, seemingly unconcerned about anything else.

Tanyll cleared his throat, and the music ceased. The crowd immediately turned their focus toward them, with some showing cheerfulness and others displaying contempt. The lord surveyed the numerous guests with a commanding gaze and finally began to address the assembly.

"I, Tanyll Zylfaren, sovereign of Cendril and the Maar provinces, extend my gratitude to Her Majesty, Queen Valera Netherborne, for the warm embrace of her hospitality. I also wish to acknowledge the graciousness of the Wynnorth Steward, Prince Farklyn Netherborne. For the first time in decades, the gates of Ryre's Keep have been opened to us, an act my people deeply appreciate. The gap that had separated our nations had nearly extinguished my hope for maintaining civilized relations with the East. Cendril extends its heartfelt thanks to you."

His words, though brief, carried eloquent weight. Observing the guests, one could witness nods of approval, their faces illuminated by contented smiles. Elyndel found it difficult to avert his gaze from Farklyn, whose arms were now crossed in a defensive stance, his expression contorted in evident vexation. The Master struggled to fathom the origin of this intense hostility. After all, he was but a child when diplomatic ties between their realms soured.

Now it was Valera's turn to speak, her gestures infused with a certain theatrical flair, befitting her character.

"I too express my gratitude, Your Highness. What joy! What an honor to have you in our midst! Your trust and goodwill mean a lot to me."

Trust. For Elyndel, this concept seemed implausible. He awaited the continuation, casting discreet glances around, ever watchful for the smallest disruption amidst the crowd. If everything was ensuing as expected, Syviis was nearing the entrance of the first dungeon. The most challenging aspect was to navigate past the guards and incapacitate them with a sleep spell. Knowing his younger sister, this likely constituted a plan that was too simple and unexciting for her. That was exactly his concern… He almost regretted not listening to Analera's proposals. Perhaps he had acted too hastily in entrusting such a perilous mission to Syviis.

Valera gently rested her hand on Tanyll's shoulder, maintaining her steadfast demeanor as she continued her address with a confident voice.

"The prospect of a lasting reconciliation between our two nations brings me immense delight."

"I share that sentiment," Tanyll replied, masking his true feelings with a well-practiced nod.

"The reality of this truce will be solidified through the imminent union of Prince Farklyn and Princess Satya," the queen of Guverl'yt proclaimed bluntly.

An audible chorus of surprised "Ahhh!" s reverberated throughout the grand hall. The reactions varied, but the element of surprise was unanimous. Elyndel's heart sank. There had been no prior agreement to announce future betrothals. Tanyll had only committed to a goodwill gesture of entering their rival's territory first. Denying Valera's claims in front of the assembled crowd would risk humiliating him and jeopardize their mission. The Master prayed fervently for Tanyll to maintain his stoicism. He focused his thoughts with all his might, hoping for a glimmer of telepathy to manifest itself in the name of justice. Fortunately, Tanyll remained composed, and Elyndel silently thanked his lucky stars, though he knew victory was not assured yet. An Eastern Kingdoms' gathering would not be complete without the customary diplomatic coup, a tactic that earned them their shrewd reputation.

Valera extended an invitation for the king to sit beside her, and he obliged without protest. The Master observed the scene apprehensively, scrutinizing every nuance of their conversation, trying to read their exchange from their lips. He was so engrossed in their dialogue that he failed to notice Farklyn's presence, the prince now standing right next to him. His demeanor was stiff, and the rim of his wine cup hovered near his lips.

"Isn't it peculiar?" Farklyn sneered, exuding arrogance. "Who would have predicted such a cordial meeting between two adversaries spanning decades?"

Elyndel merely nodded, uncertain of the young man's motives, whose reputation preceded him. Farklyn was often described as detached, egocentric, and vain, traits that did little to inspire sympathy from the Master.

"It seems like only yesterday that the notion of such an evening was utterly unimaginable," Farklyn continued.

"Politics in Balt'boec is certainly full of surprises," Elyndel responded, striving to maintain a gracious demeanor.

"Indeed!"

Both of them remained silent, allowing their eyes to drift through the room brimming with enthusiasm. Farklyn's chuckle emerged as he gestured toward Analera, who stood isolated in a corner, a cup in hand, wearing a stern expression.

"I suspect these festivities haven't fully won over certain members of your delegation."

"Don't take it personally, Majesty. We are accustomed to Analera's reserved nature," the elf replied, laughing softly in return.

"I see! She strikes me as quite different from the lively Syviis."

The mention of his sister's name sent a shiver down Elyndel's spine. The prince focused his gaze on him, a disconcerting intensity in his eyes.

"She is," the Master responded, attempting to maintain a detached air.

"I'm curious… where IS Syviis? I was meaning to get better acquainted with her," Farklyn inquired, his voice husky and smooth.

"She stepped away to her room for a moment. The heat can be challenging for us; we are not accustomed to it," the elven Master explained politely.

"What a shame! I hope she navigated the fortress' winding corridors without too much difficulty. It's easy to become lost," Farklyn continued, carefully choosing his words.

His grin broadened, causing Elyndel to swallow hard. The elf glanced at Tanyll, who showed no change in mood. At least, everything appeared to be proceeding smoothly on that front. Should he create a diversion to look out for Syviis? Or perhaps he should attempt to neutralize the prince before he could interfere with their plan? Maybe Farklyn had already alerted the royal guards...

Farklyn placed a perfectly manicured hand on Elyndel's shoulder, abruptly interrupting his train of thought.

"If I were you, I'd check on your sister's well-being. This heat can be quite... barbaric."

His gaze was unwavering, his tone sharp. There was a peculiar gleam in his hazel eyes...

He knew.

"I hope you enjoy the rest of the evening," the prince concluded, strolling away leisurely.

He knew, and he had tried to warn him. Elyndel wished more than anything to rescue Syviis before it was too late.

He maintained his composure to evade stirring suspicion. Taking a deep breath, he scanned the room for Analera. She stood alone, wearing her customary stern expression, deliberately avoiding mingling with the crowd. The Master approached her with a confident stride, putting on a facade of playfulness.

"We must stop our plan immediately. The prince knows," Elyndel whispered, forcing a smile.

"I told you!" the White Lady snapped in frustration. "You should have entrusted this task to me!"

"Now is not the time, Ana! We need to alert Syviis and the Montallis brothers before they're caught."

"Fine. I'll take care of it. My absence will be less noticeable than yours."

As she prepared to leave, the Master subtly stopped her by gently holding her wrist.

"Ana … be careful," he pleaded, gazing softly into her eyes.

Analera's cheeks flushed intensely, and she exited the room with a barely perceptible smile.

Elyndel took on the task of diverting the queen, thus alerting Tanyll about the urgent situation at hand. He seized refreshments from a servant's tray and moved toward the royal dais, assuming a swaying gait. The two monarchs were still engaged in conversation, with Valera exhibiting a more playful demeanor compared to her interlocutor. They watched the couples on the dance floor, twirling with energy to the lively music characteristic of Wynnorth.

"Ah, Master Elyndel! I was beginning to believe you were neglecting me," Valera exclaimed, breaking into a crystalline laugh.

The elf offered a solemn bow and presented her with a cup of wine, to which she responded with a charming smile. There it was again, that strange sensation, the same vibration he had experienced earlier…

"What do you think of this evening?" she inquired, swiftly downing the contents of her glass.

"I must admit, Your Highness, I've rarely witnessed anything quite like this. Our own celebrations are a bit less … shall we say… spicy?" he responded amiably, his anxiety subtly present.

He glanced behind him: amorous couples, moving in close quarters to the rhythm of the sultry melody. He felt as if he were in a brothel rather than a ballroom.

"As you can see, passion runs through the veins of the Eastern countries. I hope it doesn't make you too uncomfortable," Valera observed, noting his slight unease.

"Not at all, Majesty! The empire's diverse cultures have always fascinated me," he replied with a smile, a dimple forming on his left cheek.

Valera raised an eyebrow, her expression both mischievous and playful. She rose from her seat, swaying slightly under the influence of alcohol. Extending an arm toward the Master, she looked at him for a few seconds, leaving him uncertain.

"What are you waiting for? Don't you want to experience our culture?" she asked lasciviously.

"I'm far from being the best dancer!" admitted Elyndel, giving a subtle wink to his king, who understood the message.

"I shall part with you two for a moment," said Tanyll. "I see some acquaintances I must greet."

"Would you like me to accompany you?"

"Stay, Master Arren! I wouldn't want to deprive the queen of such a charming companion."

Tanyll slipped away while Valera pulled Elyndel into the center of the room.

The guests bowed with reverence as they passed, and the couples gracefully dispersed to yield the floor to the sovereign. A sense of distress suffocated the elf, and he struggled desperately to maintain his composure, guarding his expression from any betrayal. There was a faint hint of déjà vu in all of this. Perhaps they had shared a waltz in the past... The memory of leading an intoxicated queen onto the dance floor felt vivid in his mind. Valera turned toward him and assumed the dancing position, a flush of drunkenness adorning her face, a blessing that shielded Elyndel from judgment. She held his shoulder firmly, her other hand gracefully placed on her hip, a playful smile teasing the corners of her lips. Despite the delicate new wrinkles, she remained almost unchanged from her youth.

A melodic blend of citoles, drums, and viola da gamba initiated a mysterious and inviting tune. Elyndel was unfamiliar with Eastern dances, yet the woman before him exuded an infectious confidence that put him at ease. He placed one hand on his partner's waist, the other behind his back, as per custom. They moved in harmony with the rhythm, a bewitching and profoundly natural dance that unfolded. In a casual yet captivating gesture, Valera released her ebony hair, letting it cascade in magnificent velvety waves. The sovereign transformed into a sensual being, shedding the constraints of royalty and surrendering to her innate essence. For that moment, Elyndel set aside his discomfort. Unlike Elven women, Valera held no restraint for physical closeness, erasing the distance between them. Their bodies intertwined with the soul of the music, causing the world to fade away. The murmurs of the crowd swirled around them, eyes filled with awe, but Elyndel saw only the woman before him. He forgot the purpose that had brought him to the queen, the perils awaiting his sister and the Montallis brothers, the Oracle, the political differences... He could not explain the source of this attraction, yet he knew it transcended mere physical beauty. Brief and disjointed images began to form in his mind—moments he could not recognize. A dimly lit hall, bloodstained hands, a crimson velvet collar... These fragments flashed by at a dizzying pace, leaving the Master disoriented as he waltzed blindly through the ballroom.

The melody ceased abruptly, snapping him back to his senses. His consciousness felt as if it had just emerged from a trance. The euphoria dissipated, and he swiftly realized that something was amiss. The crowd stood frozen, their voices silenced. The queen's regal demeanor had vanished. Her lips, once parted in delight, now released a jagged breath, and her furrowed eyebrows displayed a puzzled expression. Elyndel's gaze shifted to his king, stationed at the rear of the room, his face livid. His heart raced within his chest. What could have transpired while his mind had wandered in pursuit of forgotten memories?

"What's happening?" Valera whispered, her grip tightening on the elf's forearm. Anxiety seemed to have sobered her from the earlier drunkenness.

"Syviis," he murmured back, scanning the motionless crowd.

As trepidation began to overwhelm him, he saw her pushing her way through the guests. Her sweaty face bore tense features, her quivering lips frozen in a state of shock. Elyndel was taken aback by the depths of concern etched across the countenance of his typically fearless and audacious younger sister.

He heard it too—a formidable roar, unmistakably belonging to a colossal creature.

Impossible…

A gigantic silhouette eclipsed the moonlight that once illuminated the stained-glass windows. Valera's fingers dug deeper in his arm, but he stood firm. He knew she recognized the source of that roar, just as he did. They had both heard it before. A chilling silence engulfed the ballroom as the guests held their collective breath. In that moment, the windows exploded, shattering with a tempest of wind, fire, and broken glass. Some attendees were hurled several feet away, while others took cover on the floor. Elyndel's instinct compelled him to shield the queen, pulling her to the ground without gentleness. A massive scarlet tail teasingly emerged through the remnants of the stone wall. Agonized screams echoed from the debris, mirroring those that had haunted Cendril's Master for more than two decades.

There was no doubt now…

"A dragon," Elyndel whispered in horror.

CHAPTER

13

GWENDOLINE

Elissa swore that she had dragged Wil's unconscious body for what felt like endless leagues. Finn attempted to assist, but it quickly became clear that physical strength was not one of his attributes. The weight of the stretcher strained Elissa's arms, leaving them sore and barely responsive. Wil, drenched in sweat, was on the brink of death, his feeble voice filled with incoherent pleas. The corrupting influence of the Sangre Majika had taken hold of his mind, subjecting him to disturbing hallucinations. It was a sight unlike anything Elissa had ever witnessed, and the miserable state of her protector threatened to erode her remaining optimism. Nevertheless, she could not succumb to panic. Wil's life hung in the balance, relying on her unwavering determination and composure. Aware that daylight was rapidly dwindling, she pushed herself to hasten their pace, despite the burdensome load she carried. Tirelessly, she attempted to beat the encroaching dusk. The scent of death receded as they distanced themselves from the heart of the forest. The sky came into view, and the trees surrendered to the long-awaited clearing. Before them, the village of Earnox finally materialized—or at least, the massive palisade that shielded the population gave an indication of its presence. Elissa had never seen such formidable fortifications encircling a single community. The towering consolidation of wood and stone seemed to reach absurdly high, bordering on the realm of the ridiculous.

"I wasn't joking when I mentioned how much the villagers dread the forest," Finn scoffed, noticing the mage's disbelief.

"Are they afraid of being attacked by an army of giants?" Elissa quipped.

Finn sneered but did not respond, implying that there might be more to her exaggeration than she realized. Despite this, he did not take them through the village gate. Instead, they skirted the wall and headed a little further west.

"Where are we going?" Elissa wondered, a hint of uncertainty in her voice.

"I told you, to my grandmother's."

"I thought she lived in Earnox…"

"She did, yes," the redhead replied nonchalantly, offering no further explanation.

Elissa's distress grew as she scanned their surroundings with an alarmed expression. If Finn had led her into a trap, Wil's fate would be sealed. Deprived of her powers, she knew she'd likely face a similar doom.

As the thought of fleeing for the sake of Walderlake crossed her mind, Elissa spotted a decrepit cabin a few feet away. It resembled a dwelling, albeit a worn down one, adorned with an excessive number of talismans and esoteric objects.

"Here we are!" announced Finn, releasing the stretcher and dashing toward the faded house.

"Grandma!" he yelled with almost childlike excitement.

Suddenly, he spun around, realizing that he had left all the weight of the warrior on the weakening mage.

"Grandma!" he shouted again, this time at the top of his lungs.

The cabin door creaked open, revealing a stout woman standing in the doorway, disheveled and filthy. Her greyish complexion matched her tangled hair. There was something peculiar about her features—a curious heaviness, tinged with a hint of madness, that did not inspire any confidence in the Guardian. Slowly, the old lady descended the staircase of moldy wooden steps, which seemed as though they could give way at any moment. Her gaze, visible through her unruly hair, fixed on Elissa. She sniffed disdainfully, as if detecting an odd odor from the young woman. Then, her expression brightened, and she let out a small chuckle as she approached. It was as if the hunter's grandmother recognized the mage in some inexplicable way.

"They're friends of mine," Finn declared. "They desperately need your help."

Yet, the lady continued to gaze at Elissa, her single visible eye focused intently.

"Who are you?" she inquired in a squeaky voice.

"I… my name is Nora Lothain," the Guardian stammered. "A corrupt sylvan creature injured this poor knight."

The old lady finally bowed, revealing an odd smile.

"Well, Nora Lothain… call me Gwendoline."

"Are you the village healer?"

"Kind of. At least, that was the case for most of my life."

Elissa nodded, uncertain about the enigmatic woman's words.

"Let me take a look at the wounds of this poor fellow," Gwendoline commanded, uncovering a toothless, blackened mouth.

She crouched beside Wil, who was still clearly in the grip of hallucinations. She inspected his lacerations with clinical efficiency, showing no concern for being gentle.

"Yes... I see," she muttered gravely.

"What is happening to him? Is there a remedy for this corruption?" Elissa inquired, her worry evident.

Gwendoline got up casually and headed for the cottage.

"That's not what I would fear if I were you," she said, not even bothering to look back.

Elissa struggled to interpret her words, feeling her anxiety grow. She realized that she was trembling and that Gwendoline's comment did nothing to soothe her nerves.

"What are you waiting for? Bring him inside," the woman barked, disappearing into the decaying cabin.

Finn and the mage complied, summoning whatever strength they had left to drag the wounded warrior indoors.

As Elissa stepped in, the pungent scent of aromatic herbs mixed with mold attacked her nostrils. Cobwebs covered the surfaces, and the once-grand furniture was now in a state of disrepair, cloaked in a layer of dust that could be seen from afar. How could someone live in such unsanitary conditions without falling ill? Elissa hesitated, her courage faltering. She found herself involuntarily backing away as the old lady approached her. Gwendoline gestured to a corner of the cabin, where a bunk was surrounded by crates of questionably fresh vegetables. The mage moved quickly, dragging Wil and arranging him as comfortably as she could manage amidst the patched-up blankets and worn cushions. Gwendoline brushed her aside with a stern wave of her hand and sat next to the whimpering man. It was hard for Elissa to discern the woman's expressions. Her hair still obscured much of her face, and the room was dimly lit, with the accumulated grime on the windows likely contributing to the gloom. However, Elissa could sense a peculiar smile on Gwendoline's almost non-existent lips. It was not until the old lady lit a candle that the battered features of her face became evident. Elissa wondered if the darkness might have been more forgiving. Finn appeared with a bucket of soapy water and torn pieces of fabric, delivering them to his grandmother, who wasted no time in getting to work. She gently removed the remnants of the man's shirt, exposing the full extent of his injuries on his already heavily scarred chest. Elissa could not help but gasp, horrified by the sorry state of her protector—a state for which she felt a profound responsibility.

"He'll be fine," the hunter whispered, placing a reassuring hand on the Guardian's shoulder.

She nodded in acknowledgment but remained silent.

The darkness settled in, heavy and overwhelming. For hours on end, the old lady worked diligently on the Knight of Aegis, applying oils, ointments, and potent-smelling substances. The whole process took place in complete silence. Finn had dozed off in a nearby chair, his head bobbing as snores intermittently disrupted the quiet room. Elissa, on the other hand, struggled to contain her worry and eagerness to learn more about Wil's condition. Even though he remained unconscious, she longed to be by his side, whispering words of reassurance. However, she was cautious not to disturb the woman who was deeply absorbed in her task, hovering over the knight. The healer's efforts seemed to work mysteriously, soothing the unfortunate man's spirit. He had stopped moaning and, most notably, his trembling had ceased. Despite the perspiration covering his body, his complexion appeared healthier. Gwendoline stayed close to him, murmuring inaudible words into his ear. She eventually left Wil's bedside in the early morning, her face reflecting exhaustion.

"Is it over? Will he survive?" Elissa asked anxiously.

The healer gave a nonchalant shrug and cast a glance at the knight.

"Hard to say. We'll find out soon enough," she replied, slowly making her way out of the room.

Moments later, she returned, carrying a dusty tea tray. She slumped into a seat between the Guardian and the still-snoring hunter. Gwendoline handed a steaming cup to Elissa, who was eager to inundate her with questions.

"Drink," Gwendoline commanded before Elissa could say a word.

Fortunately, the goblet appeared to be the only clean object in the house. The infusion emanated an inviting aroma—a sweet blend of blackcurrant and jasmine. The anxious mage sipped politely, her eyes fixed on the soothing concoction.

Gwendoline savored the tranquil silence that enveloped them. Her gaze remained fixed on the roaring fire in the hearth as she nursed her drink with an air of contentment. Now that Elissa could study her more closely, she noticed the condition of Gwendoline's left eye: it was dull, the iris casting a whitish tint. Gwendoline smiled, lifting a crooked finger toward the pale pupil.

"A gift from birth," the enigmatic woman shared with her guest.

"Sorry... I didn't mean to..."

"Don't worry, I'm used to it," the healer explained, a touch of melancholy in her tone. "Or rather, I WAS used to it. Villagers struggle to contain their curiosity and judgment."

"That's why you live outside the palisade?" Elissa inquired timidly.

"Among other reasons... my gifts are no longer welcome in the community. Those who have visions of impending death often frighten those around them."

Gwendoline stirred her drink with the tip of her finger, her gaze locked on the brazier. Meanwhile, Elissa could not hide her surprise.

"Are you a banshee?" she asked.

Elissa had read tales of these creatures, endowed with the power of dire prediction, but she had never encountered one before. According to legend, their shrill howl foretold death and momentarily paralyzed those unfortunate enough to be nearby. No sound equaled that dreaded cry. Until now, the mage had believed that banshees were mere myths, stories told to scare children. Observing the amazement on Elissa's face, Gwendoline chuckled softly under her breath.

"There! This is the kind of reaction I'm used to. However, I don't particularly like that term … banshee."

"I'm sorry… how should I address you, then?"

"Gwendoline."

Elissa nodded before taking another sip.

"I don't fear you… at least not anymore," she specified. "It was only a surprise. I thought your kind was just a legend."

"We are indeed very few," the woman admitted. "I remember when we were considered a blessing, when our gifts were celebrated by our fellow men. Back then, dragons roamed Balt'boec unafraid of being hunted. That era was lost due to fear and judgment. Now, we're relegated to tales and legends as abominable spirits wandering the forests."

"I don't see any monsters in front of me, if that makes you feel any better."

Gwendoline burst into a macabre laugh, causing Finn to startle in his seat.

"You flatter me," she replied with an amused smile.

"What happened to the others?" Elissa asked curiously.

"Same as the dragons… and the Oracles. Ignorance has inflicted much damage in this world. Those who possess skills that diverge from the norm are shamelessly persecuted. Demonizing the unknown is easier for many than trying to understand it."

The compassion Elissa felt for these oppressed souls resonated with the affinity she now shared with them. Her power appeared to unsettle Toran Sius. Was it possible that the Council also perceived it as an aberration?

"So? What brings you to the heart of the Pendard forest, my dear?" Gwendoline inquired, interrupting her thoughts.

"We… we want to reach Osthallvale as soon as possible," she replied, her own honesty confusing her. The second she uttered the words, she realized she had revealed too much.

"May I know your real name, Miss Lothain?" the banshee added with a mischievous smile. Once again, the flood of words escaped the Guardian's lips.

"Elissa Reinhart."

Her stomach stirred, and her heart seemed to stop for a moment. She had felt no desire to divulge such information, quite the contrary. Helpless, she realized she was now at the mercy of the old woman.

"Good," whispered Gwendoline, smugly crossing her skeletal fingers in her lap and staring at the mage with disconcerting intensity. Elissa's gaze fell with dread on the almost empty cup she still held in her hands.

"The tea?" she breathed.

The banshee's smile widened, revealing her gaping teeth ravaged by the effects of neglect. Elissa wanted to leap up, but her body remained glued to her seat.

"My apologies! It's for my Finneus' safety. The poor lad has the agility of a ferret, but the naivety of a lamb."

"I am not guilty of anything. I have no connection with Earnox or its residents," growled Elissa, unable to endure this immobility that controlled her. A traitorous anger surged within her—the banshee's frightening scrutiny of her every move, this feeling that her mind was wide open, at the mercy of an intruder… She could not bear it.

"No? So why this dire aura that you are dragging around with you?" insisted Gwendoline. "Your presence, your person stinks of death. I've seen it deviously approach this village for a while now. And here you are … a stranger radiating incredible power."

"I don't want anything from you! Simply a safe path to our destination!"

"What were you running away from? Justice for your actions?"

"No!" Elissa exploded, startling the hunter who woke up immediately.

"What is going on?" he exclaimed, jumping to his feet.

"Go back to sleep, my boy," Gwendoline commanded, keeping her gaze on the Guardian.

"Grandma … what did you do?"

"I'm watching over you," the banshee replied simply.

Finn glanced at the empty cup in front of the Guardian, then studied her snarling expression.

"Again?" he despaired, dropping into his seat.

Elissa groaned, frustrated. She now knew that this was common practice for the old lady.

"I… I apologize on her behalf! I would give anything to redeem us!" the hunter stammered, exasperated.

Elissa realized she was in no danger. The banshee was telling the truth; she just wished to protect her family. Her resistance seemed futile, so the Guardian decided to play along to end this as quickly as possible.

"Do what you want."

She leaned back in her seat, and Gwendoline's accusing expression slowly faded.

"Thank you," she answered sincerely. The mage gave her a nod, but nothing more.

"A banshee senses the life energy that remains in each of us, as well as when it will be extinguished. Generally, my gift is limited to the citizens of this village. Sometimes, it can perceive the aura of those a few leagues away. A lost druid, a poor fellow who would try to make his way through Pendard... However, some individuals possess such phenomenal power that their death manages to resonate across the empire."

Elissa knew exactly where Gwendoline was going with this. Her throat tightened, and she let strands of her dark hair fall in front of her face like a curtain, shielding her from the banshee's steady gaze.

"A powerful soul shattered, causing a tear so great it shook my entire being. I was unconscious for a moment that felt like an eternity," the woman explained with a hint of dread in her tone. Her features took on a somber air, accentuating the lines of experience etched upon it. She continued her inquiry with a composed and cautious demeanor.

"I'm sure you were there. Death pursued you more than anyone I've met."

Elissa nodded, struggling to hold back her emotions.

"Who?" Gwendoline insisted, her tone stern.

"My father... The Emerald Guardian of Walderlake," Elissa whispered, a warm tear tracing a path down her cheek.

Gwendoline's expression softened. She reached out, placing a comforting hand on the woman's wrist. The dam holding back the tears that Elissa had stubbornly withheld since Brennet's death finally broke. This simple yet profound gesture from a total stranger was the catalyst. She shared every painful detail of that tragic night, the memories still vivid in her troubled mind.

Time flew by as Elissa recounted the recent events, her burden slightly eased though the pain remained raw. Gwendoline, absorbing the tale, nodded thoughtfully at intervals.

"It seems those behind this massacre are desperate to obliterate any chance of your father's legacy enduring."

"Tell me about it," Elissa retorted cynically, her hand brushing the pouch containing the emerald, the source of her recent misfortunes.

"Those who question this attack will risk the wrath of the Council," Gwendoline continued.

"The Guardian's followers could find themselves facing the hangman's noose," Finn chimed in.

"It could be a faction uninvolved in Walderlake's politics, possibly from the Eastern lands. They might have heard of your father's condition and seized the opportunity to get rid of him and steal the stone."

"The East... or perhaps Cendril."

"Cendril?"

"A few of the attackers were elves... That surprised me greatly."

"Given the ambiguity of your assailants, it's imperative that you don't linger in this region any longer. You must reach the shores of Osthallvale," Gwendoline urged.

The old woman's thoughts drifted, and her pained gaze shifted to her grandson.

"I can help you find a swift passage to the coastline," she offered after a pause.

Elissa's ears perked up, a glimmer of hope returning.

"You must promise me you'll take Finn with you," Gwendoline implored, her face now etched with newfound urgency.

"Grandma, no!" protested her grandson, instantly sitting up straighter.

"You have to, my boy!"

A palpable sorrow tinged her words.

"Earnox and its people... we're running out of time," the banshee continued. "The world as we know it is nearing its end. I saw our demise, but not yours, Finneus. I believe this is a sign from the gods... a sign that you are meant to play a role in the pivotal moment of our history."

Finn sprang to his feet and paced anxiously across the dim room. He ran his fingers through his carrot-colored hair, deep in thought and anguish.

"There's still hope for you, Finneus Anlys!"

The man's fist collided with a wall, causing the entire cabin to shudder. It was not anger, however, but rather an uncontrollable outpouring of emotion.

"You'll take him with you, won't you?" the old lady asked once more.

Elissa, though uncertain, could not bear to leave anyone to such a tragic fate. She nodded in agreement, a gesture that instantly seemed to ease the banshee's distress.

"Come with us, Grandma!" the hunter pleaded.

He knelt before her, gently holding her shaky hands. Gwendoline managed a wry, yet resolute chuckle.

"You know very well that it's impossible for me to accompany you. My spirit is bound to the forest, and it hasn't shared its secrets with me for a while. It's an unmistakable sign that death is coming for me," she explained with unsettling calmness.

"Why not try anyway?" Elissa ventured, noticing the pain etched on the young man's face.

"The future isn't changeable. Not without divine intervention," the old woman replied, almost amused by the notion.

The Guardian resisted accepting that the future was unalterable. The idea that she could not be the master of her own destiny felt absurd to her, heavy. However, the banshee seemed so resolute in her beliefs that Elissa dared not argue.

"As I mentioned, I can help accelerate your journey to the shore," Gwendoline continued. "Those pursuing you won't give up until they have you in their grasp. Your best bet is to lead them astray, send them in the wrong direction. A Mimic spell might buy you the time you need."

Elissa had not considered this possibility, primarily because Mimic spells, aside from being incredibly intricate, required rare ingredients she could not likely obtain.

"I possess almost all the necessary components for the potion," assured Gwendoline, sensing her hesitation. "I'm missing only a few things that you can easily acquire from the village market. Finn will accompany you there."

"I'm not sure… We risk losing precious time."

"But you can't leave immediately, can you? Not while this poor young man is in such dire condition."

Elissa's gaze shifted to Wil, his strained, wheezing breath echoing through the cabin.

"At dawn, we'll have our answer," Gwendoline whispered, attempting a comforting smile.

Elissa nodded, her focus still on Wil's pallid face. He needed to recover. The thought of continuing the journey alone was a daunting prospect.

Fine. She'd give Gwendoline's plan a chance to unfold.

CHAPTER

14

MALAWET

As Farklyn regained consciousness, a searing pain throbbed in the right side of his face. He was disoriented, unsure of how long he'd been out. Was it mere seconds? Or had it been hours? The ground beneath him felt strangely warm against his cheek, and a sticky, viscous fluid clung to his skin. He recognized the metallic taste of blood, a sensation all too familiar, seeping between his lips. His ears were ringing, assaulted by an aggressive hiss that echoed within his skull. Farklyn was well aware that his semi-deafness was a direct consequence of the explosion that had hurled him several feet away. Nonetheless, amidst the chaos, he managed to discern the cries and moans of distress that filled the air in a grim cacophony.

Finally opening his eyes, he was aghast at the horrific scene unfolding before him. Ash and glass carpeted the floor, scattered with the ghastly remains of badly burned bodies. Bruised men and women lay dispersed like a somber tapestry on the shattered tiles of the crumbling ballroom. The once-glowing spark of life in the eyes of some was forever gone.

Those with the ability to walk urgently sought to flee the nightmarish tableau, while the bravest few, scarce in number, attempted to provide aid to the wounded. Farklyn grappled with the pain that stabbed through his ribs as he struggled to rise, emitting pained moans. He surveyed the room, a sense of desperation clouding his thoughts, unsure of what he hoped to find amidst the wreckage. His mother was nowhere to be seen, nor was the King of Cendril. Had they managed to escape to safety? And Braylon, that unreliable rascal, where was he now?

A familiar whimper provided the answer he dreaded. The counselor lay mere feet away from his master, his face drawn with agony. His left arm was pinned beneath an imposing wooden beam from a section of the sagging ceiling. Despite the searing pain coursing through his own body, Farklyn rushed to Braylon's side with surprising determination. He strained against the oppressive weight but swiftly realized he could not free the man on his own.

"Help me!" Braylon implored in a choked voice. Suffering painted his soot-covered, tear-streaked face. His trembling lips conveyed an apology to the prince, but the barely audible words were stifled by a second futile attempt, drawing a wrenching sob from the counselor lying helpless on the ground.

A menacing, cruel roar shattered the air once more. The winged creature returned to the attack, and Farklyn felt his very core quiver. He envisioned himself perishing in a blaze of dragon fire, his flesh melting under the scorching onslaught. There would be nothing left of him, only charred remnants, a fleeting existence among countless others. He could hear it, the reptilian beast circling high above the besieged fortress. In that chilling moment, the notion of abandoning Braylon to his fate, fleeing like the coward others saw him as, crossed his mind.

"I'm sorry," he whispered, a wave of guilt consuming him.

"Majesty!" the adviser implored, his voice broken.

A solitary tear traced a path down Braylon's dirt-streaked cheek, causing the prince to falter. He could not risk his life for a mere servant... he,

Farklyn Netherborne, the steward of Wynnorth. Duty compelled him to flee… or rather, fear urged him to flee. And yet, maybe he could prove himself more stubborn than his terror.

Farklyn was taken aback when Elyndel knelt beside him. Shattered glass covered his wavy hair, and his face, tainted by ash and blood, bore fine cuts. His demeanor appeared remarkably calmer than the prince's, and his eyes held a clear compassion.

"We must extract him from here and bring him to safety," Elyndel urged in a hoarse voice, his concern evident.

Farklyn nodded, feeling the sting of shame coursing through him like venom. Embarrassment was a sensation almost foreign to him until now. He wondered if the elf could discern his imminent abandonment of his adviser, if he could sense the terror that had consumed the young man he regarded as an adversary. However, the Master's empathetic manner suggested that such concerns mattered little to him. He transcended these power games, a perspective unheard of among the Easterners. In Wynnorth, citizens sought out opportunities to find faults in enemies, even in loved ones. Why did the Master diverge from this norm?

Wasting no more precious moments, the two men tried to free Braylon from beneath the debris. The task proved agonizing for the steward, who struggled to endure the pain radiating through his abdomen. Braylon's piercing screams filled the remnants of the ballroom, causing a sting of panic to twist Farklyn's stomach.

"Are you well, Prince Farklyn?" inquired the elf with concern. "You're almost as pale as Analera."

The realization dawned on the young prince that he had never encountered anything like this before. Contrary to his mother and brother, he had been shielded from the horrors of war and human suffering. He had been kept distant, insulated within the comforts of his golden palace, or rather, he had been pushed aside for the convenience of the one who birthed him. He shook his head, striving to dismiss these unsettling thoughts. This was not the time for self-loathing.

"I'm fine," he fibbed, refocusing on the task at hand.

They eventually managed to free the counselor, who fought to remain conscious. Farklyn averted his gaze from the gruesome wound. Braylon's arm was crushed, contorted to a degree that made it seem like it belonged to another body. The prince swallowed hard, knowing that the destroyed limb would likely necessitate amputation.

"Help me carry him," Elyndel commanded as he firmly gripped Braylon below the shoulders. The young man complied, his actions driven by instinct, momentarily disregarding his grievances toward the one giving orders.

The ground trembled once more, signaling the return of the beast. Its roar reverberated off the stone walls, mingling with the rising cries of terror within the fortress. The prince's heart raced as it never had before, to the point where his own pain seemed numbed. People jostled each other, struggling for a path to safety. The unfortunate souls who stumbled remained on the ground, trampled mercilessly by the panicked crowd. Another explosion erupted, this time impacting the western facade of the stronghold. Farklyn's hands trembled as he grappled with his own helplessness, a horrifying realization. Until now, he had deceived himself with a sense of indifference toward death. How wrong that belief had been...

"This way, Majesty!" a familiar voice broke through the cacophony. Farklyn scanned the crowd and spotted her: Jenima, his favorite maid who had often kept him company during his sleepless nights. Without a second thought, he charged in her direction, dragging the dying counselor and the Master of Cendril along. Her ebony face glistened with sweat, yet it radiated unmistakable relief.

"Jenima? What are you doing here? You must seek shelter!" Farklyn implored urgently.

"I had to find you. I know of a corridor leading to the fortress' vaults. You'll be safe there!"

With determination, she snatched a lantern from the wall and skillfully navigated through the tumultuous crowd.

Farklyn found himself in unfamiliar passages, though he swore he had thoroughly explored every nook and cranny of Ryre's Keep during his childhood. A secret corridor, without a doubt. Their brisk pace halted in a musty, damp room where the pervasive scent of mold hung heavily. Barrels covered in dust indicated its previous use as a wine cellar. However, its current contents were far from its past purpose. A table cluttered with an array of objects dominated one corner: candles, grimoires, bandages, talismans, and more. A shelf held vials of crimson liquid alongside curious bones.

"Where are we?" the prince questioned, disbelief in his gaze as he surveyed the surroundings.

Other servants huddled in the room, trembling and seeking refuge on hay piles and cots. Their battered faces, marked by terror, reflected their astonishment upon seeing their lord.

"What is the meaning of this?" he asked, glaring at Jenima, who remained silent. Farklyn advanced with a commanding presence, his demeanor authoritative. The woman hesitated, biting her lower lip before responding.

"We use this place as a sanctuary."

"We?" Farklyn queried.

"Those who cater to your needs, Your Highness. This is where we tend to those the crown has cast aside: deserters, former prisoners, beggars… those who serve you in the lowest ranks, neglected and uncared for," Jenima explained frankly.

"I don't believe I'm acquainted with the kind of healing that necessitates such talismans, such… paraphernalia," Farklyn retorted, gesturing toward the array of questionable items.

The maid remained silent, her gaze directed downward. Elyndel finally broke the silence, his tone serious, almost solemn.

"If I'm not mistaken, this is Malawet."

Farklyn's brow furrowed in surprise; he had encountered that term before. Malawet referred to a forbidden magic practiced by the Aokule desert peoples, prohibited within the eastern provinces by royal decree. Jenima lifted her eyes, fiercely locking her gaze onto her sovereign.

"Yes, Malawet!" she replied defiantly, her passion burning within, long concealed from him.

Farklyn responded with a knowing smile, appreciating the fervor she had kept hidden until now.

"Engaging in illicit activities within Ryre's Keep, are we? Do you realize that the king severely punishes those who dabble in forbidden magic?" he sneered, holding her intense stare.

"But... you're not your brother, are you?" she whispered sweetly.

Farklyn did not immediately reply. Instead, he studied her intently from head to toe, newfound interest sparking within him.

"Indeed," he said with a mischievous grin, "I am not Fabyan."

Jenima subtly sighed in relief, nodding. She attempted to maintain her composure, but a hint of vulnerability lingered.

"Put him here, so I can attend to this poor fellow," she requested, indicating a roughly prepared cot.

Farklyn and Elyndel acted swiftly, gently placing the whimpering Braylon in the designated area. The maid meticulously assessed the extent of his wounds. Unlike the prince, she displayed no trace of distress at the gruesome injury. She seized a glass flask, its contents an opaque onyx liquid, and applied a few drops to the adviser's mutilated limb.

"I've never seen anything like that... the winged creature," she admitted, getting down to business.

"None were meant to witness such carnage. We took measures to ensure it," the elf whispered with a mix of solemnity and puzzlement.

"Could someone have reopened the breach?" Farklyn questioned.

"Highly unlikely! Only a select few possess the power to accomplish such a feat," replied the chief magistrate of Cendril. "Nevertheless, there are rare mages with the capability to create a second fissure."

Anxiety seemed to creep in as this option was considered. Time and again, Valera had boasted about the achievements of those involved in sealing the portal between Balt'boec and Razakstrom. She held this triumph as unbeatable.

"Could the Masters or Guardians of neighboring lands be responsible?" Farklyn inquired.

"Perhaps... But I doubt it. It could also be someone yet unknown to us," Elyndel continued.

"You seem to have a particular suspicion," Farklyn prodded, his eyebrows furrowing.

Elyndel was well aware that revealing anything related to the prophecy was risky, especially with his adversary present.

"It's just speculation, nothing more," the Master replied simply.

The steward of Wynnorth appeared unconvinced, but a cry of pain from Braylon spared the elf from further interrogation. The adviser's shattered arm contorted on itself, accompanied by loud and repulsive cracks. Through this horrific moment, Jenima seemed completely impassive, displaying a stoic familiarity with such gruesome sights. She continued to smear a substance that looked eerily like blood on Braylon while muttering inaudible words. Farklyn put a hand to his mouth to conceal a gasp of disgust, while Elyndel stared at the scene with macabre interest. Then, the man's arm stilled, and the screams stopped. Braylon jerked, whining, clutching his miraculously intact limb.

"Well... that was some effective magic! Barbaric, certainly... but damn effective!" exclaimed the prince, his tone a mixture of uneasiness and feigned nonchalance. "I wonder why this practice is not more common."

"Because Malawet cannot exist without its share of sacrifices," Elyndel said gravely. "Isn't that right, Jenima?"

While wiping her patient's pale face, the healer nodded uncomfortably without even looking up at them.

"Would it be possible to use it to bring someone back to life?" Farklyn asked with obvious curiosity.

"Yes, it's also the main reason why this magic is prohibited throughout Balt'boec. Resurrection charms have their price… a massive price," Elyndel replied grimly, glaring at Jenima.

"I've never taken part in this practice. I can assure you!" Jenima retorted defensively.

The room shook again. Another attack had occurred. Farklyn's throat contracted, and he instinctively grabbed the Master's arm, a move he immediately regretted.

"Forgive me… I…" he began, his voice faltering.

"I understand. It's normal to be afraid," Elyndel tried to reassure him, maintaining exemplary calm.

"I'm thinking of all those who couldn't reach safety. All the wounded who remained on the top floors, those who crowded around the exits in the hope of making their way out… I don't know where to turn now," the prince confessed with sincerity, revealing his vulnerability. He felt trapped, much like a vulnerable rat.

The elf observed him for a moment, staring at the man with penetrating eyes. Was he judging him? Of course, he was! Farklyn disgusted himself. How could he have been so naive, so weak? However, the Master gave him a slight smile. It was not mockery or pettiness, but compassion.

"I understand," he repeated, his sincerity catching Farklyn off guard. Such empathy from an elf, something he had thought impossible throughout his life.

"We'll need to leave this place sooner or later. Many people still require our assistance," Farklyn stammered.

"Agreed. However, I believe it would be best if you remained here, Your Majesty."

"I am the steward of Wynnorth. Isn't it my duty to help my guests?"

"You're the only heir capable of sitting on the throne of your kingdom," Elyndel pointed out.

"So, it's in your best interest to let me follow you," Farklyn countered, a mischievous smile playing on his lips.

Elyndel gave a faint, barely perceptible grunt, but the prince could discern his annoyance.

"All right, then. I still believe that you are making a mistake. Considering that neither of us has weapons to defend ourselves, the risk is even greater."

"Don't forget to thank my lovely mother for that," the young man sneered.

"I'm sure the queen wanted to demonstrate her concern by prohibiting weapons for this ball."

Elyndel's tone sounded unconvincing, revealing that he was merely trying to be polite and did not believe his own words.

"One would think that after all these years, you would have at least learned to lie!" Farklyn added, walking past him.

Elyndel chuckled before turning toward the exit. "I have to retrieve my scepter first," he said, catching up with the prince. "Do you know how to handle a weapon?"

"I can manage with a blade."

Farklyn recognized that his limited combat skills would not allow him to survive very long in the heat of the action. Elyndel's puzzled expression confirmed that he already suspected this.

"You should stay here, in safety," the elf advised, blocking his way.

"I'd rather follow you," Farklyn insisted, a cocky smile on his lips. "It would be irresponsible of me to let the Master of Cendril roam the fortress alone while everyone's eyes are on a common enemy."

The two men remained silent, their expressions unreadable. Then, after a few seconds, Elyndel reluctantly agreed with a dry and hoarse "fine." Farklyn's smile grew wider, more condescending. Elyndel would have liked to outmaneuver him, but that was impossible without his scepter. Resorting to physical force was even more unthinkable.

"After you," the young man simpered, gesturing for the elf to lead the way.

Elyndel's demeanor darkened, his lips forming a thin line in response.

"Be careful," Jenima cautioned, a serious expression on her face.

"Look after our good-for-nothing Braylon," Farklyn replied with a half-smile, turning to leave the room.

"Stay safe, my prince. I beg you!" the counselor pleaded in a low, quavering voice before losing consciousness.

Farklyn rolled his eyes, exasperated by his adviser's unwavering drama. Then, he made his way toward the exit, muttering under his breath.

"Of course, Braylon. Always so alarmist, so…"

But then a hand grasped his neck, and he felt himself slipping away. Farklyn wanted to look over his shoulder. However, his body remained paralyzed, his eyelids growing excessively heavy. Darkness enveloped him, and a deafening silence seized his mind. His memory faded, letting the last few minutes he had just lived slowly dissolve into oblivion.

———— ··•• ·· ————

Elyndel's gaze shifted alternately between the motionless form of the prince on the ground and the tense expression on the young woman's face, who stood nearby. Jenima's hand was still extended, bearing traces of blood, marking the place where Farklyn's neck had been mere seconds ago.

"Malawet?" Elyndel inquired, his tone almost reverent.

"Malawet," confirmed the maid.

"Do you understand the risks you're facing?" he questioned, the gravity of the situation evident in his voice.

She nodded, the weight of her decision clear in her eyes.

"Why did you think I led both of you to that cave?" she confessed with a faint smile.

"Why are you helping me?" asked the elf, curiosity and recognition woven into his words.

"Because I've felt the anguish of watching one's people suffer due to the choices of others," she replied, her tone imbued with purpose.

Elyndel did not speak, but he conveyed his acknowledgment with a nod, gratitude glinting in his eyes.

"She's in the dungeons… The Oracle," she revealed.

Elyndel halted in his tracks.

"How do you know this?" he inquired, intrigued by her insight.

"A maid learns many things when she finds herself in the right bed," Jenima retorted.

It was a lie, yet the Master decided not to press further, respecting her intentions.

"Come with me," he urged. "Your safety is compromised now."

"I'm afraid I'm indispensable among the wounded," she responded, fully aware that by choosing to remain, she was putting her own existence at risk to safeguard the vulnerable. She sighed, a warm smile gracing her lips.

"I don't fear those who could end my life," she concluded resolutely.

Though it was still a lie, Elyndel felt it would be cruel to undermine such a noble act. Something about her reminded him of his younger sister—strength of character and a certain audacity.

"I'm certain our paths will cross again," the Master replied, showing his respect.

Without further words, he turned and left the cellar, the cries of pain from the numerous wounded serving as a poignant farewell.

CHAPTER

15

THE THIEF

Finn's persistent snoring provided no solace for Elissa, leaving her to grapple with her worries about Wil's condition. He appeared to be on the slow path to recovery, yet Gwendoline's warning conveyed a lingering danger. The banshee's unease, however, seemed to stem from more than just the knight's frail health. Before retiring for the night, she had relentlessly interrogated the Guardian about her behavior and history. Elissa found it challenging to decipher how these inquiries correlated with his well-being. Observing the intensity with which the old woman studied the warrior, she harbored an unsettling fear that her companion might not awaken. Still, his breathing had grown steadier, and his features had regained a certain gentleness. Perhaps it was something imperceptible to the naked eye, something linked to the banshee's powers. It felt as if death itself clung to the new Guardian, just as she sensed it might with Wil. What if he had not been completely forthright with her? What if he harbored a weighty past stained by carnage? She had dismissed the notion of a bloodthirsty Wil as absurd;

his smile and demeanor did not fit the profile of a killer. Of course, he was almost a stranger… a stranger who had repeatedly risked his life to protect hers.

As dawn broke, Wilhem remained in an unresponsive slumber, and a sense of despair engulfed Elissa. Gwendoline tried to offer consolation, proposing that she accompany Finn to the village to gather the few missing components needed for her Mimic spell. The banshee handed her a crumpled piece of parchment, which listed the necessary items: mandrake, belladonna, tulip bulb, sheep heart.

"A rather eclectic shopping list," remarked the Guardian, not daring to question its contents.

"Nothing too complicated! It should take us no more than an hour," reassured the young man. With a quick motion, he seized the list and casually tucked it into his pocket. Elissa cast one last concerned glance at Wilhem as she reluctantly left him behind.

"Don't worry, he's in capable hands," Gwendoline comforted her, observing her hesitation.

Elissa managed a somewhat anxious smile in response before trailing after the hunter. Finn led her along with a cheerful manner, humming a tune unfamiliar to her but which probably belonged in a lively tavern.

"I can't understand how you can be so upbeat after what happened yesterday," the Guardian inquired with a monotone voice. "Aren't you concerned about Gwendoline's prediction?"

The man simply shrugged, maintaining his pace without slowing or bothering to face her.

"Tomorrow is another day!" he declared with a detachment that left Elissa questioning its sincerity.

The sun ascended, casting the sky in a magnificent orange glow. Its rays filtering through the trees transformed the morning dew into a glistening river of crystal. The scent of damp earth and pine enveloped the air, momentarily easing the grip of anxiety on Elissa. They reached the entrance to the palisade swiftly. At its center stood a door adorned with a bull's-eye. The figure behind it, a tall young man with a face weathered by the sun, appeared cautious about granting them passage.

"Randon, it's me! I've been delivering my catches to your father every week for over a decade. Come on, open up!" the hunter urged impatiently.

"You, sure. But her? We're not accustomed to strangers," the doorman retorted, his voice hollow, hinting at some mental vulnerability. Finn grumbled under his breath, revealing his annoyance.

"I can go back," suggested the Guardian, who preferred to be by the knight's bedside anyway. Finn raised a finger in front of Elissa, a mischievous smile playing on his freckled face. From his coat, he extracted a delicate golden pendant, dangling it at the man's nose.

"Mellina would love something like this."

"M-Mellina?" Randon stammered, his round eyes widening in his bewildered expression.

"You're not engaged, are you? Don't let her slip through your fingers. The villagers won't ignore such beauty for much longer," Finn persisted.

The man swallowed audibly, while Elissa restrained an urge to voice her exasperation.

"What better way to show her your interest than a lovely piece of jewelry that will always remind her of you?" Finn continued persuasively.

After a moment's reflection, Randon disappeared from behind the bull's-eye.

"I'll go back to Wil," Elissa insisted, ready to leave.

The hunter caught her arm, signaling her to wait. A knock resonated from the other side of the fence, and the door creaked open slowly. The man's worn face emerged, displaying his vacant gaze, framed by large protruding ears. Finn upheld his promise, presenting the necklace to Randon, who stared at his newfound prize in wonder.

"Don't stir up any trouble," he said.

A few steps farther, the redhead sneered playfully.

"This is what happens when a secluded village refuses entry to outsiders for too long. The bloodlines get muddled, and they give birth to easily managed simpletons."

"Aren't you a native of Earnox yourself?" Elissa inquired, her exasperation doubling.

Finn burst into laughter, leaving her question unanswered.

The town's charm captivated the Guardian: a verdant expanse alive with a lively and bustling population. Elissa had anticipated an ordinary rustic settlement, but was surprised by the homes and boutiques that seemed to belong in paintings. The charming white houses, enhanced with vibrant patterns, lent a sense of unity to this picturesque hamlet. Earnox's town square brimmed with enthusiasm. Pastel pennants danced above them, converging upon a statue of a robust, bearded man at the center of a grand fountain. Elissa grasped the villagers' reluctance to welcome outsiders; they feared jeopardizing this haven they had built. She managed to nearly ignore the concerned glances and hushed murmurs as they navigated the hamlet. Adopting a discreet demeanor, she followed the hunter in silence, feeling more out of place in the crowd than ever before.

The sheep's heart was at the top of Gwendoline's list, and it was evident that Finn had a regular rapport with the village butcher. The man, a gourmand with a deep voice, caused them no trouble. Of course, he shot wary looks at Elissa and refrained from speaking to her. It did not matter! She already knew she would not be leaving this place with new friends. They then visited Ernestine, the apothecary, who appeared less than pleased to serve them.

"Mandrake and belladonna?" she inquired, scrutinizing the mage from head to toe with a stern expression.

"Nothing too complex!" Finn chimed in.

"Are you planning to brew a poison?" exclaimed the saleswoman, raising a thin grey eyebrow in suspicion.

"Gwendoline needs it to alleviate her rheumatism. You're aware how the approach of bad weather particularly affects her!"

"Her rheumatism?" Ernestine repeated, visibly unconvinced.

"Besides, she asked me to send her regards and invites you for tea whenever it suits you."

"Too much," Elissa murmured reproachfully.

"You can drop the charming act; I'm not deceived. I'll give you the mandrake, but there's no way I'll hand over the belladonna," she replied firmly.

"Really? Why?"

"Your story doesn't add up, and I refuse to have a death on my conscience," Ernestine interjected, raising her aquiline nose in judgment.

Finn attempted to change her mind, but the woman proved to be more stubborn than him.

"What should we do?" Elissa wondered dejectedly.

"I might be able to acquire some, but I'll have to venture deeper into the forest," the hunter responded with a sigh, running his fingers through his fiery hair in annoyance.

"Despite the dangers that await you there?"

"I'm not any more thrilled than you!" grumbled the man as he headed toward their final destination.

Guilt gripped the Guardian once again. How many were willing to put their lives at risk to ensure her survival?

"Don't worry! I have my methods," Finn tried with a wink, noting her apprehension.

Elissa nodded, unconvinced, and the two resumed their journey.

The florist's shop was conveniently located, just at the end of the town square. As they walked there, Finn's attention was drawn to a figure on the horizon. A young woman was headed their way, her eyes dark, fists clenched, and an air of fury about her. His smirk vanished, and he quickly grabbed the mage's arm, urging her to enter the store as swiftly as possible.

"What's going on?" she inquired, freeing herself from his grip.

"Nothing too serious... Just an old flame I have no intention of reconnecting with," he replied, scratching the back of his neck anxiously.

It was clear he was lying. However, Elissa had no desire to become entangled in the hunter's questionable affairs. Her priority was to complete their shopping so she could return to Wil's bedside.

The floral scent welcomed them into the charming boutique, basking in the morning light. Everywhere Elissa looked, vibrant displays of flowers created the illusion of an indoor garden. The white lilies near the entrance brought a smile to her face; they had been her mother's favorites.

"Miranda?" Finn called out.

A woman emerged from the greenhouse, greeting them with a radiant and warm expression. Her golden hair, adorned in a crown of braids, reminded the magician of the lovely street vendors who occasionally visited Brevic Manor to sell their jewelry. Beside her stood a blond girl, scarcely older than five years, who was thrilled at the sight of Elissa, her round face lighting up with excitement.

"Mom, look! A stranger!" she exclaimed, rushing toward Elissa.

"Brea, be polite to the lady," retorted the florist, joining her little one.

"It's alright," Elissa assured with sincerity.

"I'm delighted to meet you! My name is Miranda. May I know what brings you to my shop on this wonderful day?" she asked.

"We need tulip bulbs. A dozen will do," Finn replied.

The woman eagerly set about fulfilling their request, a contagious enthusiasm radiating from her.

After finishing arranging the flowers, Miranda handed a basket to the hunter, a bright smile on her face.

"We only needed the bulbs," Finn hesitated to accept it.

"A small gift to brighten up Gwendoline's home!" Miranda replied gently.

Elissa was taken aback by the merchant's openness, which seemed to set her apart from the other residents.

"Thank you for all this care. It's a change from the stern looks I've received since I arrived," the Guardian remarked.

"I understand. I was also seen as a foreigner not so long ago, and I moved here years before my daughter was born. Distrust runs deep in the hearts of the people of Earnox," explained the woman, nodding with a smile that revealed a touch of melancholy.

"I wonder what made you want to settle here, isolated from the rest of the world," Elissa inquired, genuinely surprised.

"Love! I used to be a peddler and roamed the continent. Alone with my cart, I traded and bartered my way from town to town. Then I met my late husband in this little village … he insisted that I be allowed in," she said, chuckling wistfully. "He was Earnox's baker and rather clumsily approached me, offering a basket of fresh donuts. He won me over through my appetite, I believe."

"Daddy made the best pastries!" Brea nodded, grabbing the mage's hand.

She slipped a bracelet braided with delicate beads and colored ribbons onto Elissa's wrist.

"For me?" Elissa asked, admiring the trinket.

The Guardian was not accustomed to receiving gifts. In Am's circle, one never gained without giving back. A simple service could not exist without some form of exchange within their community.

"I... I can't accept this," she stammered.

The little girl gave her mother a puzzled look but did not take back the bracelet that Elissa handed her.

"Brea never tires of making these, to the point that I don't even know where to put them anymore! It's a lovely way to keep her busy, so I'm not complaining. Take one at least! It would do me a favor."

"I... thank you," the Guardian whispered to the child.

"As I mentioned, I've traveled a lot. I'm familiar with the customs of certain druidic communities," said Miranda with a cheerful wink.

Elissa smiled shyly, feeling touched by the gesture as she eyed the bracelet with emotion.

"Don't hesitate to come and see us again!" concluded the florist, heading back to her greenhouse.

Elissa's throat tightened. Come back? She knew that would be impossible. Gwendoline's prediction finally hit her, and she realized, like a punch to the stomach, that an imminent end awaited the population, including Miranda, little Brea, the gatekeeper, the apothecary... and the banshee herself.

"We have to warn them!" the mage whispered to Finn, her voice trembling.

"Warn them of what? We don't even know what truly menaces them," Finn replied, arms crossed over his bony chest.

"Perhaps... perhaps we could attempt to get them out of the village or keep them away from each other to prevent the extermination of Earnox's people."

"What makes you think that wouldn't be what causes their demise?" Finn countered, his tone firm, brows furrowing.

"I don't know, but not trying would be criminal on our part."

"You'd inflict more harm than good by tormenting them like this. Do you want to taint their last moments with worry?" he whispered, holding his ground.

"How can you be so insensitive?" Elissa said, regret tingling her voice as she realized she had hurt him. Finn's face darkened, and Elissa saw the weight of his past in his eyes. He contemplated her for a second, lips pursed, his expression a mix of dejection and resignation.

"Do you think I've never tried to save those affected by Gwendoline's predictions? Since my childhood, I've had to witness most of them, whether I wanted to or not. Each effort ended in failure, and I'm convinced I've caused the deaths of some by attempting to challenge fate. After years of bearing this burden, I had to learn to detach myself from those around me… to detach myself from everything."

"I didn't know that," the woman muttered, guilt lacing her voice.

"The future is unchangeable," he stated.

In a swift motion, he placed the silver crowns he owed the merchant on a display. Elissa exchanged a look with him, finally nodding reluctantly. The hunter walked away, and the mage followed, her heart heavy.

In front of the shop stood the enraged peasant girl they had encountered earlier. She resembled a doll: short and plump, with a lovely face framed by blond braids, and big blue eyes like a summer sky. A furious expression contradicted the softness of her features, the pendant Finn had just traded with Randon dangling before her.

"Mellina! What a joy to see you again!" exclaimed the hunter, attempting a strained smile.

"Don't take me for a fool, Finneus Anlys!" the woman snapped, her cheeks flushed with anger.

Finn immediately stepped back, his head slumping between his shoulders.

"What kind of idiot steals something and then gives it back as a gift?" she cried out, her voice high-pitched.

Mellina's outburst caught the attention of the intrigued villagers, who turned to observe the unfolding scene.

"Steal?" Elissa wondered, throwing a bewildered look at her companion. As the word left her mouth, she realized the accusation did not surprise her.

"It's a misunderstanding," the hunter hurriedly responded, waving his hands in front of him in a panicked manner.

"Really? Someone broke into my house and stole my valuables."

A second woman approached, older and grimmer than the first.

"What has he done again?" she asked, judgment clear on her face.

"Thieving, as usual," the young beauty growled, her venomous gaze unwavering.

"You're very quick to accuse, Mellina. I might have just found it! You know how forgetful you can be sometimes."

"...Finn," Elissa sighed softly.

"The lock has been forced open, and the latch is broken," the young woman snapped, clearly insulted.

Several people gathered around. It was evident they did not hold Finn in high regard and quickly rallied behind Mellina.

Elissa had no doubt about the hunter's guilt, yet she could not forsake the promise she had made to Gwendoline. Duty and honor bound her to fulfill this commitment.

"Gwendoline is behind all this!" the apothecary exclaimed, joining the rest of the villagers. "Finn stopped by my shop to get the ingredients for that old shrew to concoct a poison. Who knows what she was up to with Mellina's necklace?"

"A curse, no doubt!" scolded Mellina.

"Gwendoline has nothing to do with it!" Finn retorted, shocked by their presumptions.

However, the crowd refused to hear him out. Turmoil quickly transformed into fear, then escalated into a revolt.

"Finn?" Elissa whispered, hoping he would find a way to rescue them from this mess—a mess of his own making. He desperately sought an excuse to offer the mob but seemed to have run out of words.

"We can't stay here, waiting for Gwendoline to poison us all! Chasing her out of the village didn't protect us from her schemes!" the fishmonger exclaimed in a frightened tone.

"And now Finn is bringing reinforcements! A stranger who certainly has no place here!" Mellina shouted.

"So true! The witch sends her minions to do her dirty work! We need to get rid of them once and for all before they annihilate us!" cried Ernestine.

The crowd reignited with fervor. Finn attempted to make his case, but general anger prevailed over his pleas. The commotion pushed him into a defensive step back.

"I beg you! Gwendoline would never hurt anyone!" the hunter implored, struggling against those who were grabbing at him.

Elissa could not remain passive. She wished to prevent a confrontation but sensed its inevitability. They would not listen to her, and their respect for her was scant. A villager forcibly laid hands on her, provoking an unexpected and intense reaction. A searing heat radiated from her skin, causing the farmer to release his grip and scream in pain. He fell brutally, displaying his blistered palm for all to see. Elissa was mortified, unable to grasp how she could have lost control so dramatically. The uproar subsided, and she realized that the poor man was not the sole victim of her magic. Several peasants lay on the ground, struggling to rise. They stared at the Guardian with a mix of terror and incomprehension. Some recoiled in horror, mirroring the magistrates of the Capitol's assembly. Silence enveloped the scene, not even a breath could be heard. The woman stammered an apology, but it seemed to have no impact.

"What is happening here?" growled a baritone voice from behind the crowd.

The group slowly parted, allowing a man of robust build, suggesting a past as a laborious lumberjack or carpenter, to approach them. His disapproving gaze, nearly hidden under his bushy eyebrows, focused on the hunter. He sighed in exasperation while meticulously adjusting his neat attire, which signaled a higher rank than the majority of Earnox's population.

"Tomm!" exclaimed Finn, stretching out his arms as if seeking deliverance.

"Mr. Mayor, if you please, Finneus Anlys! You've once again brought shame upon yourself," the man retorted, curtly dismissing Finn's casual demeanor.

Finn scoffed at the comment, but the lord immediately interrupted him.

"I don't want to hear your excuses. We both know that lies are your closest companions." With a tone of finality, Tomm silenced the thief. "As the mayor of this village, I cannot allow your actions to go unpunished. It's clear that your presence alone has been a burden for many, and for far too long," he continued.

Finn lowered his head, his gaze revealing a painful resignation.

"What would your parents say if they saw you today? Do you think they wished such a future for you?" Tomm inquired, his tone reflecting a personal sense of mourning.

"I'm sorry," the hunter whispered, his voice wavering with genuine regret.

"This woman is dangerous!" Mellina shouted, pointing an accusatory finger at Elissa. "She attacked us without any restraint!"

"She doesn't wield a scepter! She must be like Gwendoline... a monster, an unnatural aberration!" barked another man, spitting vulgarly on the ground.

The mayor shifted his attention to Elissa, appearing less impressed than the rest.

"Who are you?" he asked, curiosity lacing his words.

"I am a traveler with no ill intentions."

"Yet your actions suggest otherwise."

"Self-defense against a xenophobic mob!" the Guardian scolded, glaring at the villagers who had incited the chaos.

Tomm chuckled subtly but refrained from adding further to the discussion. It was evident he understood what she meant. He approached the hunter with a commanding yet measured step, then addressed him in a low, authoritative voice.

"You know I made a promise to your parents to keep you safe in Earnox, right?" Finn nodded slowly. Tomm forcefully shrugged off the crowd that was speculating about the young man's fate.

"I regret that I must now break this oath that meant so much to me. I've tried to overlook your numerous missteps, but a theft? Followed by this assault? I knew you were impulsive, yet I never imagined you could descend to criminal deeds. Do you understand that I'm left with no alternative but to take action?"

"Yes," replied the young man in a broken voice.

"And to think that it's our finest hunter I must now punish," whispered the mayor, in a tone of regret. "Finneus Anlys, I am compelled to banish you from Earnox," he announced, ensuring the villagers could hear his judgment.

The crowd began to murmur frantically. The verdict seemed sadly pleasing to the locals.

"That's all? What about Gwendoline... and this... this woman?" Mellina protested, stepping closer to Tomm.

"That's enough," he retorted coldly.

"But Father... Don't you care about the village's safety? Shouldn't you..."

"Silence, Mellina. If you persist, I won't hesitate to impose punishment on you as well."

The young peasant woman opened her mouth, but no sound came out. With that, Tomm signaled to the hunter that it was time for him to leave. Finn managed a strained bow and offered a faint smile. Without further ado, he walked away with determined steps under the scrutinizing gaze of the villagers. Elissa followed him, refusing to give anyone a final glance. She could sense Mellina's smug stare burning the back of her neck. It almost tempted her to turn around and unleash a spell, or perhaps even a slap...

———— ··●·· ————

A hushed atmosphere enveloped them as they returned to the banshee's cabin. While she understood the gravity of Finn's actions within the community, she could not fully grasp the torment he must have endured over the years, grappling with Gwendoline's visions and the harsh opinions of the townspeople. She resisted the urge to join the chorus of judgment. Elissa sought the right words to ease Finn's burden, to reassure him that he could not shoulder the weight of all these accusations alone. However, her own experiences of dealing with her troubles and anxieties left her somewhat awkward in displaying empathy, leading to an uncomfortable pat on the back, a gesture that she immediately regretted, given his lack of response.

Her gloom swiftly lifted as she entered the cottage and was greeted by

Wil's smile. Holding a bowl of soup in his trembling hands, he sat on the banshee's bed, his chest swathed in clean bandages. Gwendoline stood beside him, a glint of pride flickering in her eyes.

"You didn't need to bring me flowers!" quipped the knight, gesturing to the basket Finn held.

Elissa hurried to her companion, filled with excitement and solace, unsure of where to begin with her explanations. Although he remained weak, the knowledge that he was safe provided her with the most precious relief.

"He woke up shortly after you left," the banshee clarified.

Elissa wanted to embrace the man, but she refrained. Instead, she fidgeted nervously, showing her gratitude to the healer with a respectful nod.

"This time, I thought it was the end for me!" confessed the knight, his voice gruff with emotion.

"Thank Itos that Finn was there," the mage said. "You owe him your life."

All eyes turned to the hunter, who stood quietly in a corner of the room, visibly troubled.

"Finn? What's going on, my boy?" Gwendoline asked, concern evident in her voice.

He remained silent, red-eyed with grief, his gaze fixed on his boots.

"Finn? Did something happen in the village?" the woman pressed.

"They banished him," Elissa explained, realizing that he would not voluntarily speak up.

"Banished? Why?" exclaimed Gwendoline, astonishment evident.

For a brief moment, Elissa thought she saw tears streaming down the man's freckled cheeks.

"I think I should stay behind. My presence would be a burden to you," declared the hunter to the mage, his tone filled with sorrow as he kept his gaze lowered.

Gwendoline's response was swift, her voice tinged with deep sadness. She turned back to Elissa, her lips trembling, a pleading look in her enigmatic eyes.

"Finn possesses incredible qualities! Yes, he has his faults, but his talents more than compensate."

"I… I believe you!" stammered the Guardian awkwardly.

"You made a promise to me! You vowed to allow him to accompany you in exchange for a Mimic spell! Must I remind you that the fate of Walderlake rests on your swift journey to Osthallvale? You gave me your word!" Gwendoline asserted with unyielding determination, bordering on urgency.

Disturbed by the relentless insistence of the woman, who seemed keen on selling her grandson, Elissa attempted to ease her paranoia.

"I won't break my promise."

"Good… good… So, I'll start working right away," Gwendoline stammered in a rush.

With that, she hurriedly exited the room, as if fearing that Elissa might suddenly change her mind.

"I'll have to go for a while… we still need belladonna," Finn declared with a hint of defeat in his tone.

He promptly slipped away, leaving the Guardian with a sympathetic gaze, unable to find the right words to offer him. The cottage door slammed shut behind him, the sound echoing through the moldy wooden walls.

Elissa sighed as she slumped down on the bunk next to Wil.

"I think I might have missed something," he inquired.

"I don't even know where to begin," she grumbled.

"A Mimic spell?"

The Guardian groaned in response. They sat in silence for a moment. After all the turmoil, the accusations, and the violence, the newfound tranquility revived Elissa's spirits. Wil placed a comforting hand on her shoulder, his warmth providing solace.

"Thank you," he murmured, observing her with more attention than usual.

"You would've done the same for me."

"I've been trained all my life to protect others. You, on the other hand, simply acted out of kindness," he explained. "This tenacity you possess, this dedication... Until now, no one has displayed as much will and courage toward me."

Elissa nodded, struggling to hide the rising emotions within her. She soon realized, however, that it symbolized much more than simple relief.

"It's nothing," she said with a nervous laugh.

"On the contrary... It means everything to me."

The woman covered her mouth, attempting to suppress an unexpected sob. Why here and now?

"Elissa?" the knight questioned.

"I don't understand... I... I thought you were going to die," she admitted, surprised by her own vulnerability. "I feared having to continue my journey alone."

"You possess immense strength, Elissa. I trust you could manage without me."

His words carried unexpected sincerity, resonating with the kind of resilience he truly admired. Initially, he had mistaken her determination for mere stubbornness, a trait that seemed exaggerated due to the isolation she had endured. Now, he realized his misjudgment. She nodded in acknowledgment, swiftly gathering her composure.

"Forgive me, I'm just utterly drained. I must admit this journey is far more challenging than I ever anticipated."

"Don't worry. We'll navigate this path together," Wil assured her, a tenderness woven into his words.

"Together," she repeated, her eyes regaining a glimmer of hope, lifting to meet his gaze.

The man bestowed a warm smile upon her, as if he was seeing her with new clarity.

CHAPTER

16

BALES

Elyndel's heart raced like a wild stallion. He navigated the desolate corridors of Ryre's Keep, desperately seeking Syviis amidst the acrid scent of smoke that filled the air. Only scattered bodies lay in his wake, most of the guests having fled in sheer panic. The deafening clamor had subsided, granting the Master a glimmer of hope that the dragon might have relented. He was aware that his sister and the Montallis brothers had made their way to the southern pavilion of the fortress, believing it to be the location of the Oracle. Were they still there? Had their mission been abandoned in the aftermath of the winged behemoth's appearance? So many questions gnawed at him but time was short. Without his scepter, he was vulnerable to potential assaults. He prayed that his weapon remained safe within the royal coffers. Thus, Elyndel resolved to make his way there first before attempting anything else. And to think that what he feared was a surprise attack by the guards from the East...

Several lanterns lay shattered, casting the fortress into darkness. Elyndel, gifted with near-perfect night vision, took advantage of his familiarity with Ryre's Keep from past visits to locate the armories swiftly. Navigating with remarkable agility, he maneuvered around overturned furniture, debris, and lifeless bodies. The door to the vaults was oddly ajar, and to his disbelief, many weapons were missing, including Tanyll's and Valera's staffs. Surprisingly, there were no signs of looting; ornate swords gilded with gold and precious stones remained untouched. Chests and valuable items were undisturbed. This sparked hope in the Master and confirmed that his king had likely escaped. However, his own scepter was absent. Recognizing he had to make do with a short sword resting on a support, he grumbled in frustration, acknowledging his limited combat prowess. Nevertheless, it was better than being empty-handed.

Voices echoed from a distant hall, gradually approaching his location. They were masculine, husky, and seductive, speaking a language strangely unfamiliar to the elf. Until now, he believed he possessed near-complete knowledge of the various dialects of the empire, realizing he had been mistaken. Despite an impulse to flee, curiosity overpowered caution. Hiding in the shadows, the Master observed through the armory doorway. The two men walking the hall had a distinctly unique appearance that intrigued Elyndel. The first was tall and slender, with a striking reddish mane tied at the nape with a lace, framing the angular features of his olive-skinned face. The second, slightly shorter but more robust, had long silky hair of bluish ebony, flowing behind him. Intriguing runic tattoos adorned their bodies, both wearing dark clothes akin to privateer captains: fitted leather frock coats and high black felt boots. Their torsos remained exposed, displaying the inked marks on their athletic physiques. Pirates from the Gamar Islands, perhaps? As they passed by the moonlight filtering through the hall's shattered stained glass, Elyndel noticed what set them apart from anything he had ever seen—their pupils glowed in the darkness, one golden and the other jade.

It was clear that the two men disagreed, evident from their snarling tones and intense looks. The one with fiery hair moved toward his companion, their faces a breath away from each other.

"Rzoj rakdiev Oleth," he growled.

"Oleth amzje nak Bales," retorted the shorter of the two, maintaining a composed gaze.

The fiery-haired man's proud expression dissolved, replaced by a contemptuous stare, his brows furrowing and jaw clenching in frustration. Elyndel thought he saw a flash of something in his eyes before his lips curved into a sadistic smile.

"Vilzen wej," he finally replied, marked by defiance that even the elf could discern.

The burgundy-haired man then turned abruptly and hurriedly made his way to the back of the hall. His companion watched him depart with a sense of satisfaction, never attempting to hold him back.

The first figure came to an abrupt halt, positioned before a yawning breach in the partially crumbled stone wall. Elyndel could only discern the dark expanse of the starry sky, intermittently veiled by thick, ash-colored clouds. The stranger stood still, absorbing the smoky atmosphere that filled the damp air. He nonchalantly approached the edge, extending his arms as though preparing to dive. Elyndel found himself questioning if the man intended to jump off the fortress. After the bewildering twists the festivities had taken, nothing could truly astonish him anymore. A surge of blood-red light suddenly inundated the hall, obliterating all traces of him. Dazzled, the Master shielded his eyes and hastily shut the door. He waited a few seconds, stunned and yearning to reclaim his scepter. Nonetheless, he scanned the corridor, only to find that the stranger with fiery hair had vanished. Had he really leaped off the fortress? There was no sign of his companion either—the one with the ebony mane and jade eyes. Perhaps they were mages? If so, where were their staffs?

Elyndel waited a second, ensuring he was truly alone. Then, not sensing any immediate threat, he emerged from his hiding place to continue his primary mission: finding his sister. He hurried toward the dungeons in the southern wing, but he soon felt the uncanny sensation of being observed. The feeling became so intense that he momentarily believed someone was brushing against his neck. Elyndel turned around repeatedly. However, no one was in sight. There was something unnaturally heavy in the air, a profound silence devoid of any hints of battle or distant commotion. Only the echo of his own breath resonated across the pavilions. Finally, he halted in the middle of an alleyway that branched into several passages—a place where his memory appeared to desert him. He sighed in dejection, running his soot-covered hands nervously through his wavy hair. Each passing minute seemed to widen the gap between him and Syviis, a distance he simply could not bear. Yet, he refused to yield to panic. He was Elyndel Arren, Master of the Order of Amethyst! He had faced far graver challenges. Drawing a deep breath, he composed himself, ready to continue his sprint down the corridor to his left.

As he advanced, that peculiar sensation returned, a phantom touch that caressed the back of his neck, sending shivers down his spine. This time, he was certain he was not mistaken. Someone was watching him. He spotted the raven-haired man, a few paces behind him. Arms crossed over his bare chest, a mischievous expression adorned his face, offering little reassurance. Elyndel acknowledged him with a nod, prompting a faint smile to grace the thin, well-defined lips of the stranger.

"Are you lost?" the man inquired with a distinct accent.

"Who are you?" asked the Master, keeping a cautious distance.

"I'm Bales."

"Bales? I don't recall seeing you earlier at the ball."

Elyndel was entirely aware that he had not been there.

"Pardon my late arrival. The currents were unpredictable," explained the mysterious man.

The elf nodded, though he did not fully understand what he meant. Bales seemed to want to play with him in some twisted way, observing and calculating his every move with keen interest. His chartreuse green eyes glinted ominously in the moonlight.

"My name is Elyndel," he continued, trying to sound as neutral as possible.

"I know who you are. We've met before."

"We did?"

"It's alright, I was very different back then," Bales said with a smirk.

"And where would we have met?"

"On a battlefield, many years ago," the man replied candidly. "As I told you, I was very different back then."

Elyndel nodded without answering. He still could not remember Bales.

"Enough joking! I don't wish to keep you from your friends any longer... the ones you're desperately seeking!" announced the stranger.

"How do you know I'm looking for someone?"

"You shouldn't be wandering around here. The fortress isn't safe anymore," Bales said, turning away from Elyndel.

Then he stopped and glanced over his shoulder at the elf.

"Are you coming?"

"I... I don't think that's a very good idea."

"Yet I know where your friends and your king are hiding," retorted his interlocutor in a tone that held both detachment and weariness.

There was no way Elyndel would blindly follow him into an ambush.

"Where are they exactly?" he inquired, still refusing to move forward.

"They're sleeping in the inner courtyard."

"They're sleeping?"

Bales nodded, his smile widening to reveal his particularly pronounced canine teeth. This conversation was pointless, and the logical and pragmatic Elyndel did not appreciate it.

"As I told you, I could show you if you would come with me. However, I can see in your eyes that you don't trust me. I can't blame you; I wouldn't trust myself either."

Without pausing, he simply turned and continued his stride, his path curiously leading away from the garden. His lengthy cloak trailed behind him, creating an almost ghostly image as he vanished from the hall, resembling a shadow retreating to its resting place. The elf realized there was no time to waste, and Bales had already stolen valuable minutes. Urgency overrode his reservations about heading to the inner courtyard. It might very well have been a trap; yet he chose to embrace the risk.

As soon as he stepped outside, a wave of relief washed over him. The scent of smoke had yielded to an unexpected fragrance of lavender, a flower foreign to the eastern realms. Once again, the hushed stillness enveloped him, an eerie quietude amidst the remarkably verdant gardens, a rarity for a city of such desert-like climate. The inner courtyard appeared like a labyrinth crafted from cedars and immaculate blossoms. The elf gently plucked a small purple bloom, only to witness it disintegrate almost instantly between his fingers.

"Magic," he whispered, shaking his head. As always, Valera's desire to astonish seemed relentless, even if it entailed exploiting the sacred potency of their stone. In a Council where magic held esteemed reverence, employing it to gratify her ego felt entirely disloyal, bordering on insolence. Elyndel chose not to linger on his own indignation, resuming his hurried pace. He navigated across the cedar walls, their pathway illuminated by torches that emitted an enchanting sapphire-hued fire. Even in the night, the region's heat remained suffocating. He loosened the collar of his silver silk tunic, feeling the branches grabbing the fabric as he passed through.

Elyndel continued to meander through the gardens, disoriented, unsure of his direction. He had likely allowed himself to be duped by this enigmatic Bales, entwined in the clutches of this labyrinth for the sheer amusement of a stranger.

"Since when have you become so naive, my poor Elyndel?" he muttered dishearteningly.

Just as he contemplated retracing his steps, a suspicious light beckoned through the foliage. He approached cautiously. The glow revealed itself to be a shimmering silver mist weaving among the bushes. Elyndel's heart swelled with hope, praying this might signify his people's proximity. He pushed through the stubborn cedars and thorny obstacles, the branches grasping at him. He emerged, blinking against the thick fog. A profound weariness overcame him, causing him to lean on his sword for support.

"A trap," he murmured as his strength waned. He battled the supernatural lethargy, with only his desperation to find his sister keeping him awake. However, the enchantment eventually overwhelmed him, and his eyelids surrendered to the weight. He collapsed to his knees, beseeching the gods for the power to rise.

Just when he believed all was lost, the mist dispersed, and clarity gradually returned. Horror washed over him as he realized he was not alone. They were all there: Valera, Tanyll, Syviis, Analera... each lying inert, eyes closed. Elyndel dared not move, his gut wrenching at the sight. He had arrived too late.

"Syviis," he whispered, his lips trembling.

Without hesitation, he rushed to his sister's side. Her hand retained warmth, her face almost serene. He pressed his ear against her mouth; she was still breathing. Overwhelmed with emotion, he held the unconscious young elf close, never feeling such profound relief. Itos had answered his prayers. A swift glance at the others revealed that, aside from a few scratches, they were all unharmed. They were merely...

"Asleep," a voice said behind him.

Startled, Elyndel spun around to find Bales standing a few paces away.

"How?" he muttered, rising slowly.

The stranger walked among the still forms, studying them with an almost detached air.

"I had to intervene, or they'd have been slaughtered," Bales responded.

"By the dragon?"

Bales nodded, his detachment palpable.

"You underestimate them. Many among them have faced them before," the magistrate clarified.

"Not this one. No one is like Oleth," Bales continued, each word weighed with gravity.

"Does this creature have a name?" Elyndel asked, a touch of mockery in his voice.

"Dragons, they all have names."

For the first time in their encounter, the stranger's tone was firm, serious. Elyndel stared at his sleeping sister. He shook her, but she did not stir. He shook her harder, yet she remained unresponsive.

"It's in vain. She won't awaken until the spell that entrapped her is lifted," Bales revealed, his gaze shifting to the sky.

"Is this your doing?" Elyndel inquired, suspicion veiled in his voice.

Bales nodded casually, his attention still on the heavens.

"Who are you?" the Master whispered, an undercurrent of apprehension present.

Finally, the stranger looked down, locking eyes with Elyndel. A smile formed on his lips, and he extended his arms.

"Wokjen siek," he commanded in his suave voice.

Instantly, everyone on the ground began to stir. Before he could question further, Bales abruptly turned and vanished into the opposite pavilion. Syviis slowly opened her eyes, her hands clutching her head.

"What happened? My head... feels like it's about to burst," she muttered.

"Don't move, Syviis. I'll be right back."

Elyndel was decided not to let Bales slip away, not until he had unraveled the depths of the powers he had witnessed. He heard his sister calling out to him, but he could not be deterred.

— ··•·· —

Fortunately, Bales was within reach, just outside the labyrinth. Elyndel hurried toward him and firmly grasped his shoulder, preventing any further escape.

"Who are you?" the elf pressed, determination in his voice.

Bales sighed, turning to face him. "For the sake of your people, I strongly advise you to evacuate the city. Seek refuge in underground locations, caves, and isolated islands. A new era is on the horizon."

The urgency in Bales' words struck Elyndel profoundly, each syllable weighed with an earnestness that shook him to his core. There was a somber gravity in his tone, a hint of pity that unsettled the Master. Then, Bales took a few steps back, keeping his gaze fixed on him. He raised his arms to the sky, much like Oleth had done before, but instead of a brilliant flash of light, a thick fog enveloped the surroundings, obscuring Elyndel's vision. It happened so swiftly that fear did not have a chance to take hold.

As the mist lifted, it unveiled a colossal and terrifying sight—an inky-black dragon. The beast extended its majestic wings, emitting a menacing growl that made Elyndel tremble. The enormous reptile fixed its gleaming jade eyes on him, confirming that it was, in fact, Bales. Elyndel could not believe what he was seeing. He had heard tales of these ancient dragons, capable of taking human form, but no one had witnessed it firsthand. This revelation left him stunned, shaking the foundations of his convictions about the empire's history. Those who had faced these ancient beings always had the uncanny feeling that they were perpetually slipping through their grasp, consistently a step ahead. They had not been wrong.

Elyndel had to act, but what could he do? He stood there, a mix of surprise and dread paralyzing him. Before he could gather his wits, Bales took flight. The creature's wings, both delicate and colossal, emitted a roar akin to the winds announcing a coming storm. It streaked through the sky with lightning speed, its ebony scales glistening in the moonlight. Eventually, it vanished behind a dense, greyish cloud that obscured it from Elyndel's gaze. He remained rooted in place, as if frozen in a moment that stretched into an eternity. A peculiar blend of excitement and alarm surged within him. It had been so long since he'd felt such vitality. Without hesitation, he turned around, profoundly shaken by those fleeting moments that had irrevocably altered the course of Balt'boec's history.

CHAPTER

17

THE HOWLING

Elissa was jolted awake, her senses heightened by a chilling, piercing scream that sent shocks through her veins. She recognized the sound instantly: the mythical banshee's cry, a haunting wail that gripped the very depths of one's soul. Here? Now? She had believed there was more time... Her body tingled with an intensity akin to the bonding with the emerald, yet unlike the invigorating connection with the stone, this surge of power left her immobilized. Her remaining traces of joy seemed to evaporate in the face of this overwhelming force. She pressed trembling hands against her ears and leaped out of her bunk, panic coursing through her. She realized that Wil and Finn were mirroring her actions, attempting to shield themselves from the ear-splitting cacophony. It felt like the longest cry in the entire history of the empire, a sound that transcended humanity, echoing across the cursed forest.

"We must flee immediately," Finn urged, swiftly grabbing his bow and quiver. "Death is coming."

A void seemed to form in Elissa's stomach, and she cast a worried glance at the knight, hoping his condition would allow him to move. He appeared to have improved and managed to stand without too much instability.

"Let me heal you completely," she offered, stepping closer to him.

"No. Keep your energy," he advised firmly.

Seeing the concern in Elissa's eyes, Wil hastened to reassure her.

"I'm alright," he said in a gentler tone.

The mage nodded, though still skeptical, realizing she would have to trust his word for now.

Luckily, the banshee had managed to fulfill her promise by completing the Mimic spells. Finn swiftly grabbed the three elixir vials and handed them over to his companions.

"Cheers!" he exclaimed, downing his potion in one gulp.

Elissa and Wil uncorked their flasks, releasing a foul sulfuric odor. They reluctantly swallowed the brownish liquid, grimacing at the immediate bitter taste. The mage had to suppress the urge to spit it all out, convinced she had never ingested anything so repugnant. A sharp sensation tugged at her insides. Judging by the pained expressions contorting her friends' faces, she knew they were experiencing the same discomfort. Clutching her abdomen with both hands, she felt as if something within her was attempting to pull out every organ. Slowly, her body stretched beyond human limits. A form appeared to materialize through a symphony of viscous cracks. She separated from her own flesh, molding and distorting herself. The pain subsided, and Elissa began to catch her breath, a cold sweat forming on her pallid face. Before her stood a double, an exact replica of herself. Shaken by this surreal sight, she gazed at this strange reflection, which showed no signs of consciousness. The Mimic spells could only create emptiness, soulless vessels. These beings devoid of emotions and personality were condemned to obey, incapable of uttering a single word. Her look-alike stared into nothingness, mirroring the blank expressions of Wil's and Finn's duplicates. All three stood there, completely naked, stiff and unmoving. In deep embarrassment, Elissa hurriedly covered her double with a makeshift sheet.

"Perhaps we should dress them before allowing them to wander around like this in the woods," she stammered.

She also avoided looking at the two "men's" bodies, realizing somewhat shamefully that she was seeing the opposite sex in this state for the first time.

"Are you sure? They'll attract more attention that way," Finn retorted with a hint of mockery.

Elissa understood he could not resist making jokes even in such crucial moments, his manner of dealing with anxiety. Therefore, she refrained from scolding him.

"Uh... head north, through the forest... please," she ordered, finishing the adjustments on the rags of her double who continued to stare blankly.

She felt foolish...

"Make enough noise to draw attention, but be sufficiently quick to outrun them," Wil said, grabbing his sword.

Immediately, the doppelgangers obeyed, their vacant expressions unchanged. Finn snatched his satchel and cast one last glance around the dilapidated shack, a hidden emotion beneath his facade.

"Let's go," he whispered, leading the way out.

Gwendoline stood before the house, her gaze fixed on Pendard Forest. Her head was thrown back, and her greying hair cascaded in large locks on either side of her body, reminiscent of serpents writhing atop her skull. Elissa momentarily contemplated that strange image before her. Gwendoline appeared to hover, a few inches above the ground, in a spectral levitation. Elissa rushed out of the dwelling, urgently approaching the banshee. The piercing screams had ceased, replaced by a vaporous halo surrounding her. Her eyes were rolled back, her face decked with dark veins that contrasted starkly with the pallor of her skin. Elissa hesitated to touch the woman, sensing a malevolent mystical force engulfing her.

"No!" Finn's voice echoed, startling her. "Don't touch her... her aura is poisoned."

"How long will she remain like this?" Elissa inquired, concerned for the banshee's state.

"Several hours, perhaps until sunrise," Finn replied, his words quivering with emotion. Elissa realized that this was his chance to bid farewell to the woman who had raised him. She discreetly withdrew to grant the hunter this private moment with her.

Finn looked at his grandmother, a mix of pity and bitterness etched on his face.

"I believe you can hear me... somewhere, deep within yourself," he began. "You were the only one who truly loved and protected the disappointment I've turned into, who envisioned a future different from the path others laid out for me."

His voice cracked, and he took a deep, steadying breath before continuing.

"I don't know if I'll ever fully become the person you hoped for. Nonetheless, I promise that I will try."

Tears rolled down his cheeks, and he said no more, his gaze unwavering on Gwendoline. This moment rekindled the raw pain of her father's recent loss for Elissa. She understood the inner battle Finn was fighting, the excruciating feeling of having to intentionally break oneself to survive. She placed a comforting hand on the hunter's shoulder, aware that it could not mend his wounds. Wil, standing a little further away, maintained a solemn composure. Now, it was Elissa's turn to be strong for her new companion, just as Wil had been for her.

"We must leave. Time is running out," she urged in a gentle but resolute tone.

Finn nodded, unable to tear his gaze from the banshee. Elissa slowly guided him, gently pulling on his sleeve.

"Don't look back," she whispered.

Finn allowed her to lead him away, abandoning the only family he had left.

———— ··•·· ————

They sprinted as quickly as Wil's barely healed wounds permitted. The frigid breeze grazed their skin, carrying with it a pungent scent of damp earth. A sinister tranquility pervaded the surroundings, an unsettling calm before the impending storm. Only the whisper of the wind through the leaves and the desperate breaths of the fugitives disrupted the peace. Gwendoline's advice resonated, yet a wild urge to warn the villagers of Earnox lingered in Elissa's mind. The image of the young blond girl haunted her thoughts, and the trinket she had given her felt like a burning shackle, binding her to the situation. She stopped, gasping, unable to continue.

"What are you waiting for, Elissa?" Wil inquired, his concern evident.

"I... I can't," she stammered.

"What do you mean? We can't linger here," Wil urged.

"I understand, but... I can't bear the thought of all those innocent lives lost. I refuse to accept this as an unchangeable fate."

"It is, and there's nothing you can do about it."

"Because you were led to believe in the finality and omnipotence of a preordained future!"

"What about the rest of the world? All those people who will perish if our attackers seize the stone," Wil argued, moving closer to her.

Despite his imposing figure and the willpower in his voice that sent a shiver down her spine, she stood firm.

"Gwendoline explained it to you. Their fate is sealed now," Finn added with resolute acceptance.

"I refuse to acknowledge that fate cannot be altered. There must be a way…"

"We don't have time to delve into that," Wil insisted, gripping her hand.

Both men held steadfast to their beliefs. Elissa sensed her reluctance appeared puzzling and even out of place to them. She hesitantly continued with them, feeling as though each step was a betrayal of her conscience. She knew that if she did not turn back, her humanity would be lost forever. With a sudden motion, she broke free from Wil's grasp.

"You're free to leave if you wish," she declared firmly. "I won't force you to come with me."

The knight let out a sigh of exasperation, glaring at her.

"We can't help them all, Elissa!" he retorted, raising his voice with authority.

"I'm aware of that," she replied.

With that, she turned around, ignoring her companions' warnings. Yet, she soon realized they were following her, grudgingly accompanying her toward the village.

"None of my charges have been as stubborn as you," Wil barked, a few steps behind.

"I take it it's not meant as a compliment," she responded with bitterness.

"Those I protected in the past valued their lives above all else and acted with extreme caution. While you…"

"While I?"

"You don't seem to hesitate about rushing into danger."

"On the contrary… If you could feel the fear that's currently gripping my insides, you wouldn't make such comments."

Finn caught up with them and firmly grasped the Guardian's shoulders, urging her to stop.

"Not that way! No one is allowed to enter Earnox after dark. Follow me, there's a breach further in the palisade."

The sound of barking echoed in the distance, hostile and alarming. Their doubles had been spotted. A knot of tension tightened in Elissa's stomach, momentarily stealing her breath. She glanced at her companions, catching their reproachful looks, their disagreement with her initiative. It did not matter. She could bear their judgments if it meant saving a life or two. Finn had spoken the truth; erosion had carved out a narrow ditch beneath the massive wooden palisade. He slipped through it with the grace of an agile ferret, his lean frame providing a natural advantage. Despite not possessing Finn's slender build, Elissa discovered a surprising flexibility within herself. With a few grunts and minor scrapes, she managed to reach the other side of the wall. Then it was Wil's turn…

Impossible.

His imposing physique prevented him from squeezing through. Finn and Elissa attempted to help, but their efforts were futile. His fresh wounds added to his agony, causing him to yelp in pain.

"It's no use, Wil. Stay there and wait for our return," Elissa whispered to him, unwilling to subject him to further suffering under the palisade.

"Elissa… are you serious?" he stammered.

"We'll be back soon, I promise," she replied, then rose, eventually breaking eye contact with her distraught protector.

She could hear his frustration, but she pressed on, resolute.

———— ··•·· ————

The hamlet lay silent. Except for the moonlight, there was nothing to guide them on their path. The routes, once bustling with villagers during the day, were now deserted. "Welcome to Earnox," Finn's bitterness was palpable in his words. Although he barely knew her, he could sense the destination the mage had in mind. So, he led her quietly through the dwellings, his steps cautious, and his cloak shielding him from view. He stopped in front of a modest abode, decorated with quaint groves and pastel shutters. Elissa instantly recognized this as Miranda's home. Finn wasted no time and knocked on the door, his impatience visible in his restless movements. After a moment, the florist opened the door, her hair a mess, and a puzzled expression on her face.

"Yes?" she inquired in a hushed tone.

"Miranda... we must hurry," he urged.

"Oh... Finn. I thought the mayor banished you from the village."

"I know, but for your safety, I need to break the law again."

"What are you saying?" the merchant whispered, her eyes widening.

"You're in danger... Earnox is in danger," Elissa spoke with a solemn tone.

The young mother covered her trembling mouth with her hand.

"Gwendoline?" she asked in a barely audible voice.

Finn nodded, and Miranda's complexion paled.

"I was one of the few who believed in her goodness," she whispered in dismay.

"We must leave now," the Guardian pressed, aware that their ruse would not last indefinitely.

"We can't abandon the other villagers... we have to try something," Miranda implored.

"You said it yourself: the people of Earnox never trusted Gwendoline. How would they accept the word of a foreigner and a man who's been exiled?" Finn replied.

Miranda remained silent, but her somber expression revealed her understanding, her resignation.

"I'll get Brea," she whispered, disappearing back behind the door.

Finn's impatience manifested in sighs as he paced before the cottage.

"We're wasting precious time," he grumbled, kicking a stone. Elissa stayed silent, fully aware that she was the reason for their precarious diversion. A distant thump reached their ears, followed by repetitive knocks that reverberated through the freezing night air. The echoes penetrated the forest like a sinister omen, causing the diseased tree leaves to shiver.

"The village gates," Finn stammered, his complexion turning pale.

Already? Had their doubles been discovered?

Elissa dashed inside the house, coming face to face with Miranda, who held her frightened daughter in her arms. Miranda was trying to gather their belongings, attempting to salvage what she had managed to build in Earnox.

"We don't have time. We must leave immediately," Elissa announced, gently urging her outside.

Thankfully, Miranda did not need a second invitation and followed the Guardian and the hunter, Brea still nestled protectively against her mother.

They hurried toward the breach as distant screams filled the air. The cries multiplied, and Elissa realized that the slaughter had started. She could not fathom why their assailants were attacking the villagers who had no connection to her new title, the stone, or the Council. They were merely caught in her wake, victims of her path. The harsh truth settled in: their aggressors were eliminating witnesses. Gwendoline had been right; she carried death with her. Wherever she went, chaos and destruction followed. She had become a harbinger of disaster, a plague. The realization coursed through her like venom, an insurmountable guilt consuming her.

Why had she not chosen a different path?

CHAPTER

18

RETURN OF THE DRAGONS

Farklyn felt as though his skull was about to explode. He awoke on silken sheets, bathed in the gentle morning light seeping through vaporous curtains. The familiar scent of saline water and citrus teased his senses, instantly recognizable. Somehow, he found himself back in his villa. He began to question the events of the previous day, wondering if the death and destruction he had witnessed were mere products of an intoxicated mind, perhaps just vivid nightmares from a night of debauchery. It would not have been the first time. His gaze landed on Eamon, the aging royal family physician, and it dawned on him that this was, unfortunately, the harsh reality. The mage-healer was seated at his bedside, immersed in the pages of a thick grimoire. The tip of Eamon's pointed nose barely held up his small round glasses, while his dark eyes scanned a list of potions and spells. Farklyn attempted to sit up, but immediate regret followed as a wave of pain surged through his body, causing him to emit a low grunt.

"Majesty!" exclaimed the magistrate, noticing his awakening. "How are you feeling?"

Farklyn groaned, a mix of discomfort and annoyance. In truth, he simply did not want to answer.

Eamon approached the young prince to inspect the bandages that wrapped his bruised chest. Farklyn felt as if a drum was pounding inside his head, and the taste of blood still lingered on his chapped lips.

"Your condition had us all quite worried, Your Highness. You've been unconscious for over two days," the mage continued.

Two days? Really? Farklyn was more injured than he had initially thought. Purplish bruises marked his tanned skin, and numerous wrappings covered his body. He attempted to sit up again, but a sharp pain in his abdomen forced him to relent.

"Yes, I know it hurts," Eamon remarked, offering a drink to his master. "The healing mages tended to your broken ribs, but the soreness will persist for a few days."

"My first battle scars! How delightful!" Farklyn quipped, a wry half-smile forming on his lips.

"Let's hope they're your last! Many overstate the glory of wars, if you ask me."

"I don't recall hearing such words from a Sapphire Order magistrate before."

"Your mother's opinions greatly differ from mine, so I keep my views to myself."

"I can only imagine!"

The two men exchanged an amused, even knowing glance. Eamon's familiarity with Farklyn surpassed that of most who had come and gone in his life. With all the times he'd ended up in the physician's office due to recklessness or his penchant for one-night encounters, Eamon practically felt like a member of the royal family.

"You must know where Valera is, don't you?" Farklyn inquired, making another attempt to straighten up. He found himself surprisingly concerned about his mother, though he quickly attributed it to his throbbing headache.

"Physically, the queen is unharmed," the healer responded. A certain unease tinged his tone, a fact not lost on his listener. The elderly man nervously stroked his white goatee, avoiding Farklyn's gaze.

"I sense there's a 'but' to this," the prince prompted.

"Her Majesty is weighed down by a heavy melancholy. This blow to her pride has affected her temperament… perhaps more than usual."

"No surprise there, considering her plans were shattered by the attack on Ryre's Keep."

"It goes beyond that, Majesty," Eamon admitted, his expression revealing his shared sorrow with the queen. "For years, the populace turned a blind eye to your mother's authoritative rule. As the main force behind the dragons' departure, her popularity shielded her from criticism. But with their apparent return, Wynnorth and Guverl'yt have grown less forgiving of her methods. Many accuse her of failing in her duty. Some even go so far as to label her a tyrant."

"People's opinions can be fickle," Farklyn commented with feigned detachment. He secretly admitted a small satisfaction at finally being proven right about his mother. Even Braylon had attempted to counsel her, urging her to adopt a more flexible approach with her subjects.

"The citizens may indeed be ungrateful," Eamon replied somberly.

"Or perhaps they've only just woken up," Farklyn retorted sharply.

The healer remained silent, perturbed by the steward's words. After a pause, the young man adjusted his tone.

"Yet, I concur that Valera's actions, though drastic, often serve the people's well-being. I could never doubt my mother's intentions, hidden deep within her. Does that comfort you?"

Eamon nodded awkwardly, but still chose not to respond. No one was immune to Her Majesty's network of informants, and accusations of treason were rampant in the eastern kingdoms. The old magistrate's wisdom and experience kept him from siding explicitly with anyone.

Farklyn sighed, his gaze drifting up to the azure sky visible from his bed. As he contemplated, he struggled to recollect the moments just before his loss of consciousness. Fragments emerged: Braylon and his wounds, the Elven Master attempting to aid him, and the presence of Jenima— fiery and beautiful Jenima. Yet, beyond these glimpses, an elusive barrier seemed to stand between him and his memories. The more he tried to breach it, the sharper his headache grew. Unintentionally, he abandoned the effort, sensing an unnatural quality to the mental obstruction.

"Cendril's delegation is likely returning home already?" Farklyn inquired with a sigh.

"They remain here, accompanying the queen," came the response.

"Really? I would have presumed they'd be hastening away from Wynnorth."

"Unforeseen developments following the attack on Ryre's Keep have kept them here. I lack specific details. Additionally, your mother awaits your presence once I grant you permission."

Farklyn's absence of enthusiasm was barely veiled, his exasperation escaping as a grumble as he settled into his pillows.

"Very well," he yielded, hoping that Eamon could shield him from his duties.

"Your injuries appear relatively minor. You'll likely be fit to leave soon. It would be imprudent to keep Her Highness waiting," the physician remarked, a faint smirk gracing his lips.

Farklyn offered a strained smile in reply. He discerned the implication behind Eamon's words—a subtle penance for criticisms aimed at Valera. Very well then! To his lovely mother, he would go.

* ·•·•· *

Farklyn departed for the Capitol, where the queen had convened dignitaries from every corner of Balt'boec. Braylon, having mostly recuperated, naturally accompanied his prince. A more extensive and closely-knit guard than usual trailed them. As Farklyn's cart approached the town, he swiftly understood the reason. Clusters of enraged citizens filled the streets, voicing their displeasure in loud protests and hurling insults aimed at the crown. A chuckle escaped Farklyn, but the humor was short-lived. He was no longer a mere observer of Wynnorth's policies; he was an integral part of them today. The realization hit him like a blow as the villagers escalated from words to action, pelting his cart with rotten produce and horse excrement. The fading tranquility of the past was now a distant memory. A wave of unfamiliar emotion swept over him, and he could not quite grasp its nature. He did understand, though, that unexpectedly finding himself at the helm of an oppressed kingdom was nowhere in his plans.

"You'll get used to it," Braylon murmured, his expression attempting empathy.

In truth, Farklyn had found comfort in the citizens' prior indifference toward him. Their current hostility, however, struck a chord. He remained silent for the duration of the ride, his battered face etched with somber concern.

———— ··●·· ————

A sigh of relief escaped Farklyn as the cart finally came to a halt, distancing him from the clamor and malevolent glares. The imposing edifice of Wynnorth's Capitol loomed ahead, its dark walls rising in towers that seemed to pierce the sky like threatening spears. Banners garlanded the structure, causing the colors of the Sapphire Council to dance in the wind. Heavily armored soldiers swarmed the main plaza, guarding the numerous entrances. With a respectful bow to the kingdom's steward, they cleared a path for him. Farklyn followed in close pursuit of Braylon, who moved with an almost comical mix of haste and unease. Dabbing at his sweat-drenched scarlet face with a handkerchief bearing the emblem of their Order, Braylon muttered, "We must hurry! I hope the assembly hasn't started yet."

The murmur of the conference room reached Farklyn's ears from a distance, suggesting a direr situation than Eamon and Braylon had conveyed. As the doors swung open, Farklyn was taken aback to find that elves and men were not the only attendees.

On the left side of the hall stood the delegation of the "little people"— fierce warriors no taller than a human child. Originating exclusively from Mortenburn, an arid region blanketed in volcanic stone at the empire's heart, these enigmatic individuals were a mystery to Farklyn. He knew only snippets of Mortenburn, a once flourishing and lush land that was marred by the eruption of Mount Dogdurhal. Over five centuries had passed since most survivors had scattered to the four corners of Balt'boec, slowly losing their distinct characteristics and customs. The "dwarf-cousins," as they were known, had gradually integrated into typical human culture, rendering their true heritage somewhat elusive. The authentic inhabitants of Mortenburn, however, vastly differed from their surface-dwelling descendants. Their small stature allowed them to navigate the intricate tunnels of mines with ease, evolving over generations to possess a robust and enduring physique. Despite their subterranean existence, their skin bore a uniform dark hue, a midnight blue that was occasionally mistaken for the night itself. In stark contrast, their ivory hair cascaded in lengthy dreadlocks down their solid shoulders. Behind bushy, pale eyebrows, their piercing grey eyes radiated an intense demeanor. These Mortenburn inhabitants took pride in their role in arms trade and mineral commerce. Yet, they rarely ventured from their homeland, reserving their dealings for sea captains, privateers, and outlaws. Encounters with these proud and solitary beings were a rarity. The presence of Mortenburn's "little people" at the assembly confirmed the gravity of the situation to Farklyn.

To the right, the resonant voices of the Ukayris from the Gamar Islands rang out, carrying a distinct aura of hostility. This matriarchal tribe of seafaring warriors bore intricate tattoos upon their ebony skin. Towering over the congress, their dignitaries projected an air of athleticism and dominance. Adorned with vibrant feathered headdresses and shell-embellished spears, they captivated the eye. Among them, the tallest figure, a middle-aged fighter with greying hair, greeted the prince as he moved by. Farklyn promptly reciprocated the gesture, feeling a sense of awe in the presence of the woman who commanded respect with natural authority. This was Taaroa, leader of the Madjiwey clan and renowned as the islands' mother. Despite her maturity, she retained an impressive muscular physique. A profound wisdom emanated from her amber eyes, hinting at a life story waiting to be unveiled.

The atmosphere within the crowd appeared animated, but devoid of visible conflict. Yet, the tension etched on the faces of the delegates. These diverse groups had primarily encountered each other on battlefields for decades. Farklyn strode into the grand hall, determined to maintain a look of dignity and self-assuredness, despite the brewing ache and turmoil inside him. His gaze was drawn to the highest balcony, where his mother was positioned. Uncharacteristically vulnerable, she exuded an air of timidity. It was a side of Valera he had never witnessed before: she averted her eyes, her fingers fidgeted restlessly, and the strained smile she employed to mask her irritation was evident. As Valera spotted her son, her countenance transformed, radiating a warmth she rarely bestowed upon him. Springing to her feet, she hurried to his side, embracing him with open arms.

"I'm so glad you're safe and well," she murmured near his ear.

Not only was such behavior unprecedented for Farklyn, but he found his mother's demeanor oddly maternal. He allowed her to hold him, though he remained passive, still caught off guard by her display of emotion.

"These vultures are circling me," she confided, her words barely audible. "Please, do not let them sully our name."

With that, she clutched his hand in a clammy, trembling grip. Her plea bore into his consciousness like a dagger. He nodded, uncertain about her true expectations. Allowing himself to be guided mechanically, he paused when he realized Valera was steering him toward the central balcony, where the leading figures who presided over the assembly were gathered.

"I would prefer to remain in the background," he hurriedly whispered.

"As the steward of the kingdom, your presence is essential."

Essential? It was a term rarely attributed to him. Farklyn's throat constricted, and his hands quivered in tandem, a fact Valera astutely observed.

"What a pair we make," she remarked, a subtle smirk playing on her lips.

Upon the raised platform stood King Tanyll, deeply engrossed in conversation with Elyndel. The Master of Cendril acknowledged the prince's presence with a nod before returning his attention to their discussion. For some reason, the elf's countenance evoked an uncanny sense of déjà vu in Farklyn. Attempting to delve into his memories only intensified his headache. So, he settled beside his mother in silence, his heart quickening its pace. Valera hushed the assembly with three deliberate taps of her scepter and then gestured elegantly for Elyndel to step forward. The Master reciprocated her expression with a courteous bow and approached the balustrade. Gazing out over the crowd with his penetrating eyes, he began speaking, his words resonating candidly throughout the hall.

"The moment has arrived to contemplate the future of Balt'boec. The dragons' resurgence poses a threat to the entire empire. We remain uncertain about their numbers among us, given their ability to assume human form which cloaks their true identities."

"Have they always been confined to Balt'boec?" queried Taaroa.

"I believe so, indeed," the Master responded with conviction.

"Why now? Do we know their intentions?" she pressed.

"That's precisely what we must decipher. These creatures aren't the mindless beings we envisioned, driven solely by instinct."

"Have we identified a second breach?" Turik Thogurn, King of Mortenburn, asked.

That same question had plagued Elyndel since the attack. He had never openly admitted it, yet the furtive glances exchanged with Valera led him to believe she shared his unease.

"To be honest, I cannot provide a comprehensive response to all your inquiries," the elven magistrate confessed. "Much like you, I navigate these shadows amidst the crisis that looms. This is why we are gathered here today."

"It could also be a ploy to unite us under one roof," Lorena Bizerac interjected. "This wouldn't be the Netherbornes' first deception."

A weighty silence descended upon the audience. Just like everyone present, Farklyn was aware of the tragic history of the Bizeracs, the royal family of Ascana. He cast a sidelong glance at his mother, anticipating her swift response to such an assertion. However, her face appeared dejected, her gaze evasive. Was it remorse? After all, the Bizerac lineage's downfall lay squarely on Valera and Fabyan's shoulders. During a diplomatic visit intended to cement relations between Guverl'yt and Ascana, an enigmatic hunting accident had claimed the lives of King Theodore and his four sons, the rightful heirs to the Ascana throne. Lorena, left to steward the realm, found herself sentenced to witness the extinction of her line. The perpetrator of this massacre was no secret, with Lorena at the forefront of the accusers. Yet, she grasped the futility of seeking vengeance without concrete evidence. She, like many across Balt'boec, knew that her retribution would be a silent, internal one.

"I can personally attest to the horrors of the ball at Ryre's Keep, as the deceased can no longer speak," declared the Master in a tone that was both courteous and resolute. "I understand that the prevailing tension between our kingdoms and families makes this collaboration delicate. However, your conspiratorial notions are further burdening a crisis already beyond our grasp. I refuse to let the empire go up in flames due to the quarrels of its leaders. If anyone present finds it impossible to set aside their personal histories, I kindly ask them to leave."

Each of his words was measured, carrying a weight that made Farklyn hold his breath. No one stood up; a dense silence draped the grand hall.

"Very well," Elyndel continued. "Your cooperation is greatly appreciated."

He exchanged a nod with Lorena, who promptly returned the gesture. Elyndel radiated a benevolence and warmth that Farklyn had rarely witnessed in a leader.

In spite of all this, the declarations, now heard by the prince for the first time, did not fill him with assurance. Dragons taking on humanoid forms, the potential of a second breach... he immediately understood the keen interest that held the attention of the dignitaries.

"Reports have persisted for years... tales of colossal reptilian shapes hovering over Mortenburn," one of the little men chimed in.

"Rumors, mere rumors!" Valera retorted for the first time, her ego visibly wounded.

It dawned on Farklyn that she was genuinely feeling guilt, a sentiment he had never thought possible in her. She feared that her actions and sacrifices might be called into question, that people could accuse her of failing in her duty.

"The motivation behind these creatures remains obscure. The one at Ryre's Keep could have annihilated a significant portion of Balt'boec's monarchy in a single night if it so wished," a magistrate from the Sapphire Council expressed.

Farklyn did not know the man's name, but his face had engraved itself into his memory since the attack. Like him, this man was one of the survivors of that grim encounter with the red dragon.

"That's why we suspect it was a message ... a means to show us the extent of the devastation this beast could unleash upon us. It wants to engage in a game, the rules of which remain unknown to us," Elyndel continued, his tone taking on a somber hue.

Heads nodded in silent agreement, a shared acknowledgment of the looming menace.

"May I address the assembly?" a voice arose from the back of the room.

All eyes turned to the tall figure standing at the forefront of his seat. Draped in an emerald toga, his chestnut hair, thinning in places, was meticulously slicked back. Farklyn recognized him immediately: Toran Sius, the Master of Walderlake.

CHAPTER

19

THE JOUST

Farklyn laced his fingers in his lap, anticipation coursing through him as he waited. Toran Sius swept his gaze across the assembly and offered a self-assured grin before proceeding.

"I believe I possess certain insights that might shed some light on this unfortunate predicament," he began, his words carrying an air of intrigue.

Elyndel nodded, though Farklyn caught a subtle twitch of his lip that indicated his dissatisfaction with the intervention.

"Do you sense the tension between Cendril's delegation and that of Walderlake?" Farklyn murmured to Braylon.

"Elyndel isn't particularly fond of Toran Sius. Tanyll and Hargon still maintain a reasonably cordial rapport. In this instance, the strain exists between their respective Masters."

"Who in Balt'boec doesn't harbour an issue with Toran Sius?"

The prince did not hold the magistrate in high regard, even though their encounters had been brief. One meeting remained vivid in his memory. It was a moment when Toran Sius had grovelled himself beside his mother. Baalhan's life had just been claimed, and the search for the culprit was underway. Valera had seemed to confide in Toran, her head bowed, tears streaming down her cheeks. He had placed his hands on her shoulders, adopting a patronizing demeanor, speaking to her as if to a sobbing child. Farklyn recalled the unsettling feeling that had swept over him. Since then, he had not crossed paths with Toran Sius, as relations between their realms had soured with time.

"Ladies and gentlemen, as you are likely aware, Brennet Reinhart has been murdered," the Master of Walderlake began. "A relentless pursuit to apprehend the perpetrator of this heinous assassination is underway. Emerald Council soldiers are tirelessly chasing her, and for several days now, they have been on her trail. Following her path, they witnessed a formidable magical explosion originating from Pendard Forest, where the fugitive had taken refuge. The site has been utterly devastated by the blast, leaving a mysterious glow hanging over the woods. Additionally, the militia has stumbled upon an ancient druidic monolith, seemingly associated with the Circle of Am."

Toran Sius's words were both cryptic and unsettling. This did not sit well with the prince, who understood that the man was using grandiosity and sensationalism to advance his point.

"This isn't the first time you've mentioned the Am community. Weren't they subjects of prosecution?" questioned Madz Fogan, a prominent magistrate of the Sapphire Council.

"Precisely!" Toran immediately concurred. "It was a trial aimed at condemning their disloyalty to the empire."

"The same trial that resulted in the deaths of their entire clan, including women and children!" Elyndel retorted with fervor, his countenance more strained than ever.

"Such sacrifices are sometimes necessary to ensure the survival of our world. I believe many of us have faced similar choices at one point or another."

The Master of Walderlake's tone attempted to be understanding, yet Farklyn saw it as nothing more than deception. Being well versed in the art of manipulation himself, he easily recognized the maneuverings of others. Elyndel, mindful not to take the bait, abstained from responding to these allegations. The young prince could not help but notice that the elf was burning with the urge to counter.

"I fail to find the connection between your explanations and the reappearance of these winged behemoths," Elyndel questioned, his demeanor slowly regaining its composure.

"You don't see the correlation?" Toran responded, his cunning grin widening. "The very creatures the Circle strived to shield during the Great War have suddenly resurfaced after the activation of one of their monoliths. I consider it more than mere coincidence."

"What about this mystical veil?" Turik inquired. "My men reported observing this phenomenon from our mountain ranges—a sort of emerald wave dancing in the skies of Walderlake."

"A dimensional rift," Toran clarified.

A restless murmur swept through the assembly, and the Elven Master sighed in exasperation.

"Neither you nor I can be certain," he remarked dryly.

Yet, his statement went unheard, and Farklyn witnessed how quickly panic was spreading among the delegations.

"Do you believe that the return of the dragons is tied to this criminal and the rift?" Taaroa asked, her voice tinged with concern.

"Without a doubt! I've personally had to address her during a confrontation within our Council. Her behavior is erratic, violent."

"You have no evidence of her guilt," Elyndel corrected.

"The escape of this usurper presents an immense peril for Walderlake... for the entire empire!" Toran countered, folding his arms. "I may not fully comprehend the scope of her abilities, but I am far from reassured—especially considering she openly assaulted me in front of all Emerald Order members."

Confidence oozed from him, a certainty that the rest of the assembly would rally to his cause. Farklyn's gaze shifted to Elyndel, who stood with clenched jaw and fists, examining the apprehensive crowd with puzzlement. Perhaps he was not used to confronting the persuasive allure that human narcissism could wield? The very narcissism that the prince observed day by day within a society deeply steeped in this perversion... Unlike poor Elyndel, who seemed almost too pure of heart for the Eastern world, Farklyn understood how to counter those who thrived on emotion rather than logic.

"Did she assault you in the presence of her father? In front of the late Guardian of the Emerald?" Farklyn inquired, pretending innocence. His voice reverberated off the marble walls, creating an echo he had never heard before, one he quite relished. His mother fixed her feline gaze upon him, curiosity evident as to why her youngest son was at last choosing to speak.

"Indeed," answered Toran Sius. "The rest of the Council can verify my statements."

He placed a hand upon his heart, as though remembering these events caused him profound sorrow.

"Isn't it peculiar that the Guardian remained passive?" the young man pressed before the magistrate could resume.

"His precarious condition likely rendered him incapable of intervening," Toran Sius asserted.

"Naturally, his condition! I apologize for interrupting," Farklyn interjected with a touch of arrogance coloring his voice. Toran Sius responded with a gracious nod before shifting his focus back to the assembly.

"As I was explaining…"

"Apologies once more, Master Sius, but something nags at me."

The mage raised his gaze to meet the steward's, who returned the look with a bright smile.

"Yes, Prince Farklyn?"

"Was the Guardian residing in a sanatorium?"

"I… I do not believe so."

"Then his daughter and servants were attending to his care?"

"With all due respect, Your Majesty, I'm uncertain if this information is relevant to our discussion."

"I understand your reservations. However, I fail to comprehend why this woman would have devoted herself to nursing a mentor she ultimately desired to see succumb. Wasn't it to her advantage that he owed her his survival before his tragic death?"

"Who can decipher the intricate workings of this sorceress's mind? Perhaps she awaited the Guardian's succession ritual as an opportune moment to act?" the Master conjectured, eager to regain control of the conversation. "To return to the matter at hand, this breach could have easily…"

"Allow me to ensure I understand your line of thought. Are you suggesting that she opted to enrage her own kingdom by annihilating her entire household after achieving her goal? If, as you assert, Brennet Reinhart was in such a debilitated state, why not let nature take its course? Moreover, wouldn't this transfer ritual guarantee his demise as well?"

"What insinuations are you trying to make, Prince Farklyn?" his interlocutor hissed through clenched teeth.

"Farklyn, please," the queen chided in a chilling undertone. Nonetheless, he remained undeterred.

"I think the late Guardian understood his daughter's temperament better than anyone. He would not have endangered your Council by admitting a potentially dangerous mage. Something must have triggered her actions... or rather, someone."

Reading the expressions of those accompanying the Master of Walderlake, the prince deduced that his allegations had struck a chord.

"I never attempted to steal the emerald, if that's what you're implying. This woman deceived us all, including Brennet," Toran Sius retorted in a defensive yet controlled manner.

"Nevertheless, she didn't usurp the stone as you asserted earlier. The Guardian willingly gave it to her."

"Brennet's judgment was impaired!"

"According to your perspective."

"According to mine and King Hargon's as well! This murderer manipulated that poor, ailing man to serve as her mere puppet."

"Is that why you were attempting to take the emerald?" Farklyn interjected, his voice clear and resonant. "To protect the stone yourself?"

"Actually, I wanted to..."

He halted abruptly, his expression shifting as he realized his misstep.

"All I desire is the prosperity of my realm and the safeguarding of our Council," he responded.

"However, you do not deny that you assaulted her based on mere conjecture."

Toran Sius struggled to conceal his anger. His face reddened and his forehead wrinkled more deeply as his scowl intensified. Farklyn suppressed a chuckle as he observed the crowd's reaction. They seemed so easily swayed, so manipulable. It bordered on the absurd.

"I would never attack anyone without reason. I may not understand her motivations, but I assure you, her volatile temperament presents too grave a risk to allow her to keep this stone."

"What is her name?" the prince queried again, his voice resounding in the room like the song of a mockingbird.

"Pardon?" Toran Sius snapped, his gaze piercing the young man with fury.

His patience was rapidly eroding, and Farklyn knew that if he continued to prod, his interlocutor would soon lose his composure.

"Your proposition entails imprisoning a woman, even her execution. It would be pertinent to know the identity of this individual you're so keen on disposing of," Farklyn quipped.

"Her name is Elissa Reinhart. However, I am not eager to dispose of anyone. I am merely determined to uphold justice," Toran retorted, his arms crossed in a defensive stance.

"Quite honorable, I must say! But let me ask… did you reach this conclusion before or after the Guardian found a mere apprentice more capable than yourself?" Farklyn continued, undeterred by the escalating tension.

The Master hesitated for a moment, taken aback by the prince's audacity.

"Is that the case?" Farklyn pressed on. "Brennet Reinhart declined to entrust you with the emerald."

"He… yes… For reasons that remain unclear to me, yes."

"Do you suppose he feared that, in your possession, the stone would bring ruin to your kingdom?"

"How dare you?" Toran hissed through clenched teeth.

"Farklyn, that is enough," Valera interjected, her tone carrying both authority and unease.

"You should heed your mother's words, young man, and hold your tongue!" Toran snapped, his face flushing.

"But I wonder... is it this uncontrollable rage that potentially factored into Brennet's choice to exclude you as his successor?" the steward continued, unabashedly ignoring the protests around him.

"This woman's parents were members of the Circle of Am. I am not fabricating anything. These are established facts!"

"And now that you've successfully removed Brennet and are ready to do the same with Elissa Reinhart, I'm left pondering who might be next on your list," Farklyn provocatively mused.

"I said silence!" Toran Sius bellowed, abruptly raising his weapon in the direction of the prince.

Almost simultaneously, Elyndel lifted his scepter. A bolt of lightning fired by Toran Sius crashed against the magical shield erected by the Elven Master, who intuitively protected those on the balcony. In that instant, chairs were vacated, and Wynnorth's guards surged toward the Walderlake delegation, readying themselves for a defensive stance. Chaos rippled through the assembly, and Farklyn's self-assured grin only broadened. Both Valera and Tanyll rushed to Elyndel's side. Their weapons emitted radiant beams of light, intercepted just in time by Toran Sius. In contrast to their Master, the magistrates from Walderlake hesitated to fully engage in the conflict. Toran Sius's response appeared to shock them, causing them to exercise caution in their actions.

Amidst the commotion, Braylon instinctively positioned himself in front of the prince, his entire frame trembling as he prepared to shield his lord from any magical onslaught. Farklyn promptly pushed Braylon aside, unwilling to let his servant suffer for his own audacity. Yet, he realized that his arrogance alone could not protect him from the imminent dangers. After all, the room housed some of the most formidable mages and warriors in the empire, while he...

Still, he did not budge from his seat, his haughty expression unwavering. Common sense dictated that he should flee to save the Netherborne lineage, ensuring Valera did not meet the fate of Lorena Bizerac. Perhaps that was why he remained rooted, a strange desire to wound his mother at the cost of his own existence? Or maybe it was a morbid curiosity driving him, an urge to bear witness to the anarchy he had incited.

After a flurry of exchanges, the Walderlake delegation submitted without further resistance. A petite woman, wearing a regal purple turban, desperately attempted to stop her hysterical leader. In a sudden, unexpected move, she pressed her scepter against the man's back, murmuring words drowned in the commotion. Instantaneously, Toran Sius found himself immobilized, robbed of the capacity to contribute to the grotesque spectacle.

Despite a few injuries, Wynnorth's sentries managed to apprehend the Master of Walderlake, confiscating his scepter in the process.

"Guards, escort Toran Sius and his followers out of the Capitol," Queen Valera commanded solemnly, her gaze searing into her son with a mix of anger and disappointment.

Without further words, she exited the hall, disappearing behind the golden velvet curtain at the dais's end.

"This is an insult to the kingdom of Walderlake!" the Master of the Emerald Council roared as he was ushered outside.

The prince's eyes met Elyndel's, and the latter offered him a curious smile. There was a hint of understanding, even familiarity, in that expression—a glow of satisfaction that only he truly comprehended. Farklyn realized that Elyndel grasped the motive behind his provocation, the deep-seated urge to unveil Toran Sius's authentic nature to the rulers of their realm.

As Toran's shouts reverberated across the vast corridors of the Capitol, Braylon's voice broke through the steward's contemplation.

"What did you try to prove, Prince Farklyn?" he inquired, a hint of reproach in his tone for the first time.

"One manipulator easily recognizes another," Farklyn responded, settling back into his seat with a sense of pride.

CHAPTER

20

THE RUINS OF ITOS

Running—this was Elissa's sole purpose now. She found herself regretting the sheltered life she'd known in the villa where she grew up, the cozy featherbed, and those evenings spent reading by the fireplace with Bruna. Her dreams of exploring the world and collaborating with the rest of the Council to share her unique talents seemed distant and naive. Fate had responded to her ambitions in a way she could never have anticipated. She carried a burden of guilt, as if their sufferings were a consequence of her impetuousness, her arrogance.

Despite their weariness and the relentless ache in their bodies, the fugitives could not afford to rest. The roads were no longer safe, nor were the villages. After the tragedy at Earnox, Elissa was determined not to risk the lives of innocent people again. Hunger gnawed at her insides, a persistent reminder of their dire circumstances. Yet she and her companions pushed on. Each step was a struggle; blisters on her feet stung with every movement. Suppressing her exhaustion, Miranda maintained her composure, shielding Brea from the true weight of their predicament. Wil and Finn took turns carrying the child on their backs, weaving fantastic tales of princesses and fairies riding gallant steeds, evoking smiles from the young girl. Despite their unwavering determination, Elissa sensed that their pace could not be sustained much longer. A moment would come when they'd have to halt, to catch their breath, to regain some semblance of strength.

Breaking the silence, the hunter spoke up, his voice strained and his gaze distant.

"We… we should find a place to rest," he managed to utter between gasps. "The horses need a breather."

Brea's laughter rang out, a sound as refreshing as a bubbling stream, as she playfully ruffled the young man's hair. Reluctantly, Wil met the hunter's gaze. Sweat-drenched and scratched, his face bore the marks of their desperate flight. He nodded in agreement, acknowledging the need for respite.

— ··●·· —

Luckily, Miranda was familiar with a secluded sanctuary—the ruins of an ancient temple dedicated to Itos. They reached this destination within a few hours, or so she claimed, as they approached a fetid swamp where only frogs and leeches seemed to thrive. The air was tainted with the odor of sulfur and decay, evoking memories of their encounter with the sylvan creature. A milky mist shrouded their surroundings, obscuring the stone path they had traversed. Moss dampened the sound of their footsteps, and the chorus of toads punctuated the otherwise eerie silence.

"Here we are!" Miranda announced with a tinge of excitement.

"I see nothing," the mage remarked, perplexed.

"Exactly!" Miranda acquiesced, skillfully guiding them through the drooping branches of the weeping willows that obstructed the way.

Parting a few entwined branches, they caught sight of the weathered facade of a shrine nestled among the trees and atop a small hill. The stone structure was garlanded with climbing vines, and faded engravings marked its surface. Some of the inscriptions had eroded with time, yet they still whispered the tale of Itos, the father of the gods who watched over Balt'boec.

"This will do," the knight agreed, stepping into what appeared more like a crypt.

Curiosity pricked Elissa, prompting her to question Miranda. "How do you know this place?"

The response was a blend of nostalgia and laughter. "I used to come here as a child."

Wonder stirred further. "And what led to its current state?"

"Much like the rest of the kingdom, it fell victim to the ravages of the Great Dragon War."

A weighty exchange of glances followed—conversations held without words, understood only by those who had borne witness to horrors and experienced the aftermath of destruction.

Despite his weariness, Finn ventured out to hunt, aiming to secure sustenance for their group.

"I'm not making any guarantees… we might have to settle for toad skewers," he quipped as he departed.

Seated on the cracked and dusty flagstones, they found a moment's reprieve. The temple's deteriorated state hardly mattered; they were all safe and intact. In the context of her past experiences, Elissa considered this escape a rare success. A surge of hope warmed her, illuminating the potential for a fate she could wield in her own hands. For once in an extended while, she allowed herself this break. She removed her worn leather boots and observed, with a touch of disdain, the sorry condition of her bloodied feet.

"You'll see, you'll grow accustomed to it!" Wil offered with a half-smile.

The Guardian nodded, reciprocating the sentiment, yet secretly hoping that such escapes would not become a habit. Rising to her feet, she felt the coolness of the flagstones slightly soothe her aching soles. With careful steps, she made her way toward the rear of the temple, where an unexpectedly well-preserved bronze statue stood. It depicted a female figure, hooded, with wings akin to those of a bat. Elissa's gaze shifted to the words inscribed on the wall beside her. Despite her extensive knowledge, the narratives of Balt'boec's deities remained largely unfamiliar territory.

"A surprising goddess, isn't she?" Miranda huffed as she approached Elissa.

The Guardian smiled, uncertain about how to respond.

"Of course! I forgot about your origins!" the merchant quickly corrected herself. "Druidic communities have their own mythology, don't they?"

"It's not exactly a mythology… more of a belief in a balance that we all have control over."

"Hence the custom of accepting nothing without being able to return the favor," Miranda added with a wink.

Elissa nodded, and the two women fell into a contemplative silence, deciphering the fragmented writings.

Reflecting on it, Brennet had never attempted to impose his doctrines on her. Since arriving in Brevic, her mentor had shown immense respect for her heritage. References to Itos and his pantheon were therefore rare in their household.

"Too bad, this story seems fascinating," she whispered, tracing the words carved in stone with her fingertips.

"It tells the tale of Itos' doubts about his creations."

"His doubts?"

"Realizing the corruption and violence prevailing in Balt'boec, a world shaped by his hands, Itos contemplated its destruction. He wished to reconstruct a utopian universe, worthy of his immense being."

"I suppose he changed his mind," Elissa remarked wryly.

"Thanks to his other half, Etyja, the mother goddess of Razakstrom." Miranda placed a hand on the marble statue, regarding it with a certain fondness. "Etyja... Her perspective on the imperfect beings inhabiting his realm differed from Itos'. She believed that their strength lay in their resilience, that the will to persist despite their weaknesses held more value than the glorified concept of perfection. Steered by the words of his beloved, Itos came to understand that Balt'boec wasn't a failure, but a world with gaps needing to be filled. He desired to share his magic with them, with the disadvantaged creations born from him. He stationed immortal sentinels at the four corners of the empire, acting as guides and protectors. Inevitably, the expected occurred, and some of these sentinels, enticed by the passionate souls of Itos' children, formed bonds with them."

"Giving birth to the mages of Balt'boec," Elissa finished, mirroring the merchant's thoughts.

Miranda nodded, her eyes alight with emotion. "These sentinels... some call them Abshanishs, others refer to them as Original Bloods."

Elissa's breath left her as if she'd been struck in the stomach. This name—her father had mentioned it during their last conversation.

"Original Bloods," she repeated, her voice carrying the weight of realization.

"A lineage that has remained pure, untouched. Their gifts would differ from those of ordinary mages. A bit like yours..."

Stunned, Elissa locked her gaze with Miranda's, the woman offering an almost amused smile.

"Your little display in Earnox's public square didn't go unnoticed," Miranda pointed out.

"Where are these sentinels now?"

"Several Abshanishs have sought refuge in the Circles, which explains the persecution of druids since Galvrick's demise. The powers of the Original Bloods terrify those who cannot understand them, much like all the extraordinary beings in this world.

"I've heard similar notions from Gwendoline," Elissa confessed.

Miranda nodded thoughtfully, her gaze tenderly resting on Brea, who stood a bit further away. The young girl was crouched beside Wil, eagerly assisting him in lighting the fire—an enthusiasm only someone shielded from the world's hardships could possess.

"I often envied Gwendoline," the young mother declared with a sigh, her voice marked with longing. "Her authenticity, her courage... Not many of us succeed in truly living in the open, without hiding."

"Not many of us?" asked Elissa.

Miranda laid her hand on the stone, and a beam of golden light traced its way through the carvings, illuminating the fragmented passages of the Itos legend. The glimmering shard dissipated as swiftly as it had appeared, escaping the notice of both the young girl and the warrior. How? Elissa stared at the woman, her confusion evident, her brows furrowing as her lips formed unspoken questions. Brennet had insisted that no one shared her abilities, "at least, not anymore." Was he ignorant of others possessing these gifts, or was this yet another of his inscrutable secrets?

"And Brea?" she murmured.

"I don't know yet. Our powers typically manifest during childhood, albeit at varying paces. I can only hope she inherits her father's nature, a simpler life devoid of deceit. It's what she deserves."

Elissa's thoughts retraced to the day she had first realized her own powers, on the summer of her seventh birthday. Gazing at moonlight dancing on the river's surface, she had envisioned ethereal snakes coiling among the stars. To her amazement, delicate silver serpents wound themselves around her small hands. Her parents had been brimming with pride, celebrating with the community by the lakeside. Men and women decked in forest hues and flower crowns had danced, the only occasion during which druids accepted offerings from their kin—baskets filled with fruits, nuts, and potion ingredients.

"When you spoke of knowing our customs from your travels… Were you once part of a Circle?" Elissa inquired.

"Eir's. It was decimated right after yours."

"I'm sorry," Elissa muttered, her voice heavy with genuine sympathy.

Miranda shrugged, her expression revealing the sadness she had kept hidden for so long.

"Toran Sius… I'm convinced he's the orchestrator behind these massacres," Elissa declared, her loathing barely concealed.

"The list of possibilities is extensive!" Miranda retorted with a bitter scoff. "Who doesn't yearn for the eradication of the uncontrollable druids and the 'aberrations' they supposedly harbour? Over the years, numerous factions have emerged… That's partly why I distanced myself from anything connected to my powers."

"I find it unfair. We shouldn't have to remain in the shadows. Those who persecute us should experience their own venom for once."

"Truth be told, I pity those who hunt us. So much animosity festering in their hearts, consumed by fear that we might shatter the world they're trying to rebuild!"

Her words hung in the air as she contemplated her thoughts before continuing.

"Of course, there are mages who possess the potential to inadvertently set our realm ablaze. In a way, I can understand the roots of their worries."

Her comment struck Elissa like a hammer, a chill running down her spine. Inadvertent destruction… Was this the peril Brennet had sought to avert by confining her, and the reason for her journey to Osthallvale? If so, why had he entrusted her with the stone? Miranda's touch on her arm conveyed a sense of solidarity, perhaps even pity. She left Elissa to join Brea, who continued her spirited conversation with Wil beside the flickering fire.

Elissa stood on the fringes of her own existence, a spectator within the vessel of her body. They feared her, a revelation that engulfed her with a surge of understanding. The scope of what had been concealed from her became vivid. Divine sentinels, the orchestrated assault on her community—it was all part of a reality that had been hidden from her. The narrative she had grown up with was a mere facade. How could Brennet have entrusted her with the emerald, with guarding a world she was so oblivious to? A mixture of rage and terror clawed at her throat. Botany, astrology, potions, geography—those were the meager tools she had been armed with. Absurd. A concoction of fennel could hardly protect her against those mercenaries. Knowledge of constellations would not guide her in making informed decisions for her land. And magic, her magic, which Brennet had strived to dampen and conceal… What if her powers inadvertently razed Walderlake, as so many dreaded? The extent of her destructive potential remained unknown to her.

Lost in the turmoil of her apprehension, she hardly noticed Wil's presence beside her. He whispered her name, yet her mounting confusion drowned out his voice. Could she obliterate him like the splintered trees of Pendard Forest? The prospect made her tremble like a leaf in autumn's chill. The ground beneath her seemed to shift, and nausea gripped her. Wil's brow creased in concern, his gaze fixated on her. With a gentle yet firm touch, he cupped her head in his palms, his hands warm against her temples. The grounding contact slowly began to pull her back from the abyss. She realized her own shallow breaths had induced her dizziness. She tried to come to her senses, but anxiety petrified her. With his forehead lightly pressed against hers, Wil urged, "Focus on my breathing."

Obeying, she synchronized her inhalations with his and gradually, her panicked gasps melded into his rhythm. Her knees weakened, yet Wil's steady grip prevented her from crumbling. His embrace enveloped her, his chest against hers, and the cacophony of tumultuous thoughts dimmed to a whisper. His proximity offered reassurance, his heartbeat a steady cadence that soothed her. She relaxed, and a warm tingle spread through her limbs.

"It's alright," he murmured, his voice a balm.

His lips brushed against her forehead, a gesture that startled her. Other than her late parents, affection had been rare in her experience. Perhaps Brennet, on occasion? Surely it was not within his protector's role to offer such comfort. An unfamiliar warmth surged through her—not his, but something distinct. Despite the grime and perspiration coating them, his masculine scent enveloped her. Earth after rain, leather, and the essence of poplar trees—to another woman, it might have meant little. To Elissa, who had never encountered such intimacy, it was intoxicating. This simple, seemingly inconsequential gesture made her aware of the vast emotional terrain she had been deprived of throughout her life.

"Is it my turn?" Finn's voice chimed from a short distance away.

Elissa's gaze shifted, her focus returning to the present. The hunter's boyish grin and playful gleam in his chestnut eyes met hers. He carried a freshly caught prey slung over his shoulder. Drawing near, he joined their embrace, nudging his way into the circle. Resting his head on Wil's muscular arm, he teased affectionately. Wil, wearing a bemused expression, brushed him off with a flick of his hand. Elissa chuckled, enveloped in the restorative presence of her newfound companions.

She would find a way. She would learn, and she would master her abilities.

———— ··•·· ————

When Elissa finally managed to cleanse herself of the filth that clung to her, she could begin to reclaim her sense. Stripping off the tunic and pants Fergus had provided, she felt a twinge of discomfort at the sight of his late wife's worn garments. She kept her long, white linen shirt, a modest barrier in case any of the men happened upon her. Ordinarily, the cold water from the nearby river might have been unwelcome, but today, every droplet on her skin felt like a deliverance—a purging of the death that had tainted her soul. As she stood under the stream, her thoughts drifted to the luxurious rosewater baths that had once been part of her daily routine. It all seemed so distant now, almost surreal.

"May I join you?" Miranda's voice cut through her contemplation, startling her.

Elissa nodded, and the other woman proceeded to remove her soiled nightgown, beginning her own cleansing ritual. With a quick wave of her hand, she splashed water onto her face, emitting a satisfied groan. She offered to braid Elissa's hair and, despite her own uneasiness, she agreed.

"I'm accustomed to dealing with Brea's hair," she reassured Elissa, fingers deftly twisting the dark auburn locks.

Amidst the horrors that had recently unfolded and the darkness that had descended upon her existence, Miranda's gentle presence acted as a soothing balm on Elissa's weary body. She could not help but think back to the times she had pushed Bruna away, especially when all the woman wanted was to comb her hair. What a missed opportunity those moments had been.

"I sense that the burden you bear isn't solely about your origins," Miranda began, her fingers neatly weaving the strands. "More than anything, you worry about proving those who dread our kind right."

Elissa's agreement came in a nod, the emerald at her side seeming to weigh heavier than before.

"Most of all, I fear that this power I've harbored for so long will ultimately control me," she admitted. "It feels like it's been building up within me, just waiting to explode."

Miranda did not respond immediately, her hands paused on Elissa's shoulders as she considered the gravity of her words. Her gaze was serious and thoughtful as she finally spoke.

"Regardless of the challenges you face or the choices you must make, I believe you'll find your way. I have faith in you."

"We barely know each other..." Elissa began, a hint of doubt in her voice.

"True," Miranda conceded. "But how many would risk their lives to defy fate for strangers? While we may not know each other intimately, actions can reveal much about a person."

"What if this burden ends up erasing the part of me that still clings to my humanity?" Elissa's voice quivered with genuine concern.

Miranda's response was a pause, a contemplative silence.

"In that case, I can proudly claim that I once braided the hair of the most feared mage in Balt'boec," Miranda chuckled.

Elissa snickered softly, though her laughter held uncertainty. She found herself silently hoping that Miranda's jest would not turn into a harsh reality. In the depths of her heart, she whispered a prayer to Itos. But if indeed the father of the gods was listening to her, would he truly choose to answer a pagan soul?

CHAPTER

21

THE KNIGHT OF AEGIS

In just a few days, Elissa and her companions neared the Estriden Sea. Wil had a plan to secure their passage, intending to negotiate with one of the privateer captains bound for Osthallvale. However, the magician could not shake her concern about how they would manage to board a ship without the means to pay their way. Apart from her pendant and the knight's sword decorated with a tourmaline gem, none of them possessed valuable items. Not wanting to doubt her companion's capabilities, Elissa refrained from voicing her reservations. To her disappointment, Wil eventually announced that they would have to proceed without Miranda and Brea.

"I understand that you're not pleased with this," he admitted to Elissa. "I might be able to negotiate passage for three, but five…"

"Don't worry!" Miranda interjected before she could even respond. "I have some acquaintances in the village of Mertonbryde, very close to the Saracenne port. They will provide us shelter."

"Is this a simple lie to comfort me?" Elissa scolded.

The merchant did not reply immediately; instead, she observed her interlocutor with a mixture of surprise and disbelief.

"What do you envision for us in Osthallvale, Elissa? We're stepping into the unknown on this continent. Moreover…"

Miranda paused, her uncertainty palpable. She recognized that what she was about to say would cause pain. A peculiar weight tinged her eyes as she hesitantly continued.

"Moreover… you understand the risks we're taking by traveling with you. Despite the gratitude I hold for you, I must prioritize my daughter's well-being. We'll manage on our own."

As Elissa nodded slowly, she once again found herself consumed by guilt. It was clear that they would be better off without her…

———— ··●·· ————

As the group reached a crossroads, torn between the port of Saracenne and the township of Mertonbryde, the early autumn air turned particularly chilly and damp. Wil protested against the idea of halting so close to their destination, yet Elissa reminded him of the dangers posed by coastal villages after nightfall. She feared the inhabitants of the marinas more than their pursuers due to their reputation. Straying from the path, they moved away from potential scouts' view. This time, Wil adamantly refused to light a fire as a precaution. Instead, Elissa conjured a sphere of heat amidst pebbles arranged in a half-moon formation. The faint violet halo provided a comfort akin to a modest fire—subtle and secure. Soon, exhaustion overcame Miranda, Brea, and Finn, and they drifted into slumber. Wil insisted on taking the first guard shift, positioning himself farther back and leaning against an oak tree, his expression inscrutable.

Despite Wil's reassuring words, sleep eluded Elissa. The notion of leaving Miranda and Brea behind without ensuring their safety concerned her, though not as much as the demeanor of the one watching over her. She discreetly observed the warrior, her head resting on her travel bag. Lost in somber memories, his preoccupied expression was evident. His vacant gaze roved through the forest, his grip on his weapon's hilt tightening. She knew his anxiety extended beyond potential attacks. Elissa recognized the look on his face. She had seen it before. The drawn features and coldness in his eyes, which normally radiated warmth, now concealed an unsettling intensity.

"I wonder what's so captivating about me?" Wil grumbled faintly, catching her off guard. Her heart skipped a beat. Realizing feigning sleep was futile, she rose and awkwardly settled beside him. He did not meet her gaze, which exacerbated her unease.

"I can't sleep," she admitted in a low, uncertain tone.

"The opposite would have surprised me."

"Yet Finn seems to be managing."

"It's easier to sleep when ignorant of danger," the knight retorted with a scornful sneer.

"Without him, you'd be dead," she reminded him.

"Who would have imagined owing their life to a peasant who likely cannot wield a weapon?" he scoffed.

"Finn might surprise us… The mayor of Earnox believed him to be quite the hunter."

Wil remained silent, his skepticism evident. His eyes seemed to darken as they melded into the obscurity of night.

"Wil… may I ask a question?"

He sighed, sharply turning to face her, his gaze penetrating hers. Caught off guard, she faltered, her unasked concerns lodged in her throat.

"I understand what troubles you," he confessed. "Don't worry, it's just exhaustion."

"Really? I still sense you're withholding secrets from me."

"What makes you think that?"

"The coldness... I saw it before, when we left Fergus' cottage."

"Perhaps you're projecting your emotions onto me, Elissa."

"It's not just me... Gwendoline felt it too. She implied you're concealing something more dangerous than the sylvan corruption."

"I doubt living practically alone in the middle of the woods was healthy for an old lady," Wil defended.

Running his hand through his blond hair, he affirmed her suspicions—he was indeed shielding secrets from her.

"Wil... I must insist. This concerns my safety, Finn's, and even Walderlake's."

"We barely know each other," he responded, his tone quick and impulsive. "I owe you no explanation for my mood swings."

His retort struck her, and she recoiled within herself, consumed by a shame she rarely felt.

"Of course... I... apologize for overstepping."

With that, Elissa rose, ready to retreat to her resting spot. Before she could fully withdraw, Wil clasped her hand, halting her. Slowly, she turned back to him, noting a change in his demeanor. His gaze no longer held exasperation, but rather uncertainty and distress. Clearing his throat, he nervously traced the scar on his mouth, struggling to find the right words. She waited.

"Do you recall our discussion about the Knights of Aegis?" he ventured wearily. "When I mentioned I was part of their ranks."

He raised his turquoise gaze, and once again, she saw that warmth that set him apart from the rest. Elissa nodded, her anticipation mingling with trepidation for what he was about to reveal.

"I neglected to tell you that I was relieved of my position."

"For what reason?" she asked in a hushed voice.

"Insurrection."

Elissa observed him with clear confusion in her eyes. Wil had always appeared genuine to her, valiant...

"Why did you hide this from me?" she whispered.

He remained silent, his gaze imploring, though he did not answer her question. She grappled with whether to succumb to anger or to appreciate his current openness.

"When?" she added, her tone imperious.

"Just before I came to Brevic."

"Weren't you expected, as you told me?"

"Yes, but not so hastily. I had to outpace my father."

"So Owen..."

"...is doing well," he finished.

Elissa gazed at him in outrage. She had thought he was different from Brennet, from Bruna's account. Just... different. He had taken her for a fool.

"Why did you come to me?" she continued, her words laced with bitterness.

"Because I saw you as an avenue of escape, a way to evade the looming accusations of treason."

"Treason?"

"My ideas were deemed extremist by certain members of the Council. I questioned the orders of magistrates and even the king himself. Their course deviated from the values ingrained by the Knights of Aegis. They disregarded the needs of the people and the treaties they had signed.

There came a point where my conscience prevented me from following their directives, and that didn't sit well with them."

"I can't fault the Order for wanting to maintain their guard united," she acknowledged.

"It was no longer about unity, Elissa!" he growled with clenched teeth.

Fury emanated from him. Rising to his feet, he strode along the shadowy path with heavy steps.

"We barely know each other." True as that statement was, it did not mean she should be insensitive to his turmoil, nor that his well-being held no significance. Perhaps the connection between them was merely her imagination. She refused to allow this conversation to end like this, to accept the notion that everything about him was a facade. Glancing at her sleeping companions, Elissa pursued the fallen knight. His imposing figure materialized through the darkness. Hunched shoulders, bowed head, erratic gait—his fury had intertwined with shame.

"Wil!" she called out warily.

He slowed but did not look back at her.

"I'm willing to listen to you, without judgment or reproach."

"I've always hated scheming against neighboring kingdoms," he finally began, his tone now more pained than angry. "Yet, I could do it when required. My conscience suffered with each instance, but I could not claim that my perspective of the world was superior to that of the magistrates. I blindly obeyed their orders for a long time. However, attacking my own kin... the citizens of Walderlake... that was unacceptable. The plots, the lives sacrificed... they didn't warrant the imprisonment and slaughter of innocent people."

"All of that contradicts their code, though..." she ventured, visibly skeptical.

"You've never seen the rest of the kingdom, have you? Have you observed how our leaders strive to maintain their power, the abuses of authority coursing through Walderlake?"

"No… up until recently, I believed in their nobility, the impeccable ethics of our Council. Clearly, I was mistaken."

"Clearly," he retorted dryly, a cynical edge to his voice. Recognizing his error, he swiftly continued. "Forgive my harshness. I forgot about the influence Brennet had on you."

"I simply want to be treated as more than a fragile child and to finally understand what's truly happening," she exclaimed. "Is that too much to ask?"

Wil regarded her gravely, then nodded before resuming.

"An embargo on magic has been imposed in Walderlake for some time now. Certain adepts had their scepters confiscated, or worse. You likely know who has attracted the kingdom's wrath."

The druids…

"Some fear the emergence of individuals more powerful than themselves," he pressed on. "Though the Circles are predominantly peaceful, some have begun to rebel against the Council's actions."

"With good reason! I consider myself a pacifist, but sometimes rebellion becomes necessary against oppression."

At this, Wil's eyes darkened further, reflecting his pain.

"Wil?" Elissa whispered, her apprehension growing.

"With various extremist groups targeting the Circles, some have resorted to barbaric practices for protection… methods banned within the empire."

"Blood Magic…"

"We… we were never informed. Our mandate was to eliminate the corrupt individuals lurking in the forests … those who opposed the Council and the crown."

Each breath felt like shards of glass in Elissa's throat. She understood where Wil was heading with his story.

"You were a druid hunter," she said in an almost detached tone. "That's why you seemed so unwilling to traverse Pendard. That's where you were stationed, wasn't it?"

"I was aware of the perils awaiting us there... but they paled in comparison to this ever-present guilt. And the crows... I'm certain they knew, recognized me! I'm unsure if they were mocking me or merely waiting for their feast—the same one I had once offered them."

Wil halted, choked by emotion. He raised his fingers to his mouth, nervously stroking the thin silver scar on his upper lip. Cautiously, Elissa approached and rested a hesitant hand on his shoulder.

"A defenseless young lad, begging for mercy," he continued with a quivering voice. "A young druid, barely older than a boy. He was merely trying to protect himself. I... I couldn't obey any longer. My conscience wouldn't allow it. After refusing orders from my superiors and urging my comrades to follow me, I was stripped of my position. I knew arrest was imminent. It was only a matter of time."

"So that's why you arrived abruptly."

In spite of the freezing night, a cold sweat formed on Elissa's neck. Nausea churned in her stomach as she paced, disregarding the man's gaze fixed upon her. He dreaded her reaction, her forthcoming decision. However, she was caught in a whirlwind of uncertainty. Did this alteration in his demeanor erase the horrors he had committed, the truths he had concealed from her?

"The entire Council is complicit in this... this genocide?" she asked, her voice quivering. "And Brennet... I can't bring myself to believe he was passive in all of this."

"I think he was attempting to halt it through you, by entrusting you with the emerald."

"So, that's what you and my father discussed?"

"Among other things. I revealed my expulsion, my past. Brennet, like many others, condemned Toran Sius' behaviour. My actions seem to have convinced him that my place was beside you."

"And Hargon? Can't he intervene?"

"Hargon has remained hidden in his court for too long. I'm certain Toran Sius holds him in a tight grip."

"He's still Brennet's brother!" Elissa pressed with a mix of despair and disbelief.

"Brennet's relationship with Hargon was troubled," Wil explained. "A profound rivalry persisted between them for years."

The image Elissa had of the magistrates, the almost supernatural authority overseeing the kingdom, crumbled into illusion. Mechanically, she grasped her pendant, twirling it between her trembling fingers. Brennet should have done more... much more.

"I believe the former Guardian intended to prepare you for eventual involvement in the rebellion that many of us are desperately trying to ignite," Wil stated with a fervent intensity.

He paused, hesitating, and then clasped the woman's cold hands in his own. His grip was both strong and gentle, as though his fingers channeled all the strength within him.

"I sense that same spirit within you," he continued, his voice hoarse, resonating with a profound energy. "You embody renewal, the force that will restore justice to Walderlake."

He drew nearer, so close that Elissa could feel the warmth of his breath on her cold, flushed cheeks. Despite his eager comments, she could not help but wrestle with doubt. Memories of her last conversation with Bruna resurfaced—a warning, urging her to understand that this was how he manipulated, with honeyed words and feigned sincerity, much like his father. He had concealed the truth from her since their first encounter, and would have persisted if not for her insistence.

Still, a part of her wanted to believe him, stirred by this closeness she had longed for but now hesitated to embrace. She was uncertain of his intentions—whether that mentioned rebellion was the sole reason he presently held her hands so intimately.

"I can forgive your past transgressions," she began, attempting to assert control over her emotions. "However, restoring my trust will prove more difficult... if it's even possible."

The firmness she sought to convey seemed to waver the moment her words left her mouth. She sensed her tone might have hinted at her doubt, even her yearning. Wil did not hide the faint smile that curved his lips, acknowledging the fragility in her resolve. She loathed herself, despising her own lack of strength.

Before she could further articulate her thoughts, a chilling scream pierced the forest. Elissa's blood ran cold as emerald beams of light sliced through the trees. She recognized their source immediately.

"Miranda..."

CHAPTER

22

ASSAULT

Without pausing to contemplate the prudence of her action, the Guardian instinctively sprinted toward the camp's location. Wil led the charge, sword drawn and ready for combat. Amidst the night's hush, death had stealthily descended upon them. Elissa had not realized how far they had drifted. Perhaps it was mere frazzled nerves that made this chase seem eternal.

Upon reaching the camp, they were met with the sight of Finn desperately fending off two cloaked assailants with his bow.

"Get back!" he commanded, his voice trembling as his entire form quivered.

Miranda and Brea were nowhere to be seen, but agonized screams echoing through the forest indicated their proximity. Elissa yearned to dash toward them, yet more hooded mercenaries materialized from the shadows, compelling her to halt. Their opponents outnumbered them significantly—perhaps by a dozen. A wave of helplessness washed over her as she braced herself for the impending clash.

Wil wasted no time, launching himself at their assailants with ferocity. His blade cleaved through the air like an untamed beast, yet their adversaries eluded his strikes with unsettling ease. These mercenaries appeared more adept than those responsible for the Brevic massacre. Evidently, their pursuers no longer underestimated their capabilities. Wil redoubled his efforts, swiftly wresting control of the skirmish.

With a deft flick of her wrist, Elissa conjured a surge of magic that toppled the enemies menacing Finn with their sword tips. Then, she promptly dealt with the assailants who lunged at the knight, his focus still unwavering on his own duel. Finn, in turn, did not hesitate to let his arrows fly toward those struggling to rise.

Wil's expression momentarily soured at not being able to conclude the fight single-handedly, yet a smile tugged at his lips when he noticed the largest opponent still standing. Unlike the rest, this giant donned cumbersome leather armor and brandished a bastard sword that would have daunted even the most accomplished foes. But not Wil. He appeared poised, almost eager, to engage with a formidable adversary. With a flourish, his rival swung the blade, the weapon hissing menacingly through the air. Yet, the knight proved markedly faster than his towering opponent, who loomed over him by at least a head's length. Several parries later, the mercenary emitted a feral snarl before launching into another assault. However, the weight of his weapon compromised his movements. Fatigue set in, and Wil's smile broadened.

Fascinated by his companion's graceful agility, Finn was oblivious to the volley of crossbow bolts hurtling their way. Elissa, acting on instinct, interposed herself before him, palms extended. The arrows halted just inches from her, their iron tips almost within caressing distance. Suspended for a heartbeat, they then abruptly pivoted toward their shooters, who grasped too belatedly the gravity of their predicament. The bolts whizzed ominously through the frigid wind, ready to pierce their intended victims' flesh. Elissa shut her eyes, though the ensuing moans of agony reached her ears regardless.

A radiant flash of emerald light coursed through the forest once again, rekindling hope that Miranda might yet draw breath. The Guardian realized the urgency of the situation. Without wasting a second, she lunged at her lone visible opponent, conjuring a blast aimed with determination. The energy hurtled toward her foe with lightning speed, yet remarkably, the individual managed to intercept it with a flourish of their scepter. In that moment, Elissa caught a glimpse of the woman's face, a smirk dancing on her lush lips. A mage, clearly, and around her age, if not younger. For an instant, Elissa hesitated. However, seeing the mercenary prepared to retaliate, she knew she had no choice but to unleash her powers.

Soon, arcs of magical energy erupted in a symphony of vivid lights, painting the air with a constellation of sparks. The Guardian parried powerful assaults with one hand while launching her own counterattacks with the other. Her adversary wielded spells that rivaled her own, perhaps even those of Brennet. Was this young woman a member of the Council? No… she was too young for that. A flicker of childish grimace twisted the enemy's mouth as she aimed her next volley not at Elissa, but at Finn. The arcane blast struck him with brutal force, hurling him to the ground as the dark energy coursed through his body. The forest echoed with his agonized screams as he writhed in torment. The sight of her dying friend constricted Elissa's throat, her heart aching at his suffering.

Until now, she had wielded her powers with restraint. After the Pendard incident, she understood the perils of succumbing to unrestricted emotions, fearing for the safety of her companions. But moderation had no place here. Her hand found the pouch hanging from her belt, feeling the iridescent energy pulsating within. In an instant, it swirled inside of her, an almost unbearable heat passing through her veins. Without a second thought, she harnessed all her rage, all her torment, whispering her incantation. Flames erupted around her, yet she felt no pain. From her very being surged a torrent of molten lava, hurtling toward her adversary. The enemy hastily conjured a magic shield, visibly straining to maintain it. Elissa intensified her assault, her determination unwavering. The foe's arrogance dissolved into sheer panic. The woman's hood fell back, revealing her face in its entirety. Her strong features twisted in terror, quivering lips seeming to utter silent pleas. Yet, Elissa knew there could be no mercy. She saw the woman would not hesitate to annihilate her if given the chance. Her acolytes had sown horrors beyond measure, a reality too grim to risk sparing her.

And so, Elissa persisted.

Panic consumed her enemy, who lost control of her enchantment. The shield shattered, allowing the lava to surge forth, engulfing her. Elissa's spell dissipated, leaving no trace of the mercenary.

Wil continued his dance with his weary adversary, a macabre waltz akin to a cat toying with a mouse. However, time was a luxury they could not afford, and Elissa's mind was plagued with worry for Miranda and Brea. This fight could not be allowed to drag on. Acting swiftly, Elissa hurled a ball of fire toward the colossal foe. The projectile struck the bastard sword head-on, forcefully disarming the surprised man. In response, a quick exchange of glances between Wil and Elissa communicated a shared seriousness. The knight let out a resigned sigh and hurried to conclude the duel.

With an intense surge of fury, Wil lunged at the mercenary. He might have expected the confrontation to be more prolonged, yet his exhausted opponent seemed to accept his imminent defeat. Wil's attack was a fusion of grace and brutality, the blade piercing through the enemy's breastplate with an almost casual precision that made Elissa quiver. The henchman crumpled to the ground, his last breath escaping his lips in a single exhale. A few weak moans, the pallor of death painted across his face, and his gaze locked into an eternal, empty stare.

Satisfaction radiated from Wil as he cleaned his blade on his trousers. Unlike Elissa, his demeanor remained detached, as though dispensing murder was as mundane as any other routine action. His role within the Aegis guard demanded this.

Abruptly, a magical projectile erupted from the forest's depths, ramming into Wil and sending him crashing to the earth. Finn reacted instantly, an arrow whizzing into the woods. The resulting roar of agony reverberated, soon replaced by an eerie silence.

"Not bad for a mere hunter," Finn's voice was tinged with a triumphant note as he offered a defiant glance at the warrior.

The injured mage lay nearby, agonizing as life slowly drained from him. An arrow from Finn had found its mark, embedding itself next to his heart.

"Good work," Wil cheered, gently patting his companion's shoulder.

With measured steps, he approached the subdued assailant and swiftly unveiled the cloaked face. A cascade of golden curls framed the thin, angular features of a young man. He seemed almost angelic, the image of an aristocrat's son, too pristine to be involved in this grim tableau.

"Who sent you?" the fallen knight inquired, his upper lip curling in a mixture of disdain and seriousness, his voice a low, gravelly undertone.

The young man, appearing scarcely older than a teenager, sneered. Wil's hand hovered over the embedded arrow, and Elissa knew she would not like what was about to happen. In one swift, merciless motion, he twisted the iron spike within the attacker's chest, tearing a gut-wrenching scream from him. The ephebe, panting and weakened, spat in defiance, his silence unyielding.

Exasperated, Wil sighed, while Finn turned his gaze away, and with a practiced gesture, he drew a dagger from his belt. Elissa too wished to avert her eyes, but a morbid curiosity held her transfixed. Unrestrained, Wil drove the blade into the young man's shoulder. Pain radiated through the assailant, yet his weakness rendered him only capable of stifled groans.

Annoyed, the fallen warrior urged, "Speak."

"The leader of the Alliance," the mage finally confessed in a quivering voice, his words fraught with fear.

"The Alliance?" Elissa prodded. "Toran Sius?"

"It's her!" the young man stammered. "The one who will shatter our empire… the one from the prophecy."

"Answer her," Wil's demand was sharp, aggression lacing his tone. "Is it Toran Sius?"

Yet, the mercenary's gaze remained distant, and as tears traced solemn paths down his cheeks, his expression held. Wil nudged him with the toe of his boot, but the captive's visage stayed static, his breath forever stilled. Frustration welled up within Elissa. So close… She had been so close to getting answers.

"We must find Miranda and Brea," she asserted, her tone loaded with gravity.

"You can't be serious, Elissa!" Wil's incredulous exclamation reverberated. "We have no idea of their numbers. My obligation is to keep you safe, not lead you to danger."

"I can make my own decisions. You may claim to be my protector, but I will never serve as one of your subordinates."

"I pledged to your father that I would defend you, and I will uphold that vow."

"Given your recent revelations, your promises carries little weight."

Elissa's acerbic words left Wil momentarily speechless. She was beyond listening, beyond reasoning. Despite the knight's stern expression, her focus was solely on locating Brea and Miranda. She would not accept defeat in the face of allegedly inevitable destiny.

Before her companion could mount a further protest, Elissa surged forward in pursuit of the two peasant women. Finn followed without a word, abstaining from questions or interjections. Elissa remained oblivious to whether Wil was doing the same. She no longer cared. A muted moon peeked through dense grey clouds enveloping the night sky. The air bore a faint trace of magic, the scent of petrichor and heated metal. Amidst the obscured vision, Elissa's pace inevitably slackened. Without any sound or scream to guide her, she began to believe that the florist and her daughter had simply vanished.

"Careful!" Finn's warning came too late. Elissa collided with a large, motionless form and stumbled onto the cool, damp soil. A yelp of pain escaped her lips as she sought the reason for her fall. Horrifyingly, her touch revealed a lifeless body. Summoning a sphere of light with her free hand, she bathed the surroundings in radiance. The cascade of blond hair confirmed her dread.

"Miranda," she whispered in a broken voice. Her lifeless form, cloaked in blood and mud, sprawled across the grass like an abandoned prey, forgotten by a disinterested predator. Finn knelt beside the woman, his ear pressed against her chest, yearning for even the faintest flutter of a heartbeat. Nothing. With gentle care, he swept aside the hair obscuring her features, revealing the grievous gash on her throat.

"They likely ended her life once they realized she wasn't you," Wil's voice held a blend of seriousness and heartache. "This emphasizes the urgency of reaching Osthallvale without delay."

Fury welled within Elissa, an ink staining her emotions like a blank parchment. Gwendoline's warnings echoed—she could not alter fate. Despite her fervent efforts, she remained powerless. Pain gripped her as she surged to her feet, her gaze scanning for the missing girl, her sphere of light intensifying with her turbulent feelings.

"What are you trying to do?" Wil's voice was edged with frustration as he lowered the woman's arm. "Do you want to attract them all to this very spot?"

"Brea needs us," the Guardian's retort was unwavering.

"We must leave before reinforcements swarm in," The man's exasperation intensified the mage's desire for defiance, causing her to start ignoring his pleas.

"Wil's right... we can't stay here any longer!" insisted the hunter.

"Nobody's forcing you to stay with us, Finn," she shot back, her words cutting.

Wil groaned and halted her by gripping her shoulders. This did not please her in the slightest. A surge of energy erupted from her chest, violently pushing her protector away. Taken aback by the audacity she had just displayed, he stared at her with a perplexed expression.

"Do you want to abandon a child to such a fate?" Her voice was a thundering bark, her eyes brimming with tears—fury, exhaustion, and grief mingling.

"She probably met the same demise as her mother," Wil's retort was a vehement plea for reason.

"If you truly knew me, you'd understand I can't leave her."

"Why thrust yourself into such danger? Brea is not the little girl you once were! You can't change the past by saving her!"

"And if Brennet had thought the same? Why me and not her?"

"She's not you. Neither was Miranda."

"Miranda was like me... she was..."

She halted, her voice strangling on the words she could not articulate. Sobs overtook her, her gaze avoiding her companions. Wil cautiously attempted to bridge the gap.

"It's not about where they came from or their abilities. The stone isn't meant for them. Brennet chose you... YOU! Your survival is essential. Think about the looming crisis."

"Oh, the crisis! You mean the rebellion where you intend to play me like a pawn?"

"I never said... Elissa, I don't want to use you."

His stern expression crumbled into desolation. He drew nearer, but she instinctively withdrew.

"Understand, I'm well acquainted with this agonizing dilemma you face. But sometimes, the greater good demands certain sacrifices. You know I'm right, Elissa."

Wil extended a hand, an invitation to continue their journey. She contemplated it briefly, but frustration and guilt held her back from embracing what he offered.

"I can't," her voice was unyielding, her jaw clenched.

This is when the magician initiated her search for Brea, a young girl like her, shackled by her origins.

After just a few steps, a powerful blow struck the back of Elissa's head. Was it a fist? A weapon? Dazzled and disoriented, she plunged into the abyss of darkness. Falling seemed endless, a never-ending descent. The faint glimmers of light disappeared as the earth vanished beneath her feet. Then, all was swallowed by obscurity, and she lay motionless on the ground, unconscious.

Sheathing his sword, Wil turned to Finn, who wore an expression of disbelief. A stoic mask covered Wil's face as he grasped the Guardian firmly and lifted her onto his shoulders.

"Let's move," he directed the hunter.

CHAPTER

23

MEMORIES

For the past few days, Elyndel had been absorbed in the arduous task of pacifying the various delegations unsettled by Toran Sius' tantrum. Walderlake branded it as foul play, an orchestrated scheme to erode their reputation within the empire's gaze. The Mortenburn faction criticized the leniency bestowed upon Sius, while the Gamar Isles mocked the juvenile animosities dividing the East and West. The Master of Cendril, on his part, deplored the absence of solidarity among the nations of Balt'boec in the face of the looming catastrophe. He grudgingly acknowledged that Prince Farklyn's boldness had caught his attention. For ages, he had harbored the fantasy of provoking a loss of composure in the chief magistrate of Walderlake, of exposing him as the tyrant he truly was. Yet, his position and wisdom had restrained such impulses. He sighed deeply, rubbing his bloodshot eyes. The ceaseless cycle of crisis management left little room for reprieve.

A knock echoed on his quarters' door, eliciting a frustrated groan from him, wondering what catastrophe he would have to deal with now.

"Yes?" Elyndel grumbled involuntarily.

Analera entered with a determined stride, pausing as her amethyst gaze settled upon the Master's fatigued face.

"I've never seen you in such a wretched state," she remarked.

Elyndel scoffed, familiar with the White Lady's forthright manner.

"Good morning, Ana."

"Morning? The midday sun hangs high in the sky!"

Without waiting for an invitation, she seated herself in the armchair opposite his cluttered desk.

"I don't wish to sound rude, but I don't particularly have time for discussion."

"How surprising!" she retorted with a mischievous grin. "I merely intended to offer support, whether or not we indulge in conversation. I know a way that, intriguingly, requires no words…"

Elyndel observed her, his ocean-blue eyes growing deeper as his slender eyebrows knitted into a solemn expression.

"We agreed to maintain a professional and amicable relationship," he responded in his deep voice.

Analera rolled her eyes and emitted a sigh of exasperation.

"You know as well as I do that we never manage to keep this agreement. Besides, a little distraction seems necessary, in your case."

"And you know why we've reached this accord," the Master reiterated, his tone both gentle and earnest. "I don't want to hurt your feelings."

The White Lady compressed her lips, causing two subtle furrows to form between her ivory brows.

"My feelings are remarkably intact," she feigned, conjuring a smile.

"I am serious, Ana… Ever since Tanyll departed for Cendril, it feels as though I'm the sole caretaker of this dragon mess. If I'm to rally the diverse powers of the empire, I can't afford to waste my time."

" I don't know how you're going to do it. All these requests, these fragile egos..."

"Syviis persists in her search for Aelrie as though her life hangs in the balance. And I've dispatched Nilyan and Gareath to speak with the Mortenburn leaders. The words of proud warriors will carry more weight than those of an old diplomat."

"Truly?" she pondered, her reluctance quite noticeable. "We're yet to unmask the traitor, and you delegate such crucial tasks?"

"I have unshakable trust in them."

"There lies the problem! The intricate mess we're ensnared in would be vastly different if some of us weren't so plagued by gullibility."

"Do not believe for a moment that I do not carry my share of guilt, quite the opposite," he confided in a weighty tone. "I fully acknowledge this weakness. However, I won't isolate myself entirely from my carefully chosen allies. Prudence shouldn't be confused with antagonism."

"I agree with you. My temperament often contradicts itself... sometimes involuntarily," she conceded, her features softening. "But across the ages, I've witnessed enough disloyalty to fuel a kingdom."

"Of course," he continued, a hint of unease threading his words. "I understand that given what you've endured... what you've..."

Analera raised her hand imperiously, a signal begging him not to complete his sentence. She persistently refused to let anyone utter the name of the one executed for the gravest betrayal in Cendril's history— the one to whom she had given her heart before Elyndel.

" ...that after your experiences... you simply desire self-preservation. I understand, Ana. It's this resilience in you, this profound commitment to justice that I find so endearing."

She nodded, bowing her head, yet refrained from responding.

Then, without ceremony or explanation, she stood up. With measured but resolute steps, she approached Elyndel, who observed her from his seat with a puzzled expression. Looking at him, her gaze ablaze with resolve, she unfastened the golden brooches that held her olive silk dress at the shoulders. The satin fabric cascaded down gracefully, like the gentle caress of wind on bare skin. Her alabaster body blended seamlessly with the radiant light that bathed the Master's chambers.

"Analera, I don't think…" Elyndel's protest was silenced by her fingertips gently pressing against his mouth.

"You're the only one I still have faith in," she whispered, her voice filled with vulnerability.

Her lips met his, and Elyndel knew, as he kissed her back, that he was treading a treacherous path. Yet, his resolve to maintain immaculate behavior wavered. Like so many times before, he deceived himself, believing this moment would yield no pain. Urgently, he drew the White Lady closer, guiding her into his embrace on the sapphire velvet chair. The fragrance of lavender enveloped him as he buried his face in her neck, relinquishing all notions of decency. She was right: he needed a distraction.

———— ·•●·· ————

Analera was still peacefully sleeping in the massive four-poster bed when Elyndel got dressed. The confines of these unfamiliar walls weighed heavily on him. Guilt ravaged his conscience once more as his connection with Analera remained shrouded in ambiguity. He dreaded the inevitable forthcoming conversation. Therefore, the elf silently slipped away, like a thief in the night. Fresh air had always soothed him.

Wynnorth presented an absolute contrast to the lush landscapes of Cendril. The red and cobalt blue tiles of the rooftops formed a picturesque mosaic as seen from the apex of the hill where Elyndel was quartered. From this vantage point, the sea stretched out on one side, while Ryre's Keep loomed over the city on the other. The incongruity between grandiose villas and cramped stone houses was stark. Unlike Cendril, where the distinction between nobility and commoners was subtle, here, the divide was glaring. Impoverished elderly men slouched on blistering flagstones, famished mothers with infants at their breasts pleaded for sustenance from passersby—the haunting tableau pained Elyndel. If Syviis could witness the state of this enemy kingdom! Fortunately, her focus remained devoted to her search mission, and since the assault on Ryre's Keep, Elyndel rarely caught a glimpse of her.

He strolled aimlessly, his steps guided by an enigmatic impulse. After a while, the familiar blend of sandalwood and saline ocean drifts reached his senses. The Eluin market was nearby. Elyndel attempted to be discreet; Wynnorth's populace was not renowned for their respect toward Elves. However, the unexpected revelation was the name on everyone's lips—Valera. It was not a chorus of adoration, but one of disapproval. Despite the oppressive heat, Elyndel pulled his hood over his head and deftly navigated through the crowd to gather information. It was a risk he typically would not consider. Nonetheless his curiosity got the better of him.

"Valera will be the ruin of us!" a youthful fishmonger proclaimed to his patrons. "They've imprisoned my brother. He just wanted to be paid what was due for his services at court!"

"You'll never see him again!" countered the spice merchant at the adjacent stall. "No one returns from Ryre's Keep, especially since the disappearance of King Fabyan."

"Watch your tongue!" growled another. "Reckless babble like that will land us in the dungeons."

"Let them try!" retorted the first, undeterred. "The people can no longer suffer the schemes of the queen, who promised a realm free from the scourge of dragons."

"Well said!" chorused several citizens, evidently at their wits' end. As Elyndel continued to navigate through the crowd, a prevailing consensus became apparent. Valera's authoritarian rule appeared to be teetering on the brink. His hopes were confirmed, yet he felt no satisfaction from it. Leaving the market behind, the Master surrendered himself once more to his subconscious.

Normally, the stifling heat of the city and the steep incline of its streets would have intensified his fatigue. However, an uncanny ease enveloped him here, as if each step drew him closer to what he had yearned for, an absence endured for way too long. Harmonious voices surged, singing an ode that mimicked the serene yet commanding waves. He followed these choral melodies, like a sailor surrendering to the guiding call of a siren. To his astonishment, he found himself near the Narbane sea, far from his villa. A temple dedicated to Iva, the goddess of oceans, stood before him. Hesitantly, he considered turning around. He weighed the risk of venturing deeper unaccompanied, particularly in hostile territory. Nevertheless, a peculiar curiosity overpowered his caution, compelling him to enter. Remarkably, few were participating in this ceremony. Had the Eastern City's populace lost its faith? The scent of olive oil, utilized for consecrating the marble and bronze statues, hung in the air. An altar, garlanded with grapevine leaves and flickering lanterns, marked the temple's end. This place, he had visited it before. Apart from the priestesses intoning their prayers and a handful of guards donning the regalia of the royal militia, only two others remained there... two women. The first, statuesque yet overly slender, occasionally cast furtive glances at her companion on the left. Her fair hair was pulled tight into a precise bun, and her aquiline nose that defined her aristocratic profile bore a familiarity that did not elude the Master. The second figure, her back turned, revealed an ebony cascade of hair and graceful bared shoulders. That aura... Elyndel recognized her instantly.

"Valera?" he breathed.

He remained concealed at the rear of the room, tucked near the towering Ionic columns. Amidst the entire kingdom, she had to be in this very temple. The notion of slipping away briefly crossed his mind, but the woman seated next to the queen glanced over her shoulder. Her eyes locked with Elyndel's, causing him to flinch like a child caught misbehaving. Retreating now was not an option—pride would not permit it. Just as he anticipated, she swiftly murmured something to Valera, who quickly turned to look at him. Elyndel extended a tentative smile toward her. Awkwardly, of course, but he smiled nonetheless. Unlike him, she seemed almost delighted to see him. With a subtle wave of her fingers, she invited him to join her, and he complied hastily.

"Master Elyndel!" she exclaimed, her voice filled with warmth. "What a pleasant surprise to find you here!"

Elyndel sometimes forgot the charm inherent in the diverse Eastern accents. Their words exuded romance, a melodious and sensuous timbre.

"The surprise is mutual," he responded, offering a bow. "Considering recent events, I'm intrigued to see you in such a public place."

"Raina has been at my side since the assault on Ryre's Keep," the woman murmured with a certain embarrassment, casting a sideways glance at her adviser.

"Given your reluctance to adhere to my security protocols, I see no viable alternatives," Raina retorted, her tone chilly.

The queen grazed her fingertips against her subordinate's knee, giggling. Raina stifled a laugh that told the Master that they were used to this kind of exchange.

"To be candid, I come here often," Valera disclosed. "The temple of Iva has long provided me solace."

"I never imagined you to be so pious," Elyndel quipped with a half-smile.

"Honestly, I couldn't care less about Iva," the sovereign responded, her detachment palpable.

Her voice carried beyond her intentions, and the priestesses halted their singing, rebuking her with stern gazes.

"I… that's not what I meant… you understand what I meant, don't you?" she fumbled, her embarrassment evident.

Yet, Iva's acolytes never wavered in their scrutiny. Elyndel suppressed a chuckle at the queen's unease, a rare instance of her control slipping.

"Ah! Why even bother!" she exclaimed, standing up. "Why not continue this conversation elsewhere, in a less restraining setting?"

Extending her arm toward the elf, she welcomed his company, and he complied willingly.

"You can leave us," the queen addressed her adviser, who lingered.

"Your Majesty… you should not wander through the city unescorted. Consider your safety," Raina implored, leveling a suspicious gaze at the Master.

"Don't worry! I could incapacitate Elyndel before he manages to utter Itos's name," Valera scoffed, her eyes rolling.

"You're quite confident in your skills," the elf responded, a trace of laughter in his voice. "Interested in testing my assertion?" she teased.

"Perhaps another time," he answered, his grin infused with amusement.

Raina paused midstep, her expression one of confusion. She watched as her mistress departed in the company of a man who, merely days prior, was considered an adversary.

——— ··●·· ———

Elyndel allowed the queen to lead him, a sense of déjà vu reverberating within him. The warmth of her fingers on his forearm, the gentle whispers of the waves synchronizing with her voice as she prattled about the agreeable weather—it all stirred a disconcerting familiarity in him. His thoughts raced, attempting to breach the barrier that kept him estranged from this part of himself that he had lost.

"Am I boring you?" Valera quipped mockingly.

Elyndel had not even realized they had stopped on the beach.

"My apologies! My mind was wandering," the man confessed with a small smile.

"Outsiders often find the weather tedious."

He nodded, not offering further explanation. He knew well enough that his current state had little to do with the heatwave, Valera let out a sigh as she released his arm and turned her gaze toward the Narbane Sea. The waves mirrored in the sovereign's deep blue eyes, and for the first time since his arrival, Elyndel sensed a genuine comfort emanating from her.

"The water will revive your spirit," she proclaimed, raising the hem of her dress spontaneously.

Under Elyndel's perplexed stare, she slipped off her shoes, intricately embroidered with gold filaments, and cast them aside without restraint. She darted along the pebbled shore with a lively step, as if her status and decorum had evaporated. Elyndel scanned the surroundings, wary of any potential onlookers. What if Eastern informants or even those from Cendril were spying? The place seemed desolate, and Valera signaled him to join her with a casual gesture. He hesitated, unaccustomed to such unguarded behavior. Yet, the lingering scent of lavender on his skin reminded him that this was not the first time he had acted out of character today. With a sigh, he begrudgingly removed his black leather boots. His demeanor exuded discomfort. This man inherently grounded and self-assured now struggled with every movement, as they seemed utterly foreign to him.

"Be careful! The pebbles can be slippery," Valera cautioned, her own steps a tad unsteady.

"I am an elf. We can tread as lightly as a feather, with no sense of weight or difficulty."

"Anywhere you step?" she asked incredulously.

"Anywhere we step."

"Convenient for escaping after your romantic conquests!"

Elyndel smirked, his cheeks flushing at the thought of the person who might still be asleep in his bed.

"Indeed, quite convenient."

Valera chuckled as well, tilting her head back to relish the sunlight against her porcelain skin. The woman before Elyndel appeared strikingly different from the tyrannical, self-absorbed ruler her kin condemned. She emanated a simple yet passionate exuberance.

"I can't recall the last time I allowed myself to be so carefree," the elf confessed, dipping his toes into the water.

"Some leisure might do your kind some good," Valera mused humorously.

"Do you find us dull?"

"I wouldn't say that... more... aloof? Snobbish?"

"Is that right?" Elyndel chuckled. "I admit our ways might be perplexing. I understand the effect my people often have on the rest of the empire."

"Perhaps you could learn a thing or two from us," the queen teased, her words dancing playfully.

"We might lack a sense of festivities, but our streets aren't crawling with beggars."

He instantly regretted those words. Valera froze, her smile vanishing along with her cheerfulness. Her gaze bore into him, more serious than affronted, making Elyndel feel smaller than ever.

"Our cultures are different," she began with measured composure. "The East's citizens don't possess the privilege of near-immortal existence. Yours have an eternity to amass wealth and perfect knowledge. Meanwhile, the lives of some of my subjects are destined to be consumed by repairing the immense damage caused by dragons... damage that was limited in Cendril, I might add. Those wandering the streets, scavenging for their next meal, are a result of the empire's indifference. Ever wonder why the relations between our nations soured after the Great War?"

"Cendril fought as fiercely as anyone during that grim period."

"I don't dispute that, but where were you when the world struggled to rebuild? We deserved more than your detachment."

"We faced our own challenges," the Master replied simply. "Also, our assistance appeared unnecessary amidst the frequent celebrations and balls you seemed to indulge in."

"Aha! Just as I thought! Swift judgments that characterize your kind... a kind that deems itself superior in every way!" Valera retorted, this time with more bite. "A pity. I believed you to be different from your compatriots."

"Tell me I'm mistaken."

"You view our celebrations as mere entertainment. I see them as a method to lift a broken society, or at least what remains of it. Sacrifices among the lower ranks were necessary; I had to leave behind this lost generation in order to ensure the East's continuity."

This concept struck Elyndel as odd, even barbaric. Forfeiting a social class to rebuild a realm was unthinkable to him. Yet, she had a point— the elves harbored judgment...

It was not about cruelty... no... Valera's decisions had not been easily made. He no longer wished to challenge her when she accused him of elitism.

"I spoke out of place," he conceded humbly. "I apologize, Valera."

He stared at her with a penetrating gaze. To his utmost surprise, the queen remained silent.

A peculiar distress shaded her expression, reminiscent of the one that clouded her face during their reunion in Ryre's Keep's throne room. She glowered at him, her eyes unwavering and laden with concern.

"Is everything alright, Your Highness?" Elyndel inquired, visibly worried.

"Yes... just a sensation of déjà vu, nothing more," she replied, promptly recovering her smile.

"Déjà vu?"

"That feeling you get when a moment seems too familiar to have not experienced it before. I appear to have lost several such moments over the years, so this isn't new to me."

So, he was not alone.

"This sensation... it has grown stronger since my arrival, hasn't it?"

She stared at him, her eyes widening in shock. He had hit the mark.

"I've been sensing a similar disturbance since I set foot in Wynnorth," he explained, "vivid images and a profound impression... so profound."

He thought of the outrage Syviis and Analera would feel if they knew how open he was to her. However, he was done hiding his turmoil.

"Who hasn't experienced déjà vu, Elyndel?" the queen retorted, feigning a casual laugh.

"Not like this, I assure you. It feels more than a simple sensation," he continued, advancing toward her with a fervor that made her freeze on the spot.

Valera's nod was slow, her expression growing somber. She contemplated him for a second, her lips parting as if teetering on a response. Nonetheless, she turned on her heel and hastened back toward the shore. She seemed to understand him, holding pieces of the puzzle that made him estranged from his own memories. He refused to let her leave like this, to endure another moment of relentless agony.

"Valera!" the elf called after her, quickening his pace to catch up.

"You have no idea of the torments that plague me!" she replied, her voice trembling.

"I understand more than those around you... those who let you believe in your own madness, those who choose to remain blind to your pain rather than stand by you. I might not grasp every obstacle you've battled throughout your reign. Nevertheless, I'm certain some connection exists between us. I'm unsure how… but your presence has stirred something dormant within me."

Valera finally halted, as if the weight of her denial had become too heavy to bear. She exhaled, and a painful smile tugged at her lips.

"Do you know why I frequent the temple of Iva?" she questioned.

"I don't."

"Nor do I. I can't understand why it draws me so much, why it's the only refuge where this ache inside me subsides. I am sure it's not faith that fills this void. Yet, your presence… a voice echoes in my mind, whispering your name."

Her smile held a profound melancholy. The queen's facade crumbled, and her candor shook Elyndel.

"You're right," she pressed on. "Maybe we should follow our instincts."

He restrained himself from reaching for her hand, though every fiber of his being urged him to do so. It felt as if touching her would bring him closer to uncovering his goal. Yet, he could not overlook who she was. Tears welled in her doe-like eyes, and she chewed on her lower lip, struggling to contain her emotions.

"Forgive my fervor," he breathed. "I hadn't meant to distress you."

"Don't worry about me. I suspect it's the stress of these past days. The people are less and less forgiving of my cause."

"I understand the weight of public opinion resting heavily on your shoulders. Having encountered numerous rulers throughout my life, I know how this pressure can bear down during one's reign. Maybe you should view it as a rite of passage."

"If only my son were here by my side," she lamented. "My dear Fabyan… His presence would alleviate the burden of their disdain."

"Fortunately, Farklyn seems to embrace his role as steward."

The woman remained silent, merely shrugging.

"Prince Farklyn appears determined to prove his usefulness," he persisted.

"Farklyn is indeed courageous, astute, and charismatic. I believe he's yet to recognize his own potential."

"Why not involve him more in the kingdom's affairs? He seems to possess a knack for deciphering people... as was evident with his performance at the assembly."

"'Performance' is an apt term! His audacious and unpredictable nature might spell trouble for us," the queen retorted.

"I used to be like him," Elyndel admitted with a nostalgic smile. "Careless, forthright... With some guidance, these attributes can be employed well."

"I don't doubt it. Yet, Farklyn's viewpoints often diverge from mine and those of the king. I can only sense his constant disagreement. Besides, I would prefer to avert sibling rivalry. How many rulers have witnessed their throne seized by relatives?"

"Nonetheless, opposing perspectives are crucial for informed decisions. They facilitate growth and self-improvement, offering a broader understanding of reality."

Valera eyed the elf, a blend of irritation and contemplation in her gaze. He anticipated a retort, but none came. Instead, she nodded, calculating her next remark.

"Brilea is under Cendril's authority, correct?"

"In a manner of speaking," the Master confirmed, predicting her train of thought.

"A single word from you could secure my son's release."

"I'm afraid it's not that simple."

"Of course... I understand that the tumultuous years between our nations prevent you from coming to my aid. The queen before you would never presume to ask such a favor of you."

They shared a lingering gaze, a suspended moment. Unexpectedly, Valera drew nearer, closing the gap between them. Elyndel recognized that unhurried, graceful step from when she had led him to the dance floor. Her hand found its place on his right arm, and she looked up at him, pleading, distressed. It was as if his heart sank, the same effervescent sensation he had experienced on several occasions now returning with full force.

"The mother in me implores you to rescue my son," she murmured, her voice breaking.

The queen was recognized for her skill in manipulation, a truth Elyndel was well aware of. Such knowledge was common throughout the empire. Yet, the vulnerability in her eyes seemed so genuine... Could it be that this time, she was speaking from a place of humility and sincerity?

"I can attempt to appeal for clemency, but I'm uncertain if anyone will listen. I can't promise anything."

"Really? Perhaps a reward could render you more persuasive?" Her tone shifted, taking on a suggestive note—a tone that stirred that paralyzing feeling within him.

Images swirled again in his mind, fragmented memories from his obscured past. The bare back of a woman sprawled on sheets of ruby silk... a bloodstained dagger clutched in her hands... the dark gaze of a young man... hazy yet strangely familiar... Long hair, robust stature. His head churned, his body shivering as these vivid fragments shook him to his core. Valera's soft touch on his arm snapped him back to reality.

Her eyelids fluttered with a coquettish charm, her deep wine-red lips curving into a seductive smile. Every aspect of her exuded charisma, lust.

"If you were to assist me, Elyndel, I could make you very... satisfied."

Any other man might have been swayed by such appeals. She possessed a certain gift... But before the queen's fingers could grace his cheek, Elyndel halted her by gently grabbing her wrist. His gaze, however, was not one of desire, but rather of disappointment.

"You clearly don't know me," he retorted with a low growl, releasing his grip.

Valera's smile vanished instantly. The elf did not linger for her response, instead turning away with determined steps. He strode past the queen, who stood still at the water's edge. He was resigning himself to the absence of answers, so near to unlocking his elusive memories. It did not matter. His integrity was more valuable than any revelations, even if they held his deepest desires.

"Elyndel!" Valera called out, her voice carrying across the expanse.

He halted, reluctantly turning back to face her.

"I'm sorry," she exhaled without pretense.

"It's not a lack of will on my part, believe me. As I told you, I will see what my influence can grant you."

A slow nod from Valera carried a weight of gratitude. Acknowledging her with a nod of his own, he retrieved his boots that lay upon the pebbles. He left the shore without even bothering to put them on.

CHAPTER

24

CORRUPTION

In the aftermath of his intense conversation with the queen, Elyndel stumbled upon a note resting on his pillow. He recognized the elegant handwriting immediately: Analera's. As he had feared, she had departed hastily for Cendril, convinced that he would proceed better without her presence. Why had he not listened to his own judgment? He sighed, chastising his lack of self-control, and tasted the bitterness of yet another unanswered question. After his conduct with the White Lady, perhaps he truly deserved this outcome. Just as he was sinking into self-pity, a distinctive knock echoed on his door. Those three precise knocks served as a reminder that his responsibilities left no room for weakness. His relief was unmistakable when Nilyan entered, his perpetually amiable demeanor in tow.

"What a face you make, my poor Elyndel," the warrior quipped, dropping a stack of parchments onto the desk.

"You're not the first to mention it," Elyndel muttered. "What do you bring me?"

"The treaties sealed by the leaders of the Gamar Islands and Mortenburn. They've agreed to form an alliance to confront the menace of the dragons."

"What a feat, Nilyan!" The Master sighed with a blend of relief and gratitude. "I hardly deserve such loyal friends."

With a heavy heart, he lowered his head, his thoughts clouded. Nilyan only had to glance at the unmade bed to see what was bothering him. After centuries of camaraderie, the seasoned fighter could read Elyndel like an open book.

"Again?" Nilyan questioned wearily.

"I'm not exactly proud of it, believe me."

"You're being too harsh on yourself, my friend."

"Easy to say for someone who's shared centuries with the same partner!"

"Marriage has its own set of trials, and remember, I had my fair share of romances before Wynn." Nilyan's grin carried a knowing edge. "Besides, I understand the challenge of distancing yourself from her."

Nilyan's smirk broadened as he continued, "Analera frightens me more than those winged monstrosities."

"Because of me, she's gone."

"To Cendril? I wonder how she managed that! Valera has reserved the griffins for the Mortenburn delegation."

"As you so aptly put it, saying no to Analera is not an easy task."

"True enough!" Nilyan laughed, his camaraderie soothing. "To lighten your mood, I've heard that Toran Sius is far from happy with this… situation. Word has it that he nearly demolished half his villa in a fit of rage. Waiting does not sit well with him, it appears."

"Poor man!" Elyndel quipped with a dismissive, sarcasm-tinged tone. "I suppose Valera is making him wait as a form of punishment."

"Given his theatrics during the last assembly, he's been strongly advised to stay within his estate. A contingent of the royal militia surrounds his residence day and night until arrangements for his departure, along with his entourage, are finalized."

Aware of his own immaturity, Elyndel could not help but secretly relish the thought of the old Master's tantrum. His rapport with Walderlake had grown increasingly strained with each encounter. The fading bond with allies he had fought alongside was a source of sorrow. Recollections of Hargon's earlier, simpler times, when everything was straightforward and sincere, only intensified his disappointment. He attributed this dramatic shift to Toran Sius's ascent to power.

"I mourn the loss of Brennet. He made nurturing this relationship seem effortless. Now, I must turn to Toran Sius and try to speak to him before his departure. Perhaps I can miraculously secure his signature. I hope a common adversary might mend the political divide... or, at the very least, spark some effort on his part."

"Reopening the dialogue seems vital to me," Nilyan chimed in with a playful wink.

Elyndel emitted a frustrated growl. He knew he could not allow Toran Sius to leave Wynnorth without a meeting, even if it meant enduring excruciating conversations.

"All these obstacles... I almost lose sight of our initial purpose in coming to Wynnorth."

"Don't fret," the fighter countered, "Syviis is pursuing the search with a dedication worthy of her spirit. But if you really want my opinion, Aelrie is no longer here."

"I tried to dispatch Syviis back to Cendril to accompany the king, but she refuses to listen to me."

"And would you follow such counsel if she were the one missing?" Nilyan inquired with a knowing smile, already aware of the answer.

Elyndel nodded, sighing in resignation. His companion approached, his large warrior's hand finding its place on Elyndel's shoulder.

"I'll leave you to your task. I must rescue Gareath from the clutches of Lorena Bizerac. She seems to have developed quite a special interest in my unfortunate brother... or maybe she's plotting to turn him into her newest bodyguard. Either way, he's undoubtedly cursing my absence."

"Nilyan... I understand I'm asking a lot of you, but..."

"Never," his colleague interjected with a blend of sincerity and fondness. "Assisting you will never burden me."

"Perhaps your perspective will shift after this."

"Challenge accepted!"

"Alright," Elyndel mumbled with apprehension. "The Brileans... Is your rapport with their queen still pleasant?"

"Azura and I maintain a loyal friendship."

"We should approach them and seek their endorsement for our alliance treaty."

"Naturally."

"This would also be an opportune moment to negotiate King Fabyan's release."

"The release of Fabyan?" Nilyan echoed incredulously. "Why would we want this tyrant back in a position of power?"

"Because global harmony can't be achieved if the Brileans keep their neighboring ruler captive. Moreover, Valera will perceive it as a gesture of goodwill and will likely be more cooperative."

"What assurance do we have that the queen won't exploit Fabyan's liberation to betray us and obliterate Brilea?"

"My gut feeling," the Master replied simply.

Nilyan stared at Elyndel, his chocolate eyes revealing an unusual blend of astonishment and concern.

"I warned you that this request wouldn't sit well," the chief magistrate continued in a hushed tone.

Nilyan ran a hand through his dark mane with a sigh.

"Very well," he answered with a touch of sarcasm. "I trust you, Elyndel. So far, your guidance has been sound, and I've no reason to doubt your decisions."

"Thank you, Nilyan. I understand the sacrifice this involves for you and your integrity."

A thoughtful "hmm" escaped Nilyan's lips, resembling more of a growl.

"Best of luck with Toran Sius," he muttered, his deep voice echoing as he departed the room.

In haste, Elyndel made his way to the villa assigned to the Walderlake delegation. Fortunately, Toran Sius had not left yet. Based on the guards' exasperated expressions, his rage had not subsided either. Such childishness! A chuckle escaped the Master as he approached the militia. Their surprise at seeing him without an escort was obvious.

"Does Master Sius receive visitors?" Elyndel inquired politely of the sentries stationed at the entrance.

"I can't say, you're the first to make such a request," replied the man, a stout fellow sporting an impressive mustache.

"Let's see if luck is on my side," the elf responded with a genial smile.

"U-uh, alright… follow me, Master Arren."

The sentinel guided him begrudgingly, stroking his mustache.

No surprise awaited Elyndel as he entered the villa. The scene before him was one of shattered objects, torn paintings, and overturned furniture. Given Toran's explosive reaction during an assembly, this extension of his violent temper behind closed doors was not surprising. Alone in the parlor sat the chief magistrate of Walderlake. A collection of books was spread out before him, but he was not reading. His forehead rested against his palm, his back more hunched than ever, as if the weight of loneliness bore down on him.

"If you've come to remind me once more that those accursed griffins are late, I swear I'll set this villa ablaze," Toran grumbled without looking up.

"I hope you'll allow me a chance to exit before that happens," Elyndel retorted with cheeky levity.

The Master of Walderlake snapped his head up, his expression a mix of bewilderment and disdain.

"Why are you here?" he inquired dryly.

Elyndel observed the judgmental gaze, a look that reflected all the contempt the old mage harbored toward him. It was a familiar derision.

"I wished to speak with you. How have you been since the recent events? Your dramatic display didn't go unnoticed by the audience."

"So, you're here to mock me?" Toran Sius barked, his scowl deepening.

"I'm here to understand your intentions."

"My intentions?"

"Indeed. This entire affair with the Guardian's daughter seems to have profoundly affected you. Her unexpected appointment, her extraordinary abilities…"

"Sure," the human admitted with a weary slump, his annoyance evident.

"The fact that the emerald is now in her possession must be quite unacceptable to you."

"Hmm," Toran grunted.

"We both know that Brennet was an obstacle for you. Your efforts to remove him must seem futile."

"What are you implying? That I orchestrated Brennet's murder myself?"

the old mage fumed, straightening up.

"Precisely," Cendril's Master admitted, his words direct.

A flush crept across Toran Sius' face, similar to the color that had tinted his features during his last outburst. Elyndel felt no intimidation. He was more than capable of defending himself if need be. For a fleeting moment, he even wished his interlocutor would attack. It would have provided the perfect opportunity to finally put an end to the old magistrate's popularity. Yet, Toran's fury gradually gave way to a profound desolation. A genuine sorrow, something Elyndel never thought he would witness in this man.

"I considered the notion of eliminating Brennet. I won't deny it. In my wildest fantasies, he'd recognize that I alone held the key to granting the kingdom the freedom it deserved."

"Your version of freedom vastly differs from mine!" the elf countered, raising an eyebrow.

"Brennet yearned for a dictator to return to Balt'boec's throne. That seemed to be his dearest wish and the source of our conflicts since our first encounter."

"You can't deny that Galvrick's era was a boon for our empire. It's also due to individuals like you that Galvrick's legacy remains essential."

Elyndel's tone bore a hint of hostility, an icy venom. Such insolence was a rarity in his life.

"And was this prosperity worth the tyranny and fear that oppressed the citizens?" Toran challenged, his voice escalating.

"Where were you during this so-called distressing period? Ah, yes! I remember... nowhere! Galvrick was long gone before you ever saw the light of day," the elf countered, his haughty expression unmasked.

"I may not have witnessed that era firsthand, but my knowledge is sound," Toran replied.

"Why not let those who lived through it, those who shaped history, decide?"

"Whether present or not, Galvrick allowed dragons to menace our lands and nurtured the rise of powerful individuals like himself. Are you willing to overlook this?"

"So, you think it would be wiser to lock up and torture poor innocents for fear that they'll dominate the empire?" Elyndel prodded.

"Those we must restrain pose a danger to our entire kingdom. Just consider the risks presented by people wielding unstable and excessive powers."

"The druids, you mean?"

"Among others."

"Is that why you pursued Brennet?" Elyndel pressed. "Because he was shielding one of them?"

Toran Sius' eyes darkened, and for a moment, Elyndel swore he saw grief within them.

"Despite my resentment toward Brennet's choices, toward this woman... I'm not responsible for that massacre. I would express my indignation at these accusations, but I understand that my actions invite suspicion. Trust me, it's not me you should be wary of."

Elyndel realized he was treading on delicate ground, that this line of argumentation would lead him nowhere. He had momentarily lost sight of the primary reason for his encounter with the elderly Master: to secure his support.

"Admit it, you don't truly believe Elissa Reinhart was responsible for Brennet's death," Elyndel eventually responded, his tone now more empathetic.

"I believe several individuals had valid motives for targeting him. I also think that if this woman were to hold any position of power, the repercussions could be catastrophic."

"What exactly alarms you about her?"

"Everything," Toran Sius confessed, his voice strained. "You're aware of the prophecy, and yet you seem so determined to shield a complete stranger."

"I'm not attempting to shield her. I merely think that we're all too quick to attach significance to a vision that might have multiple interpretations. This woman could potentially hold the key to our salvation."

"I see! Keep your friends close and your enemies even closer," the human sneered with a smirk. "And if this vision does indeed take the ominous turn we fear? What if she does prove to be a threat?"

Elyndel remained silent. Toran's words resonated. He knew that should Elissa Reinhart reveal sinister inclinations, he would have to… address the situation…

"That's what I thought. We're not so different, you and I," taunted the Master of Walderlake.

"I recall what Aelrie, our Oracle, stated before her abduction. She wanted to keep this prediction hidden. She considered that bringing her visions to light compelled those who heard them to manipulate the future, shaping them to fit the interpretations they desired. My belief is that Elissa will become the subject of this prophecy, not because she was born to fulfill it, but because we have attributed this destiny to her."

"That's true! Yet few possess the same heritage as Elissa Reinhart. Or should I say, Lothain?"

"Original bloods?"

Toran nodded, his expression almost fearful. This marked the first instance when the Elven magistrate sensed trepidation from him.

At that moment, the guard who had led Elyndel to Toran Sius entered the room, instantly defusing the tension between the two men. Even before he announced himself, his desperate demeanor hinted to Elyndel that he had been the focal point of Toran Sius' temper in recent days.

"The griffins are back and ready for your departure," he said with a trace of relief.

"Finally!" Toran exclaimed, springing up from his seat.

Elyndel did not want their conversation to conclude in this manner. He reached out and caught the man's arm, detaining him. Toran Sius froze in place, and the sentry's expression edged toward horror, fearing a clash between the two magistrates.

"Your signature. That's all I require to ensure your safe return," Elyndel whispered.

"Is this a threat?" asked the Master of Walderlake, a hint of a snarl on his lips.

"I'd rather regard it as a suggestion."

Elyndel no longer recognized his own demeanor. He tried to reassure himself by remembering that his motives were driven not by personal gain, but by Cendril's safety.

"Leave us alone for a while," Toran directed dryly at the guard.

The soldier immediately complied, and the two Masters maintained unbroken eye contact.

"What leads you to believe that I would be inclined to sign your treaty after the last assembly? After the way you unfairly accused me of heinous crimes?" the human inquired with arrogance.

"It would be unfortunate if you lost Hargon's respect, wouldn't it?" Elyndel countered, a faint smirk emphasizing the dimple on his left cheek.

Toran Sius fell silent for a moment.

"You're bluffing. What could you hold against me that the king doesn't already know?"

"Do you recall a particular conversation with the late Balhaan? Right after his coronation?"

The Master of Walderlake's face paled, his crystalline eyes widening in surprise.

"Where should I affix my signature?" he replied, feigning detachment.

Elyndel had not anticipated that he would be so easily provoked. Certainly, anyone would shudder at the thought of revealing their treachery to their sovereign. Without further protest, Toran Sius marked his sigil on the parchment that the elf held out to him.

"I must admit, I find it difficult to understand why you're so fixated on me," grumbled the man.

"Individuals who manipulate their lord's mind don't instill much confidence in me," Cendril's Master confessed without restraint.

"I'm not the one whispering in Hargon's ear."

"Then who is?"

Toran sneered, revealing his gaping teeth, his face momentarily resembling that of a reptile.

"The measures I take to secure my realm may appear barbaric to you. Yet, I'm the first to prioritize justice and fairness before condemning anyone. Granted, I've made mistakes in the past... mistakes I still deeply regret. This hunt for the Abshanishs... it's not Council-directed."

"The Abshanishs," the elf repeated, his brow furrowing in puzzlement. "I didn't expect you to have such an affinity for legends."

"And I did not anticipate you to be so uninformed."

"Are you referring to the tale of the sentinels of Itos? The ones dispatched to Balt'boec to guide its lost souls?" Elyndel chuckled.

The Master of Walderlake then curved his lips into a Machiavellian smile.

"A fictional narrative, true, but grounded in reality."

"According to you, the Original Blood would signify them?" Elyndel asked, a touch of judgment in his tone.

"Of course."

"If the Abshanishs are indeed scattered throughout the empire, why focus on Elissa? Why base your prophecy on her?"

"Ah! Finally, an intelligent question!" Toran hissed through his teeth. "Upon our first meeting, I sensed that something about her was... off... beyond the ease with which she wielded magic. The way Brennet concealed her, where he found her... it was more than pride or pity. So, I began digging into her history."

"And?"

"What I uncovered made me tremble. I knew Brennet was planning to reinstate someone onto Galvrick's throne. I would have staked my life on it!"

"Cut to the chase," Elyndel urged with a sharp tone.

"The emperor had no descendants or heirs. That's why the throne remains vacant. At least, that's what we thought until members of Valler's druidic community traced their lineage."

Elyndel stared at Toran, aghast, though the old man attempted to conceal it. He wanted to appear composed, assured. Yet, his breathy voice betrayed him.

"You... you believe Elissa Reinhart is Galvrick's descendant."

"Elissa Lothain, a name Brennet hastened to erase, replacing it with his own. If my suspicions are correct, this woman could reign over the empire without even getting her hands dirty."

"*Bound by the Original Blood, mastery over the stones she shall have,*" the elf whispered, recalling the prophecy.

"I won't permit a second Galvrick to rule over Balt'boec!" Toran Sius ignited, almost pleading for his counterpart's support.

"I won't unjustly target an innocent as a precaution. I'm not like you."

Toran did not explode as the Master of Cendril anticipated. Instead, he sighed, shaking his head with a despondent, melancholic expression.

"When the world goes up in flames, remember that I warned you."

And so, the Master of Walderlake left the parlor, without so much as a backward glance.

CHAPTER

25

LADY FORTUNE

When Elissa opened her eyes, she was met with concern as she found herself in an unfamiliar place. Alone in an oddly unstable room, she groaned in pain, clutching her skull with both hands. Distress gripped her as she recollected her last moments of consciousness. She did not know who had attacked her or if she was now in enemy territory. She had not been bound, and no one appeared to be watching her. This indicated that she was not imprisoned. A rush of apprehension overwhelmed her as the faces of her companions flashed in her mind. No, she could not allow herself to believe that Wil could have assaulted her. The thought seemed preposterous.

Suddenly aware of her surroundings, she realized her dizziness was due to more than the blow she had suffered. The walls around her were curved, featuring small portholes. Numerous hammocks swung rhythmically, suspended by ropes. Overhead, the wooden ceiling creaked with the activity from above. A strong blend of sweat and tobacco, far from alleviating her nausea, permeated the air. The rising clamor of dozens of voices, boisterous yet playful, reached her ears. Certainly not the atmosphere that would prevail in a dungeon. Listening intently, she could hear the distant roll of the sea, confirming her suspicion that she was confined within a ship's hold.

Summoning her courage, she rose clumsily, grasping whatever support she could find. The room was dimly lit, but not enough to hinder her navigation between the grimy and odorous hammocks. Trunks were positioned in front of each, bearing the names of their owners: W. Hagley, L. Mitrik, R. Sweete, S. Daamon, P. Lazarus... Elissa immediately stopped reading, feeling bile rising in her throat. Hastening her pace, she fought to suppress the ignoble sensation. She could not be sure if she was fit enough to defend herself if need be, but she preferred venturing alone through the ship rather than waiting for an unexpected encounter. Slowly, she ascended the creaking stairs. And to think that she was counting on the element of surprise...

Before her stood a group of stern, filthy-looking men. Nothing resembled the dignified naval militia Brennet had mentioned in his tales. These sailors bore no uniform; their sun-bronzed arms were covered with tattoos. One of them smiled, revealing teeth that were both rotten and unwelcoming. Elissa took a step back, ready to defend herself. The man, however, tipped his tricorn hat in a gesture of politeness that struck the mage as absurd. Silver rings intertwined with his tangled, long hair. His eyes, already too severe, were painted in a smoky ash hue.

"The young lady is awake!" he declared enthusiastically, his voice greasy with amusement.

"Where am I?" Elissa inquired cautiously, still on her guard.

"Aboard the Lady Fortune! The pride of the West Seas!"

"And you are...?"

She hesitated to utter the word hovering on her lips.

"Pirates? Without a doubt!" her interlocutor responded, his laughter resonating through the air.

His companions joined in, leaving Elissa uncertain if she should feign amusement in return. Opting for a nervous nod, she recalled her father's stories about these lawless souls who roved the seas, seeking their next plunder. In each of those tales, encountering one of their ships never led to fortune.

"I honestly have no idea why I'm here... Sir?"

"Swarlee Daamon, but folks just call me Lee. This here is Blackbird, Weasel, and Percy. You'd do well to stay clear of these rascals, especially Weasel. He'll sweet-talk you and then have your pockets empty before you can bat an eye," the pirate declared, pointing in succession at his accomplices with a finger darkened by gunpowder.

"Slander!" Weasel retorted with a smirk.

His teeth, mostly gold, gleamed in the dim light. Towering over Elissa with his lean frame, he sported wide eyes, tousled brown hair, and prominent ears that likely earned him his unflattering moniker. Both Percy and Blackbird had sturdier builds. Percy's bald head beaded with sweat and featured finely scarred skin that created the illusion of scales. Elissa was careful not to linger on him, not wanting to offend him. The latter boasted a full beard, a sizable ring adorning his right nostril, and a black dragon tattoo that graced his exposed abdomen.

"May I inquire... where are we headed?" the woman asked, her words somewhat awkward.

"Osthallvale! That's where we're bound," Lee announced, his expression brimming with excitement. "Lady Fortune is the only vessel capable of traversing from Walderlake to the Minotaurs' continent."

His tone carried a certain pride, his curly mustaches wiggling with enthusiasm.

"The Sea Hook sometimes manages to reach Osthallvale's shore," Blackbird corrected in a mocking voice.

"The Barracuda too!" Weasel chimed in, raising a long, skinny finger into the air.

Lee shot them a stern look, and both men immediately fell into silence.

"None of them possess the speed and strength of Lady Fortune. We'll get to Osthallvale in no time, at most two weeks!" barked the mustachioed sailor.

"And my companions? Where are they?" Elissa asked apprehensively.

The pirates exchanged uncertain, uneasy glances but remained silent.

"Where are Wil and Finn?" she pressed with concern, studying their faces.

"I'll inform our captain that you're awake. Percy will show you the way," Lee said with obvious nervousness, brushing off her inquiry.

"Why me?" Percy exclaimed, stepping back.

"Because you're the favorite!" Blackbird taunted.

"Bullshit! I've managed to keep out of the captain's thoughts. It sure as hell won't change today! Weasel can go instead," Percy retorted, shoving the puny man forward.

"Why me over someone else? Isn't Lee the officer here? He should be the one escorting the girl."

"Alright then! As the superior, I order you to bring her," Lee settled on a firm tone.

Weasel wanted to argue but held back. He knew that refusing to obey the command would invite unfortunate consequences. He groaned in displeasure, then grabbed the mage by the arm and forcefully began dragging her along.

"Fine, then! Follow me!"

———— ··●·· ————

The terrified manner in which the sailors spoke of this infamous captain did not provide Elissa any reassurance. She pictured a bloodthirsty and ignoble man awaiting her for reasons that she deeply feared. A dark and venomous gaze, a colossal stature, and a sadistic smile… this was the portrait she sketched in her anxious mind. The pirates glared at her viciously, shamelessly blowing kisses and making perverted comments. She felt like nothing more than a piece of meat thrown to a pack of wolves. Gritting her teeth, she looked down and kept walking, trying to ignore their degrading behavior.

"What does your captain want from me?" Elissa cautiously asked Weasel, who skillfully avoided her gaze.

"We've been ordered to take you to the captain's quarters as soon as you wake up."

"That doesn't answer my question."

"That's all I'm allowed to say," the man defensively replied.

"Fine," the mage muttered, a hint of annoyance in her tone. Her hands trembled with apprehension, and she pondered if escape was still possible. What if she neutralized Weasel? But then what? The ship was swarming with pirates. Could she eliminate them all? She could not sail the vessel herself. Drowning felt like an almost tempting option…

Too late. Weasel halted in front of a door marked with the letters M.R.. He shuffled nervously, avoiding eye contact with the mage. Elissa's palms were clammy as she nearly longed for the company of the pirates. Weasel let out a nervous squeak and timidly knocked twice. After a moment, a woman emerged from the doorway, her expression intense and imperious. Despite her uninviting demeanor, Elissa could not help but admire her physique: a buxom beauty, captivating, honeyed eyes, and dark hair cascading over her shoulders, partially veiling a neck adorned with an ivory silk scarf. The roundness of her features gave her a simultaneously mature and youthful appearance. If she was older than Elissa, it could not have been by much. A servant or a concubine? Perhaps an unfortunate woman torn from her family to exploit her charms…

"Captain Redding," Weasel bowed to the lady.

Elissa's jaw dropped. She had anticipated Redding, the bloodthirsty sailor, the sea monster of unparalleled cruelty… The captain eyed the man with obvious impatience and folded her arms.

"What do you want, Weasel?"

"Here… here is the girl. The one we rescued at the port of Saracenne."

Rescued?

"Excellent," Captain Redding snapped, turning away.

Elissa and Weasel exchanged perplexed looks. After a few seconds, the mage took the lead and entered the cabin hesitantly. Weasel seized the chance to slip away, leaving her alone with the woman everyone seemed to fear.

The surprisingly spacious room was nothing like what the Guardian had envisioned: violet velvet curtains and sheets, a large mahogany desk supporting several leather-bound books. Paintings adorned the walls, framed by shimmering fabrics that bestowed an air of warmth and luxury. Furs and vibrant silk cushions decorated the bed, reminiscent of the nomadic merchant caravans that occasionally passed through Brevic. Unlike the smoky aroma that tainted the rest of the ship, the cabin carried a pleasant scent of incense.

"Myrrh and cypress," the woman remarked casually.

Elissa regarded her warily, still on edge.

"The incense. They can be found on the trading islands around the Aokule Desert," the captain explained.

Seating herself near the central windowsill where moonlight reflected off the sea, she studied Elissa from head to toe with an unusual expression—not disgust, but rather perplexity. She gestured for Elissa to take the chair beside her with a nod.

"The Iron Hands by Grasia Lorabella," Elissa ventured, pointing to the book on her desk. "One of my favorites!"

The woman chuckled softly.

"So... you're Captain Redding?" Elissa continued, trying to maintain her composure.

"Or Meggy the Butcher, or the Black Widow of the Islands... I go by many names. But yes, on this ship, that's the appropriate title," she said with a half-smile.

There was an undeniable aura of confidence in every move she made. The way she settled into her seat, the casual cross of her legs... Elissa could not pinpoint what set her apart from the other swashbucklers, but something about her commanded respect and authority.

"And you? What names are given to you?" the pirate inquired.

"Elissa. Elissa Reinhart," she replied candidly.

This time, no truth serum had been administered. It was an honest admission, one she almost regretted immediately.

"I believe, like me, you're granted various nicknames. Is that the case, Elissa Reinhart?"

"I don't know what makes you say that," Elissa answered, a tad too defensively.

"Few request passage to Osthallvale," Meggy commented, withdrawing a dagger from her boot. "Even my fellow sailors hesitate to embark on such a journey."

A chill crept through Elissa's veins, and her breath caught. Though the captain's gaze was focused on her own fingernails, which she was cleaning with the tip of the dagger, Elissa could not help but shudder in apprehension.

"Obviously, you're not a pirate," the captain continued nonchalantly. "Your purity sets you apart, a quality rarely encountered by us privateers. You're not a farmer either. Only someone from a well-to-do family could afford such fair skin and delicate hands. Perhaps a rich man's betrothed? A lord's daughter?"

"I don't understand why my social status matters so much to you," Elissa snapped.

"It's crucial for me to know whether those who step onto my ship pose a threat to my crew."

"I mean no harm. My father recently passed away after months of illness. I promised him that I'd journey to Osthallvale to fulfill his obligations in his stead."

"His obligations? In Osthallvale?" Meggy raised an eyebrow, skepticism evident in her tone.

"Yes, to pay respects to a few acquaintances... people he hadn't managed to speak to before he died."

Captain Redding rose from her seat, her dagger swiftly finding a resting place in the arm of Elissa's chair. She leaned in close to the mage, whose shock immobilized her.

"I'm not a forgiving person," Meggy murmured, baring her teeth. "Trust me when I say I don't typically give those who lie to me a second chance. Next time, this blade will find your throat if you refuse to cooperate... Guardian."

Elissa's insides constricted as the captain's warm breath grazed her cheek. Instinctively, she reached for the pouch hanging from her belt, prepared to strike to defend the stone.

"Don't worry. I have no intention of taking that responsibility from you," Meggy reassured with a smirk.

"How can I believe that?" the mage growled. "Many would desire to steal it."

"And I'm a pirate! Therefore, naturally, I would wish to seize it from you."

Elissa merely nodded, her unwavering gaze locking onto the captain's, who chuckled in response. With a swift motion, the woman retrieved her weapon and resumed her seat, nonchalant.

"Those possessing a stone must grapple with the attached consequences... consequences I'm not keen on dealing with," she continued.

Her demeanor softened, and for a moment, Elissa thought she detected a glimmer of pity.

"The notion of selling it didn't cross your mind?" she inquired skeptically.

"I know what would befall this kingdom if that emerald fell into the wrong hands. It might sound strange coming from me, but I have a very valid reason to wish prosperity upon Walderlake."

"Really?"

The pirate did not reply directly; instead, she observed Elissa with a curious expression.

"Reinhart, hmm? Your reputation precedes you. According to the Council's declarations, I stand before a monster capable of slaughtering her own family."

"I didn't kill anyone!" Elissa retorted before realizing the truth. "At least... no innocent people. I'm not responsible for my father's murder."

"I believe you," the captain said with a solemnity that caught Elissa off guard.

"So easily?"

"You're a terrible liar, and your reaction has told me what I needed to know. Plus, I don't put much trust in the Emerald Council."

"If you don't wish to take the stone, as you claim... What do you want from me? What will you do to me?"

"That's a rather ungrateful way to address the woman who saved you," Meggy shot back, her laughter filling the room.

"So... you didn't abduct me?"

"My dear, if I had intended to, you'd be gagged and restrained deep within this ship's hull!"

"So, where are my friends?"

"Your *friends* encountered me at the port of Saracenne, pleading with me to allow you on board. However, that blond fellow who was carrying you confessed to knocking you out to bring you here. I thought it best to confine him to a cell until you awoke," the captain explained with a benevolent smile.

The air seemed to evaporate around Elissa. So, it was true... Wil had attacked her. The man who had held her tightly, who had shielded her from panic, had struck her.

And Brea... Wil had prevented Elissa from assisting her. This poor, gentle child left in the clutches of mercenaries... She likely lay in the woods, much like her mother. Something within Elissa broke. She swallowed hard, her eyes stinging from overwhelming grief.

"And Finn? Where's he?" her voice sounded distant.

"On the bridge, lending a hand. Brave lad!"

With that, Meggy Redding strolled over to pick up a silver flask engraved with an octopus twined around a ship's anchor. Raising the container to her lips, she took a hearty swig, her demeanor utterly composed. She offered it to Elissa, who accepted it politely. The spiced rum coursed through her like liquid fire. She was not well acquainted with alcohol's taste, but that did not matter. The warmth soothed the pain that had settled in her chest. The captain chuckled and sat on the armrest of the very chair she had stabbed just minutes ago. Close... much closer than Elissa was accustomed to.

"Where... where is he? Wil, I mean."

"I told you! I've confined him."

"Captain Redding... I understand your motives, but..."

"Meggy," the woman interjected. "Call me Meggy."

"Alright… Meggy… but Wil is harmless. We are… we're good friends," she pressed on, trying to ignore the turmoil raging within her.

"An unusual friendship, wouldn't you say?"

"Wil had his reasons…"

"The man who beat me throughout my childhood must have had reasons too. The one who seared a hot iron into my skin after snatching me from my family certainly had his reasons. They all did," Meggy responded, revealing a thick scar shaped like the letter G on her left forearm.

Elissa's throat tightened as she regarded the painful mark on the woman's skin, a stark contrast against her tanned complexion. It was hard to fathom that such a strong, commanding figure had once been subjected to such cruelty against her will.

"While I understand your perspective, your harrowing experiences don't equate to the present situation."

"Don't they? If you say so. Nevertheless, I believe a woman should be able to make a decision without being attacked," Meggy's voice bore a hint of aggression.

Elissa nodded, feeling torn. She knew Wil, knew the kindness he harbored, but the captain's words had sown a seed of doubt. After all, she had misjudged him before.

"I still want to see my friends," Elissa asserted, meeting the pirate's gaze.

Meggy smiled, sensing Elissa's internal conflict. Her expression turned comforting, even warm. Before Elissa stood not the Butcher, but Meggy Redding. They exchanged a look, affirming the woman's willingness to comply with her request.

"Good! I suggest we allow this Wil some time to simmer overnight," Meggy advised.

Resentment prompted Elissa's reluctant agreement. After all, what harm could a night of reflection do?

"What do you want from me now?" she inquired, her anxiety palpable.

"As I mentioned before, your companions have already settled your debt. You're free to do as you wish."

"How? We possess no valuables…"

"Don't bother. It's no longer your affair. But if you truly want to be of use, perhaps you could amuse me a bit."

"Amuse you?" the mage repeated, skepticism evident. "I don't think that's my forte."

"You underestimate yourself greatly. I've got a few notions of how you might do just that."

Elissa shot her a piercing look and abruptly stood from her chair.

"I don't care how things work on this ship. Back in Brevic, no one would dare suggest such arrangements! We're not… animals!"

"I didn't realize discussing poetry was taboo in your quaint hometown," Meggy remarked with a suppressed laugh. "I thought an avid reader of The Iron Hands collection might appreciate it. Does philosophy provoke the same reaction?"

"Oh! The Iron Hands, yes… a marvelous piece!" Elissa blurted out, her cheeks flushed. Captain Redding passed her the flask once more, and she took another sip without protest.

"We'll get along famously, Elissa Reinhart," Meggy quipped.

CHAPTER

26

NETHERBORNES AND VERINAS

A persistent crowd had gathered in front of Queen Valera's villa. Their discontent echoed day and night, prompting the sovereign to remain hidden within her quarters, avoiding confrontation. Their demands for respite from the Capital's relentless toil and sustenance for the starving peasants rang loud. Farklyn advised that she extend a gesture of kindness to appease them, assuring that such a simple act would quell their fervor. Raina, however, offered a different perspective to Valera. She insisted that the tumult would eventually subside on its own, and acknowledging their grievances would only stoke their anger. Rarely had the queen been subject to such vehement hatred. One who thrived on cultivating her subjects' admiration could not fathom enduring this for much longer. The Easterners' swift shift against her baffled her. After all, they owed her their safety from the dreaded dragons. Of course, she denied any involvement in their resurgence.

She had also heard whispers of accusations regarding her supposed heavy-handed approach, often coupled with the term *tyrant*.

"Absurd," she mused, chuckling incredulously. The populace could not possibly grasp what was truly best for them. Valera compared herself to a strict parent, guiding her children onto the path of virtue and prosperity. Her own sons had never complained about her parenting. The citizens should do the same. At least Elyndel treated her kindly, even charmingly. She knew his duty mandated exemplary politeness and diplomacy, yet his night-blue eyes bore a particular interest. His manner of speaking to her, observing her... It seemed to transcend the realm of her beauty and the assets she had unashamedly wielded to her advantage. Valera sensed an uncanny connection between them, a déjà vu of sorts. She pondered why her torment had found solace in Elyndel. The partition in her mind, the barrier she had long neglected... It was a vulnerability she could no longer tolerate. Yet, the Elven Master was candid, open. Who could be so willing to share such vulnerability with a rival? Elyndel Arren. Almost regretfully, she recalled the way their conversation had concluded. Almost.

Valera sprang up from her work desk, a desk that seemed to trap her day after day.

"More like a prisoner!" she exclaimed in exasperation, arching her back to alleviate the stiffness.

Raina inundated her with manuscripts for review and endorsement: death penalties for betrayal, numerous arrests for incitement... It was ceaseless. She questioned if tightening her grip was truly the answer to the simmering rebellion. She remembered her aunt, Auda Verina, and the dire fate her despotic actions had met. She refused to follow suit, to encounter the same end. Fortunately, their personalities were vastly different. Their worldviews, their dispositions, their awareness... Worlds apart! She mentally rejected the contrary notion. But what if they tried to manipulate her, just as they had with her unfortunate aunt? Would she descend into paranoia and madness? After all, she had once fallen prey to the same man who had annihilated Auda, the man to whom she had previously given her heart...

Impulsively and violently, Valera swept the various objects from her marble desk. She heard glass shatter, but did not bother to assess the extent of the damage. A servant would clean it up soon enough, as usual. She paced restlessly across the room, her gaze drawn to the paintings hanging on the terracotta walls. They depicted the Netherbornes and Verinas, who had reigned over the Eastern lands for generations. It was as if they were observing her, captured in their eternal grandeur. The portrait of Balhaan was conspicuously absent from the line of monarchs. Valera had ensured that all physical traces of his brief presence in their lives were erased. Her father's painting, that of Valerius Netherborne, particularly caught her attention. She swore his icy blue eyes sought to penetrate her very soul. In the image, his left hand clutched the jeweled hilt of a glorious sword, while his right rested upon his heart. As always, he projected valor and courage, traits Valera knew he lacked. Just like his daughter, a cascade of ebony hair framed his face. The disdainful smile on his rosy lips still managed to unnerve her to this day. To those who did not know him intimately, his charm was evident. Yet, his corrupted soul tainted her perception. A shiver ran down her spine as she recalled fragments of her youth, a childhood squandered in ceaseless attempts to gain his approval, to compensate for her gender.

"Feeling nostalgic?" Raina's voice cut through from behind.

"Let's hope that's sarcasm," the queen retorted, taken aback. "A man whose existence revolved around debauchery, who drove my mother to suicide and pushed his people to the brink? Who could miss such a character?"

"Nonetheless, he's the progenitor of Guverl'yt's most celebrated heroine," the adviser explained, offering a wink to her sovereign.

Valera chuckled coquettishly before defiantly meeting the portrait's gaze.

"See, Father! It is ultimately a woman who wears your crown."

She savored her vindictive words as if they were the finest wine. The day she had discovered the lifeless king, his face pallid and his eyes frozen in a tormented expression, remained etched in her memory. Foam had collected on his well-formed lips, while one hand clung weakly to the bedsheets. He must have attempted to rise before succumbing to the poison's effects. Although Valerius' demise was officially deemed accidental, Valera knew it was Balhaan's doing. He had always taken pains to erase all traces…

Yet, Valera felt no sympathy for her father. If anything, she believed he deserved a more agonizing fate… a much harsher one.

"I must admit, I miss my mother," Valera confessed, a note of melancholy in her voice, her gaze fixed on the portrait of Lilion Verina.

"If it offers any solace, the people still hold her memory dear," Raina replied.

Valera nodded, her attention lingering on the immortalized visage of the late queen. Like her older sister Auda, Lilion wore her chestnut hair in a wreath of braids, decorated with delicate roses. Both possessed captivating dark eyes, reminiscent of the now-scarce deer that once roamed the Eastern regions. However, their similarities ended there. While Auda's appearance might have been termed ordinary, Lilion exuded an unmatched elegance. The Princess of Wynnorth's incredible beauty had garnered numerous suitors from across Balt'boec. Yet, her allure was in no way proportional to her kind and magnanimous spirit. She preferred the company of creatures and the less fortunate over the insipid and hollow courtiers. During that time, King Urius had openly exploited his daughter's loveliness to bend his rivals to his will.

"Legend holds that a single glance from Lilion could divert entire armies from their course," the queen added with a half-smile.

"Likely the reason Valerius abandoned his betrothal to Auda Verina. Who could not fall in love with such a charming princess?"

"Love?" Valera hissed, her tone almost indignant. "No, my father was a collector, a hunter of beautiful things. My mother was merely another prized acquisition for him to add to his treasury. I'm also convinced that Valerius harbored disdain for women. His disappointment in Lilion for bearing a daughter instead of a son, his humiliation of Auda Verina… I was but a child at that ball, yet I still recall the anguish in Auda's eyes.

How Valerius ridiculed her attributes before his guests... the brutal degradation he subjected her to... It's hardly surprising that poor Auda despised him so vehemently."

Valera shook her head, cursing her father in a voice barely above a whisper before continuing.

"I often pity my aunt. Despite the heinous acts she committed during her reign... I mourn the destruction of her spirit. There was a time when she was my only ally... a time when I was estranged from my mother."

A cough from Raina prompted Valera's immediate realization of her slip.

"One of my only allies," she corrected with an affectionate glance. "I can't fathom where I'd be today without your invaluable counsel."

She recollected the initial encounter with Raina. The day she entered the College of Magi, Batilda Fiore, the headmistress, had made it plain that neither rank nor youth would shield her from hardship. Perhaps it was a form of revenge against the royal family or merely a method of maintaining control over her apprentices. Batilda had cast magical blows upon her for simply inquiring about her training. Subsequently, Valera, a solitary and bewildered child, had found herself unable to stem the flow of her tears. Then appeared Raina, her new roommate. Slightly older, Valera immediately perceived in her the elder sister she had always wished for. Raina's composed demeanor and pragmatic spirit entranced her. Without seeking reciprocation, Raina had offered solace to the young princess on that first chilly night in the apprentice dormitory.

"I know this might sound strange, but I miss those times," the queen admitted. "As a child, I believed those were the most trying moments of our lives. How wrong I was..."

Darkness veiled Valera's eyes as she swiftly turned away from her adviser. She faced the portrait of Valerius, the despicable man who had robbed her of her innocence and tenderness. She resolutely stifled her tears, a burning fury churning in her stomach, while the chants of the crowd reached her ears. Raina's hands rested firmly on her shoulders, her grip unwavering despite her slight frame. Though she could not witness Raina's expression, Valera sensed the compassion the adviser had always extended to her.

"Do you remember when the great Batilda attempted to punish you for accidentally knocking over your inkwell?" Raina queried with a more familiar tone. "In your distress, you instinctively deflected her laceration spell, and she ended up seated on her own rear several feet away."

"How could I forget?" Valera smirked, her voice mixed with emotion. "It's also the sole instance I managed to wield magic without my scepter."

"The apprentices present were torn between fleeing and bursting into laughter."

"Batilda never dared to target me again after that... nor anybody else."

"I understand doubt clouds your thoughts, but the Valera I know wouldn't permit anyone to shatter her life. She wouldn't be defeated by adversity. The crowd that assembles outside the villa is mere clamor."

"I don't know... I have a feeling that my choices led to this crisis. Perhaps... perhaps a change in approach is required."

"If we yield now, we'll appear feeble to the people... to the world."

"Similar to all those who vanished into obscurity before me? Like the Netherbornes and Verinas who succumbed to pride and obstinacy?"

"These same qualities allowed the East to establish an impressive presence within the empire."

"Perhaps you should preach this to the citizens who suffered under my aunt's haughty vanity... or to my unfortunate mother, condemned to endure my father's fragile ego!"

Valera's fury ignited as the image of Lilion, gagged with an iron muzzle, pierced her like a blade. According to Valerius, she smiled excessively in his absence; he had remedied that.

Distant shouts resounded within the villa, a blend of anger and desperation. Likely another insurgent striving to infiltrate and attack her. Assassination attempts appeared to be a part of her family's legacy…

On instinct, she grasped her scepter and tensed, awaiting a threat. The screams escalated, then ceased abruptly. The guards' work, without a doubt. Valera sensed anxiety rising within her like an encroaching tide.

"Elyndel… I believe his presence could soothe their anger," she mused aloud, lowering her weapon.

Raina pursed her lips, emitting a barely perceptible snarl. "I fail to fathom how our adversary's influence could render this situation tolerable," she disdainfully retorted.

"Perhaps we should release their Oracle. After all, we've obtained what we wanted from her."

Raina's arms crossed over her chest, a glint flitting through her golden-rimmed gaze. "Maybe we should also offer them the remnants of our treasury? Surrender our weapons?"

"Keep your sarcasm to yourself," the sovereign growled.

"Think of what you are actually proposing! How many times has this Oracle been wielded against us? Only a fool would disregard this opportunity!"

Valera raised her scepter, pointing it at her adviser, who promptly fell silent, though her unyielding expression persisted. The flame within the ruby flared, menacing and eerie.

"You're the sole person to whom I authorize such familiarity and candor. Yet, do not take this privilege for granted."

Raina did not respond immediately, observing the woman she considered a sister for a moment. Never before had she been threatened in such a manner.

"My apologies, Your Highness," she replied, her tone cautious and calculated. "I shall return to my duties."

She offered a slight bow, yet did not lower her gaze. Finally, she turned, leaving Valera's anger as fiercely ignited as before.

Without waiting for Raina to close the door to her apartments, she briskly paced to her bedroom's balcony. Leaning against the stone railing of the expansive mezzanine overlooking the sea, she exhaled, striving to regain command over her emotions. The scent of sea salt, always therapeutic, managed to offer a degree of solace. Why did they all provoke her like this? Perhaps she should have listened to Farklyn instead of Raina. At times, she questioned why she was so tough toward him. His sons had inherited their father's disposition: brilliant minds yet devoid of magic. But this was not the root of her discontent with him. Farklyn differed from his brother in ways she could not define. Their audacity responded to different invitations, and their desires diverged. Farklyn's morality was unlike the values cultivated in the East, a morality she lacked. Alone with these ruminations that compelled her self-reflection, Valera grumbled. She swept her dark mane aside, and a breeze tenderly grazed her moistened nape. Anger always held such control over her. With surprise, she noticed the air's freshness—an unusual occurrence in this region, particularly at this hour. Curious…

Valera discerned that the clamor of the crowd had diminished. She had not recruited the finest sentinels in the citadel for nothing. Yet, a sting of guilt for her unyielding conduct toward her subjects struck her. Ordinarily, she delegated the handling of revolutionaries to her adviser. She sighed, her thoughts retracing to Elyndel. What if she were to release the Oracle she held captive back to her people? Irritated by the inner conflict, she groaned. Farklyn, Elyndel… they sowed doubt within her. Gazing upon the tumultuous waves of the Narbane Sea, she found their usual shades of green and turquoise replaced by an oddly somber grey.

Could it be…

She looked up, taken aback by the sight of the sky darkening, clouds converging. A droplet grazed her forehead, succeeded by another. In a heartbeat, a true downpour engulfed her, accompanied by an ominous wind promising a storm. Here? Now?

Valera erupted in laughter, her arms outstretched in a triumphant gesture. Euphoria swept through her as she embraced the rain, seeing it as a sign that her prayers had been heard and the long drought was finally over. She understood that this deluge offered her people respite, perhaps signifying the preservation of divine favor.

Her ecstasy was interrupted by Raina's entrance, her countenance grave and her expression unreadable. The queen halted, her satisfaction instantly fading.

"What is it, Raina?"

"Your Majesty… news from Brilea," the counselor responded, her demeanor serious. "Your son, the king…"

With those words, Valera's stomach churned.

"Fabyan?" she stumbled, panic coloring her voice.

"His Highness has returned."

Valera covered her mouth, stifling a gasp of astonishment. Tears of relief streamed down her cheeks, mingling with the warm raindrops. Perhaps this day would not be a catastrophe. Pride and confidence swelled within her. She, alone, had ended the drought and brought her son home—or so she would convey to the people.

CHAPTER

27

THE RETURN OF THE KING

Disarray reigned as King Fabyan's arrival inspired preparations for a celebratory ball in his honor. Another tiresome event arranged by his dear mother, Farklyn guessed. Valera could not resist orchestrating grand spectacles at the slightest pretext, hoping to sway the populace in her favor. How convenient a distraction the king's return was! The prolonged drought had also ended with recent days' torrential rains. Boldly declaring that Itos had bestowed his blessing upon them, Valera sought to exonerate her own transgressions. Farklyn simmered quietly, hardly able to believe the nonchalance with which his mother brushed aside any skepticism. Adding to his frustration was the passive demeanor of those surrounding him. Despite the looming threat of a common adversary, they were immersed in arranging celebrations. In just a matter of days, the fervor over dragons had disappeared, replaced by a tense political atmosphere. However, the newfound alliances Valera coveted would be rendered null if the empire were to literally go up in flames. This, it seemed, did not concern her.

Farklyn had yet to encounter Fabyan since his return. His twin reveled in the adulation of his subjects and seized every opportunity to appear in public. This fueled Farklyn's suspicion that something was wrong. Unlike when he was indifferent to Valera's machinations, he now harbored an intense urge to discover the secret dealings occurring behind his back. As usual, he set his sights on Braylon to initiate his investigation. The poor counselor had evaded him as best he could, but was aware that his master was invariably relentless. After all, Farklyn possessed an almost innate knack for manipulating his servant's vulnerabilities. Protesting and grumbling, Braylon reluctantly departed for Ryre's Keep to gather intelligence on Valera and Fabyan's whereabouts.

Awaiting his return in his chamber, the prince considered countless scenarios concerning his twin brother's condition. He had to admit that this anxiety was disconcerting him. The days of carefree existence seemed to be relics of the past.

"I'm eagerly anticipating Fabyan's reinstatement to the throne! My tranquility has never felt so distant!" he jeered at those in his vicinity.

He tried to overlook the discomfort his remarks were provoking. In these rants, he recognized his own attempt to persuade himself that he did not mourn the prospect of returning to his obsolete life. He needed to silence the inner voice taunting him, the one whispering words like disgrace, inept, worthless. And what better way to numb the soul than by resorting to old habits, immersing oneself in indulgence? His anticipation necessitated good companionship, as well as the soothing embrace of mead's sweet nectar.

Farklyn called for Jenima to join him. She had always possessed a unique talent for diverting his mind. As he reclined on his chair, contemplating his existential void, he was garbed in loose cotton trousers and a muslin bathrobe of the same shade, leaving his chest exposed. Jenima had previously complimented him on this attire... Restless, he kept his eyes, painted with dark colors, fixed on the door.

After some time, three gentle, almost inaudible knocks echoed. "Enter!" he called, his lips curving into a lustful smile. However, the woman who timidly stepped into his chambers was unrecognizable. It was Jenima, yet her typically vibrant countenance appeared dull, even sickly. Her chestnut eyes were red, perhaps from sorrow or weariness. The spirited demeanor he so adored seemed extinguished. An air of disquiet surrounded her, difficult to decipher.

"Your Majesty requested my presence?" she inquired, her gaze fixed on the floor.

"I was hoping to meet Jenima," Farklyn stated with nonchalance.

"Your Highness?"

"I do not recognize the person before me. The Jenima I know is spontaneous, passionate. This fragile figure is not her."

"I… I apologize for my temperament. I shall try to please you," the maid murmured, avoiding his gaze. Her submissive timbre struck the prince's ears as unsettling.

"You may go," he uttered casually, yet disappointment stained his tone. Jenima curtsied and turned to exit the room. However, as she was about to retire, her lord's voice reached out to her in an almost sing-song manner. Slowly, she pivoted, still refusing to meet his eyes.

"You seem eager to leave. I admit, I too would feel anxiety if I had attacked the man I am supposed to serve."

The maid looked up in dismay.

"What is it?" Farklyn grumbled, observing the woman from his velvet chaise.

"I am not sure I understand…" Jenima's breath hitched, and she swallowed hard. She ultimately sank to her knees, lowering her head humbly in submission.

"I await your judgment, my prince."

"My judgment?" he mused.

"Spare me the torture, please."

To her, he must have seemed solely an executioner, a detached noble. She pictured Fabyan.

"I am not my brother, let alone my mother," the young man retorted.

"I... I apologize... I assumed..."

"I know what you believed," he continued, adopting a more composed tone. "I am aware that something happened within the dungeons of Ryre's Keep. I don't know what, exactly; my memory remains foggy despite my efforts to reclaim clarity. However, Master Ancel informed me that Malawet possesses diverse uses... including the manipulation of minds. A remarkably convenient coincidence, wouldn't you say?"

He scrutinized her with a peculiar, indescribable gaze. Slowly lacing his fingers, his imposing presence seemed to dominate the surroundings. For a moment, Jenima appeared to cease breathing.

"And here I believed you were on my side," he murmured with a smirk.

"I am on the side of justice," she asserted, her voice unwavering. Raising her head defiantly, she fell silent once more. Farklyn detected a sense of resignation in her demeanor. Through that outburst, she had perhaps sealed her fate.

His lips twitched at the corners, and he arched an eyebrow in amusement. "Don't worry. Unlike many men in this realm, I recognize the worth of women with character."

Casually, the prince poured a second goblet of purplish wine and extended it to her. She hesitated, but Farklyn's smile widened, encouraging Jenima to step forward. He gestured for her to settle beside him on the long, padded armchair, patting the seat with his fingertips. She refrained from touching her drink, her gaze resting on it dubiously.

"I haven't poisoned it, if that's your concern," Farklyn stated in an almost monotone manner.

She let out a nervous giggle and took a timid sip. Observing her more closely now, he noticed her complexion was paler than usual, with dark circles under her eyes.

"Are you unwell?"

"I don't think so... I... If I may, Majesty... why summon me to your chambers if not to reprimand me?" she ventured, avoiding his inquiring gaze.

Ordinarily, he would have responded with a devastating smile... but she seemed so fragile today. The desire for company evaporated, and he sighed.

"I am no longer certain," he admitted, placing his cup down without taking a sip.

Farklyn leaped on his feet, startling poor Jenima. He paced the room like a caged wolf, agitated and tormented.

"I apologize for wasting your precious time. You may leave," he intoned with a heavy note in his hoarse voice.

The servant nodded and rose discreetly.

"Jenima?"

She paused.

"I recognize when a person commits an act of rebellion with noble motives. I am also the first to celebrate the courage of such actions. I consider myself a merciful man. I dare hope that this fear consuming you will eventually fade, and I will once again encounter the woman with whom I have spent such delightful hours."

"I am certain of it," Jenima retorted with a flirtatious tone.

With a graceful bow, she departed, a smile gracing her generous lips.

"Oh, and merciful does not equate to foolish," the prince clarified. "My compassion can readily transform into cruelty if my forgiveness is misused."

Each word he weighed was laden with seriousness, causing her to tremble. Without waiting for her reaction, he turned back to the bedroom window. He knew she understood. Moments later, he heard her exit, the door gently closing behind her.

Farklyn strolled to the balcony, hoping the fresh air might rejuvenate his spirit. The downpour was intense, as if the rain they had long been denied was finally catching up. The waves of the Narbane Sea crashed against the rocky shore with fervor. The prince felt an affection for the tumultuous dance of the waters, sensing an almost intimate connection. The sky, draped in somber, threatening clouds, was rent by lightning from all directions. An air of power hung; an omen rooted in more than mere bad weather.

Braylon burst into the room, neglecting even the pretense of knocking, leaving Farklyn puzzled by his abrupt return. Paler than ever, the man appeared as if he had seen a ghost. His lips quivered, and beads of sweat dotted his forehead.

"What news do you bring, Braylon?"

"Your Majesty... your mother requests your presence," he uttered in an almost queasy voice.

"And what of my brother?"

"Precisely... Her Highness wishes to speak with you about... the king's condition."

Farklyn dashed out of the room without a second thought.

"Let's go," he whispered, his expression heavy with torment.

They arrived at Ryre's Keep in no time. Farklyn was thoroughly soaked, but did not care. Braylon led the way, guiding him through the fortress's halls and toward the royal wing. As he thought about it, Farklyn realized he had never truly felt the bond everyone spoke of—the connection twins were said to share, enabling them to endure each other's pain. This connection had not manifested between them. Even during their childhood, despite all the wounds and sorrows, Farklyn had never sensed the slightest tingle, the faintest hint of his brother's emotions. He almost felt guilty for this absence, as if he had failed to experience something he should have. He had often attributed this lack to the distance that had separated them from birth. Fabyan, as the elder twin, had always been elevated above him. They both had been acutely aware of the differences between them. The first existed to rule, the second to serve. Despite the special attention Fabyan had received, Farklyn had never harbored bitterness or envy. He would not have wished misfortune upon his brother for anything in the world.

"Have you seen Fabyan?" Farklyn inquired with evident concern. He tried to rein in his imagination from deviating into wild speculation. Nonetheless, the adviser's panicked attitude made it difficult.

"Briefly, Majesty… very briefly," Braylon stammered.

He hastened his steps, almost as though attempting to flee from his lord's probing questions.

"In what state is he? Is he well?"

"I… I think we should wait for Her Majesty's presence before… before…"

Farklyn's patience wore thin. Amidst his inner turmoil, he seized Braylon by his silk purple jacket and forcefully pinned him against the nearest stone wall.

"All this secrecy is becoming infuriating. I demand answers," he hissed through clenched teeth.

"My prince… I implore you!"

The adviser squeezed his eyes shut, as if bracing for a blow. Yet Farklyn had never raised a hand to him, though there were times he felt tempted. Slowly, he released his grip and drew a deep breath to quell the flames of anger raging within him.

"Farklyn?"

He turned to see Valera calling out to him from the far end of the corridor.

"Mother?" he whispered almost involuntarily.

"Finally! There you are!" she exclaimed, extending a hand toward him.

Without a second thought, he rushed to her. Her eyes were red, weary. If he did not know her better, he might have believed he saw her discreetly wiping a tear from her cheek with her fingertips. Valera enveloped him in her arms, and for a moment, he hesitated before reciprocating the embrace.

"Oh, Farklyn! These monsters! They will pay for what they did to your poor brother."

The queen's tone held both fiery anger and profound pain. A queasy sensation gripped Farklyn's stomach as his breath seemed to catch in his chest.

"Where is he?" he whispered.

Without further delay, Valera led him down the corridor. For an instant, he thought he heard the sound of a stifled sob. He resisted the urge to question her or offer his support. He knew she wanted to maintain the illusion of invulnerability. Silence was the best relief he could provide. As they neared the farthest room in the villa, a cacophony of screams and moans assaulted Farklyn's ears. He recognized his brother's voice immediately, and his blood ran cold in his veins. Fabyan was suffering. He rushed to him, as if his very presence could alleviate his twin's pain. He swung open the door to the bedroom, revealing a gruesome scene. Hunched on a chair was Fabyan... or at least, Farklyn assumed it was him. The figure had long, dark hair cascading over its rough, scaly shoulders. The face was grotesquely contorted, unrecognizable. In his past, he had come across individuals with atypical appearances, but his brother's visage bore little semblance to those cases. There was almost nothing human left in those features. Torture itself could not have created such a catastrophe. The nose was gone, replaced by a pair of gaping holes. The left eye was swollen shut, while the right revealed a large, yellowish iris reminiscent of a predatory bird. The skin was a patchwork of pustules, resembling a combination of leather and scales. And the mouth… it sent shivers through Farklyn. Filled with sharp teeth akin to a beast's, it sat unnaturally low in the face, as if about to fall off. His once-charming lips were nearly erased.

Farklyn swallowed hard, repulsed and horrified by the grotesque sight. Fabyan was gone. The prince eventually registered the commotion in the room. Several healers from the Sapphire Council attended to the king. They prodded and measured him. Some cast healing spells, while others sifted through dusty grimoires. Fabyan wailed, whether from pain or despair, Farklyn could not discern. But he was suffering, and that was what mattered most to him. The young sovereign emitted a heart-rending cry as Master Ancel thrust a small metal instrument beneath one of the scales on his chest.

"Stay away from him!" Farklyn roared, charging toward his brother.

They scattered like vermin discovered in a pantry, retreating from the prince's fury.

"No… let them do their work, Farklyn," his twin muttered.

His distorted mouth hindered him from articulating well. He wiped the saliva dripping from his chin with a delicate silk and lace handkerchief, monogrammed with his initials. This image unsettled Farklyn more than anything else. Everything seemed so surreal. For the first time in his life, he pitied Fabyan.

"Believe me, my appearance has improved since my return. Hard to fathom, I know!" the king explained, catching Farklyn's discomfort.

The prince cast a wary glance at the mages who lingered nearby.

"For days, they have struggled to restore your brother's original physique," Valera said from the doorway.

"Useless!" Fabyan grumbled, his brows furrowed.

The queen of Guverl'yt did not challenge his assertion. Farklyn realized she was trying to convince herself that such an affliction might be rectified. With a subtle nod, she signaled for the healers to resume their efforts.

The scene troubled Farklyn deeply. He aimed to exhibit strength, not necessarily because he believed Fabyan would have done the same for him—probably not—but because it seemed the honorable thing to do. He stepped forward, suppressing his own discomfort, and settled down near the king.

"Who did this to you? The Mistress of Brilea?" Farklyn queried.

"Those seeking vengeance, naturally! One after another… they twisted my body with their insidious magic. Day after Day… I… I lost track of what sunlight even looked like, Farklyn. The taste of wine, the touch of gentle skin… All faded from my memory. I was… defeated."

As these words left his lips, the king's composure crumbled into tears. It struck Farklyn that he might not have witnessed his brother cry since… forever? Even in childhood, Fabyan had been a model of strength and courage.

One of the mages partly drew back a curtain, allowing in what little daylight this somber afternoon had to offer. Fabyan jolted from his seat with a bloodcurdling shriek, retreating to a corner of the room between his grand four-poster bed and the stone wall.

"No! Not the light!" he moaned, his disproportionately large hands concealing his face.

"Close the curtain!" Farklyn commanded, hurrying toward him.

"Fire! They mean to burn me!" Fabyan sobbed as he began to slap himself.

Farklyn tried to intervene, but Fabyan's frantic clawing injured him. Blood streamed from the gash on Farklyn's left cheek. His handsome face… the one thing most people only saw in him. Unwavering, he made another attempt to calm his distressed brother.

"Help him!" Valera directed the guards stationed outside the room.

They came swiftly, though their apprehension at restraining their own king was evident.

Eventually, Fabyan yielded to their firm grasp, his breath ragged and his mutterings incoherent.

"It's alright. You're safe," Farklyn whispered.

He clasped Fabyan's agitated hand. A sense of helplessness enveloped him, reminiscent of the dragon attack. The twins stood in that manner for a moment—Fabyan softly weeping, Farklyn grappling with his own inadequacy.

"I promise, we will work toward restoring your former self," Master Ancel declared, almost with arrogance.

Yet Farklyn recognized that his brother's physical state was of lesser concern. While his body appeared shattered, his soul seemed even more fragmented.

Recollections of the torments Fabyan had inflicted upon Brilea's people resurfaced. Their resentment was understandable. Valera exhibited no leniency toward the bordering kingdom's dire circumstances. Above all, she sought to expand her dominion and amass wealth. That, at least, was Farklyn's perception. Brilea's military strength paled in comparison to its neighboring realms. It had maintained its privileged position within the empire owing to its abundant resources. The Wynnorth king had been especially harsh to the citizens of this trading nation. They had been afforded little respite, facing war after war, their troops dwindling. Fabyan perceived them as vermin, a plague that aimed to deprive Balt'boec's countries of its primal riches. Naturally, this was not the case... but any price demanded was an affront to the rulers of the East.

Farklyn's attention was drawn to the outfit laid out on the king's bed: an ivory frock coat paired with cropped trousers, adorned by gold buttons. A puffy midnight blue silk shirt and sapphire-gilded shoes completed the ensemble. It was the sort of attire he reserved solely for special occasions, like a ball.

The upcoming ball…

Farklyn offered an apologetic glance to Fabyan and rose, summoning a strained smile. He made his way to his mother, his courteous expression shifting to one of reproach.

"Why go on with the festivities? Can't you see the state your son is in?" Farklyn's voice grew low and gruff.

"We should tend to that wound before you end up disfigured like your brother," the queen countered, her finger gesturing toward the bloody gash on the prince's cheek.

"Answer me!" he demanded.

"We can't afford any hint of vulnerability… especially not now. Furthermore, I have faith in the healing abilities of my mages. I'm sure they can considerably improve Fabyan's appearance."

"And what about his mental state?" Farklyn questioned incredulously, pointing to the man who still seemed lost in his own ramblings.

"The mages are trying to address this… situation. They understand the urgency to do so before our festivities."

"When is the ball?" he inquired.

"During the new moon."

"Mother, you're ruthless! You're giving them only a few days to work. Can't you see the agony your own son is enduring?"

"Yes, he's my son… a son who also rules over Wynnorth. As king, his personal struggles must wait. We need to project unity and strength to our people."

"You can't be serious! And to think I was beginning to have faith in you…"

Valera observed Farklyn with resolve… but also sorrow. He knew his words struck a chord, yet he could not refrain from defending Fabyan. For a moment, she seemed to weigh her choices. As she often did when confronted with her own missteps, she nervously nibbled her lower lip. Perhaps there was still hope for her after all…

As Farklyn waited for her mood to shift, the queen redirected her attention to the healing mages.

"Until the new moon. Is that clear?"

With a final look at Fabyan's pained form and the chorus of "Yes, Majesty," Valera's gaze returned to her son's, now darker than ever and filled with defiance and arrogance. Then, she abruptly left. The prince could not allow her to withdraw, not with the potential repercussions of her hasty decision.

"Mother!" Farklyn called out, hastening his pace to catch up.

However, she continued her stride, dismissing his plea. Without further thought, he reached out and grasped her arm, attempting to halt her progress. She immediately shook off his grip with a quick, aggressive movement.

"If you dare lay your hands on me again, I won't hesitate to summon my guards to arrest you."

Her words reverberated like a declaration of war, sharp and merciless. Recognizing the futility of his efforts, Farklyn let her go. His arms dropped limply to his sides, and he lowered his head. He had wished to believe in her fairness, her maternal compassion. For the first time in his life, he envied his brother's position … the position that granted him authority. And so, he turned back to Fabyan with a heavy heart, uncertain of how much longer he could endure those agonizing screams.

CHAPTER

28

SANTABRIA

In the company of Meggy Redding, Elissa's duties seemed to fade into the background after just a few days. Almost. Brea's image persisted in her thoughts. She still hoped that the child had survived the attack, even though it appeared highly improbable. Perhaps death was a kinder fate than captivity... Meggy had generously offered Elissa private quarters, although she rarely found herself there in the evenings. Instead, the two women dined together, savoring a lavish spread— roasted chicken, warm buttered bread, candied fruits, and pork stew flavored with rare spices. Contrary to expectations, the pirate was not only courteous but surprisingly playful as well. Elissa struggled to recall her last truly uplifting discussion before meeting Meggy. Interactions with Brennet lacked passion, those with Bruna depth. As for the conversations with Wil... she deliberately avoided those thoughts. Despite their differences, Meggy and Elissa delved into a multitude of subjects—politics, poetry, philosophy, literature. Elissa realized with a sting in her heart that these were topics she rarely engaged in for the sheer pleasure of it. Her life had always been a quest for utility, representing an elite society she felt detached from. The magician now eagerly anticipated the arrival of sunset, a time that marked Meggy's return to her quarters.

On the fifth day aboard the Lady Fortune, Lee delivered a neatly bound package along with a note bearing the words:

Same time, same place?

—M.R.

P.S. This piece of art cannot remain hidden any longer.

The parcel contained a stunning creation that left Elissa speechless. Unfolding it revealed a gown of such opulence it could rival royal attire. The sweetheart bodice, resplendent in emerald hues, was adorned with glistening crystals. The skirt billowed with tiers of soft tulle, reminiscent of the fashion sported by the grand ladies of Walderlake's court. Mouth gaping, Elissa tore her gaze from the magnificent fabric to meet Lee's equally astonished expression.

"Well... That's unexpected!" he muttered, his brow furrowed. With a puzzled shake of his head, Lee exited the cabin, leaving Elissa to confront this unexpected gift whose significance eluded her.

Tentatively, she discarded her worn clothes in favor of the resplendent dress, a creation that starkly contrasted with the rugged backdrop of the pirate ship. The gown complemented her flawlessly. Its verdant hue harmonized with her eyes, its intricate details enhancing her porcelain skin. Most of the bruises from her past hardships had faded, leaving her complexion visibly rejuvenated. Undoing the braid she had worn since Miranda's passing, her auburn locks cascaded freely down her shoulders. For the first time in too long, she felt elegant, even beautiful. If only Bruna could see her...

As the sun finally dipped below the horizon, Elissa mulled over changing her clothes on several occasions. Yet, she feared that declining Meggy's gift might offend her, so she approached the captain in her splendid attire. Meggy greeted her with a smirk, assessing her from head to toe with a self-assured expression. She was dressed in a more refined outfit: dark suede trousers, a light cotton shirt in the same hue, and an emerald silk corset gilded with black pearls. Her ebony curls were held back by a velvet ribbon, revealing the bronzed skin of her neck and shoulders. She extended a courteous invitation for Elissa to join her at the table and gallantly pulled out her chair. Something felt amiss. Why this extra attention, this simpering? Meggy clearly had some ulterior motive… but what?

"You look especially beautiful tonight," the captain remarked as she settled into her seat.

Perhaps she did want to steal the stone, after all. Elissa's throat tightened.

"Thank you," she responded, carefully managing her tone.

Alert and watchful, Elissa remained mostly quiet, focusing on her meal. Her mind raced. What if Wil and Finn were not truly on the ship? She had not seen them since the attack. She hastened to empty her dish, avoiding eye contact. Meggy observed her intently, her gaze inquisitive, attentive.

"Enjoying the food?" she inquired, lifting her glass of rum to her lips.

Elissa ceased chewing and glanced at the untouched contents of Meggy's plate.

"You seem nervous," Meggy probed again.

Suspicion ate at her. Poison? But if Meggy had intended to harm her, she could have easily done so during their first meal together… right?

"I'm fine," she lied, putting her fork down.

Though Meggy appeared unconvinced, she did not press the matter. Seemingly, she was not considering getting rid of Elissa… at least, not yet. So what exactly did she want from her?

"Tell me... How does a young Guardian like you spend her leisure time?"

"My leisure time?"

"Your hobbies?"

Elissa regarded her as if she had spoken in a foreign tongue. She wished to retort, but her mind was cluttered with memories of training and lessons.

"Sometimes, I visit the gardens to read some of the books my father gave me."

"So, literature is your passion?"

Elissa hesitated, her disbelief apparent. "I... suppose. Why the sudden interrogation?"

"Interrogation?" Meggy queried.

"All of this!" Elissa gestured toward the sumptuous feast and her ornate dress, too extravagant for the occasion. "What's the purpose? What do these courtesies mask?"

Meggy's expression turned a mixture of irritation and surprise.

"These are simply tokens of goodwill toward the first educated, intriguing, and charming person I've encountered in quite some time."

She reclined slightly in her seat, fingers entwined in her lap, sighing. A soft chuckle escaped her lips before she continued.

"I'm a headstrong woman, Elissa Reinhart. I don't shy away from pursuing what I desire."

There were no ulterior motives, no assassination attempts. There was just them... and the connection Meggy was trying to form. Elissa had never considered this possibility, and that realization left her disconcerted. Was she truly so broken?

"Alright then," Meggy resumed, her tone lighter. "What ignites your passion? What drives you?"

Elissa wrestled with the question, her mind a tumultuous sea of both emptiness and fullness. A weight settled in her stomach as she grappled with her answer, laced with an underlying distress she struggled to mask.

"I... I don't know."

Meggy nodded, a smirk quirking her lips.

"Fair enough. I shall take it upon myself to rectify that."

———— ••●•• ————

Elissa awoke to the pounding of drums in her head. She had ignored moderation over the past few days, though not to the extent of the previous night. Rum did not sit well with her. Still, she found its effects preferable to the relentless torment within her. Swiftly, she realized that she was not in her own quarters, but rather in Meggy's cabin... more precisely, in the woman's bed. Wrapped in a bearskin, she recoiled in horror at her own nudity. How? What had she done? She struggled to remember anything beyond vague, hazy fragments of images.

"A bit of self-control, Elissa," she chided herself with a sigh.

"You don't say!" came a mocking voice that caught her off guard.

Meggy stood by the window near her desk, holding a book. Her eyebrow arched in a mischievous expression as she observed Elissa. The Guardian's throat tightened as certain moments flashed back into her memory—the warm breath on her cheek, the scent of citrus and jasmine that Meggy exuded.

"Don't worry, I'm not an animal," Meggy scoffed, closing her novel. "I can manage my impulses quite well."

Unlike Elissa, Meggy was fully dressed. Her booted feet rested on the desk, displaying their tall, flared leather elegance.

"Apologies… I… I must have fallen asleep in your quarters," Elissa stammered, attempting to cover herself.

"I must admit, the comfort of my bed might surpass that of your cabin. That's why I arranged for you to be carried here."

Carried? Elissa's eyes darted around for her clothes, but they were nowhere to be seen.

"They're not here," Meggy remarked, moving across the room.

"Should I even ask?"

"Let's just say that Weasel is taking care of cleaning them. You don't handle your drink as well as the rest of the crew. And such a lovely dress…"

The Guardian emitted a mortified groan, her head sinking between her shoulders. She wished she could bury herself in the sheets, vanish from the Lady Fortune, and never return. Meggy chuckled as she tossed a stack of clothes in Elissa's direction.

"You can wear these while you wait. Unless you're overcome by the urge to dance naked again to beseech the Moon God?"

Consumed by shame, Elissa mechanically dressed in Meggy's garments. The ensemble consisted of a loose white shirt, cinched by a wine-red bustier enhanced with delicate black roses. Completing the look were tall, flared thigh-high boots and solid greyish trousers. Elissa could not help but smirk at her unusual reflection in the mirror.

"What's amusing you?" asked the captain, drawing closer.

"I look like a true pirate."

Meggy disappeared briefly, only to return with a tricorn hat that she placed atop Elissa's head. She then handed her a dagger with a twisted black leather grip. Elissa accepted it hesitantly, as though it were the most peculiar object on earth. Inscribed on the blade were the words "Honor binds us," the motto of Walderlake.

"Now you look like a true pirate," Meggy quipped with a smirk.

Despite the embarrassment, Elissa sighed with an odd sense of contentment, the pleasure of no longer being the girl molded in Brennet's image.

—————— ··●·· ——————

After savoring a hearty lunch, Meggy informed Elissa that Lady Fortune would be making a pit stop to replenish its food supplies. The chosen location was a small trading island nestled within the expanse of the Estriden Sea. Elissa, largely unfamiliar with its existence due to its near absence from most maps, inquired about its secrecy.

"Corsair captains must safeguard certain places of business," Meggy explained. "In case the Councils attempt to intrude upon our affairs… Santabria Island offers us rest and sanctuary."

The idea of stopping before Osthallvale, and worse yet, departing from these quarters where she had sought refuge since her arrival, filled Elissa with unease. Though the fear of those pursuing them weighed heavily, the thought of encountering Wil proved even more daunting. She did not know how to react, what words to say in his presence. She fervently wished she could erase their last moments and start anew. However, her newfound companion was determined not to let her forget. She perceived Wil's actions as an unforgivable affront, even if Elissa insisted upon his typically amiable disposition.

"If it eases your anxiety, I'd be more than willing to toss him overboard," Meggy joked, stepping out of the cabin.

She was teasing, of course… but Elissa knew that merely uttering such a desire could make it come true. Consumed by nerves, she stared at her reflection in the mirror. The purplish half-moons under her eyes had faded, and the sparkle in her gaze had regained its vibrant forest green hue. Her clothes no longer wore her, and her once pallid cheeks now exhibited a healthy flush. The sea suited her, as did Meggy's company. She took a sip from the flask her new confidante had provided. The liquid instantly warmed her throat and spirit.

The sun momentarily blinded her as she ascended to the deck, alive with bustling pirates. The horizon was clear, the vast blue sky awe-inspiring. Anchored close to the shore, Lady Fortune offered a breathtaking view of the island. Santabria, unexpectedly sizable, was teeming with towering coconut and banana trees. Crystal-clear waters lapped the white beach tenderly, akin to a lover seeking affection. Simple wooden homes with thatched roofs dotted a small verdant mountain that bore resemblance to an ancient, dormant volcano. Boats were already headed to the coast, and Elissa even managed to spot Blackbird and Weasel among them. She searched anxiously for Wil, but instead, her gaze found Meggy and Lee gesturing for her to join them on the starboard side. Without hesitation, she hastened toward them, hoping to evade the impending meeting that caused her such apprehension.

"Don't panic, he's staying on board to watch over the ship," the captain reassured her with a wink.

Elissa nodded, her expression belying her unease. Swiftly, she climbed onto one of the canoes with Lee's assistance, her anxiety somewhat alleviated.

Awaiting her on the shore was Finn, his fiery hair visible from a distance. Elissa worried he might be upset with her for her absence, but the wide grin on his face suggested otherwise.

"Elissa!" he exclaimed as she disembarked.

She had to admit, seeing him again lifted her spirits. There was something endearing about his youthful enthusiasm, his prominent ears practically vibrating with excitement. The young man rushed forward to greet her, embracing her with exuberance.

"Finally out of your sulking, are you?" he teased in a jovial tone.

Elissa chuckled. Upon closer observation, she noticed a certain change in him, a newfound ease. He seemed content, as though the sea breeze had brought about a transformation. A faint red beard was starting to form on his once-boyish face, lending him a more mature air. She also finally spotted the tattoo on his right forearm: a fox clutching a thistle. The ink appeared fresh against his slightly reddened, swollen skin.

"What's this?" she inquired.

"Oh, that? Percy's gift!" he explained, pride evident in his gaze as he admired the design.

"The fox symbolizes you, I presume," Elissa chuckled, ruffling her friend's hair.

"That's what we call him here! Fox!" Percy chimed in with his booming voice, passing by with a crate on his shoulders.

He affectionately thumped the hunter, causing him to momentarily lose balance.

"Much better than Weasel, in my opinion," Elissa whispered. "And the thistle?"

"The emblem of Earnox, a reminder of where I come from," Finn explained.

Elissa detected a note of sorrow in his voice—the sense of grief for his devastated home.

"You seem to be enjoying life on board."

"I believe so," he admitted. "Here, no one fixates on my past, on the mistakes I've made. I'm free from the constant judgment of those around me."

"I never judged you, Finn. Forgive me if I ever gave you that impression."

"You haven't done anything wrong, truly. Your morals seem so impeccable, and you... so noble, unblemished... while I... The outlaws, the undesirables... that's where I belong."

"You're too hard on yourself."

"Maybe," he shrugged. "Only time will tell."

"Are you thinking of becoming a pirate?"

"Who knows? Perhaps once all this mercenary and Council business is behind us, we'll set sail to join Lady Fortune's crew."

"Who knows!" Elissa responded with a forced smile.

She understood that her status as Guardian would limit her choices, let alone allow her to wander across oceans. She needed to come to terms with it.

As the crewmen loaded the canoes with supplies for the upcoming journey, Meggy led Elissa, Finn, and Lee to the island's sole tavern, La Reina. An uncomfortable blend of tobacco, alcohol, and sweat permeated the air, a scent oddly akin to that aboard the ship. Despite being a haunt frequented by the empire's outlaws and rogues, Elissa curiously felt a sense of security there. Perhaps it was due to Meggy's presence or the distance that now separated her from Walderlake. In any case, her mind seemed calmer. She followed Meggy to an unoccupied table in the back, aware of the room's collective gaze fixed on the captain. Everyone in this seedy establishment recognized her. Some nodded with respect, while others glanced away almost fearfully. The woman Elissa had grown acquainted with over the past few days was so remarkably different from the fearsome pirate that the world perceived her to be. The group settled at the table: Elissa beside Meggy, Finn adjacent to Lee. A black velvet pouch, filled with clinking coins, was placed before the captain. Without delay, the innkeeper, a middle-aged woman of robust build with eyes as blue as the lagoon, hurried over.

"The fearsome Meggy Redding!" she exclaimed, a grin lighting up her face. "A pleasure to see you once more! What can I get for you?"

"The usual, Cixtia! And some food, please."

"The cook's absent today... perhaps..."

Meggy paid no heed to the end of the explanation, promptly plunging her hand into her frock coat. She retrieved a necklace decked with black diamonds and placed it before the innkeeper.

"Right… right away," the older woman stammered, her eyes widening.

In a blink, an ample feast appeared before them, accompanied by several dusty wine bottles.

"No rum?" Elissa pondered, raising an eyebrow. "I'm shocked!"

"I have easy access to rum on my ship. The alcohol in Santabria, however… Cixtia runs the finest wine cellar in the entire empire."

"I propose a toast!" Lee exclaimed, lifting his cup. "To our captain who guides us toward good fortune every day!"

With enthusiasm, they joined in, while Meggy remained quietly beaming, a subtle smile gracing her lips.

"I'd like to propose a toast as well," she eventually added, refilling her glass. "To new friends, those who drink, fight, and fornicate by our side!"

Elissa choked on her sip at those words, and Finn and Lee echoed Meggy, emptying their goblets in one swig.

"Oh, I almost forgot! People of Brevic are not animals!" Meggy smirked, casting an ardent look at Elissa.

Heat surged into the Guardian's cheeks, something within her igniting. She did not know whether it was the wine's effect, but she met the captain's gaze with a smile.

"There's a first time for everything, right?" she whispered in a flirty tone she had never employed before.

Meggy did not respond verbally but looked at her approvingly, an inviting gleam dancing in her amber eyes.

"Wil!" Finn exclaimed, motioning toward the tavern entrance.

The fire within Elissa waned, her excitement replaced by a crushing sensation as she spotted him through the crowd at the back. His expression seemed melancholic, his eyes fixed on the ground as his fingers nervously raked in his blond hair. The mage's heart raced, fighting her urge to rush over to hug him, or hit him… or maybe both. She was unsure how to react, whether to speak or flee. Her mind scrambled, needing silence. She swiftly grabbed Finn's glass and downed its contents. Finn seemed about to protest but thought better of it upon seeing her agitation.

"What are you doing here?" Meggy barked before the knight even reached their table.

"The crew was considering bringing more cattle on board Lady Fortune."

"You were meant to stay on the ship," the captain added dryly.

"Percy begged me to assist in moving the supplies," he replied simply, his voice hushed.

"Percy? I'm the officer in charge!" Lee retorted sternly.

"They couldn't find you," Wil clarified, glancing at the table laden with drinks. "They seemed desperate and worn out. With no higher authority present, we had to make a decision."

"W-well," Lee muttered with slight embarrassment. "I'm going before that fool loads a whole barn onto the ship."

The officer excused himself with a hat tip and exited promptly.

Wil finally met Elissa's gaze, causing her to freeze in her seat. She felt acutely aware of each breath, every flutter within her. He said nothing, but she sensed a tale hidden behind his lips. With a nod of farewell, Wil broke their eye contact.

As he prepared to leave, Meggy's voice rang out, halting him in his tracks.

"Wil Strongbow, isn't it?" she queried.

Slowly, he turned, his gaze shifting between the two women.

"Sit," she ordered, gesturing to the vacant seat beside Finn.

Elissa was sure she glimpsed a flicker in the knight's eyes. The set of his jaw, the crease that appeared between his brows… it was clear that the command, one more fitting for a dog, insulted him deeply. Nonetheless, he maintained his composure and complied. Meggy regarded him for a moment, a trace of arrogance in her gaze, while Wil remained motionless. Settling back into her seat, she filled a cup and handed it to him with an irreverent gesture. Finn, now more uneasy than ever, cleared his throat, breaking the silence.

"This wine is quite something, Captain Redding."

"Pleased you enjoy it. Courtesy of Brilea's most renowned vineyard!"

Her attention shifted back to the warrior, akin to a predator spotting its prey.

"Brilea! Have you ever set foot there?" she inquired.

"Once or twice," he responded cautiously.

"A splendid country! Its survival owes much to your father, doesn't it? Owen Strongbow?"

Wil blinked, his pause stretching a fraction too long.

"Indeed," he replied dryly.

"So you're following in his footsteps? Aiming to become a hero?"

"I wouldn't dare compare myself to him."

"The weight of such a famous father must be quite frustrating! Is that why you appear to struggle to control the anger that consumes you?"

His glare could have set her aflame and Elissa trembled. Was it fear? Or desire? The alcohol clouded her judgment. The urge to intervene surged, yet the electric tension between them kept her in check. Finn, with his wide eyes and lips drawn into a thin line, seemed to share her sentiment.

"I'd be honored to be half the man my father was. But I am my own person," Wil responded cautiously.

"A man who thought it appropriate to strike a woman who refuses to submit to him?"

Meggy maintained her unwavering stare on Wil, drawing Elissa closer and draping an arm over her shoulders. Despite his seething anger, he held himself back, his jaw clenched even tighter. He then turned his imploring gaze to the mage.

"Elissa, you know me... I..."

He let out a resigned sigh, aware that his words would likely carry little weight. She had expressed her sentiments during their last encounter in the forest. He shook his head, continuing in a tone both sincere and defeated.

"I'm so sorry. Panic took hold... I thought you were willingly walking into danger. I pictured the downfall of Walderlake... of all of Balt'boec! I couldn't stand idly by. I couldn't let you go, not when the fate of our kingdom rests in your hands!"

Oh, the kingdom's fate! Not hers. Elissa edged closer to Meggy, defiance lighting her inebriated and emotional expression.

"Naturally, your life means more than Walderlake," he added, visibly irritated by the proximity of the two women. "The thought of finding you lifeless like Miranda... of losing the person I once pinned hopes on... I couldn't bear it."

Better.

"So you justify your actions while cowardly blaming her? Is that your stance?" Meggy continued, seemingly unimpressed by Wil's words. "Isn't it ironic? You employ anger and brutality to regain control over situations slipping from your grasp, yet in the process, you relinquish this control to that very rage."

"Think you know everything about me?" he growled.

"Men like you hold no secrets from me," the pirate retorted, her hand stroking Elissa's arm.

"This arrogance, this superiority complex… and yet! You can't deny that violence shapes our lives. Unlike you, I'm aware of my vulnerabilities." he replied.

Meggy erupted into a cruel laughter, and Elissa sensed that he had struck a nerve.

"A deserter who still aims to serve the nation! Why through her, though? Guilt, perhaps? Or righteousness?"

A cunning smile curled her lips as she fixed her gaze on Elissa.

"Ah, I see! It's not logical thinking when it comes to her. You fear something might be taken from you, something you haven't yet managed to put your mitts on."

Wil's expression darkened, his struggle to contain his emotions evident.

"What's wrong, little man? Did I hit a nerve?"

Her fingers danced provocatively along Elissa's thigh.

Caught between two storms, Elissa found her voice drowned by their intensity. Throughout the conversation, she had not uttered a word. They spoke on her behalf… for the timid and uncertain Elissa. Yet, she could easily overpower anyone at this table if she chose.

"Enough," she growled, her tone low but firm.

Wil, Meggy, and Finn all turned to her.

"Enough," she reiterated, her voice gaining strength. "I'm not a commodity to be won. Nor will I participate in this odd rivalry between you two. This game you're playing holds no interest for me."

"I'm not playing you," Wil countered swiftly, his expression earnest. "I only wanted…"

"I know," Elissa interrupted, her tone colder than she intended. "I understand your rationale, the way you believed you were protecting your homeland. That's what you were taught. But it doesn't excuse your actions."

He nodded slowly, his bewilderment evident. A heavy void seemed to expand in her chest. Her attachment to him remained unwavering despite the resentment that suffocated her. Meggy chuckled, subtly but audibly. Wil glared at her with fury, leaning closer to his rival.

"You didn't tell her the truth, did you?" he said, his teeth bared. "You didn't clarify the real reason why you keep her so close to you?"

Elissa immediately turned her gaze to Meggy. Meanwhile, Finn's head dropped, and he seemed to contemplate escaping the scene. The pirate remained silent, and for the first time since their initial meeting, Elissa noticed unease in her demeanor.

"Why did the illustrious Meggy Redding agree to let us set foot on her ship? Kindness had little to do with it, believe me!" Wil's voice persisted.

A drawn expression appeared on the woman's face, and she withdrew her arm from around the Guardian's shoulders.

"Answer him," Elissa interjected with an icy command.

Clearing her throat, the captain carefully distanced herself.

"When your companions asked me for passage to Osthallvale, I sensed immediately that this was no ordinary group of travelers. No sane person would undertake such a journey... unless driven by an entirely unconventional purpose. I saw in you a woman of exceptional abilities, a force of nature. You... you seemed like a pivotal asset in my own quest."

"We're not heading to Osthallvale," Wil revealed gravely.

A queasiness churned in the Guardian's stomach, and for a moment, the room appeared to sway.

"At least, not directly," Meggy added, as if this statement might quell the mounting anger.

Elissa was not sure what expression she wore, what furious scowl distorted her features, but it seemed to frighten those around the table.

"Give me an explanation," she snarled through clenched teeth.

"Perhaps I should join Lee," Finn muttered, as if contemplating an exit strategy.

However, the look Elissa gave him froze him in place.

"Or I can stay put!" he quickly amended, his chuckle tinged with unease.

Meggy cleared her throat once more before proceeding cautiously.

"There's a man... a despicable individual who deserves to be eradicated from this world."

Elissa's laughter erupted, startling everyone at the table.

"A personal vendetta, is it?" she retorted with a touch of disdain.

"I suggest you let her finish," Wil responded, his tone weighty.

The mage waited anxiously, taken aback by the knight's sudden alliance with the captain.

"This man... he goes by the name Alden Grenbryel," she explained, shuddering with disgust. "He's the reason I embarked on a life at sea."

She paused, her expression becoming laden with a tormented heaviness.

"For years, I've scoured the oceans, driven by one goal: to make him pay for the unspeakable crimes he perpetrated against my village... against me."

"What sort of crimes?" Elissa inquired.

"Atrocities borne of a twisted mind," she replied without elaborating further.

Elissa's thoughts raced through the possible horrors those words encompassed, yet she decided it was best not to press for details.

"I don't deny the agony Alden inflicted, but this is not my battle to fight. I can't keep the stone away from our land for too long."

"On the contrary," Wil countered. "His family's influence is growing within Walderlake. Their voices resound in the court. His uncle, Zaff Grenbryel, leads Aegis' troops in their campaign against the druids."

"Your former commander?"

Wil's back stiffened as he nodded, continuing his explanation.

"Livius, Alden's father, wields power on the Emerald Council. Cloven, Alden's younger brother, is also a member. Parrish Grenbryel, his cousin, commands the nation's naval militia. I'm convinced they orchestrated the massacre of your household."

"But... what about Toran Sius?" Elissa stammered.

"Toran Sius is corrupt, yes. I'd pay a high price to see him face retribution from the kingdom! However, the Grenbryels pull his strings. Especially Livius..."

"Why didn't you share this with me earlier?" she interjected, her voice carefully controlled. "Isn't this the kind of information that should be disclosed? We've discussed so many topics, Meggy... why not this one?"

Wil's gaze shifted to Meggy, and Elissa sensed a tinge of mockery in his expression. The captain's eyes briefly dropped before she replied.

"Considering your state at the time, I was afraid you'd decline my offer."

"So, you chose to hide your true intentions and decide for me?"

"I was only waiting for the right moment to reveal it."

"And you thought La Reina was the best time and place to do so?" Elissa shot back, gesturing toward the encroaching patrons.

Her breath quivered, and her lips, her fingers... her whole being. The right words eluded her, yet the fire... that surge of lava she felt, the same that obliterated the young mage in the forest. And the warmth that coursed through her...

"Elissa!" Finn exclaimed, staring at the fiery glow emanating from her hands.

She saw it too: her palms ablaze, scorching the oak table like a red-hot iron. With horror, she snatched her hands back, realizing her loss of control. Panic doused her anger, and she sprang to her feet, her gaze locked on the burned imprints etched into the wood. Their eyes fixed on her—Wil, Meggy, Finn, even Cixtia, who approached with a fresh bottle. She needed to leave, right now.

"Where are you going?" Wil questioned before she could slip away.

"Back to the ship."

"Elissa!" Meggy called out, standing up. "I just didn't want to rush you."

"I survived the massacres of the Cercle of Am, Brevic, and Earnox. I escaped the clutches of that cursed forest and those assassins. I'm no fragile child in need of unwavering protection. Right now, I have to rest. I want to wield my powers with full control when we confront Alden Grenbryel."

A smirk tugged at the corners of Meggy's mouth as Elissa strode toward the exit.

"Tomorrow, we'll initiate a plan to rid our land of those destroying Walderlake's spirit."

"Finn!" the mage beckoned, urging him to follow.

The hunter sprang to his feet, saluting the captain with a sheepish grin before hastening after the Guardian, who stormed out of La Reina.

CHAPTER

29

UNCONSCIOUS

This family, the Grenbryels, perhaps they were the architects of the massacre that claimed her household. Meggy was offering her retribution on a silver platter. Yet, the clandestine nature, the manipulation, the games... it all diverged starkly from the world she envisioned. What she anticipated from Wil or Meggy did not align with this reality. At least, there was Finn. Finn, the scoundrel, the liar, the outcast. Oddly enough, he was the one who shared the most unfiltered truths with her. Her friend. She had led him to her quarters, her sole intention being to drown her disappointment in alcohol. Seated on her bed, the ginger-haired lad prattled on, discussing everything and nothing, judiciously avoiding the altercation in La Reina. She was grateful.

After two cups of cider, her inner turbulence was not suppressed. Amidst Finn's playful antics, Elissa observed a subtle scrutiny in his gaze, a reluctance to voice his thoughts frankly.

"Go ahead," she slurred in her inebriated state. "I can tell you're itching to share what's on your mind."

He hesitated, then flopped onto the bed with a sigh, nervously tousling his fiery locks.

"Do you really want to hear what I think?" he asked, his tone tinged with apprehension.

Elissa nodded. She was resolute about her friends not censoring their words around her.

"I think you underestimate yourself," he began. "I'm not talking about your abilities... the ones that unnerve you so. I mean you, the person—devoid of magic or facade. You're fading, Elissa."

"I'm trying," she murmured. "Believe me, I am."

"I don't doubt it," he replied, a kind smile gracing his lips. "Maybe if you saw yourself through my eyes, a woman who risks her life for strangers without flinching, you'd realize the place you genuinely deserve."

She nodded, letting his words linger. Downing the contents of her cup, she then stretched out beside him.

"I didn't anticipate friendship being so challenging," she mused.

"So, our conversation annoys you?" Finn inquired with a hint of amusement in his sleep-laden voice.

"Not ours. The one at the tavern, though..."

"Are you sure you're really talking about friendship?" the drowsy man quipped.

Touché. A wry half-smile curved the Guardian's lips.

"Why is it so complicated?" she pondered aloud.

"Maybe you become too attached to anyone who offers even a bit of attention," Finn replied, stifling a yawn. "You seem so eager to fall in love with those who give you their devotion and protection that you don't take the time to truly get to know them."

A frown knit her brow.

"I might do the same if my past were like yours," he added with a scoff.

He placed a comforting hand over hers.

"There. A touch of genuine, platonic affection."

Was it true? Was she quick to fall for those who bestowed the attention she had once yearned for? The knight's shielding, his support—and the embrace he had shared with her within the temple of Itos... Such sensations were so new to her. What did she perceive in him? What could truly develop between a deserter and a Guardian hunted by her own realm? And Meggy, who appeared so willing to bare her soul? She promised adventure and revelation, ardor and flames. Yet, perhaps it was all too idyllic to be genuine.

"I'm frightened, Finn... I dread falling short of expectations, of being blinded by vengeance rather than fulfilling my duty. Brennet urged me to hasten to Osthallvale, yet now I'm on the trail of a man I didn't even know existed this morning."

"You heard Meggy and Wil. The emerald will never be safe with him lurking."

"I understand... but my father had a reason for wanting me on the Minotaur continent."

"Do you think Meggy's cause is ill-timed?"

"Believe me, this is a battle I wish to defend... but when the moment is right. I sense something unsettling about this..."

As her words ebbed, she realized the pulse within her belonged to anxiety, to uncertainty. A voice warned her that she was not prepared for this confrontation, that this rendezvous would unleash chaos.

"Finn?"

But the hunter was already lost in slumber. Elissa sighed, surrendering to the embrace of her own dreams.

———— ··●·· ————

Elissa woke to the sensation of a warm, slightly rough hand caressing her cheek, a hand accustomed to wielding weapons. In the dimness, she beheld Wil's face next to hers. The sight did not startle her; it felt like the most natural thing in the world. His breath brushed her lips as his thumb traced the line of her jaw. The exhilaration she experienced at the tavern paled in comparison to this.

"Elissa, I..."

She silenced him with an index finger on his mouth, preventing him from delving into explanations. Her rationality and resentment seemed to have evaporated. The man who typically took charge now looked hesitant. Guilt was not his usual companion. Acting on impulse, Elissa bridged the gap between their lips. He appeared taken aback, and a soft moan escaped him as her fingers weaved through his silken hair. She realized she had yearned to touch those wheat-blond locks since they first met. Wil's restraint dissipated as he explored the contours of her body. Her heart raced as he lifted his mouth from hers, descending to her neck. For a moment, nothing else existed.

Then, a throat clearing disrupted the scene. Elissa's gaze locked with Meggy's, the captain observing from the cabin entrance, a mischievous grin playing on her lips. With languid grace, she advanced, clad in a simple, almost ethereal nightgown. In different circumstances, Elissa might have been unsure about such displays, which still felt novel. But her longing overpowered any hesitation. Wil assisted her in straightening up, wrapping an arm around her. Meggy approached, as if the discord between them had vanished, as if the trio had been lovers for ages. Why? That thought dissolved quickly as Meggy's lips met hers without constraint or shame. Natural. It all seemed so natural. Amidst these beings radiating fiery passion, Elissa surrendered control. Time ceased to matter, along with her inhibitions. She tore off Wil's shirt, revealing his scarred, muscular torso. Among the scars was the one inflicted by the sylvan raven, a mark she tenderly traced with her fingers. Thanks to Finn, only that ivory mark remained from the horrifying attack on Wil's skin.

Finn... Where was he? He had dozed off next to her in her cabin. A startling realization hit her; she was no longer in her quarters. Fairly unfamiliar surroundings met her eyes. Based on the bamboo structure above and the canvas walls, she was in an elaborate hut. Colorful veils and golden coin garlands enhanced the ceiling. Jade trinkets shaped like various animals decorated the furniture. The fragrance of agarwood and eucalyptus filled the night air, distinct from Lady Fortune's scent. She was unfamiliar with this place... and the man who now stood where Wil had been...

Gasping, her eyes widened. The stranger's face, perhaps the most captivating she had ever seen, seemed to glow in the shadows. A cascade of dark locks framed his slightly gaunt cheeks and well-defined jawline. He was young, younger than her at least. He appeared as stunned as she was, remaining motionless, almost nude, and staring.

"Who are you?" he inquired, his voice melodic.

More curious than astonished, he seemed. Pulling herself together, Elissa could not avert her gaze from his dark, indescribable eyes.

"E-Elissa..."

"Elissa," he echoed, nodding as though her name held meaning. "How did you find your way into my chamber?"

"Your chamber?"

The hut dissolved, replaced by a grand room in a luxurious villa. The bed they occupied could comfortably accommodate three more people. She noticed the sapphire-colored blankets, upon which the man knelt. Embroidered in silver thread was a raven in the center of a crescent moon—the emblem of Wynnorth.

"I must be dreaming, right?" he queried.

He extended a hand to touch her face, as if contact would confirm his suspicions. Elissa gently clasped it, an intense jolt coursing through her, akin to the sensation during her bonding with the emerald. Her surroundings tumbled, leaving her uncertain where her body ended and his began. Amidst this almost unbearable distortion, his features blurred, and his face finally dissolved into darkness.

Nothing remained; only emptiness. Anxious, she shut her eyes, attempting to wake. Her efforts were futile, and panic seized her. Tearfully, she searched the void, not quite sure what she sought.

"Wake up, wake up, wake up…"

Her pleas echoed unanswered, and she was trapped in shadows. She was a prisoner of this darkness.

"Interesting," a small voice spoke behind her.

Swiftly turning, she saw a woman… an elf. Her angular face framed by almost silver-blond hair showcased pointy ears. Vibrant garnet eyes regarded her with a nearly inquisitive curiosity. It was a dream; all of it was a dream.

"For now," the elf whispered, seemingly aware of Elissa's thoughts.

"Who are you?"

"Aelrie," the odd interlocutor replied simply.

The name sounded familiar…

"The Oracle of Cendril. My father told me about you."

She nodded, a glimmer of hope dancing in her large, bulging eyes.

"Are you… are you still alive?"

"I think so… sometimes I wonder," the elf confessed.

"Where are you imprisoned? Perhaps I can help you."

Aelrie offered a pained but grateful smile.

"Wynnorth! But I fear you cannot help me. The queen... she will keep me captive until my sanity shatters and my mind breaks."

"Wynnorth," Elissa whispered.

Once more, a whirlwind formed, shrouding her in darkness. Breathless, she felt herself traverse the universe, yet remained motionless. Shadows eventually gave way to the villa from moments ago. The handsome young man still stood, as she left him, bewildered and concerned as he gazed at her.

"How... how are you doing that?" he mumbled hoarsely.

She did not know and had no words for him. Aelrie materialized in a corner of the room, her expression just as baffled as the stranger's.

"The Oracle... of Cendril!" Elissa exclaimed, pointing at the blond woman. "We must free her."

The man turned to look but seemed oblivious to the elf clearly present.

"I... I don't see anyone," he breathed, his concerned gaze locking onto Elissa's.

"We need to assist her!" she insisted, drawing nearer to him. "You're in Wynnorth, correct?"

Though unfamiliar, he brought a sense of ease and familiarity. Could he be a manifestation of her subconscious?

Or perhaps...

"Why, for now?" she asked with a touch of despair, turning her question to the elf. "Is this just a dream?"

The Oracle regarded her solemnly, but the man's response came before Aelrie could speak.

"Wynnorth, yes. Elissa... why do you..."

His words were interrupted as he placed a hand over hers, disappearing again into the swirling abyss of darkness.

The Guardian found herself once more facing Aelrie, her breath ragged and full of anguish.

"Why, for now?" she pressed, her tone insistent.

"I don't fully understand how, but you managed to enter a part of my mind through your dreams."

"Why is this young man also here?"

"I've seen him in my visions before. I imagine you somehow connected with him and pulled him into one of them."

"So he's real?"

Aelrie nodded slowly, her expression veering toward a troubled vacancy.

"You say that I drew him into your mind. But why him?"

"I believe a special force binds you, an unchanging power."

"Destiny?"

"No, destiny is changeable."

The air seemed to escape from Elissa's lungs, the impact of realization akin to a punch in the stomach. She had been right all along. All this time.

"Elissa..."

The voice resonated from every direction, an intense echo within the vast void. A shared glance with the elf conveyed their mutual understanding—someone was attempting to rouse her from this state.

"Elissa..."

Not now, not when Aelrie could potentially provide so many answers. Her body trembled, mirroring the expanding darkness around her. The Oracle's face clouded over.

"Who is this man? Why are we linked?" the Guardian exclaimed.

"You must awaken," Aelrie's words echoed, disembodied and haunting.

"ELISSA!"

Finn's voice reached her, piercing the void as Aelrie vanished. The urgency and fear in his plea made her heart leap in her chest. What was happening? She had to open her eyes.

NOW.

CHAPTER

30

TREACHERY

Elyndel's return to Cendril transpired uneventfully, although his inner emptiness seemed to intensify with each mile that separated him from the East. The scent of lilacs and lush greenery, a stark contrast to Wynnorth, greeted him upon his homecoming. He had missed his residence, but not as much as the familiar faces he had encountered daily for centuries. Nemeryn, his valet, emerged from the Arren family mansion with an air of eagerness to welcome him. The broad smile that adorned his androgynous face, framed by cascades of fiery-red locks, conveyed the deep affection the valet held for his master.

"Here you are!" Nemeryn exclaimed, punctuating his words with a brief but respectful nod.

Elyndel had no inclination to be addressed in the manner befitting powerful lords. The exaggerated bows and elaborate curtsies were foreign to him. He cherished the authenticity and ease that came with interacting with his people.

"How was everything during my absence?" inquired the Master.

"It went well. However, Lady Naefiel paid a visit a few times."

"Analera? What for?"

"It appeared she wanted to confirm you were still abroad. Regrettably, I couldn't glean her intentions as she kept her distance from the residence. She cast glances toward the windows and then departed swiftly."

A sigh escaped Elyndel. Memories resurfaced, reminding him of the reasons he had chosen to sever any ambiguous ties with Analera.

"A missive arrived yesterday morning," the servant informed, handing Elyndel an envelope.

The Master immediately recognized the intertwined symbols of a willow tree and a snake, confirming its sender: the emblem of Guverl'yt... Valera's. With a nod of gratitude to the valet, Elyndel waited until Nemeryn's fiery tresses disappeared within the mansion before he opened the letter, an odd sense of trepidation settling in.

"The queen, the mother, and the woman thank you.

—Valera."

Surprisingly, he found himself more taken aback by the brevity of her message than by its content. He had expected a lengthy missive from her, yet this concise note carried an unexpected weight of acknowledgment. It dawned on him that this letter must have been dispatched before his departure from the East, indicating that Valera had been unable to convey her sentiments to him in person. Nonetheless, it was evident that Nilyan's persuasive powers over Brilea's queen had yielded results. Elyndel resolved to reward Nilyan generously for his efforts, acknowledging the burden it must have placed on the man's conscience.

Elyndel spent the following two days attempting to dispel the rumors swirling around Cendril. Toran Sius's outburst had cast doubt on Walderlake's true allegiance, overshadowing any previous suspicions about the Emerald Council's intentions. The growing apprehension among the Elven community made it challenging for Elyndel to convince Cendril's influential citizens that war with their neighbor was not imminent. He recognized the shortcomings of his people—despite their noble and scholarly temperaments, they often hesitated to embrace other cultures and were prone to self-centeredness and arrogance, leading to their self-imposed isolation from the outside world.

Despite their indifference, Elyndel focused on crafting defense strategies to present to the Amethyst Council. From his desk, he gazed out the window at the changing colors of autumn across the moors, contemplating the need to protect the land from marauding creatures intent on its destruction.

"Looking for someone?" Analera's sudden appearance startled Elyndel, who had been lost in thought. She stood in the doorway, wearing a diaphanous jade gown, her hair pulled back tightly.

"Forgive the intrusion," she continued with an inscrutable smile. "Your charming valet let me in."

Approaching with feline grace, her amethyst eyes fixed on him, Analera seemed to regard him as her prey.

"Hello, Ana," Elyndel replied evenly. "I trust your return went well. You left rather abruptly…"

"The atmosphere of Wynnorth did not suit me," she said, trailing her fingertips across the desk as if searching for something.

"Nemeryn mentioned your frequent visits."

"Nemeryn exaggerates. I merely stopped by once or twice."

"Is something wrong?"

"No. Your informants were simply awaiting your return."

She handed him a parchment marked with the initials E.R., followed by what appeared to be coordinates.

"They've finally located her," he murmured.

With relief, he discovered that Elissa Reinhart was no longer in Walderlake; instead, she was situated near a cluster of trade islands amidst the Estriden.

"I'll dispatch a militia to ensure her safe passage. According to Toran Sius, the pursuers of the new Guardian are particularly formidable. Hopefully, we'll reach her before they do."

"That will have to wait. The king has summoned us."

Her suggestive tone had dissolved into acerbity, an air of menace settling over her delicate features.

"Is everything alright?" Elyndel queried, rising from his seat.

Stepping back, she averted her gaze from him. In that instant, Elyndel understood the reason for her sudden change in demeanor. Valera's missive lay open on his desk, in plain view of the White Lady. For a moment, guilt gnawed at him, even though nothing but a political alliance remained between him and the Eastern ruler. Though he knew he owed Analera no loyalty, he could not help but harbour a degree of compassion for her.

"The king insists that we join him at our lair as soon as possible," she responded in a curt voice.

"I was already en route."

She nodded, feigning detachment, though a faint purse of her lips betrayed her true intent.

"Ana, I…"

"We should hurry. Bad weather approaches."

Her tone was sharper than ever, yet Elyndel lacked the patience or energy to delve into the matter. Their relationship had often been marred by unspoken grievances and wounded emotions. This recurrent pattern was likely why their romance perpetually waned. The Master required no further urging and hastened to the secret chamber, trailing Analera in silence.

———— · • ● • · ————

"I'm surprised she allowed you to leave. The queen, I mean," Analera suddenly remarked as they strolled down the path leading into the forest.

"Valera has no authority over me. I can do as I please."

Analera chuckled ahead of the Master, her brisk strides projecting an air of defiance. Though her face was hidden from view, Elyndel could perceive the bitterness etching her features.

"Did her coquettish smiles and doe-like eyes not enchant you?" she mused. "The memory of you two dancing cheek to cheek still lingers vividly."

Ah.

"Why harbour such jealousy toward the queen?"

"Jealousy? How could I possibly envy someone as loathsome as Valera Netherborne?"

"Nothing happened…"

"Of course," Analera interjected with an acerbic edge.

"I share no intimate relationship with her, and even if I did…"

Elyndel paused, recognizing that saying more would only inflict further ache upon the White Lady. She eventually turned, her eyes reflecting a blend of pain and reproach. Naturally, she guessed the direction of his thoughts.

"You are free to do as you please, Elyndel."

With those words, she pivoted on her heels and strode away without waiting for his response. After a moment's hesitation, he followed suit, yet he refrained from catching up to her. He understood that distance and silence were the only balm he could offer.

———— ··•·· ————

Surprisingly, Tanyll was already in their lair and accompanied, moreover. Princess Satya sat next to him, her lovely face etched with concern. She wore a golden chiffon dress that harmonized beautifully with her ebony complexion, a white cape held in place by delicate gold chains. Bronze dragon scales enhanced the shoulders of her cloak, trophies of her father's battle prowess. Her hair was woven into a dark crown, revealing the delicate expanse of her neck enhanced with a pendant—a deer surrounded by stars—the emblem of Cendril. Her olive eyes met the Master's gaze, instantly conveying her distress. This expression was a rarity, given that Satya usually radiated joy and vivacity. Elyndel paused briefly to collect himself and hide his surprise at this unexpected intrusion. He exchanged a glance with his king, unveiling the evident toll that recent events had taken. His eyes were red, swollen, and wearied. The once fresh and vibrant complexion now appeared pallid, even sickly.

"You wished to speak with me, Your Majesty?" the Chief Magistrate inquired cautiously.

"Yes. Please, have a seat, Elyndel."

No pleasantries, no smiles. Tanyll's voice held a peculiar monotony and fatigue. There was a certainty in Elyndel's mind now; something had deeply unsettled the king. He obliged and took his place at the table, aware of the scrutinizing gaze of both the sovereign and his daughter. Analera lingered at a distance, her silence laden with an air of sternness.

"Are you well?" Elyndel inquired, his empathy evident.

"We need to strategize on how to track them... the traitors," Tanyll replied, his voice low and breathy, as if he was speaking more to himself.

"I understand the urgency of that matter," Elyndel affirmed, nodding. He could sense Satya's shared discomfort. Usually, the king and his daughter seemed united, in league.

"I've compiled an extensive list... a list of potential traitors," Tanyll continued, his intensity unsettling.

Elyndel had seen this expression before among the various rulers of Balt'boec. This paranoia, the tendency to teeter on the precipice of madness... perhaps it was an inevitable progression for those who held power for too long.

"While I acknowledge your concerns, I believe that recklessly hunting down presumed adversaries would only squander precious time needed to fortify our defenses. A dragon assault on our realm would be catastrophic... infinitely more dire than internal traitors," Elyndel reasoned.

"Reckless? I've spent the past few days investigating, and I'm convinced that I've pinpointed those who pose a threat," Tanyll countered, his gaze unwavering.

Elyndel's eyes scanned the parchment handed to him by the king. It was exhaustive—shockingly so. Several familiar names caught his attention. Leaders from the most influential Cendril families, magistrates of the Amethyst Council, commanders of their armies who had historically been loyal... The list bordered on the absurd, the insane.

"I... I'm at a loss for words," he admitted, his astonishment palpable. "What are these suspicions based on?"

"Talk of rebellion against the crown, acts that betray our nation... collaboration with our enemies," Analera declared firmly from her position across the room.

Despite his efforts to remain impassive, a shadow passed over Elyndel's features. He was aware of the implications of her words. Analera rarely spoke without a specific aim in mind. Still, he found it difficult to accept that she would support Tanyll in this madness, frustration or not. Her actions were usually guided by reason, which was why he frequently turned to her for counsel.

"Father ... you cannot continue to track all these individuals," the princess interjected. "You seem oblivious to the toll it's taking on your health... your well-being."

"I understand your concerns, my child, but the safety of our realm holds greater significance to me than my own condition. We must eliminate the traitors on this list before they commit an irreparable act," Tanyll stated with an ominous gravitas, his expression resolute and unwavering.

"You intend to target our allies based solely on suspicion?" Satya exclaimed in disbelief. "It contradicts the principles our dynasty has upheld throughout the ages."

"Times change," the king replied, detachedly.

Elyndel shifted his gaze between Tanyll and his daughter. It was difficult to fathom that the man he had served for so long could utter such words. Tanyll was just, fair. A few weeks ago, he would have never chosen this path. Elyndel knew he had to prevent this nonsensical conversation from spiraling further. He attempted to remain calm, to persuade.

"I believe we could explore a less... drastic alternative," he ventured.

"The imminent perils necessitate drastic measures," Analera countered.

"Since when does that involve murdering innocent people?" Elyndel retorted. "I seem to have missed the moment such a proposal gained approval."

"Likely while you were in the embrace of the Queen of Guverl'yt!" Analera spat.

"I reiterate, Valera and I maintain a strictly diplomatic connection."

Analera scoffed, her aggression palpable.

"Quite diplomatic, considering she sends you letters directly to your residence as tokens of gratitude."

Elyndel sighed. How did they get here? While he had tried to spare Analera's feelings, he understood his attempts were futile, and perhaps even perilous. He refused to become a pawn in their rhetoric, in this madness that had gripped them during his absence. For the first time in ages, he wanted to allow his frustration to dictate his actions and leave the room immediately. However, he remembered his privileged position, his title that he aimed to honor. Thus, he regained his composure and continued.

"Tell me, where are the Montallis brothers? And Syviis? This is a conversation that would benefit from their perspectives," he asked with measured calm.

"Regrettably, my trust in them has faded," Tanyll replied, exchanging a secretive nod with the White Lady.

"What does that imply?"

"Don't feign such astonishment, Elyndel. Wasn't it Nilyan who orchestrated Fabyan Netherborne's release, a ruler hostile to us?" Analera retorted, her pointed gaze oozing with disdain.

"Under my directive! The kingdoms mustn't clash while a common adversary threatens the realm."

"A directive on which you should have consulted me," the king rebuked.

"I admit my intervention was hasty, and I'm willing to accept your reprimand. Nilyan was hesitant to engage with the Brileans. He deserves no condemnation."

"I will determine who warrants chastisement," Tanyll growled in a tone rarely employed. "While the decision may have been yours, Nilyan acted based on his loyalty to you... the same loyalty that guides Syviis and Gareath."

"Do you question their allegiance to you, my king? My sister has dedicated herself wholeheartedly to the Council, just as Nilyan and Gareath have to the crown."

"I've never denied that," Tanyll countered, yet his intent was unmistakable.

"Is this why you summoned me?" the Chief Magistrate inquired dryly. "To debate the loyalty of your closest allies?"

Tanyll smirked irreverently, a jarring contrast to his usual demeanor.

"You're likely curious about why my daughter is present," the king chuckled, brushing a hand against Satya's cheek. Elyndel saw the bewilderment in the princess' reaction, signifying that she, too, was unaware of the motive behind this meeting.

"I have a plan that involves her... all three of you."

Anxiety and confusion hung in the air, and Elyndel waited, uncertain.

"We never responded to Queen Valera's proposition," Tanyll began. "I intend for Prince Farklyn to join us soon to formally announce his engagement to Satya."

The young elf turned toward him so swiftly it seemed as if an invisible force had slapped her.

"Father, you can't possibly..."

"Fear not, child! It shall be a brief marriage," Tanyll interjected with a sadistic half-smile.

"You would you wish to end his life?" Elyndel immediately questioned. "Farklyn hardly appears threatening to me. If there's even a slight chance of restoring amicable relations between the East and the West, I'm certain the prince holds the key. He possesses greater reason and pragmatism compared to Valera or Fabyan."

"What devotion to the Netherborne, Elyndel!" Analera exclaimed. "Do you forget the kingdom you're obliged to serve?"

"I could direct the same question to you, considering your own jealousy is clouding your judgment."

"I believe that I more than amply demonstrated my loyalty to Cendril the day I executed Taegen for his treachery."

Her lips trembled, and Elyndel swore he saw a glimmer of tears forming in her eyes. Analera must not have spoken that name since that fateful day. Taegen of Miraynore, the traitor of Cendril...

The king's gaze bore into his, stern and intense. He awaited his response, disregarding his daughter's pleas. Elyndel grasped that rational discourse with Tanyll or Analera was futile. Bringing Farklyn into this conflict was unthinkable, especially at this moment. He needed to conclude this meeting swiftly and reach out to those whose sanity still held.

"Very well. I will investigate the matter and strive to provide you with results that will alleviate your concerns."

The king inclined his head courteously, his attention then drawn back to the list he grasped tightly. Elyndel's eyes met the princess's gaze. In an instant, she regained her composure. She understood the reason for his hastened departure. Without a second wasted, the Master rose and rushed to the exit.

"Elyndel!" Analera's voice called out.

For a fleeting moment, he thought about ignoring her plea. What other scheme was she concocting?

"I believe you forgot to relay the latest developments regarding the Guardian of Walderlake."

"Elissa Reinhart?" Tanyll interjected, immediately lifting his gaze from the list.

"We have located her," Elyndel confessed with a hint of reluctance.

"And?"

"She is situated on the Estriden Sea, south of the Callac Islands."

"Estriden! Excellent... excellent!"

The king's reaction to this revelation puzzled the Master. Tanyll suddenly appeared overly concerned about the fate of a woman he had no personal connection with. Then, Elyndel discerned a glint in the monarch's eyes, faint but visible. Delirium? Out of habit, he turned toward Analera for some sort of affirmation, only to realize in a split second that their once-tight bond had fractured. The exchanged glance carried an undertone of rivalry, an element foreign to their prior relationship. Between the Master and the White Lady, things would never be as they once were. Perhaps, in a way, this was for the better...

Tearing his gaze away from his once-faithful confidante, Elyndel left the room with a heavy heart. He shut the door to the secret chamber gently, symbolically ending an era that was no more, and descended the staircase that led him back into the forest.

CHAPTER

31

BEHIND THE KING'S EYES

After a few minutes of walking, immersed in his own thoughts, Elyndel detected movements drawing nearer. Inaudible to a human ear, these sounds were as soft as the caress of a breeze. He halted, hoping it might be Analera, ready to offer an apology. However, it was not the face of the White Lady that emerged from the trees, but Satya's. Breathing heavily, she hastened toward the Master, scepter in hand. The evident distress in her eyes concerned him deeply, prompting him to move swiftly closer to her.

"Princess Satya? What is happening?"

"I slipped away quietly. Analera... I believe she noticed my unease. One thing is certain, I cannot return to that room."

"For what reason?"

"I... I no longer feel safe by my father's side. Something insidious has taken hold of him. I am convinced of it."

"Exhaustion? Given the recent events, that wouldn't be surprising."

He intended to remain vague, avoiding the premature acknowledgment of his own apprehensions. Satya might be playing a double game, sent by Tanyll to test his loyalty.

"It's much more than mere fatigue, Elyndel!" she burst out. "I can't fathom that no one else but me senses this disturbance. You understand me, I saw it in your eyes!"

"I admit this drastic shift does perplex me a bit."

"I know him better than anyone. I can assure you that my suspicions are founded on more than just a feeling of discomfort. I strongly believe that it's no longer my father's essence behind his eyes. Since his return from Wynnorth, his actions seem... different. Like... like a painting that's been faintly altered. For those who catch glimpses of it now and then, it appears clear. However, those who observe it day after day perceive the subtlety of the change. That's what I sensed in him. And this hunt for traitors... The Tanyll I know would never have initiated such deeds."

The sincerity in her tone touched Elyndel, prompting his defenses to lower.

"Regardless of His Highness's justifications," he began, "we cannot allow these threats to take root."

"Do you believe Analera is the cause of this madness?"

"A few days ago, I would have assured you that Analera couldn't possibly be capable of malice. I'm uncertain what to think now. I fear that many innocents might fall victim to the jealousy that seems to consume her."

"What do you propose?"

"I must first inform Syviis and the Montallis brothers about this meeting."

"I'm with you. I refuse to return to Tanyll."

"He will find your absence suspicious..."

"He'll be suspicious of a smile, a word, a gesture. In his state, I'm afraid he's seeking any opportunity to turn against those around him. Remaining by his side seems far riskier, in my opinion."

Elyndel nodded, albeit with hesitation. He sighed before resuming his path. Despite the growing rift between them, he hoped Analera was not in peril in the presence of the king.

———— ··●·· ————

The weather over Cendril's court bore a murky and grim tone. The fragrance of damp grass and earth after the rain infused the air, while a dense mist veiled the moors. A shiver rippled through Elyndel as the biting breeze sneaked beneath his too-light tunic. The very atmosphere seemed to resonate with an ill omen, a portentous promise. He quickened his pace, keenly aware that the princess's attire left her even more exposed than his own. Along the river's course they walked, guiding them toward the yard typically bustling with fishermen and merchants, now eerily abandoned.

"My father has commanded the palace access roads be emptied. Hunters are also barred from entering Loraven Forest.

Elyndel's incredulous expression evoked a snicker from Satya.

"I know, it's utterly mad!"

As they arrived at the courtyard gardens, both the Master and the princess perceived an unsettling absence in the landscape.

"Where are the nobles?"

"Perhaps they've taken shelter inside? The storm appears to approach hastily."

Hurrying to the apartments assigned to Elyndel within the palace, where he intended to gather his companions, they navigated through corridors shrouded in a pervasive darkness akin to nighttime. Strangely, none of the lanterns or candlesticks were aglow, the servants having inexplicably omitted their lighting. Then, the Master realized the sentries were absent...

"Stay behind me," he advised, extending his scepter before him.

Within the silence enveloping them resided a strange familiarity, an otherworldly weightiness Elyndel had encountered before. He foresaw what stood ahead, yet he withheld it from Satya, not wanting to unnecessarily alarm her. The answer awaited beyond a partially open door. A guard lay sprawled on the ground, eyes closed, weapon resting at his side. Satya involuntarily stepped back, her hand covering her mouth in horror.

"Is he..."

"No, he's asleep," the man responded in a low, deep voice.

Perhaps Bales was nearby. At least, Elyndel hoped it was him...

Upon reaching the Master's quarters, a radiant light emanated from beneath the doorway, contrasting starkly with the mansion's prevailing gloom. He readied his staff, prepared to confront whatever lay beyond. In an armchair sat a figure, arms crossed over a bare chest, countenance illuminated by the roaring hearth's blaze.

"Bales," Elyndel whispered.

However, he did not lower his weapon. The dragon greeted him with a smile reminiscent of an old friend.

"Master Elyndel!" he exclaimed, springing up with agility from his seat.

"Why are you here?"

"I was flying around," he replied with unsettling simplicity, while the Master's tone remained sharp. Bales then turned his attention to the woman still framed in the doorway. The princess's striking jade eyes bore into him, a profound resentment evident.

"Ah, this must be the sublime Satya Zylfaren!"

He offered her a bow, but she proceeded to regard him with such animosity that Elyndel felt a chill.

"I've heard much praise about you," the dragon continued with a grin.

"Why are you here?" the Master interjected firmly.

"Is he always this serious?" Bales inquired, ignoring the question. "I hope he's more friendly with your kind."

The princess's lips trembled with anger, her fists clenched as she advanced toward the creature.

"How dare you set foot in this palace, dragon?"

At no point did she attempt to conceal the loathing in her quivering voice. This reaction seemed to amuse Bales, his smile widening.

"I see you've been informed about me. Just know that being here holds no greater appeal for me than it does for you. I prefer the solace of my forest."

"I won't reiterate: what do you want?" the Master scolded, stepping between them.

"What an interesting manner to address someone who merely wishes to warn you of impending catastrophe," Bales retorted.

With a casual brush, he removed a speck of dust from his long black coat, not bothering to meet Elyndel's gaze.

"The other dragon? The one who was with you at Ryre's Keep?"

"Do you think this bad weather will continue? I hate flying during a downpour!"

Satya pushed Elyndel aside and faced Bales, her delicate features twisted into an intimidating expression.

"Your kind has wiped out thousands of innocent lives, including my own mother's! I suggest you answer this question for your own safety. Dragon or not, I won't hesitate to confront those who jeopardize my homeland. Savages like you hold no regard for life."

Bales studied her with a mixture of amusement and contemplation. He seemed pleased by her defiance, despite the derision she directed at him.

"Your kind, Princess, is responsible for the murder of my family and those I've considered friends for millennia. I'm not the one who parades another's loved one as a trophy," the creature growled, gesturing toward the scales adorning her shoulder pads. "If I were you, I'd think twice before labeling us as savages."

She wanted to retort, but Bales had a point. So, Satya sealed her lips and swallowed her frustration. Finally, Bales redirected his attention to Elyndel.

"I'm indeed referring to Oleth, the one who attacked you during your celebrations. Like me, he hails from the Razakstrom Empire. We've remained concealed in Balt'boec since the breach closed."

"Why now?" the Master questioned.

"I believe he was simply waiting for the right moment to reveal himself."

Finishing his sentence, he reached for a crystal goblet from Elyndel's pantry and filled it with mead. He extended the cup to the elf who looked at him reproachfully, declining his offer.

"As I said... so serious," the dragon commented, siting on the Master's desk.

Elyndel brushed aside the remark, well aware that Bales' arrogance was the least of his concerns. The memory of the fiery-haired man remained firmly etched in his mind, the destruction and bloodshed serving as a grim warning. This creature seemed more powerful than any he and his loved ones had encountered in the past, a realization that troubled him deeply.

"So, where is this Oleth now?"

"He's always had a fascination with your kind. It wouldn't be surprising if he's concealed himself among you," Bales responded.

"Why Cendril?" Satya's question dripped with venom.

"After the horrors inflicted upon his family, it's clear he seeks to initiate his revenge here," the dragon replied.

"We need to ready our armies without delay," Elyndel urged the princess.

"I don't believe the threat will come from the skies. No, I know Oleth. His penchant lies in hunting and savoring the torment. His approach won't be direct slaughter; rather, he'll strike at the heart of the Elven people's vulnerabilities."

"Which are?" the princess challenged.

"Your pride, your assumed invincibility. He aims to assail you from within, exploiting the ranks you deem impenetrable."

"The traitor... the one we've sought for months," the Master murmured.

"You mentioned he waited for the right moment. What was it?" Satya probed.

"We sensed a tear between our worlds, the emergence of a new breach. Oleth spoke of a woman... one capable of restoring equilibrium between our realms."

"Equilibrium?" Elyndel quizzed.

"Come now, Elyndel. I thought you had a more discerning mind. Without us, the magic that sustains Balt'boec can't thrive. The drought plaguing the East, worsening each year, started when the rift sealed. Your precious empire was fractured and weakened even before our arrival. You've merely begun to comprehend the drain of our energy. Naturally, Oleth doesn't strive to restore our powers to your world; he seeks to seize your lands for our race."

"So he intends to annihilate us..."

"I can't say if his aim is extermination... or to keep you all enslaved. Regardless, it doesn't bode well for you," Bales stated lightly, taking a sip of his drink.

Elyndel and Satya exchanged a worried glance. According to him, there seemed to be no escape. The resurgence of the dragons spelled their destruction, while their absence signaled the end of prosperity.

"Please don't look so dejected, Elyndel. There's a solution for everything, if you play your cards right. Yours is sailing to Osthallvale."

Elissa. Elissa Reinhart held the key to their salvation, the source capable of restoring equilibrium within the empire. She was the one who would protect the people of Balt'boec.

"Why reveal this to us? Why help us?"

"To be perfectly candid, I quite enjoy my current existence… an existence that would undoubtedly be jeopardized if certain associates of mine controlled Balt'boec."

"How can we be sure you're reliable? You might be sowing discord among us, making way for an easier attack by your companion," the princess interjected.

"A hint of mistrust! I expected nothing less, my dear Satya. Go to the highest mountain, north of Loraven Forest. Near a rocky mound encircled by shrubs, you'll find the verification you seek."

As Bales uttered these words, the stifling heaviness in the air dissipated almost instantly.

"Now I must take flight," he declared, chuckling.

With a nonchalant grace, he rose and sauntered toward the window. A congenial nod was offered to the Master, while Satya was met with a sly smile.

"Until we meet again, I hope," he remarked.

Stretching out his arms with an aura of elegance, revealing more of his tattooed chest, Bales transformed. But it was not into the majestic dragon Elyndel expected. Instead, he morphed into a small, winged lizard, hardly larger than a palm. The inky creature seemed to cast an amused glance at the Chief Magistrate before taking off into the air.

As he vanished, the door swung open. In haste, Syviis, Nilyan, and Gareath burst in, their faces etched with fear and sweat glistening.

"Elyndel! And... Princess Satya? What a surprise to find you here!" Syviis stammered, offering a respectful bow.

"I believe I'm as taken aback by these developments as you are," Satya conceded.

"Sentinels pursued Nilyan and me. Somehow, we managed to outpace them," Gareath panted, breathless from their flight.

Above all, the Master prayed that this was not the consequence of threats laid out by Tanyll and Analera.

"I encountered them purely by chance while fleeing the magi college," Syviis clarified, a note of urgency in her voice. "Tanyll's guards tried to arrest me without justification. I had no choice but to incapacitate them with a spell."

"What's happening, Elyndel? Why is the royal brigade after us?" Nilyan questioned, struggling to catch his breath.

A shared glance passed between the Master and the princess before she started with her explanations. Without reservations, she recounted the final days spent by her father's side, his suspicious demeanor, and the drastic measures he aimed to enforce. Elyndel detailed the encounter with Bales, relaying his exact words.

"We need to verify the implications of this dragon," Syviis declared, her anger palpable. "Our first maneuver should be to search Loraven Forest."

"I agree!" Satya concurred, moving toward the exit.

"Your Highness... I'd strongly advise you to remain here," Elyndel recommended.

"I'm capable of defending myself if need be. Let's not forget I am the future heir to our kingdom's crown and stone," Satya reminded.

"I hold complete faith in your skills as a mage. However, you also stand as the sole successor to the Cendril throne. As Chief Magistrate, I would counsel you to stay here, in safety."

"Your duties are confined to the guidance of the Council of Amethyst—a council of which I am not a member, Master Elyndel."

Satya concluded this exchange with a determined, proud gaze. Her presence was commanding, befitting her position. Elyndel relented to the inevitable as Syviis cast him a subtle, mocking smile.

Just before leaving, Gareath raised a hand, silencing them all. Listening intently, the warrior approached the door with caution.

"They're coming... the guards," he murmured solemnly.

What followed occurred with astonishing speed. Gareath and Nilyan seized their weapons—a longsword for the elder and a keen axe for the younger. Elyndel dashed into the bedroom and signaled for the others to follow. Kneeling before the hearth at the room's end, he employed his scepter to shift the low stone wall within it. A cloud of soot arose, unveiling a hidden passage that the Master quickly crawled into. His companions wasted no time and entered the crevice, hurrying through the concealment. The guards' footsteps approached, resonating in the corridors like an impending danger.

The cramped and grime-covered tunnel proved challenging for the Montallis brothers, who struggled to navigate it due to their imposing frames. Light was scarce, nearly absent when the stone wall sealed behind them. Luckily, the small passage led to a hallway that, while narrow, allowed them to stand. Swathed in ash and dust, Elyndel, Syviis, and Satya promptly conjured beams of radiance at the tips of their scepters. As a group, they advanced through the passageway in silence, the scent of damp and mildew clinging to their noses.

At the corridor's end lay a wooden door—the sole exit. The rusty locks bore cobwebs and thick limestone deposits, indicating that they had not been used for a considerable time. Without a keyhole, only Old Elvish inscriptions marked them. Elyndel recognized a few words, but no more.

"Don't tell me the Master of Cendril can't unlock a door!" Syviis teased, peering over her brother's shoulder.

"I suspect this latch requires a precise enchantment…"

"I suppose you don't remember that incantation at all," the young mage jibed, shaking her head.

"I hate to spoil the moment, but we need to hurry. The guards will soon discover this passage," Nilyan urged, casting an anxious glance behind.

Elyndel muttered a series of enchantments, resting his scepter on the locks. No response. He attempted another. Still nothing. Exasperation welled within him. He enjoyed puzzles. However, he could have done without one now. Syviis grumbled, nudging her brother to take his place. She invoked a spell, but it yielded no result. The three mages debated the right incantation, yet their combined efforts left the latches locked. Meanwhile, the turmoil seemed to intensify. Gareath maneuvered through the group, his broad frame pushing them one by one against the wall. Without uttering a word, he swung his axe forcefully at the gate, the decaying wood offering little resistance. Everyone froze as the warrior systematically dismantled the barrier. Finally, light burst forth, promising an escape from the dusty corridor.

With the door breached, Nilyan made his way past his companions, casting a small smile to his brother.

"Let's go," he urged, placing a hand on Elyndel's shoulder.

However, the fresh air was not the sole thing that greeted them upon emerging. The castle's northern facade was surrounded by soldiers from the royal guard, weapons poised, arranged in an offensive formation. They were outnumbered… severely outnumbered.

"Master Elyndel, Princess Satya!" began Enaril Kelkian, the militia's leader. "We are here to apprehend the traitors to the crown, by the decree of King Tanyll Zylfaren."

His voice wavered, the unease within him palpable. They all knew one another well, almost intimately. They had fought side by side, stood together for common causes. Enaril had watched Syviis and Satya grow up. His eldest son was still serving under Nilyan.

"Traitors? I don't know to whom you refer," the princess queried, her resolve firm.

"The king... the king has ordered us to arrest Syviis Arren, along with Nilyan and Gareath Montallis."

"Nonsense! We cannot comply with such baseless instructions," Satya countered, displaying no sign of faltering.

"Your Highness ... these orders are directly from your father. I'm in no position to challenge them, even on your behalf. If you cooperate, no harm will befall you. You have my word."

"You know us well, Enaril," the Chief Magistrate insisted. "None of us would turn against Cendril."

"Our orders don't pertain to you, Master Elyndel. Your name isn't on our list," the soldier clarified.

"Not yet, but it likely will be. Yours might be as well, if we don't halt the king's madness. This isn't disloyalty. It is sound reasoning. Our realm's ruler is no longer fit for his role."

"Elyndel is telling the truth," the princess snapped. "My father has lost his senses."

"We're not in a position to defy our instructions," Enaril reiterated, his conviction faltering.

He had spoken with Tanyll... he had witnessed the strange behavior firsthand. Yet, he did not lower his weapon...

"Don't push us into facing you," the guard warned.

"You realize you won't win this battle," Elyndel said calmly.

"Our... our orders come directly from His Majesty..."

The turmoil raging within Enaril was apparent. The Master's gaze softened, compassion evident. They were not their adversaries; they were victims of Tanyll's instability.

"I understand you believe you're fulfilling your duty," he responded, "but your lord is no longer himself. I implore you to trust us, to rely on our judgment even if it contradicts your instructions."

The commander hesitated, pondering the Chief Magistrate's words. His men exchanged worried glances. Elyndel knew they were waiting for his signal to lower their weapons. However, Enaril looked up with a steely expression.

"You must comply."

The day had transformed into a nightmare. Elyndel could not grasp how his world was crumbling around him.

"Enaril… we're not your enemies."

"You will be if you hinder the Royal Guard's mandate."

"Very well. I regret what I'm about to do," the Master concluded, dejected.

Immediately, he aimed his scepter at the elf, who in an instant transformed into an adversary. A silver streak shot forth, striking the soldier head-on. He froze, his body turning as lustrous as marble—a living statue. The rest of the guards remained immobile, shock mirrored on their faces. They knew that even a hint of retaliation would lead to their downfall. They stood before some of the most formidable individuals in the kingdom. While they might outnumber them, they were certainly overmatched in power.

Silence descended upon the militia, followed by murmured whispers and anxious glances. Then, one by one, they began to drop their weapons, starting with a robustly built elf with a mature face. Elyndel observed the fatigue in his eyes, the weariness of someone who had seen his share of battles and refused to turn against his own. The others followed suit, until thirty swords lay strewn on the damp earth. An intense emotion surged within the Master, and he did not conceal it from those who displayed their loyalty to him. Maybe, in this matter, the king was correct after all...

The princess stepped forward, and the soldiers made way for her to pass.

"This wise decision won't be forgotten," she declared, her voice a blend of strength and gratitude.

Syviis, Nilyan, and Gareath followed her, wordlessly. Elyndel perceived the fear in his sister's eyes. The way King Tanyll had berated her despite her devotion seemed to rattle her more than the two warriors. Some might attribute this to her youth, yet the Master believed it was due to her strong sense of justice. He followed her, placing a reassuring hand on her shoulder. She did not turn to him, but he knew the gesture comforted her. He stopped in front of Enaril's petrified form, sighing with mixed emotions. He then cast a grateful look to the guard standing beside him, the first to surrender.

"From the bottom of my heart, thank you."

As Bales had directed, they ventured northward into Loraven Forest. Elyndel's heart raced, his scepter slipping through sweaty fingers. For the first time, he had defied his king. In some way, Analera was correct...

In less than an hour, they reached the prescribed location, thunder growling in the distance. The sky darkened progressively, a harbinger of the impending storm. Wasting no time, they all set out in search of the rocky pile mentioned by the dragon. Trying to cover as much ground as possible before the tempest hit, they scattered—Nilyan and Gareath on one side, Syviis and Satya on the other. Elyndel proceeded alone, an unnerving dread settling within him. An odd scent lingered in the air, a mixture of rust and burning iron. Magic.

After a while, Nilyan's voice boomed in a startled curse. The Master halted, a chilling sensation coursing through his veins.

"Over here!" Gareath shouted.

Elyndel found them, the most horrendous stench infiltrating his nostrils... the smell of death and decay. The two warriors stood together, their tanned faces marked by concern. Gareath remained speechless, his hand covering his mouth. Nilyan pointed with a trembling finger toward what lay concealed behind a thicket of gooseberry bushes. Elyndel approached carefully, parting the branches with his ivory staff. Slowly, the figure of a man on the ground came into view… and then his face.

At his feet lay Tanyll Zylfaren.

Time seemed to suspend, Satya's scream reverberating like an echo in his ears. The king's visage was ashen, terror etched onto his features. Puncture marks, forming a large crescent, marred his chest. Clotted blood stained his torn white tunic. Decay had ravaged his body so mercilessly that they soon realized that Tanyll… the true Tanyll Zylfaren… had met his end long ago.

"Who… who sits on my father's throne?" the princess sobbed.

CHAPTER

32

THE CALM BEFORE THE STORM

"Wake up, Elissa!"

As she opened her eyes, Finn's face materialized through the darkness, a mask of terror. This time, she found herself in her cabin, but distant explosions hinted at an escalated situation while she had been asleep.

"What's happening?" she inquired, quickly rising from her bed.

"The Kraken! Meggy finally located it."

"Alden Grenbryel's ship?"

Finn nodded and urgently pulled the Guardian by her hand out of her quarters. She let him guide her, still shaken by the vivid dream. A cannon blast from the Lady Fortune sent a jolt through her. Were Wil and Meggy on the island of Santabria? How much time had elapsed since that strange vision? And the visage of the stranger who now accompanied

365

her every step...

They passed Weasel, who appeared unusually composed. The pirate sat on the stairs leading to the deck, cleaning his blackened nails with the tip of a dagger.

"Where are you rushing off to?" he inquired, scarcely glancing up.

Elissa and Finn exchanged puzzled looks as another explosion rocked the ship.

"I forgot, it's your first boarding!" he chuckled.

"Shouldn't you be mustering the crew?" Elissa panted.

Weasel's shrugged nonchalance baffled her.

"It's not the first encounter like this with the Kraken. He's been toying with us for months, so most men don't take these warnings seriously anymore."

Months...

Meggy had informed her that they would not set sail for Osthallvale until she had dealt with Alden Grenbryel. Elissa could not afford to wait indefinitely...

"The night will be long, mademoiselle. You should return to bed. Fox, you can be useful with the cannons."

Finn nodded and cast an uncertain glance at Elissa before leaving her. Weasel's indifference alarmed her. She could not fathom being held away from her destination for so long. She understood the reason for this detour and the desire to claim her vengeance herself... but at what cost? She could not remain passive and had to express her feelings to Meggy.

"Where's the captain?" she demanded.

Weasel gestured to the top of the stairs, which she hastened to ascend.

The moonlit deck was deserted, a stark contrast to the supposed vigilance of the crew. Blackbird, at the helm, appeared indifferent, his gaze distant. Despite the gravity of Meggy's vendetta, the sailors went about their tasks calmly, almost relaxed. The Lady Fortune's pirates seemed to have lost their sense of urgency. Meggy stood near the hull, scanning the horizon with a spyglass. Elissa approached, her fury palpable.

"If you want to talk, Elissa, it will have to wait. The Kraken is within my reach, and I can't afford distractions," the captain said.

"I don't care! I must get to Osthallvale. That's all that matters now," Elissa insisted.

"We had an agreement, remember," Meggy reminded her.

"Do you think I don't worry about Grenbryel's fate? This man deserves punishment, absolutely! But the realm is weakened without the emerald... the East will exploit it," Elissa argued.

"Well, no one's forcing you to stay aboard," Meggy replied sharply. "Though I doubt your swimming skills!"

"This vendetta could jeopardize the fate of an entire kingdom. And for what? Your impatience?" Elissa's tone was charged with frustration.

Meggy lowered her spyglass, glaring at her with menace. "Leave us, Lee," she ordered, her voice dripping with aggression.

The officer nodded tensely and quickly withdrew. Meggy and Elissa locked eyes, bitterness festering between them. Meggy reached for the gold chain around her neck, retrieving an oval locket from her bodice. Enhanced with a single pearl, she opened it to reveal a portrait of a young boy, hardly three years old, with crystal-blue eyes and caramel complexion.

"My son, Helios." she murmured.

"You've never mentioned him before... Where is he?" Elissa inquired.

"Walderlake. A sheltered village near Murtfort, along the coast. I've scoured the seas for months in search of Alden Grenbryel, for Helios and for the unfortunate women who would cross his path. You have no idea of the devastation this man can cause," Meggy explained, her voice tinged with emotion.

"I can imagine," Elissa replied, haunted by memories of her own past.

"I assure you; his actions are much worse than you can conceive," Meggy added.

"I understand, Meggy. Though our experiences differ, I know this feeling that drives you. For a long time, I woke up in the middle of the night, desiring to erase those memories as much as those who caused them. However, I chose to move forward, to not let them restrain me any longer," Elissa said, offering empathy.

"How do I move forward when the one I'm pursuing wants to take my Helios away and make him a part of his corrupt family?" Meggy lamented.

"His family? Grenbryel is... Helios' father?" Elissa asked, shocked.

"Father? No. A father deserves that title. Alden is merely the monster who sired my child during his brutal intrusion into my life... a creature to whom I refused to submit. Rejection wasn't a concept he was familiar with, though..." Meggy's voice trembled with rage as she revealed the brand on her arm once more.

G.

The symbol of the man who sought to break Meggy Redding but instead created a storm.

"I can't let him haunt my thoughts any longer," Meggy murmured.

Elissa understood Meggy's burning desire for vengeance. But she also feared the consequences of Meggy's reckless pursuit.

"I have a bad feeling, Meggy. The battle you intend to wage... it could risk the survival of Walderlake. Let me complete this journey first. If this family is as powerful as you say, do you realize that others will fill his void? That we'll soon be vastly outnumbered?" Elissa pleaded.

"Walderlake means nothing to me if Alden Grenbryel can get his hands on my son," Meggy retorted, her resolve unwavering.

"Yet, by bringing the emerald closer to this man, you're compromising his safety!" Elissa argued desperately.

"I'm sorry, Elissa… but I can't risk losing track of the Kraken again," Meggy replied, her voice firm.

With that, Meggy turned and walked away, abandoning Elissa and her pleas, consumed by her fiery determination.

———— ••●•• ————

The cannon fire had ceased, leaving behind a daunting silence that only heightened the mage's distress. She felt trapped, suffocated by the impending confrontation, and found herself unable to retreat to her cabin. Instead, she remained on deck, despite the chill of the night. Blackbird, noticing her unease, offered her some rum to warm her up. Acting on her frazzled nerves, she drank too hastily, hoping to find solace in the sky above. However, the vastness of the firmament only seemed to amplify her turmoil, and soon the stars began to spin before her eyes. Nausea gripped her, her breathing became erratic, and she clung to the ship's railing for support, struggling to steady herself. Why had she shown so little restraint? Gunpowder lingered in the air, offering no respite from her unease. A captive—that's what she was aboard the Lady Fortune. The rumble of the sea was her undoing, and she leaned over the side, vomiting profusely.

Thankfully, Meggy was nowhere to be seen, spared from witnessing her embarrassing plight.

"Pitiful," she grumbled between hiccups.

She wiped her mouth with the back of her hand and groaned. Slowly, her strength returned, and she took a deep breath, allowing the cool sea breeze to soothe her clammy face.

A hand landed on her shoulder, causing her to jump. Suppressing a scream, she swiftly turned around.

"Wil…"

There he stood, right beside her. His expression bore a mix of solemnity and remorse, teetering between uncertainty and shame. Hours earlier, she might have urged him to leave. But now, with a bit of hindsight, after that vision…

"I understand that I'm probably the last person you want to see. However, I'd like to offer my apologies. I let down your expectations. I made you feel insignificant when the opposite is true. My actions were inexcusable, and I deeply regret them. You have no idea how much…"

Elissa listened in silence as he delivered this heartfelt speech, her gaze fixed on the sea. She wanted to believe him—her heart did, at least. Wil moved closer and hesitantly took her hand.

"I'm sorry, Elissa."

Whether it was the effect of the alcohol or sheer exhaustion, she burst into laughter. Wil stared at her, bewildered.

"It's ridiculous, don't you think?" she chuckled. "Amidst all this death and danger… I'm here holding the fate of our kingdom, and we're busy with feelings and endless apologies. I don't have the energy for all this anymore."

Her amusement overcame her, and she laughed uncontrollably. After a while, the fit subsided, leaving her exasperated. She knew her words had wounded the knight. She could clearly see his dejected look, illuminated by the darkness that enveloped his eyes. He deserved it, and more.

"Maybe she'll reconsider. Meggy, I mean," she said, peering up at the night sky.

"I highly doubt it."

"This fight… she seems to be ignoring the consequences. She appeared so reasonable. I suppose I let my initial impressions cloud my judgment. It wouldn't be the first time."

Her gaze held a hint of accusation, and Wil's brows furrowed immediately. No matter. She found satisfaction in these minor revenges.

"She's been good to me since we boarded."

"I wonder why!" Wil retorted stiffly.

"Jealous?" she taunted, a smirk playing on her lips.

He did not respond, but his head drooped. She did not care. She felt an urge to provoke him, an almost visceral desire to assert dominance. She did not know what force, what spirit had taken hold of her, but she approached him without hesitation. With a swift movement, she gripped his chin and turned his face toward her.

"Jealous?" she challenged.

Wil's breath escaped him as though he had been struck in the gut. Yet, it was not pain that marked his features…

Just as the knight was about to answer, an explosion resounded in the distance.

"Get down!" Blackbird yelled, diving to the ground.

A piercing whistle cut through the air, followed by the impact of a cannonball on the Lady Fortune's starboard side, slicing across the deck like a knife through butter. Elissa shouted, protecting her face as wood splinters flew around them. Another shot echoed, and Wil lunged at her, shielding her from a barrage of debris. A mast collapsed, crashing dangerously close with a deafening noise. The cries of sailors erupted from below deck, and a dozen crew members swarmed onto the area. Some hastily donned their attire, while others prepared for combat. Finally, the Kraken emerged from the shadows, a menacing titan. An intricately carved wooden octopus clung to the ship's prow, painted a deep charcoal hue. Banners decked with the insignias of Walderlake and the Emerald Order fluttered in the wind.

A third shot rang out, shattering the vessel's structure with impunity. With horror, Elissa watched as a pulley struck Blackbird, hurling him into the sea like a discarded doll. Chaos reigned as the pirates prepared to engage. They appeared bewildered, taken aback by this long-awaited moment. Meggy stepped onto the deck, saber in hand, a near-mad gleam in her eyes. Despite her disadvantage, the excitement of nearing her goal was palpable. Wil seemed equally eager to confront one of the pillars of the Grenbryel family—those responsible for his desertion. Elissa knew she should savor the prospect of finally exacting revenge, but a peculiar sensation lingered within her. Wil dashed to her side and embraced her briefly.

"Remember who you are, Elissa Reinhart," he murmured in her ear.

Amidst the chaos, those words reverberated louder than a cannon's roar. He was right—she was the daughter of Brennet Reinhart, Nora and Jeon Lothain, the Emerald Guardian of Walderlake. Her breathing eased, and she exchanged a fleeting glance with him. Elissa fought against the urge to kiss him—a feeling stronger than common sense.

The Kraken rocked Lady Fortune, striking her without mercy. The frenzy on deck had reached its zenith as Meggy mounted the railing. Her dark curls billowed in every direction, her powerful physique, her fierce allure... This sight sent shivers of both fear and admiration through the Guardian's body.

"No prisoners, no pity! But Grenbryel is mine!" Meggy's voice boomed.

"Yes, Captain!" the crewmen roared in unison.

"Prepare for boarding!" Meggy the Butcher bellowed.

Lady Fortune's crew cheered her with raised fists. No prisoners... Meggy was set on a massacre to satisfy her thirst for vengeance. In an instant, the mage witnessed the initial wave of pirates leaping onto the enemy deck with astonishing agility. Those they encountered did not get a chance to mount their own defense. Amidst the chaos, Elissa spotted Finn, his fiery, disheveled hair easily standing out in the crowd. He was ready to jump aboard with his companions, radiating pride and determination. It was difficult to believe this was the same frail, fearful man she had met in Pendard Forest.

"Don't be reckless, Finn," she whispered as the adversaries neared the railing.

Her breath caught in her throat. The crew looked young, almost childlike. Fear was etched on their faces. In a heartbeat, Elissa grasped that these youths likely had not chosen this path willingly. She pondered who might be aboard that ship. Who would be destined to become victims of Meggy's vendetta?

She rushed toward the pirate without even taking the time to think, without calculating the words to offer to such a stubborn person... a woman who was obviously about to commit the irreparable.

"Meggy! These men seem hardly old enough to wield swords."

"Those behind them are more than capable."

"I beseech you to show them mercy."

"They serve under a monster's command and shall pay the price. You, of all people, should know they don't hesitate to harm the innocent."

"Think of your son! Think of Helios! Would you hold the same stance if he were in their place?"

Meggy's expression tightened. An internal struggle waged within her, violence tugging at her mind. Her gaze darkened, grew ruthless. In that moment, Elissa discerned which side had triumphed.

"Meggy," she quivered. "This assault is senseless. I implore you to see reason!"

The captain seized Elissa's chin, drawing their faces close. A cruel grin crept onto her lips, and the Guardian swore she saw flames flicker in her eyes.

"I respect your choices. Now respect mine."

With those words, she claimed Elissa's lips, stealing a hungry kiss. The mage stood frozen, Meggy releasing her. A gentler smile graced her mouth before she turned back to those awaiting their turn on deck. With a brief nod, she beckoned Wil to follow, and without hesitation, he did.

In a heartbeat, captain and knight were overboard, weapons raised, ready to engage. Soon, the clash of blades and fierce roars reverberated across the vast expanse of the sea.

CHAPTER

33

FLIGHT

"Don't disappoint me," Valera commanded.

The servants gathered in the throne room of Ryre's Keep nodded hesitantly. The queen watched them slip away, reminiscent of a satiated cat allowing a mouse to escape. That very temper of hers irked her youngest son, those tantrums and that air of superiority. Donned in her finest attire, a broad crimson smile adorned her face. She seemed to revel in making the populace yearn for their king's return. And then there was this peculiar promise of triumph on her lips. Triumph over what? Farklyn was clueless. He dreaded even more her covert schemes brewing in the shadows. He now understood that she was limitless in her quest for gratification. If the queen's demeanor appeared more serene than ever, apathy had settled in Farklyn as a response. He stood in the room's corner, quiet, a starkly austere expression chiseled onto his face. With a mere look of disdain, he felled his mother, unable to support her yet again in her antics meant to mend her bruised ego. A ball? Had she not learned anything from the recent events? Fabyan could not be seen in public, and Farklyn did not know how much longer he could sustain this tangled masquerade. He groaned as his mother burst into laughter. Raina must have whispered something in her ear, which brought amusement—nothing more. Undoubtedly, weariness had intensified his already foul mood. Sleep had eluded him since that remarkably vivid dream.

Elissa…

The face of the woman who had visited him was etched into his mind, as if seared by a scorching brand.

Farklyn waited until Raina had moved away before approaching Valera, steeling himself to voice his discontent.

"As the steward of Wynnorth, I deemed it prudent to bolster our defense in case of an attack… The aspect that nobody seems inclined to oversee, you see?" he began, his tone dry.

"I don't care for your sarcasm and arrogance, Farklyn. The situation is well under my control, trust me," the queen replied, rising from her throne.

Farklyn refrained from retorting. Trust her? Of course not! Despite the renewed hope he had held for her over the past few weeks, she had managed to shatter everything in a blink. The way she obstinately disregarded Fabyan's anguish was a glaring testament to that.

"I intend to consult with Elyndel shortly. I wish to discuss with him the fortifications necessary in the event of dragon attacks. He, too, seems inclined to prioritize the safety of his people above all else," he continued.

"Well, well! Now who's deeply impressed by the Master of Cendril? Quite the turnaround!" Valera jeered, her tone mocking.

"My stance toward the elven folk remains unchanged. Nonetheless, I believe collaborating with them could prevent the Eastern realms from confronting this looming threat in isolation. It's the lesser of two evils," Farklyn replied.

"No matter your thoughts or reasoning, now is not the time to burden me with such affairs. Moreover, your brother has returned. This obligation no longer rests upon your shoulders."

The prince struggled to formulate a retort, knowing he could not allow her to triumph once more. Before he could find the right words, Valera gently enclosed her son's hand within hers, her touch eerily gentle.

"I need you, Farklyn... your sharp mind, your strength... I've been spiraling lately and it terrifies me. Elyndel has suggested I entrust you with more responsibilities within the kingdom's administration... a move I intend to make. I'm pleased that you're finally interested in the realm's affairs, and I encourage you to reach out to him. However..."

Her gaze clouded, and she bit her lower lip before continuing.

"Stay with me a while longer," she pleaded. "You can depart for Cendril once I'm in better spirits."

Her doe-like eyes could melt even the coldest hearts, particularly Farklyn's. At that moment, he loathed himself almost as much as he despised her.

"Of course, Mother."

In spite of himself, his voice assumed a reassuring, gentle tone. Valera beamed at him, her mouth framed by those delicate wrinkles Farklyn found charming about her. With her graceful fingertips, Valera ruffled her son's silken mane.

"Such magnificent hair... cascading so beautifully over your shoulders!" she mused with an admiring sigh. "I hope you'll keep it like this for the ball tomorrow night."

"I wonder who would dare set foot in Ryre's Keep again after the recent turmoil. Wynnorth's aristocracy isn't renowned for bravery."

"The Do'wis will be present... Madz Fogan and his associates too. Floriana Loprehk and her sons have also pledged not to miss this event for all the gold in the world," Valera enumerated proudly.

"Do'wis, Fogan, Loprehk... these families command the largest troops in the realm."

Her smile broadened, and Farklyn finally grasped her intentions.

"You plan to sway them to enlist their militias against the dragons, enticing them."

He felt a pang of guilt toward his mother for doubting her cunning yet again.

"I'm afraid the world at large is hesitant to rally alongside us," Valera revealed. "The Eastern clans have paid dearly, defending the realm against these winged giants. Their resurgence casts skepticism on the sacrifices they've borne under my banner."

"And who better to win back their favor than you!"

Farklyn watched her exit the room with a mix of wonder and reluctance he scarcely admitted to himself. As she turned back for a final glance, a mischievous grin curved on her lips.

"Who else?"

———— ··•·· ————

Farklyn prepared for the festivities with the meticulousness of a soldier readying for battle. Despite the queen's explanations, he could not shake the profound unease surrounding the entire affair. Donning the clothes chosen for the occasion proved troublesome—not because he found them repulsive, but because the satin silk shirt seemed to him nothing more than a veneer, a disguise. Pretenses had always been integral to his role, yet after these past few weeks, they appeared futile, even ludicrous. For the first time in his life, he glimpsed a world beyond the snug cocoon he had inhabited.

His thoughts turned to that woman, the name on everyone's lips... Elissa Reinhart. Following that peculiar dream, he could not shake off the curiosity, the yearning to establish contact with her. Whether she was real or a construct of his imagination remained a mystery. Her face, though new to him, felt strangely familiar. The pallor of her skin, the green forest-like gaze, the very essence of spring she radiated… He needed to locate her, be it for his realm's sake or his own tranquility.

With meticulous care, he finished grooming his wavy hair, reserving special attention for this festive night. After smudging his hazel eyes with smoky ash, he observed his reflection in the mirror. It had been reiterated to him often that he had inherited Valera's beauty. Now he recognized that it was possibly the only shared trait. Their ideologies diverged, yet her brother and mother harmonized so effortlessly. What was it that set him apart from Fabyan? At times, he contemplated how his life might have differed if fate had granted him magical abilities. Bitterly, he tried to shift these intrusive thoughts. He would, alas, need to rely on his keen intellect and silken eloquence.

———— · •●• · ————

As the ball started, Farklyn remained engulfed in unease, his reflections consuming him. He failed to detect Braylon's arrival, the man entering his room like a foreboding raven.

"Is everything alright, Your Highness?" Braylon inquired, his tone laced with genuine empathy.

"I simply wished to abstain from the festivities tonight. Nothing more," Farklyn replied, his voice subdued.

"I apologize, Majesty. I will try to uplift your spirits," Braylon responded, though his concern was palpable.

It dawned upon Farklyn, with a tinge of dismay, that his servant appeared to be the sole individual concerned about his emotional state.

"Are there many attendees?" he asked, his tone softening.

"Relatively… Thankfully, the designated families have graced us with their presence. It shall bring satisfaction to the queen and your brother," Braylon replied.

"So, is Fabyan recovering?" Farklyn inquired.

The counselor nodded, though a trace of apprehension lingered in his expression.

"Yes?" Farklyn prodded.

"Majesty?" Braylon hesitated, clearly unsure of whether to divulge further.

"You're not here without a purpose. Something is bothering you," Farklyn pressed.

"I... I shouldn't speak of it... If Her Majesty were to discover..." Braylon trailed off.

"Do not fret over her. It is to me that you shall be accountable if you remain silent," Farklyn asserted, his tone firm.

"The king has voiced complaints on multiple occasions about specific... entities?" Braylon finally relented.

"Entities?" Farklyn echoed, his curiosity piqued.

"He... he expressed discontent about the presence of beings that only he seems to perceive. When the attendants tried to understand what His Highness was alluding to, he succumbed to a frenzied rage... uncontrollable. Several guards attempted to reason with him, to no avail. They had to restrain him on numerous occasions. Among other claims, he swears that a woman with serpent-like tongue and hair of rubies aimed to immolate him... a sort of chimera haunting the corridors."

Without further ado, Farklyn pivoted on his heel and advanced toward the exit, his expression ablaze with fury.

"Majesty? Where are you going?" Braylon called after him, his voice filled with concern.

"To Valera's room before she destroys what's left of her credibility," Farklyn replied curtly, his resolve firm.

Against Braylon's objections, Farklyn had a strong feeling he would find his mother in a state of ease within her quarters, likely holding a glass of wine and gazing at herself in the mirror. Sadly, his intuition proved correct. Her penchant for grand entrances often meant punctuality was beyond her.

Dressed in a stunning gown of black and silver taffeta, she swiftly rose upon spotting her youngest son. Advancing to meet him with open arms, her expression lit up with enthusiasm that only served to intensify his exasperation.

"Farklyn! I assumed you would already be waltzing, given your fondness for such gatherings!" she exclaimed, her voice dripping with false cheer.

"Mother, you must be joking!" Farklyn snapped, pushing her away, his frustration palpable.

The queen's grin faded, as if she had been slapped across the face by his harsh words.

"You don't honestly think Fabyan is ready to mingle with a crowd in his condition," he added, his tone softer but no less firm.

"I am quite well, dear brother," a voice emanated from behind the wicker screen at the room's rear.

The king emerged, adjusting a leather belt around his lean waist. Though his features still bore traces of his ordeal, his former allure managed to transpire through the marks, his eyes brimming with their customary appeal. Given the horrible state he was in just days before, this was a major victory for the healing mages.

"Fabyan... I didn't know you were here," Farklyn muttered, feeling a flush of embarrassment at being caught off guard.

Observing his brother's slightest movements, his unsteady gait and stooped posture, Farklyn discerned the subtle tremor in his hands.

"It is astonishing what the mages have achieved in such a short time," Fabyan mused, his index finger caressing his cheek absentmindedly.

Though his faculties might have wavered, his vanity remained intact.

"Indeed, remarkable. Are you well, brother?" Farklyn inquired, genuine concern evident in his voice.

With a chuckle, Fabyan adjusted the golden crown atop his head.

"He is quite well. The populace longs to see their king again," Valera remarked nonchalantly, attempting to shift the conversation away from Fabyan's condition.

"Mother, word has it that a peculiar woman has been spotted wandering the corridors. It would be wise to fortify your security. One can never be too cautious," Farklyn interjected, his tone serious.

"A woman?" Valera's interest was piqued.

"Though I have not personally seen her, some claim to have glimpsed her scarlet locks in the shadows," he continued, his gaze steady.

"Scarlet?" the king breathed, immediately roused from his casual demeanor.

"They say she probably sneaked between the different apartments in the evening, hissing with her serpent's tongue," Farklyn added, watching as Fabyan's eyes widened with fear.

"She is here," he repeated in panicked whispers.

Valera glared at her son. She understood what he was trying to do.

"Farklyn… a word," she interjected, her controlled tone thinly veiling her vexation.

He complied, suppressing a smug grin as he followed her to a secluded corner, leaving Fabyan to cope with his composure.

"Why are you tormenting your poor brother?" she demanded, her voice edged with frustration.

"Is it not you who disregards his well-being? You who would thrust him into a sea of judgmental gazes? Fabyan is far too unpredictable to withstand the scrutiny of your guests," he retorted sharply.

"I know that!" she snapped, reigning in her tone's intensity. "I am not an imbecile, Farklyn."

"Ah!" he exclaimed unabated. "You seek to exploit your son's state to elicit sympathy from your guests."

"We wield the upper hand over Brilea. Families that refrained from the conflict on moral grounds can finally see the true cruelty of these so-called gentle people. The citrine of this degenerate realm is now within my grasp, courtesy of your brother's sacrifice," she explained, her tone resolute.

"So, the topic of dragons' defense is off the table? From the beginning, your intent was to subjugate neighboring kingdoms... to dominate our empire!" he accused, his frustration boiling over.

"If seizing Balt'boec from them is the sole means to shield us from other rulers' incompetence, I shall do so. In my possession, their gem will give us unparalleled support against the dragons. Brilea has never proven itself worthy of such a jewel! Galvrick acted out of pure pity when he entrusted it to them," she countered, her resolve unwavering.

"Are you questioning the reasoning behind its creator?" Farklyn shot back, his eyes rolling. "The Grand Master... our emperor... the man who bared his soul to aid his loyal subjects? Galvrick owed this benevolence to none, yet he granted it without hesitation. Your ingratitude knows no bounds!"

"The Mortenburn deserved the citrine more, in my opinion," she sneered unabashedly.

"You are insufferable! I implore you to reconsider your plan! I believe that you are thinking of the prosperity of your country. However, you must understand the impact that such actions would have on the world, on your family... on yourself! I know you don't desire to be labeled a tyrant," he pleaded, his frustration giving way to desperation.

Her demeanor softened, as though her child's words had struck a chord.

"Farklyn…" she uttered his name tenderly, stroking his lustrous locks.

"How handsome you are, my Farklyn! I'll never grow tired of looking at you," she murmured, her voice filled with a strange mixture of affection and detachment.

With that, she spun around and departed, leaving Farklyn feeling impotent and frustrated. Despite his explanations and supplications, Valera's narcissism remained unyielding. In his gut, a void materialized, followed by a peculiar sentiment.

Grief.

Enveloped by a cloud of somber thoughts, he surrendered control to his feet, allowing them to guide him mechanically to his chamber. Neither the lively music that reached his ears nor the alluring aroma of the feast managed to stir his senses. Before the mirror on his dresser, he gazed at his reflection with an almost visceral disgust. His sole worth seemed confined to a bestowed title and this physique that everyone appeared so eager to admire. Acting on impulse, he withdrew a dagger from his belt. The candlelight shimmered upon the blade, etched with the amaryllis, the emblem of the Netherborne family. Fueled by a fierce determination, he raised it to his scalp and, with a swift movement, initiated the obliteration of the mane his mother cherished. Almost savoring the moment, he watched as the locks fell to the floor, each strand a step closer to his liberation. Equipped with a cedar-handled razor, he meticulously finished the task, leaving no trace of hair on his head. A sense of contentment settled as he stroked his now bare skin, a near terrifying smile curling upon his lips.

• —————— • •●• • —————— •

His travel bag was ready in no time. Devoid of any lingering remorse, he stepped across the threshold of his room, his course set toward the least frequented west exit of Ryre's Keep. The anticipation of the gala provided the perfect diversion for his escape. Like a shadow, he navigated the deserted corridors. The prospect of being apprehended carried a thrill more intoxicating than his recent conquests combined.

"Where are you off to, my prince?"

For a moment, his blood seemed to turn to ice, but he soon recognized the voice.

"And what brings you here, Jenima?"

She too was attired for travel, draped in a mink cape, inappropriate for the season.

"I should ask you the same question," she retorted with a mocking attitude. "It is rare to see you with clothes on."

At last, he recognized her.

"I'm leaving for my country estate for a much-needed break. Some fresh air might do me some good."

Unconvinced, her gaze rested upon his newly shaven head.

"A new look?" she inquired. "For what occasion?"

"Is it not to your liking?" he jested with a smirk.

"Frankly, I find it better. It makes you look less... how shall I say? Netherborne?"

A genuine laugh finally emerged from him after days of disquiet.

"You seem to be in a hurry," she added.

"Wishing to escape before the ladies at court get their hands on me," he fibbed. "My mother apparently overlooked separating my former lovers from one another."

"It never bothered you before."

A soft chuckle rippled through him, though Jenima's demeanor remained cold. Anxiously, she bit the inside of her cheek before stepping closer.

"Take me with you."

Her voice carried a mix of eagerness and desperation.

"I can't," he replied.

"I need to accompany you… to Cendril, I mean."

"Why would you think I'm headed to Cendril?" he questioned, taken aback.

"Given Fabyan's return and the queen's stance on the impending crisis, I… I believe that's your likely path. Your convictions deviate from your family's, while Master Arren shares your views."

Mere weeks earlier, such a comparison would have ignited his fury. A lifetime of scorning the elves left him dealing with his own xenophobia.

"Why are you leaving Wynnorth?" he inquired.

"Why stay in Wynnorth? That's the better question."

"You understand that I cannot protect you if we're caught."

A solemn nod followed, and he sighed. Time was slipping away, and his anxiety warned against further deliberation. The moment Valera noticed his absence, she would dispatch guards to track him.

"Very well… come with me."

As he moved to leave, the face and pleas of Elissa Reinhart spread through his thoughts.

The Oracle… Cendril's… We must rescue her.

"You know the fortress like the back of your hand, don't you, Jenima? I'm sure you know more about what it hides than the queen herself."

"For a man in such a hurry to abandon the citadel, you seem eager to stay," the woman mocked, her voice shaded with nervousness.

"I must retrieve something before I leave… or rather, someone."

CHAPTER

34

THE KRAKEN, THE ORACLE, AND THE DRAGON

Elyndel paced beside the lifeless body of his fallen king. The wounds inflicted were unmistakably the work of a colossal creature, the bite marks on his chest mirroring those etched onto battlefields during the Dragon War.

Oleth.

Amidst the princess's mournful sobs, Elyndel struggled to maintain a clear mind. His friends' heated debate served only to worsen the situation.

"We must strike while the impostor remains unaware of our intentions," Syviis declared fervently, her very being radiating fury. Despite her small stature, her temperament was potent enough to unsettle even the most determined adversaries, save perhaps Nilyan, who showed no hesitance in opposing her.

"We can't risk for that Oleth to shapeshift right in the middle of the palace, Syviis," Nilyan added.

She hated when he ended an argument by mentioning her name in such a paternalistic way. With a venomous glare, she took an assertive stride toward the elf, who stood almost two heads above her.

"Sometimes, risks are essential, NILYAN," she retorted sharply.

"Your temerity once more leads you astray," he replied with composed authority.

"This same temerity that got us out of trouble on numerous occasions. I'm trying to regain control before the situation spirals," Syviis insisted.

"It already has spiraled," Gareath interjected somberly, gesturing toward their fallen king.

"What does this impostor seek?" Syviis inquired. "What is his real motive?"

"Bales told us that he aims to sow discord among us," Satya replied amidst her sobs.

"An objective he seems to be achieving splendidly," Nilyan commented dryly, his gaze unwaveringly fixed on Syviis.

"Yet, that is not his primary goal," Elyndel stated before his sister could retaliate. "I am certain he seeks something more, beyond wreaking havoc. What motive prompts him to draw so close to Analera during my absence?"

"Analera is the one who has received intelligence from your spies in Cendril, during your stay in the East," Nilyan deduced.

Elyndel's countenance paled, recalling his recent discussion with the White Lady in his office.

"I have already granted his desire."

"The Guardian of Walderlake?" the princess inquired.

"We cannot allow Oleth to escape," the Master affirmed. "Syviis is right; we must swiftly return to the palace, before it's too late… before he gets his clutches on Elissa Reinhart."

The young elf nodded, her gaze reflecting gratitude. That upturned nose, those rosy cheeks, and the large brown eyes harboring unadulterated courage… she bore a striking resemblance to their mother.

"Analera is still with him," Gareath reminded them. "We must be cautious not to endanger her."

"She deserves the same fate as that dragon," Syviis retorted sharply.

"Ana believes she serves the monarchy," Elyndel explained. "According to her information, we are the ones betraying our homeland! If only I could explain everything to her…"

"It is for her to clarify how she so readily turned against us!" Syviis interjected fiercely.

"No wonder she did after her torment at the hands of Taegen," the Master replied.

"I don't care about that! We have all survived significant ordeals without forsaking our allies."

At that moment, the wind rose, and a deathly omen caressed the nape of Elyndel's neck. He immediately sensed it was more than an impending rainstorm; an otherworldly force was closing in.

"Quiet!" he commanded.

They all fell silent, and a distant roar was heard. Holding his ivory scepter upward, Elyndel scanned the horizon with trepidation. Despite the coolness of the air, beads of sweat formed on his back, conjuring an involuntary shiver.

"What is happening, Elyndel?" the princess questioned, her voice mixed with anxiety.

"Take cover."

His gaze never wavered from the sky, and the group grasped the looming threat. The Montallis brothers drew their weapons, seemingly useless against such an adversary yet potent in their experienced hands. Syviis and Satya gripped their scepters. Though unaccustomed to facing such foes, Elyndel placed his faith in their capabilities, particularly his sister's.

Amidst the tension, a colossal figure of resplendent ruby descended from the clouds. Horns protruding from its head, a thorny crest tracing its spine, the creature's roar echoed across the hills.

"Stand behind me!" Elyndel commanded.

He did not care for his own existence. There was no way Oleth would prevail. With a gesture, Elyndel conjured a protective dome above them, a greyish mist shrouding them from view. Without wasting a second, everyone braced for the dragon's fiery attack, charging furiously in their direction. The creature roared again, flames dancing through its gaping maw. Elyndel shivered. Apparently, he never grew accustomed to the anguish of facing a larger-than-life opponent.

• —— · •●• · ——— •

Elissa vaulted over the Kraken's railing, her eyes wide with horror as the bloodshed unfolded before her. Pained cries, sword strikes cutting through adversaries who were too paralyzed to fight back—the scene assaulted her senses. The air was thick with the acrid scent of gunpowder mingled with death and the tang of sea salt. The atrocities she had witnessed at home paled in comparison to this macabre display.

Amidst the chaos, Elissa struggled to locate Wil and Meggy. She was jostled from all sides as she tried to navigate the crowd without losing her balance on the slippery bridge slickened by viscous blood and strewn corpses. The thought of being trampled to death in this turmoil was not how she envisioned her end. A desperate urge to scream or cry tugged at Elissa. Her hands shook as she clutched the dagger the captain had given her. She had no clue how to wield it effectively, but merely holding it provided a semblance of protection.

Among the fallen bodies, Elissa spotted Wil's blond hair. He was shoving his way under the blows of Meggy's saber. She hastened after them but was abruptly confronted by a burly man with rugged features. His uniform bore the emblem of a white octopus, yet unlike the others, fear did not sketch lines on his battle-hardened face. A commander, perhaps? His arm raised, ready to strike down the Guardian mercilessly. But Elissa was quicker. She thrust her hand forward, conjuring a potent force field that sent her assailant hurtling through the air. He staggered to his feet, cursing, then charged once more. Elissa replicated her defensive maneuver with an instinctive motion. The man slammed into a mast with brutal force, the sickening snap of bone breaking likely drowned out by the tumult. He crumpled to the ground, motionless.

Elissa's attention returned to her friends, only to find Meggy and Wil vanished amidst the turmoil. Frustration gnawed at her as she scanned the frenetic crowd. She caught sight of Weasel, engaged in combat with a Kraken crewmate a short distance away. Weasel's offensives were relentless, and blood streamed from the young pirate's right arm, evidence that he had not escaped unscathed. He seemed scarcely older than a boy, and his trembling lips uttered pleas in an unfamiliar language. The terror in his eyes struck Elissa like a blow. Weasel pursued his adversary with a ferocity reminiscent of those who had obliterated the children of the Circle of Am. Without hesitation, she conjured a magical projectile that intercepted the pirate's blade. The weapon spiraled through the air before coming to a rest several feet away. With an incredulous gaze, Weasel stared at Elissa who stood frozen in place. Then, the hostility returned, this time directed at her. Undeterred, flames flickered at her fingertips. She would not allow him a chance to retaliate. The pirate drew a dagger from his leather boot, his emaciated features twisted into a feral expression.

A fool. A wretched, desperate fool…

Fortunately, Jenima maneuvered the secret passages of the fortress with skill, evading detection. Laughter and voices surged through Ryre's Keep like a distressing melody—now soft and harmonious, now rapid and strident. This heightened the blend of excitement and trepidation churning within the prince's heart. It was as if he almost desired to be discovered!

Descending the main courtyard that separated the stronghold's four wings, they ventured into a tunnel previously unknown to Farklyn. Jenima navigated it deftly, her familiarity evident.

"It appears this dungeon exploration isn't your first," Farklyn jested.

"I oversee the unfortunate souls awaiting trial," Jenima responded, her voice laced with a touch of gloom. "In Wynnorth, that often equates to a perpetual waiting game."

"I wasn't aware," Farklyn admitted.

"Of course, you weren't," Jenima retorted, her tone carrying a hint of bitterness. "The fact that you know nothing about your realm's corruption stems from your own detachment. Few can claim educated insight into their environment when hidden in a gilded palace. You lived for indulgence and desire."

"So, you hold quite a bleak opinion of me," Farklyn remarked, his curiosity genuine.

"I... no... I blame your mother for the upbringing she gave you."

"I find your generosity in calling it an upbringing rather amusing," Farklyn chuckled briefly before growing serious. "I understand your disdain. Realize, though, that I strive to rectify some semblance of justice in Balt'boec, even if it means threading through this dim corridor at the risk of my life. It won't absolve my family's wrongdoings, but I am committed to dedicating my existence to amending their offenses."

"Amending? Why not try to halt them altogether?"

Farklyn's brow furrowed, creasing his typically smooth forehead. He held Jenima's penetrating gaze, uncertain how to respond. The idea of confronting his mother and brother horrified him. His position was no match for theirs, and he lacked an army.

"Let's not waste any more time," he muttered hoarsely, hastening his pace. Who would lend an ear to him, except, perhaps, Elyndel Arren?

———— ··●·· ————

A surge of lava erupted from the red dragon's maw, crashing against the Master's magical dome. The searing heat momentarily cast doubt upon the resilience of his spell. The mental strain required to sustain it became a torment to bear.

"I won't hold out much longer," he muttered, his teeth clenched.

Gareath hurled a massive dagger at the creature. Despite the precision of the throw, the blade failed to leave even a scratch. Unfazed, Gareath launched a second knife, its barely audible hiss slicing through the air. This time, the blade found its mark between the dragon's scales. The reptile growled in fury, but the dagger embedded in its neck did not stop him. Claws poised for attack, its gaping maw displayed formidable teeth, nearly as fierce as the fire that threatened to spew forth. The ruby gaze settled on Syviis, causing Elyndel's stomach to knot. Yet, his sister remained astonishingly composed, a smirk curling her lips. She leaped from the dome, much to her brother's dismay, who was left within to sustain their protection. She knew flames posed no danger to a red dragon; they reveled in the hottest of infernos. Fortunately, Syviis was a disciple of earth. Eyes shut, she drove her scepter into the ground like a conqueror planting a flag. In hushed tones, she beckoned the elements to their aid. The earth trembled and quaked. Her free hand ascended slowly, and the hill fragmented into massive rocks. The resulting explosion rattled them, but not as much as the dragon, which understood Syviis's intent. Projectiles sped toward it, its attempts to evade them proving futile. Despite its reptilian shape, Elyndel could sense the panic in its eyes, its aerial maneuvers betraying its distress. Ultimately, the deluge of debris overwhelmed it, piercing its mighty wings. The creature bellowed into the sky. The scent of earth saturated the air, and a dusty haze formed overhead. For a brief moment, the dragon vanished, its wings' fluttering the only indication of its presence.

Debris cascaded around the group, exposing the beast, which struggled to regain altitude. Just as Elyndel thought it might have met its end, he saw a gleam in its eyes—a malevolent and savage gleam. Clearly, it was readying for another assault.

"Syviis!" he shouted in desperation.

Unbeknownst to him, his sister was already in motion. A colossal boulder struck the beast's skull, sending it hurtling toward them in a daze. Shaking off its stupor, it was met by Satya's charge, invoking the stormy sky for assistance. A blinding lightning bolt crashed onto the dragon, eliciting a piercing roar. Its descent spiraled out of control, tumbling downward at a perilous speed. Elyndel held no doubts—the impact would be brutal. Straining to maintain the dome, he braced himself for the impending collision.

———— •• ● •• ————

Weasel charged once more, saber in hand and vengeance burning in his eyes. Elissa sensed that same bubbling fervor within herself that always announced her moments of toppling those who opposed her. She did not want it to come to this, not against someone she had regarded as an ally. However, a fleeting look at the rag-clad young boy cowering behind him reminded her that Weasel was not her comrade, let alone her friend. She did not belong to Lady Fortune's crew, the Council, or any Circle. She was alone… alone with her duty and her unswerving commitment to justice. The bodies continued to crumple around her. Elissa knew she had to take immediate action to halt this bloodshed from persisting.

The sailor charged toward her, and the emerald flames dancing between her fingers surged in intensity. Weasel showed no signs of relenting… and neither did Elissa. In a heartbeat, a conflagration consumed her adversary, who managed only a pained cry. The fire subsided, leaving nothing of the pirate but a mound of ash mingling with the pool of blood on the bridge. This time, the Guardian was spared from guilt. The crewmen exhibited no compassion for their victims, and she had no choice but to reciprocate.

Elissa seized the young adolescent and hauled him away a few paces. She pushed aside those who stood in her path with unwavering force, politeness having no place amidst this chaos.

"Where is your captain?" she demanded.

He gave no answer, his lips quivering so intensely that speech was beyond him.

"Where is he?" she pressed with urgency.

His haggard gaze met Elissa's, and in that moment, she realized he did not understand her words.

"You don't speak our language," she murmured, while his expression remained unchanged.

His olive complexion, ocean-like green eyes, and the way his hair was braided… He brought to mind the depictions of the nomadic tribes that wandered the heartlands of the empire.

"Aokule? Are you from the Aokule desert?" she ventured.

His face lit up at the mention of that distant region. With childlike fervor, he nodded, then pointed at himself with a trembling finger, softly uttering the word "Manakkea." Little had Elissa known that one day, studying these languages would prove invaluable. She regretted not having paid more attention to Brennet's desire to teach her.

"Manakkea… Itu dibe? Your name?" she inquired.

He extended his arm, unveiling a prominent burn scar shaped like the letter G… the same emblem she had noticed on Meggy.

"Manakkea… slave," the horrified Guardian whispered.

Around her, time seemed to hang suspended. She cast a glance at the battered bodies of the Kraken's crew. Each bore the same branding, that abhorrent G that had stripped them of all autonomy. Slaves… Elissa was aboard a slave ship.

———— ··•●·· ————

The passage opened up into the damp, cavernous dungeons of Ryre's Keep, a place Farklyn had never deemed worthy of his presence before. They were not far, and the nauseating stench that wafted from them confirmed his premonition that he would not find pleasant sights there. In the shadows, the prince and the healer surveyed their surroundings. Several sentries stood watch, more than Farklyn had anticipated.

"Valera has been exceptionally vigilant since the last ball," Jenima murmured, her voice barely audible. "I'm not sure how we'll manage to rescue the Oracle. Her cell's security is nearly impenetrable now, even to the guards tasked with its protection."

Farklyn shot her a smirking glance, then shed his traveling cloak, still concealing his evening attire. He handed it and his satchel to the woman, who immediately grasped the ruse he intended to employ.

"Your Majesty, consider the risks…" Jenima began, but he paid no heed to her warnings, gesturing for her to follow. With resolute steps, he emerged from the shadows and approached the sentries with an aura of authority.

"Prince Farklyn?" one of them asked, genuine surprise in his voice. "We haven't seen you in this dungeon before."

"And with good reason!" the young man retorted, raising his head with a disdainful air. "This place reeks of death."

The guards exchanged uncertain glances, their gazes shifting to the maid who stood slightly behind her lord.

"What brings you here, Your Highness? None of our detainees currently require medical attention."

"I'm here by my charming mother's decree. I need to relocate a prisoner away from the capital."

"A prisoner? Which one?"

"You're well aware of whom I'm referring to! Now, lead me to her. Your sovereign insists on the urgency."

"Without questioning Your Majesty's authority, the queen specifically instructed us not to leave the Oracle unattended without her presence... except for the king and Master Ancel, naturally."

Maintaining eye contact, Farklyn advanced with a graceful, predatory stride. A cruel smile graced his lips as he approached the guard, so close that he felt the man's breath on his skin.

"Do you honestly think my brother and my mother have the luxury to venture into the dungeons, while the nobility of Wynnorth and Guverl'yt are assembled above? The situation is already precarious enough for the mighty Valera to entrust her own son with the task of descending into these filthy depths! I'd much prefer to be back upstairs, amidst the company of a few courtly ladies, rather than wasting my time with such imbeciles."

"I understand your frustration, Your Majesty. However..."

"However? Who are you to challenge Farklyn Netherborne in this manner? Ah, I see! The one who will lose his head for defying the queen's orders and jeopardizing our nation."

Despite the fear etched on his interlocutor's face, Farklyn knew his threats would not easily bend the guard to his will. He hoped his own apprehension and the beads of sweat on his forehead were not as evident as they felt.

"My prince... we can't..."

Farklyn did not let the sentry finish his sentence, producing a bronze key from his pocket, its surface engraved with ancient runes. This key had taken him weeks to steal. He had nearly been caught during the elven delegation's visit. Initially, he had planned to loot it from his mother's quarters and implicate them, sowing doubt. He wanted to eradicate all notions of forced marriage plaguing the queen's thoughts. But then he had met Elyndel, and his intentions had shifted… for a time. However, his initial schemes had resurfaced after that poignant dream. The king's unexpected return had provided the perfect diversion.

The soldier's eyes widened, his complexion paling.

"My apologies, Your Highness," he stammered. "Please, follow me."

Farklyn did not bother acknowledging the words with a nod, striding forward with a demeanor both proud and imperious.

CHAPTER

35

LOSSES AND OFFENSES

Elyndel was consumed by searing pain, as if a dagger had been driven into his abdomen. It went beyond a mere broken rib, leaving him unsure how he would manage to rise. A muffled gasp escaped his bloodied lips as he attempted to sit up. His protective magic dome had crumbled under the weight of the creature. Leaning against the white birch that had broken his fall, the Master's pain-clouded gaze sought out his friends. The thought of finding them mutilated twisted his gut with paralyzing dread. His eyes first settled on the princess. Unconscious and several feet away, she lay near the bushes. The silver tiara she had worn just moments before was now replaced by a sizable gash on her forehead. Suppressing his own pain, he crawled toward her, the sole heiress of the kingdom. What if she had already died? The notion sent his stomach churning, mingling with his own agony. He fought back a surge of nausea, a cold bead of sweat tracing a path down his temple.

Miraculously, Satya still breathed, but her shallow inhalations and pallid complexion hinted that she demanded urgent attention. He needed to stabilize her and frantically searched for his scepter to administer a healing spell. His gaze briefly met Syviis', a bit farther off. She struggled to aid Gareath in rising, bearing only minor scratches. Relief washed over him.

Nilyan, on the other hand, limped toward a prone figure. The naked form displayed a fiery mane that partially obscured a physique covered in runic symbols of the same hue as the hair. The deep furrow etched into the earth beside the body bore witness to the force of impact. With his sword gripped tightly in his left hand, Nilyan nudged the dragon, now in its human shape, seemingly unconscious within a circle of scorched grass. Raising the weapon above his head, Nilyan prepared to put an end to this strife, this menace hanging over Cendril.

In that very instant, the creature surged upright.

Its movements defied reality, preventing the elf from evading the strike. The dragon's hand, armed with razor-edged claws, plunged into Nilyan's exposed abdomen as if slicing through butter. Gasping, the warrior's weapon slipped from his grasp as he staggered backward, blood spewing from his gaping wound and staining his adversary's face. The creature offered a macabre smirk as it licked its lips.

"NILYAN!"

Gareath's anguished cry seemed to shake the very hill, the forest.

Time suspended. Nilyan Montallis crumpled to his knees, bewilderment crossing his features. He fixed his wide, chocolate eyes on his younger brother. A semblance of a smile graced his face, his gaze growing vacant. One final gasp escaped his lips before he collapsed, life abandoning the body of the famous warrior. The humanoid creature turned its attention back to the Master, a sadistic grin twisting its face, now flecked with crimson. Elyndel's shock, as he stared at the dragon's partially scaled form, was palpable, stealing his breath.

"It's not Oleth," he whispered, horror reverberating in his voice.

"Stop! They are slaves!" the Guardian's panicked shout echoed through the chaos.

Bloodthirsty pirates, blinded by their orders, failed to comprehend that their assault was gravely misplaced. How could they obey Meggy's commands without questioning why only terrified individuals stood before them? Innocents fell, and those who had the audacity to defend themselves met an even worse fate. Elissa's gaze swept over the crowd, her heart aching with helplessness. Except for Captain Grenbryel's few lieutenants, these were not all Kraken crew members. She pieced together the truth—while the Kraken sailors had vanished, Meggy's crew had abandoned their ship. Lady Fortune was a deserted trap.

Worse still, the emerald remained on board. In her haste to awaken, the Guardian had left it in her cabin. An amateur's mistake. Duty screamed at her to return to the boat, to retrieve the stone. Yet, she knew that would mean sacrificing the innocent. A choice she refused to entertain but had to make. Heavy-hearted, she cast one last glance at the frightened young man beside her. "Hayane... forgive me!" Her voice quivered as she whispered before bolting away.

Climbing over the railing, she rushed back to her cabin, avoiding looking over her shoulder. The pleading gazes might sway her, and she could not allow that. The ship lay abandoned as her fears predicted. An eerie, somber aura replaced the vibrant life that had pulsed through Lady Fortune moments before. Elissa's sprint to her cabin mirrored the weight pressing on her soul. An impending sense of doom deepened with the unusual silence. Thankfully, the gem remained where she'd left it. Her touch on the precious emerald was gentle, as though soothing a frightened creature. Shivers wracked her body. Tears mixed with sweat, and splatters of blood adorned her cheeks. Seated on her bunk, she gathered strength, forcing herself to rise, to return to the fury of the battlefield.

"Get up, Elissa... get up," she murmured.

"To go where?"

The Guardian tensed. Her mouth felt dry. The cabin door creaked open, impossibly slow. A man entered, grey eyes gleaming with amusement. His raised eyebrow oozed satisfaction. With a proud step, he advanced, towering over her.

"Well! What do we have here?"

His deep voice squeaked slightly. Slender and confident, he wore a vivid green hat atop coppery hair, golden shoulder pads ornamenting his uniform. One look was enough to know who stood before her: Alden Grenbryel.

— · •●• · —

Farklyn and Jenima trailed the guard, enveloped in an uneasy quietude, while curious glances from the other sentries bore into them. He had a nagging sense that they could see through his ruse, sense the anxiety he concealed beneath the veneer of arrogance and pride—the mask he shared with his mother. Amidst the passage by the cells, Farklyn pressed on with his charade, despite the prisoners' pleas.

"My trial? Is it time, my king?" The frail voice caught Farklyn's attention, and he glimpsed an elderly man on the ground. He had fallen from his bunk and was attempting to get up using his frail forearms. The image stirred a tremor in the prince. He could not fathom the time this poor old soul had spent within these putrid walls, but his feeble appearance spoke of years robbed. Against his better judgment, Farklyn stopped.

"I am not the king, only his brother."

"Are you here for me, Your Highness?"

The earnestness in the man's gaze provoked unexpected empathy. The cruelty and disregard of King Fabyan had never been this apparent. Farklyn swallowed the lump in his throat, maintaining a front of stoicism.

402

"Your Majesty… you shouldn't pay them any attention," the guard interjected. "These bandits don't merit acknowledgment of their existence."

"What has this man been charged with?"

"I don't know," the sentry replied.

A glance at Jenima revealed pity engraved on her features, her eyes harboring suppressed fury that made Farklyn shudder. He suspected that if Jenima possessed the means, she would bring fire and blood to the kingdom and its rulers. The thought strangely thrilled him.

"I'm innocent, Lord!" The prisoner slumped, defeated. "If the court would hear my defense, I… I could go back to my family."

"He has not received a fair trial?" Farklyn inquired, feigning detachment.

"Do criminals even deserve such?" the guard questioned, eyeing Farklyn suspiciously, signaling the need to move on before the act crumbled.

"Indeed," the prince affirmed, controlling his tone.

With a casual flick to remove an imaginary speck from his silk shirt, he pressed on.

"Let's proceed."

———— ··•·· ————

The dragon ascended as Gareath charged with a wild scream, his axe raised. Yet, the creature struck him with effortless force, sending the fighter sprawling backward. Undeterred, the flame-maned stranger bypassed Gareath and moved a few paces toward Syviis. Bereft of her scepter, she scanned the ground with frantic gaze. The beast's sadistic stare met Elyndel's, draining the color from the Master's face.

"Not my sister," he growled.

Seizing Satya's weapon, he staggered upright. Agony tore through him, but determination overrode the pain. A beam of light surged from the staff, hitting the monster square on. The creature crashed to the ground, convulsing in uncontrollable spasms. The torment drawn on his features seemed almost unbearable. Good. A glimpse at Nilyan's lifeless body obliterated any lingering empathy Elyndel might have harbored.

The aftershocks of the discharge dwindled.

"Who are you?" the Master demanded, his jaw clenched.

"Sakariel," the monster responded in a malevolent, hissing tone.

A smirk twisted Sakariel's lips, revealing pointed teeth reminiscent of his reptilian form. His human guise paled in comparison to the transformations of Bales and Oleth. Hints of scales remained visible beneath his hair, and his diamond-shaped pupils betrayed his mediocre appearance.

"Where's Oleth?"

"My lips are sealed."

Another bolt erupted from Elyndel's scepter, eliciting twitches of agony from Sakariel. He would torment the creature. Though he already suspected the answer, a surge of rage pushed him toward vindication. After a while, the spasms subsided in Sakariel's trembling form. Panting, the dragon spat in disdain on the ground. Elyndel's faint chuckle rang out as he took a few measured steps forward, staff still aimed at his adversary.

"I can play this game all day if needed. Yet, I doubt your endurance will match. Hence, it would be wise to share the whereabouts of Oleth and spare yourself from this suffering."

Fear eclipsed the young dragon's arrogance, rendering him uncertain. Slowly, his gaze lifted to meet Elyndel's, revealing a hint of madness lurking within his eyes.

"My father has ventured to find the one who will mend the rift between our worlds."

"Your father..."

"It's merely a matter of time," the creature growled, pupils ablaze with ominous fire. "The descendants of Razakstrom will triumph over your feeble empire."

A gust of wind swept over them, and Elyndel knew immediately that reinforcements were coming.

——————— ··•·· ———————

Elissa's reflexes kicked in as she instinctively raised her hand, hoping to strike the man before he could make a move. But his swiftness outpaced her, delivering a masterful blow to her face. She tumbled off the bed, her head colliding harshly with the floor. Intense pain exploded through her, mingling with the metallic tang of blood flooding her mouth. Her jaw throbbed, a rhythmic pulse of agony as if her heart had migrated there, and the room started to spin around her.

"My apologies!" Grenbryel burst into laughter. "But I couldn't risk leaving you in full command of your powers, could I?"

Elissa wanted to retort, but her battered face only allowed her to mumble a few unintelligible curses. She struggled to regain her bearings, attempting to rise, when Grenbryel seized her arms and yanked her close.

"Nothing brings me more delight than witnessing a woman fighting for survival. That fire within you, the disheveled hair, that fierce look... What a thrill it is!"

His grip on her wrists tightened to the brink of breaking, but she stifled her cry. She could not show him her vulnerability, no matter how excruciating the pain. She needed to incapacitate him, to cast a spell that could save her and alert Meggy... yet her mind felt vacant, her thoughts a hazy swirl.

"I was hoping to toy with our beloved Captain Redding a bit longer! But when I learned that the Guardian of Walderlake was aboard... the reward promised by Toran Sius was too tempting to let slip through my fingers. Wish me luck! Your capture might just mean a promotion for me."

"I wish you to rot in the underworld where you'll soon find yourself," Elissa snapped, her fury blazing like fire.

"Shame we're running out of time," he muttered with a sneer.

With that, he licked the bruise forming on Elissa's cheek. She yearned to fight, but fear seemed to paralyze her, holding her captive in its grip.

———— ··●·· ————

They eventually arrived where the Oracle was supposedly imprisoned, or so the guard claimed. All Farklyn could see was a stone wall at the end of a dusty corridor. He exchanged a puzzled look with Jenima, who stepped forward decisively.

"If you'd allow me, Majesty. I fear your splendid attire might get soiled," she suggested.

Farklyn nodded, all the while aware of the sentry's unsettling gaze fixed upon him. Their suspicion was unmistakable. Jenima gently took the key from his hand and approached the wall with her head lowered. Sliding the rune-covered end of the key between the bricks, she conjured luminous inscriptions on the surface. A low rumble resonated through the dungeons, and the structure split apart, revealing a swath of darkness before them.

"After you, Highness," Jenima said, bowing respectfully.

Farklyn cleared his throat, casting one last glance at the guard before stepping forward. The wall sealed itself behind them, plunging them into complete obscurity. He felt Jenima's fingers entwine with his, guiding him cautiously through the passage.

"I don't know where we are going," Farklyn admitted, his steps hesitant.

"I've been here before... when she first arrived in Wynnorth. It was I who tended to her injuries."

"So, my mother showed no mercy to the Oracle?" Farklyn questioned, bitterness evident in his tone.

Jenima chose silence as her response. Yet, in that silence, amidst the encompassing darkness, he sensed the weight of her emotions. Of course, Valera had not held back...

Then, a glimmer of light appeared, and the corridor opened up into a surprisingly spacious chamber. The cell resembled a miniature forest: apple trees and lilacs flourished, birds perched on branches, and an otherworldly glow akin to moonlight radiated from the space, despite the absence of windows. Alongside the scent of blooming bushes, a sweet mystical fragrance wafted in the air—a fragrance of magic.

"Hello, Prince Farklyn."

In one corner of the room sat the elf, set upon the trunk of a willow tree. Her chin rested on her knees and her fragile arms, marked with several lacerations, encircled her legs.

"What have they done to you?" Farklyn breathed in shock.

"Is this another illusion of my mind?" she questioned, her finger welcoming a chaffinch that perched upon it.

"We are quite real. I wish to take you home... to Cendril."

"Cendril?"

Her countenance brightened, her eyes closing as if she were savoring the very name of her distant homeland.

"I saw you in a dream," she continued, her voice ethereal.

"We're running out of time. We must hasten," Farklyn urged. "Elyndel is waiting for you."

CHAPTER

36

THE END OF ALL THINGS

Grenbryel gripped the mage by the back of her neck, a short sword poised at her throat, and forcefully dragged her across the ship. He showed no restraint. Though the man remained silent, his face bore a self-assured smile that seemed to carry both youth and age. Elissa had attempted to repel him with her powers but quickly realized that the iron handcuffs she wore emitted a faint glow, preventing her from wielding her magic.

"My father's invention," he commented, tapping the cuffs lightly with his index finger. "He gifted them to me on my last visit to Richeroc. You are the first to experience them. I hope you feel honored!"

"Your father... working under the orders of Toran Sius, I presume?" Elissa inquired.

Alden burst into laughter, as though the magician had just shared the world's most humorous joke.

"This pompous old fool no longer wields any authority over his Council! He clings to the belief in his supremacy, but it is the Grenbryels who rule now. The Alliance will soon eclipse the power of the Master of Walderlake, and the kingdom will reclaim its former glory."

"The Alliance..."

Her heart sank. The very ones who had slaughtered her household, the ones who had killed Miranda, who had relentlessly pursued her—Meggy and Wil had been right.

"As always, your spirited captain has been exceedingly reckless," Alden continued, paying her no mind. "Leaving her ship behind for us to board! Ha! A few discreet rowboats and a simple diversion were all it took. I had expected better."

"You appear to be quite enamored with the sound of your own voice," the mage retorted steadily.

The Kraken's captain raised his hand as though to strike her, but retracted. Instead, he ran his fingers languidly over her face. There was something excruciatingly aggressive in this innocuous caress. His face, too close to hers, his warm breath on her jaw... she wanted him far, far away from her. She did not know what he had in store. However, she knew she needed to eliminate him before he could harm her friends.

They finally reached the ship's bridge. Elissa realized that Alden Grenbryel's real crew was now on board the Lady Fortune, armed to the teeth and prepared for action. The captain chuckled, taking obvious delight in this moment, which he undoubtedly regarded as the pinnacle of his supremacy. He cast proud glances at his men, savoring their admiring expressions with perverse satisfaction.

His gaze then shifted back to Elissa, his grey eyes piercing through the mental defenses she had erected to maintain her composure.

"Now, let's have some fun," he sneered, running his hand beneath her bodice.

Elissa attempted to resist, but Grenbryel instantly tightened his grip, the sword's tip pressing against her skin, freezing her in place.

"Any sudden movement from you, and this blade will find its way to your throat. If only my father could see me now… he would be so proud! Your capture promises me great wealth, Guardian. A bounty of riches!"

"Is the length of your speeches a way to compensate for a certain aspect of your physique that I'd rather not mention?" Elissa retorted, her voice carrying an arrogant tone previously unseen in her.

The captain's face contorted with anger, and once again, his blade drew perilously close to Elissa's throat. However, she responded with a defiant smile.

"Go ahead! Kill me. I know you're itching to," she taunted.

"It's not the desire that's lacking… but no. I am quite certain that what awaits you in Richeroc will not disappoint. Traitors of Walderlake tend to receive little mercy."

The Guardian remained silent, her urge to strike him down growing more intense.

"Don't worry, you won't be making the journey alone," he added, his smile returning.

She had to destroy him.

"REDDING!" Grenbryel bellowed, his voice echoing across the sea.

———— ··●·· ————

Elyndel watched as the wyrms sped through the dark clouds, their ominous presence unsettling the sky. He counted five, though the dense forest could easily conceal more of these half-snake, half-dragon creatures. They seemed to be hurtling toward them with unwavering determination, as if their sole purpose was to shield Sakariel. While their size paled in comparison to the colossal winged giants, their ferocity was undeniable. Elyndel refused to accept that it would all end here. For the chance of his sister's survival, he would battle to the bitter end. Bracing himself for the impending confrontation, he summoned the suppressed strength that had slumbered within him for far too long. The wyrms landed, using their fearsome tails to propel themselves at their master's side. Sakariel chuckled wickedly before setting his monstrous minions upon the elves. A surge of magical energy coursed through Elyndel's veins, ready to be unleashed. Yet, he restrained the torrent, holding it in, letting waves of power crash gently against the borders of his being.

Beside him, Syviis knelt, casting an imploring look at her brother. The monstrous wyrms were closing in rapidly, their presence growing ever more menacing. But Elyndel did not strike prematurely. He allowed the magic to swell within him, filling every fiber of his being with its radiant force. Gareath, the seasoned warrior, leaped toward Syviis, his powerful frame serving as a shield for the two women. Words were unnecessary between them, as they had fought side by side in countless wars, their understanding unspoken.

The wyrms drew perilously near, their hissing breath hot and foul, reminiscent of the stench of decaying bodies on sun-scorched battlefields.

NOW.

Elyndel unleashed the contained torrent of luminous energy upon the oncoming creatures. Their agonized cries echoed through the hill, a triumphant fanfare of victory. Hope surged within Elyndel as two of the wyrms lay incapacitated on the ground, mouths gaping with menacing teeth. However, the remaining monsters staggered to their feet, resilient and relentless, as Sakariel advanced with an ominous expression.

———— ·•●· · ———— ·

Aelrie leaned heavily on Farklyn, her strength waning to the point where her legs could barely bear her weight. Darkness cloaked them, and the man could hear the elf's labored breaths, struggling to push herself forward. His throat constricted with worry. How would they ever manage to escape the fortress or even make it to Cendril with her in this fragile state? Perhaps he had overestimated his own abilities…

"Forgive the words that come from my mouth, Aelrie," he whispered. "I must maintain this charade until we're out of danger."

"My name," she replied in a murmur, her voice filled with emotion. "It's been so long since I've heard it spoken, except in my dreams."

Her grip on his arm tightened, and Farklyn could sense the recognition in her eyes, a feeling so rarely directed toward him.

Jenima took his place as Aelrie's support and opened the cell door. A wave of light greeted them, along with the judgmental gazes of the guards. Farklyn held his head high, projecting an air of conceit and detachment as he approached.

"Let no one follow us," he commanded imperiously. "The location where we're taking her must remain a secret, and I have a feeling the queen doesn't trust your militia anymore, especially after the last ball."

"Majesty?" inquired the guard who had led him to the cell.

"You know full well that Cendril's delegation nearly succeeded in reaching her," Farklyn continued. "Only that cursed dragon stopped them. Valera hasn't forgotten."

The sentry's face paled, and sensing he was about to offer an apology, Farklyn impatiently pressed forward. He quickened his pace but made sure to listen for the footsteps of the two women close behind him. The exit from the dungeons came into view, and his heart skipped a beat at the thought that they might have successfully rescued the Oracle on their own.

Pushing open the door, he exhaled in relief, turning to Jenima and Aelrie.

"I was convinced that we were going to f—"

Suddenly, something sharp pressed against his back, digging in like the tip of a sword.

⎯⎯⎯ ·•●·· ⎯⎯⎯

"REDDING!" Grenbryel's voice thundered again.

Meggy emerged over the railing, trailed by Wil and Finn. At the sight of her arch-nemesis, her features twisted into a potent mask of hatred.

"Megara Redding! Finally found you, I see. I was beginning to miss you!" Grenbryel taunted.

"So, you were eager for death?" Meggy snapped back, baring her teeth menacingly.

"I must say, I expected more from you. Falling for such a ruse… quite uninspiring! I should have known better than to overestimate the simple harlot that you are."

A few of Grenbryel's crew members burst into laughter.

"Release Elissa," Meggy hissed.

"The Guardian? Far too valuable to simply let go, my dear," Grenbryel sneered. "I intend to take her with me. But I understand your eagerness to have her back. I believe I know your preferences quite well, after all," he added, running his fingers through the coppery strands of Elissa's hair.

Wil had an overwhelming urge to leap at Alden Grenbryel, to drive his sword into the man's flesh, to strike him with all his might to ensure he'd never touch her again. Finn and Lee had to restrain him forcefully as their adversary laughed heartily at the fallen knight's furious reaction.

"Well, well! It seems you're quite popular among the crew!" Grenbryel chuckled as he turned his attention to Elissa. "Should I find out for myself what sets you apart from the others?"

With a hand on the woman's reddened cheek, he immediately felt her spit in his face, her defiance unwavering. In response, he backhanded her with brutal force. Her nose throb as blood trickled from her lips. Despite the pain, she had no regrets.

"I'm pleased to announce that Lady Fortune is now mine. Or rather, it belongs to Walderlake!" Grenbryel declared. "Did you honestly believe we'd allow a band of pirates to sail the seas without us eventually seeking justice?"

"An exchange of ships? I never took you for such a generous soul, Alden!" Meggy taunted.

"A gift that will be short-lived," Grenbryel retorted with depraved pride.

Meggy's expression darkened, her face going pallid.

"You and your crew stand atop barrels of gunpowder cleverly placed by my men long before your pitiful arrival," he continued, relishing the shock that crossed Meggy's eyes.

"You'd destroy your own ship?" she exclaimed incredulously.

"Why not? I'll be awarded a new one when I deliver this traitor to the Council."

"You're a monster," Meggy spat, her revulsion palpable.

"Unless..." Grenbryel paused, his sadistic grin widening. "Reconsider my offer, and I'll let your crew go unharmed."

"Are you still obsessed with making me your slave?" Meggy shot back.

"I prefer the term *lover*," he retorted.

"I don't see a difference."

"It's your choice, Megara. Become mine, and your crew will leave unscathed. Refuse, and you'll all meet the ocean's depths."

$$\bullet \quad \cdot \cdot \bullet \bullet \cdot \cdot \quad \bullet$$

Gareath leaped onto one of the monsters, delivering a masterful blow. The beast's rock-hard scales absorbed some of the damage, yet the warrior pressed on undeterred. The Master joined the fray, sending arcs of silver lightning crackling toward another wyrm. It took several attempts until one of the creatures lay prone on the ground, weakened but not dead. As he prepared to deliver the final blow, one more wyrm crept close and swung its tail with force. Elyndel was sent sprawling, his head impacting the earth. A loud groan escaped him, and for a moment, he feared he might never rise again. He watched helplessly as the wyrm advanced, its menacing red eyes locking onto his own while its forked tongue flicked between its teeth.

"Elyndel!" Syviis' desperate cry rang out.

The creature loomed above him, its foul breath stealing the air from his lungs. It spread its wings and screeched, a final warning before lunging at its helpless prey. The Master knew the end was near. Covered in blood, Gareath appeared behind the wyrm, swinging his axe with a vengeance. A shrill scream emanated from the beast's maw as its head was severed from its body, rolling to the ground.

Rain suddenly began to pour, catching them by surprise. Elyndel lifted his battered face to the heavens, letting the cold droplets cleanse his mud-and-blood-streaked body. Despite the suffering and weakness, he knew he could not allow Sakariel to triumph. He was the Master of Cendril, the kingdom's hope. A surge of determination flooded his being, giving him the strength to rise to his feet. Gareath sighed, his bruised face reflecting his pain.

"For Nilyan," he muttered.

The warrior charged at Sakariel without restraint, engaging the dragon in combat once more. Sakariel countered, regaining its formidable form. Gareath managed to evade the fiery breath that spewed from its mouth. Swiftly, he darted beneath one of its raised paws, slicing deep into its left flank. The reptile roared and ceased its assault, allowing the Master to muster what little strength he had left. He cast an entanglement spell, causing roots to burst from the ground, ensnaring his foe. The bound dragon was now at their mercy.

Elyndel staggered closer, Nilyan's lifeless body still haunting his vision. He stopped just within earshot of Sakariel, determination gleaming in his eyes as he addressed the creature.

"Balt'boec will not fall. We will defeat those who seek to destroy us."

With a simple wave of his hand, he signaled Gareath to move forward.

———— ··●·· ————

"What a surprise to find you here, my dear brother!" Fabyan exclaimed, his sword edging deeper into Farklyn's back. Frozen in fear and weighed down by failure, Farklyn dared not move.

"Funny! I'm surprised that you've suddenly taken an interest in my whereabouts," Farklyn replied with a veneer of cool disdain.

His eyes locked onto Jenima's, finding not just dread but a hint of connivance. She had a plan, possibly involving Malawet. All he needed to do was buy her some time.

"I know you better than anyone!" Fabyan snarled. "Even a brief period wearing my crown gave you ideas of grandeur."

Farklyn smirked, "I thought it was a prerequisite for donning it?"

The king's response was a sinister silence, punctuated by a menacing glare. Stepping forward, he confronted Farklyn almost nose to nose. Their personal guard formed a tight ring around them and, for a moment, Farklyn stopped breathing.

"Would you really betray your own blood? Denounce our mother?" Fabyan hissed, his voice carrying an unfamiliar threat.

Farklyn scoffed. "Defending Valera now, are we? You were always the first to critique her parenting style."

"People change! To demonstrate my newfound generosity, I'm offering you mercy," Fabyan continued, a wicked smile stretching across his scarred face.

"Oh, truly?"

"Yes, truly! You see, I understand you. We are more alike than you'd admit. I know your deepest desire is to leave a lasting legacy, to be revered. Swear your allegiance to me now, and I'll overlook this treasonous escapade. We'll imprison the Oracle and execute the servant, of course. But you, dear brother, you will live a life of luxury and indulgence, surrounded by courtesans and drowned in the finest spirits. I even intend to elevate your functions and the honors attached to them."

As Fabyan spoke, Farklyn's gaze drifted thoughtfully toward Jenima. But within moments, his expression morphed into something ruthless, something cold.

"Honor? All the courtesans I desire?" he asked.

"And the most handsome of valets!" Fabyan added, eagerly.

"Your Majesty!" Jenima cried, her face a portrait of shock.

Ignoring her, Farklyn approached her with a look of arrogant disdain, a reflection of his past self. His hand subtly moved to his belt, a signal Jenima noticed immediately.

"Why should I forfeit my comforts for a mere servant?" Farklyn mused aloud, a sinister edge to his voice. "Though, I must admit, I will miss your... particular skills."

Jenima's face morphed into one of utter revulsion. "You're just a coward... a petulant little nobleman with no value except for his fleeting beauty."

With a laugh that bordered on a growl, Farklyn grasped her throat, the Oracle staggering behind her, fear blossoming in her wide eyes.

"I wonder who will retain their allure the longest," he whispered dangerously.

"You're repulsive," she spat back.

Ignoring her, Farklyn drew her into a harsh, possessive kiss. To Fabyan and his minions, Jenima seemed to be struggling at the hands of a petty lord. In reality, he discreetly passed her the dagger he had hung on his belt before his departure… the same one he had used to get rid of his mane. When she grabbed it, he tore his lips away from hers and gave her an apologetic look. Then, he pointed at one of the guards and snapped his fingers to order him to seize the healer.

"Fabyan, you overlooked one detail," Farklyn announced with feigned sweetness.

"What might that be, dear brother?"

"I am not, and never will be, you."

In an explosive moment, Jenima drove the dagger into a sentry's throat, blood erupting from the wound. Using the ensuing chaos to their advantage, she began chanting, a powerful force emanating from her blood-streaked hands. Guards were sent flying, including the king, who now wore an expression of stunned betrayal.

"Seize them!" Fabyan roared, his face contorted in rage.

Springing into action, Farklyn scooped up the Oracle, making a dash for safety. Jenima grasped his shoulder, her voice rising in a crescendo of ancient words. A blinding light swallowed them, the ground disappearing beneath their feet. Energy pulsated around them, vibrating with an unseen force as their surroundings dimmed to a faint whisper.

———— · ·●· · ————

As tension mounted, Meggy hoisted herself over the Kraken's railing, determination burning in her honeyed eyes.

"No, Captain Redding…" Lee's voice cracked, his arm reaching futilely toward her.

Ignoring his pleas, she approached Grenbryel with resolute steps, her demeanor somber yet steadfast. Elissa and Wil exchanged a glance, an unspoken conversation of words and promises hanging between them. In that moment, Elissa felt an unbearable burden descend upon her, a poignant realization of the companionship Wil had offered, sparing her from loneliness.

"I'll find you," Wil murmured, a vow tinged with regret for the kiss that never graced her lips.

As Lady Fortune drifted away, the plank connecting the two ships plummeted into the water, shattering the grim silence. With a heavy heart, Meggy bestowed a final lingering gaze upon her crew, fighting back tears of fury and despair. Grenbryel shackled her wrists, and she offered no resistance. Steeling herself, Meggy bit her lower lip to steady its quiver. Her plan had failed, and her appetite for revenge had doomed them. Yet, Elissa understood her. Meggy's actions were not born of selfish desires, but a fervent need to mend her wounds and safeguard her son's future.

The Lady Fortune became a distant silhouette, soon lost in the fog along with their comrades. The Kraken resembled a spectral entity haunting the sea's expanse. Elissa felt her heart sink but swore that this could not be their last meeting. The gods would not be so cruel...

After a moment, Grenbryel approached Meggy from behind, causing her to stiffen. He placed his hands on her shoulders, his touch like the talons of an eagle closing in on its prey.

"I lied," he whispered, brushing his lips over her ear.

A thunderous roar eclipsed his words, and in the distance, the ship erupted in flames. Elissa's heartbreaking cry reverberated across the sea. Meggy crumbled to her knees, tears rolling down her cheeks. The skyline turned into a morbid canvas of smoke and fire blending with the fog. The macabre laughter of Grenbryel and his men punctured the chaos, fueling the tempestuous fury building in Elissa. The stone vibrated, as if trying to dictate her next move. Energy surged within her like water through a broken dam. She quickly became one with the emerald, and the bonds restraining her melted as easily as wax in a scorching blaze.

Grenbryel recoiled in horror.

"Stop her! She's breaking free!" he shouted to his men, who remained frozen in fear.

In an instant, the grey sky turned inky black.

"Elissa?" Meggy's voice barely reached her amidst the turmoil.

The mage remained still, her eyes rolled back, her stoic face marred by green-veined markings.

Chaos ensued as the Kraken's crew scattered, their captain's commands drowned by the howling winds and encroaching doom.

"Hold your positions!" Alden protested.

But none of them obeyed. Emerald lightning tore through the sky. Time seemed to halt, giving way to a deafening silence. Soon, the rhythmic rolling of the sea resumed, announcing the approach of a monumental wave that surged toward them like a titan ready to ravage the world. The last sight before it crashed into the ship was the grateful smile blossoming on Meggy's lips.

And then, there was oblivion.

The monstrous wave struck with brute force. Yet, amidst the chaos, Elissa did not register any pain from the violent impact or the salty water flooding her lungs. In the pit of her soul, she knew she had succumbed to the depths. How could it be otherwise? Her body descended, battered by the tumultuous sea. Surrounding darkness embraced her, as an eerie tranquility subdued everything.

Before her consciousness slipped away, she perceived a sensation of being seized, as though massive claws encircled her waist, lifting her toward what she presumed was the surface. She reclined, unable to muster the strength to open her eyes, entertaining the thought that perhaps death was ushering her to an eternal slumber. The resonances of the waves gradually receded, replaced by a whisper of air that caressed her. In this surreal state, Elissa harbored the peculiar notion that she was floating above the restless sea, somehow removed from danger. The idea seemed absurd, too convenient, yet she felt her body ascending with an ethereal grace, almost as if... as if she had taken flight.

———————— ··●·· ————————

Elyndel beckoned Gareath forward to claim his revenge. The fierce elf obeyed, weapon ready, his face a canvas of palpable shock. With a flick of his wrist, the Master signaled his colleague to proceed. The dragon, weakened and in its human form, attempted futile resistance, gasping for life. This did not deter Gareath, whose rage fuelled his actions. After several forceful blows with his axe, he brought the foe down.

At last...

Elyndel exhaled deeply, his gaze drifting sorrowfully over the lifeless bodies of Nilyan and Tanyll. Sakariel had fallen, but triumph eluded him. A significant fragment of his world had shattered, leaving him on the verge of collapse, engulfed by exhaustion and agony. Soaked to the bone, he trembled uncontrollably, the gnawing void within his soul growing ever vaster. He yearned to rush to his sister's side, to embrace her tightly, yet found himself immobilized, unable to take a step.

"Pull yourself together, Elyndel," he urged himself in a hushed tone. As the Master of Cendril, he could not succumb to his anguish. He needed to assist the princess, to lay his friends to rest, to bear the weight of his people's grief upon his shoulders, dedicating his being fully to his role until nothing remained of him, until...

His breath came in ragged gasps as a torrent of emotions submerged him, the ground swaying ominously beneath his feet. Overwhelmed by a wave of debilitating nausea, he recognized that the refreshing rain against his skin was the only barrier preventing his descent into unconsciousness. He could not afford to falter, not now.

Suddenly, a luminous flash momentarily robbed him of sight, followed swiftly by another surge of light. Blinking rapidly, he beheld Farklyn before him, a picture of shock and exertion, his entire body quaking. In his arms, he cradled Aelrie. Flanking the prince was the servant who had aided his escape during the ball at Ryre's Keep. Her linen dress bore scattered stains of fresh blood, yet her evasive eyes revealed it was not hers.

"Farklyn?" Elyndel uttered, his tone colored with disbelief.

"Elyndel!" the young man greeted, his voice quivering with unrestrained emotion. Despite his reassuring smile, Elyndel could sense the turmoil within him, a maelstrom echoing his own internal chaos. His eyes landed on the servant girl's hands; in one, she wielded a dagger, while the other... blood dripping from it mingled with the rain-soaked grass. She remained silent, her attention fixated on the elf.

"Malawet?" he inquired, seeking confirmation.

"Malawet," Jenima affirmed with a solemn nod.

Syviis dashed to aid the woman in Farklyn's arms, carefully brushing the grime-coated hair from the Oracle's face. Tears welled up, threatening to spill, as she stifled a sorrowful cry.

"Is she..."

"Merely unconscious. She succumbed to sheer exhaustion," Farklyn clarified, offering a measure of reassurance.

"I... I don't understand... why?" Elyndel murmured, his voice barely rising above a whisper.

"Because I can no longer deny who I am meant to be," Farklyn declared, his face a mirror of genuine conviction. Elyndel nodded, a solemn comprehension reflected in his gaze.

"Things will never be the same again."

"I certainly hope so," Farklyn responded, a wistful half-smile gracing his features.

———— ··●·· ————

Elissa had lost track of time. Were those seconds or days that had passed? Her thoughts gradually cleared as a familiar touch grazed her numb skin.

"Breathe, Elissa."

It sounded like Brennet, his voice gentle as a whispering breeze. A comforting warmth enveloped her, the sensation on her cheek growing increasingly tangible. She was convinced that she was dead, that she had joined her mentor in the afterlife. Strangely, this brought her a sense of relief.

"Open your eyes," the entity urged again and again.

So she did. Gradually, Elissa opened her eyes. The sun's brilliance momentarily overwhelmed her, but she embraced it eagerly. A towering figure loomed over her.

"Father?" she managed to utter, her voice weak and raspy.

As her vision adjusted, the distinctive features of a Minotaur crystallized before her.

"Take it slow," he urged softly, a hint of concern outlined across his face.

"Am I dead?" she queried.

"No, but waking you was no easy feat," he admitted, aiding the Guardian to a sitting position.

"Who are you?"

"I am Kal-Oden, a healer from the Circle of Torim."

Elissa cast her gaze around, absorbing the pristine white sands, the lush tropical surroundings, and the crystalline waters gently lapping at her feet.

"Where am I?" she inquired, though a part of her felt she already knew the answer.

"Osthallvale," he responded.

The name echoed in her ears, sounding like a harbinger of long-awaited freedom.

Impossible. Impossible. Impossible.

She was certain she had died, lost to the ocean's depths far from any shoreline. She recognized that drifting to Osthallvale on her own was unlikely. Fate rarely showed such kindness. Someone must have brought her here. She scanned the surroundings once more, seeking any sign of her savior, but discovered no one.

Her mind raced to her companions—Meggy, Wil, Finn... Her heart stumbled, a crushing realization settling in that they likely lay at the sea's bottom.

Her hand instinctively found its way to her neck, where it met the pendant her mentor had given her. It was his last legacy. She could feel the emerald of Walderlake pulsating gently against her skin...

Almost his entire legacy.

She took a deep breath, emotion constricting her throat.

"Father... we made it."

The saga of An Empire of Stones will continue in Volume 2...

ACKNOWLEDGMENTS

This novel saw its first lines in the basement of a tiny house in Saint-Dorothee. I was barely fourteen at the time, and I remember isolating myself for months and going to bed at odd hours to write. It was a period when, like Elissa, I felt particularly reclusive, an overly well-behaved child who wanted above all to excel, but whom many called weird. Luckily, there were Gabrielle and Tanya, two friends with whom I was able to share this world. They got invested in this story, Gabrielle sharing characters' illustrations with me while our teacher had her back turned and Tanya who was the main inspiration for Bales. Our roads may have parted but know that you were the triggers for this adventure!

From the beginning, my mother, Jocelyne, pushed me to pursue this novel. She was the one who believed in it for me during these long years… even when I no longer paid attention to it, when I thought my words were worth nothing. Mom, you have been my most faithful reader, and your support has allowed me to find this place that I had never wanted to take.

To my husband, Luc, who is the first to pull out his cheerleader pom-poms to cheer me on. Thank you for all these dates during which we discussed Balt'boec, for all these evenings when you listened to me tirelessly talk about these fictional characters that I treated like family members. Never has anyone supported, encouraged, and valued me as much as you, Luc.

To my children, Wesley and Dean. Being your mom granted me the patience to focus on what was truly important. You have allowed me to see more clearly, to use my time more wisely. You gave me the determination to persevere, the desire to become who I am today, and I now have a new understanding of the world because of you.

A sweet thought for my friends who supported me during the many crises and questionings. Kim, Marie-Ève, thank you for these precious corrections. Cynthia, Alexanne, Sophie, Claudele… I send you love for your inputs. Thanks to Lesly for your enthusiasm and for bringing to life with such care and accuracy these characters who only resided in my mind. Analera owes you so much!

Finally, thanks to Kimberly who offered me her editing services. Your encouragements gave me the confidence to complete this project, and your precious advice pushed me to expand this universe. Because of your judicious work, An Empire of Stones did not end up on a dusty hard drive. I look forward to sharing the sequel with you.

ABOUT THE AUTHOR

Stephanie van Rijn, born Vincent, is an actress and author from Quebec of Dutch and French-Roma origin. After completing her studies in theater and arts and letters, she lived for several years in New York. There, she developed a love for writing and worked as a screenwriter for several independent feature films and series. Her passion for all things geek and the birth of her twins eventually led her to fantasy novels. You can find her on social media to discover her  upcoming projects in various artistic mediums.

Instagram.com/stephvanrijn

facebook.com/stephvanrijn

photo by Marisa Parisella

Printed in Great Britain
by Amazon

46310169R00245